I0585493

❀ Formatted with Vellum

POWER AND MAJESTY

BOOK ONE — THE CREATURE COURT

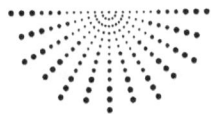

TANSY RAYNER ROBERTS

PRAISE FOR POWER AND MAJESTY

For the Friends of the John Elliott Classics Museum, who were there at the beginning.

CONTENTS

THE CREATURE
COURT CONTINUES

THE WORLD

Inglirrus

Camoise

The Green Isles

Atulia

Edore

Isharo

Orcadia Stella

Nova Stella

Ammoria

Zafir

ORCADIA Atulia

REYENNA

Tierce

LATTORIO

Aufleur

Barony of Diamagne

SILANO

Bazeppe

AMMORIA

© Jilli Roberts 2009

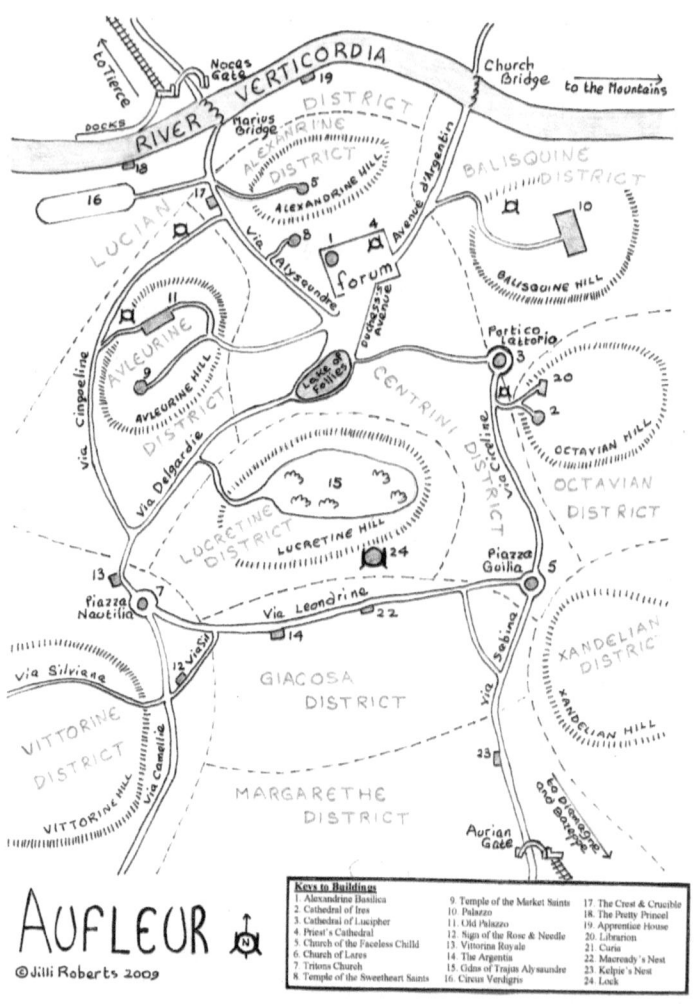

to Tierce
DOCKS
Nocos Gate
VERTICORDIA DISTRICT
19
Church Bridge
to the Mountains
RIVER
Marius Bridge
ALEXANDRINE DISTRICT
18
16
17
ALEXANDRINE HILL
5
BALISQUINE DISTRICT
10
LUCIAN
Avenue d'Argentin
8
1 4
Via Calysoundre
forum
BALISQUINE HILL
Via Cinpeeline
11
AVLEURINE
AVLEURINE HILL DISTRICT
Lake of Follies
Portico Lattorio
3
20
2
Via Delgardie
CENTRINI DISTRICT
OCTAVIAN HILL
OCTAVIAN DISTRICT
Pedrossia Avenue
15
LUCRETINE DISTRICT
LUCRETINE HILL
24
Piazza Guilia
5
13
7
Via Leondrine
22
Piazza Nautilia
14
XANDELIAN DISTRICT
Via Silviane
Via Camelia
Via Camelia
GIACOSA DISTRICT
Via Sebina
XANDELIAN HILL
VITTORINE DISTRICT
VITTORINE HILL
MARGARETHE DISTRICT
23
to Diorna and Baninie
Aurian Gate

AUFLEUR
N
©Jilli Roberts 2009

Keys to Buildings
1. Alexandrine Basilica
2. Cathedral of Ires
3. Cathedral of Lucipher
4. Priest's Cathedral
5. Church of the Faceless Child
6. Church of Lares
7. Tritons Church
8. Temple of the Sweetheart Saints
9. Temple of the Market Saints
10. Palazzo
11. Old Palazzo
12. Sign of the Rose & Needle
13. Vittorine Royale
14. The Argentis
15. Gdns of Trajin Alyssundre
16. Circus Verdigris
17. The Crest & Crucible
18. The Pretty Prinsel
19. Apprentice House
20. Librarion
21. Curia
22. Macready's Nest
23. Kelpie's Nest
24. Lock

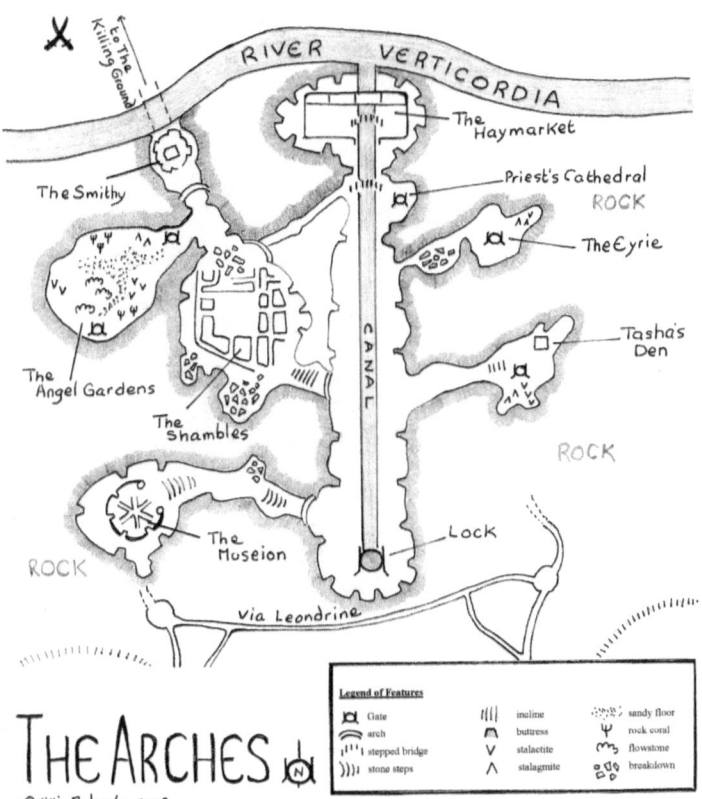

X ← To The Killing Ground

RIVER VERTICORDIA

The Haymarket

The Smithy

Priest's Cathedral

ROCK

The Eyrie

The Angel Gardens

Tasha's Den

The Shambles

CANAL

ROCK

The Museion

Lock

ROCK

Via Leondrine

THE ARCHES

©Jilli Roberts 2009

PART I
THE YEARS OF
THINGS FORGOTTEN

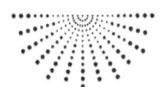

1
ONE DAY BEFORE THE NONES OF CERIALIS

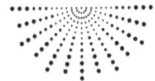

NOX

*V*elody couldn't sleep in this city. The ancient, gothic weight of it pressed around her, through the walls of the rented room.

No one else had this problem. The other demmes were asleep on their makeshift cots, while the chaperones (including Velody's Aunt Agnet) snored lightly from the larger beds. Every room in Aufleur was packed like this, so their landlady claimed. The apprentice fair drew in crowds from every town and village from coast to country, the dust from the railways still clinging to their clothes.

Velody missed home. She missed the warmth of her room above her papa's bakery, and the familiar sleepy sounds of her sisters and brothers. Every street and canalway in Cheapside and the market district of Tierce was known and safe and hers. Aufleur was so much huger and darker and more foreign.

I can't live here, she thought desperately. *Not for seven years. This city will eat me alive.*

A mouse ran over her pillow.

Velody sat up in a rush, pushing off the thin blankets and scrambling out of her cot. One of the other demoiselles — Rhian, she thought her name was — muttered and sighed at the noise, but quickly fell back to sleep.

There was no sign of the mouse, but Velody would now rather die than return to the cot. It was warm despite the darkness — Cerialis was the last month of summer. Wearing nothing but her cambric noxgown, Velody slipped to the window and let herself out onto the balcony.

The city was no less oppressive out here, but at least she could see the looming domes and towers instead of merely feeling them in her bones. Velody breathed in the calm air. Four hours until dawn? Six, at most. It wouldn't do to have shadows under her eyes in the morning — what kind of mistress would take an apprentice who looked ill and shaky? Perhaps if she calmed herself out here a little longer, she would be able to sleep.

There was a soft sound beside her, and Velody turned to see a little brown mouse creep across the balcony. She was prepared for it this time and managed not to behave like a damsel in a musette melodrama.

A second mouse emerged from the shadows, and then a third. Velody was beginning to feel outnumbered. Her eyes were so fixed to the rodents that she almost missed the sight of a naked youth falling out of the sky.

He crashed, shoulders first, into the roof of the house across the street, shattering slate tiles. He rolled and dropped onto the cobbles below, bare limbs splayed in all directions. Incredibly, he was laughing, his head thrown back in hysterical giggles. He was long and lean and muscled. He was also completely off his face.

The sky came alive with colour — iridescent green with the occasional splash of pink and gold. Velody had heard of such strange light effects, but never over a city. Colours rolled off the skin of the naked, laughing young man. He was beautiful, if utterly shameless.

Velody pressed herself against the window of the boarding house, hoping he would not see her. Then again, she doubted he could see his hand in front of his face, the state he was in.

The sky flashed brighter than before, in colours that Velody couldn't even name. Was this normal?

A second naked man stepped out of the sky, and Velody lost her breath. Normal, it seemed, had been flung out with the scraps.

This man was dark where the laughing youth was fair, and he walked down from the sky as if there were stairs beneath his feet instead of empty air. He wore his nakedness like armour, and his skin had a lantern glow about it. And really, the fact that he could walk on air was far more important than the fact that he didn't have a stitch of clothing on, but Velody couldn't help blushing. When her mother lectured her on the dangers a fourteen-year-old maiden might face in the big city, this wasn't quite what she'd had in mind.

'Garnet,' said the dark-haired man, his bare feet brushing the cobbles as he stood over the other. 'Are you hurt?'

The fair one, still sprawled in the street, whooped as if this were the funniest thing anyone had ever said to him.

'Are you drunk?' demanded his friend, crouching down to his level. 'Are you high?'

'I might — might, I say — have had a tiny pinch of surrender in my flame-and-gin,' said Garnet, enunciating carefully.

His friend smacked him. 'You went into the sky with that shit in your blood? What were you thinking?'

'Can't all be perfect little saints and soldiers, Ash-my-love.'

'Tasha's going to kill you,' Ash growled. 'She'll cut your frigging balls off.'

'A fine nox's work then.' Garnet tipped his head back and stared up at the blazing sky. 'Think the gin might be wearing off.' He shivered.

Ash glared at him. 'Where are your clothes?'

'One of the roofs around here.' Garnet waved an arm aimlessly, and stared at it as if it were fascinating. 'I was sort of looking for them when I got sideswiped by that... that... was it a lightweb or a cluster?'

'The things I do for you,' said his friend and — this was the bit that had Velody pressing a fist to her mouth to stifle her gasp — his body exploded into a cloud of black shapes.

Not shapes. Cats. The cats separated and swarmed up the walls on both sides of the street. One came up to Velody's balcony, and blinked with interest at the small horde of brown mice that had gathered there. She pressed herself further back against the wall, hoping not to be seen.

The cats returned to Garnet, several of them dragging items of clothing with them.

Garnet snatched the garments from them and pulled on a pair of trews. 'Claw marks. Lovely.'

The cats came together and glowed briefly before reshaping into the tall, muscled and still very much naked figure of Ash. 'Grateful as ever. Shoes?'

'Didn't bring any.'

'Fine. Just stay out of the sky for the rest of the nox. Crawl home if you can — sleep in the gutter if you can't, and I'll come drag you home after.'

'My motherfucking hero.' Garnet shrugged into the shirt,

but didn't button it, staring instead at his hand. 'How many arms did I start with?'

Ash groaned. 'You're too smashed to make it down to the undercity without killing yourself.'

'It's a warm nox, I'll manage.' Garnet slumped back against the nearest house, almost comfortable.

'Arse,' said Ash. 'Why do you do this to yourself?'

'Know you'll catch me when I fall,' said Garnet with a yawn and a smirk.

'Aye, and someday I won't.' Ash spun apart again into his swarm of cats, and took off into the sky in a blur of paws and tails and raw power.

Velody breathed out and closed her eyes for a moment. Someone should have warned her that the city of Aufleur was rife with flying naked men who transformed into cats.

When she opened her eyes, the street was empty and Garnet was gone.

Velody pushed herself up onto her feet, wanting to escape back to the safe confines of the dormitory. Something grabbed her wrist, dragging her back against the railings of the balcony.

'Little mouse,' hissed a voice in her ear. 'Did you enjoy the show?'

Fingers dug into her wrist. Garnet's fingers. She gazed up into the strange, beautiful face of the youth who now stood on the outside of the balcony railings, his eyes blazing at her. What did he do — fly up here? Oh, saints, he probably did.

'I have to go inside,' she said in a small voice.

'Not yet, little mouse. I want to talk to you.'

He slid a slender leg over the railings, jumping properly onto the balcony. It occurred to Velody that she should be grateful he had put his clothes on first. He grasped her other arm as well, holding her fast.

'If I scream,' she said, 'the whole boarding house will come awake.'

'Good luck with that,' he drawled. 'Daylighters sleep deeply in this city.' He squeezed her wrists cruelly.

'What are you doing?'

'Mostly? I'm wondering what a little mouse like you is doing out on a fine nox like this.'

Garnet's eyes were a little crazy and Velody wondered what sort of potion "surrender" was. It sounded like the kind of thing Sage, her eldest brother, had been into that first year after the dock accident.

'You see me, yes?' Garnet asked.

'Of course I see you.' She pulled, but he wouldn't release her wrists.

'And you see the sky?'

'Hard to miss.'

'What colour is it?'

She looked blankly at him. 'What?'

'What colour is the sky, little mouse?'

Velody looked up, just as veins of rose and lilac threaded across the clouds. 'Pink... purple,' she said. There were three flashes in quick succession, as bright emerald as the spun silk she had admired in a shop several days before she left Tierce. 'Green.'

'And my friend,' Garnet said in a whisper, 'what is his animal?'

'Cat,' she said.

He wetted his lips a little. 'Poor mouse. Didn't see this one coming, did you? You're one of us. And it's going to eat you alive.'

Velody was angry now. Close up, this boy wasn't even as big as her brother. Who did he think he was, trying to terrorise her like this? 'And what are you?' she flung at him. 'Am I supposed to be afraid of you?'

8

Garnet laughed, and was lit up from behind by a sweep of bright white light in the sky. His hair was red-gold, not blond, and he had tiny freckles on his throat. 'Small town demme,' he said. 'I know your type. Here for the apprentice fair, I suppose. You want to spend your days as a thread-smith, or a ribboner, or —'

'A dressmaker,' Velody said.

'A dressmaker.' His hands loosened their grip on her wrists, still encircling them lightly. 'You can kiss that good-bye, my sweetling. You belong to the nox now. No apprenticeship for you, no shilleins to send home to your family, no warm husband and children in your future.'

To her horror, Velody saw her hands darken as soft brown fur tufted out from her fingers. Her ribs squeezed her, as if she was about to burst apart. 'Stop it!'

'That's not me, little mouse,' said Garnet. 'It's all you.'

She concentrated on her hands and the fur diminished until the skin was clear and moon-pale again. 'Am I going to turn into... cats?' she asked.

'Not cats,' as if she was stupid for suggesting it. His eyes brightened. 'I can take it away. Take the curse from you right this minute. Leave you to your little daylight life, just as you want. You'll never see me or my kind again. Never see the sky light up with colours.'

Somewhere along the way, Garnet had let go of Velody's wrists. She rubbed them now. 'What's in it for you?'

'Sharp. I'll admit, it will do me no harm to hold your power under my skin.' He stared seriously at her. 'You don't want this, mouseling. You don't want the nox in your blood and your life. I've seen too many children burned by it.'

'I'm not a child.'

'Are you not?' He seemed amused. 'Don't think I was ever as young as you.'

Velody's mind raced. She was scared of this strange youth

9

and the things she had seen. She didn't want any part of it. A dressmaking apprenticeship, shilleins to send home... that was what she wanted.

'You'll have to give it willingly,' said Garnet. 'There's only one way I can take it by force, and I'm really not that much of a bastard.' He eyed her body up and down, far too appreciatively.

'What is it you will take from me?' Velody asked.

'Animor,' he said, and his mouth curved around the word like a lover's lick. 'You won't feel its loss.'

She closed her eyes. 'Take it then.'

Something warm brushed against her mouth and she realised too late that he was kissing her. She had never been kissed like this before. His mouth swamped her and his tongue flicked deep against hers.

For a moment, her chest felt itchy and strange, as if a creature was inside, scrabbling to get out. Every vein in her body hummed. Something left her, and at the time it didn't feel particularly important.

It was the best kiss of her life, and within an hour of returning to her little cot in the dormitory, Velody had entirely forgotten it.

2
NONES OF CERIALIS

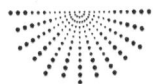

DAYLIGHT

*V*elody was the last one to rouse. She was exhausted, as if she had been running races in her sleep, though she remembered none of her dreams. When she got out of her cot, her body felt strange, slower than usual, and the world a little less bright.

A blonde demoiselle, Delphine, who had a cut-glass accent and had brought a family servant along as her chaperone, held court in the midst of the other demmes. 'Of course, Madame Mauris is the best dressmaker in Aufleur,' she was saying loudly. 'She only takes one apprentice every seven years. My mother expects me to catch her eye with my fine stitching.'

'Not to mention her fine vowels,' whispered a tall demme near Velody, whose dark red hair was pulled back in a tight braid.

Velody covered her laugh with a cough.

'My father still thinks sending me here is some sort of

punishment,' Delphine went on, shaking her long golden curls. 'Learning about the value of hard work, and all that. As if it's going to stop me flirting with the gardener! My mother is in on the conspiracy, of course.'

'Conspiracy?' asked one of the demoiselles who had gathered around Delphine like beetles on a rose.

Delphine rolled her eyes dramatically. 'To make me a world-famous dressmaker, of course. Weren't you listening?'

The tall demme snorted at that.

Delphine glanced up, her eyes hardening. 'Rhian, isn't it? You're the one who brought a boy as your chaperone.' Her laughter had a cruel edge, and the demmes around her giggled dutifully.

Velody remembered Rhian's brother — a gangling boy with spectacles and auburn hair like his sister. Their landlady had been flummoxed by his presence — chaperones were usually female and middle-aged — and sent him to sleep in the attic with her sons and nephews.

Rhian set her chin squarely. 'My brother was the only one who could be spared to come all this way. We don't all have family retainers. I can't imagine someone like you lasting ten minutes as an apprentice. You won't be allowed servants to bring you rose oil and sweetmeats, you know.'

'And what are you going to be?' Delphine sneered. 'With shoulders like yours — a carpenter, perhaps?'

'I would if they let women practise the hard crafts,' Rhian said, which set the beetles giggling again. 'I'm going to be a florister.'

'How sweet, to care nothing of wealth and status,' said Delphine, dismissing her. 'I wish you well of it.'

THE AUFLEUR FORUM was a hive of activity. It was a huge area, more than six times the size of the piazza at the centre of Tierce. The council provided trestle tables upon which the prospective apprentices could display samples of their work. The boys' fair had been two weeks earlier; today the Forum was awash with demoiselles and their handicrafts.

Rhian was chosen early, her floral arrangements catching the eye of several respectable floristers. She gave Velody a grin as she packed up her stall, and even her brother offered a smile as they left for the apprentice registry to declare which offer she had decided to accept.

There was far more competition for the needlecrafts, and Velody waited for most of the day. Her Aunt Agnet was supposed to stay at her side, but kept darting off to peer at the other stalls, or to gape at the huge public buildings that surrounded the impressive Forum.

Delphine had the stall beside Velody. The two of them eyed each other discreetly for the first few hours, but finally cracked and examined each other's wares with every appearance of amity.

'This stitching is very fine,' said Delphine, fingering a soft noxgown. 'Did you knit the lace yourself?'

'Never again,' said Velody. 'Work like that would turn me blind in a year.'

'Lacemakers make great sacrifices for their craft,' Delphine agreed with a wicked smile.

Velody relaxed a little at this evidence that her ladyship had a sense of humour. 'The ribbons on that festival gown are marvellous,' she said.

Delphine shrugged. 'Ribbons are easy.'

Velody was dreadful at the finework required for ribbons, but did not say so. 'I've heard that Mistress Sincy the ribboner is looking for apprentices this year,' she said, then bit her lip. 'I didn't mean —'

'Well, yes,' said Delphine. 'Ribboning is hardly the most prestigious profession, is it? But I suppose it's better to be a first-class ribboner than a second-class anything.' She eyed Velody. 'You never said what kind of apprenticeship you were hoping for.'

Velody opened her mouth to say something like 'Anything with a needle, really,' which was half-true. But why should she cower at the feet of this demoiselle just because she had pretty hair and spoke like a lady? 'Dressmaking,' she said. 'I want to be a dressmaker.'

Delphine gave her an amused look. 'Luckily for you, I thrive on competition.'

Rhian returned some time later sporting a scarlet band on her wrist. 'I'm to report to the Apprentice House tomorrow morning,' she told Velody with glee. 'My new mistress seems nice enough — though she has a mouth on her. I hope she's not the type to reach for the birch rods the first time I drop a plate.'

'If she is, you're doomed,' said her brother. He came forward to shake Velody's hand. 'I'm Cyniver.'

'Nice to meet you,' said Velody. He seemed nice enough, and her palm was warm where he had touched it. 'Not too bored?'

'Not now I've got our Rhian off my hands,' said Cyniver. 'I can visit the librarion in peace tomorrow, before I return home.'

'You and your books,' Rhian scoffed. 'Velody, can we fetch you some lunch? You must be starved by now.'

'Anything, please,' said Velody, not trusting her aunt to remember her.

Rhian hesitated, then glanced over at Delphine. 'Shall I fetch you something while I'm at it?'

Velody waited for Delphine to say something cutting, but

the other demoiselle surprised her. 'That would be kind,' she said.

After bringing pasties and cider to the others, Rhian insisted on dragging Cyniver the entire breadth of the Forum to look at all the stalls. Velody didn't mind. All the apprentices would be living in the Apprentice House by the river for the next seven years, so assuming she got a position, she would have time enough to get to know her new friend.

There were plenty of seamstresses and needleworkers among the crowd during the afternoon, and Velody was delighted to receive three tokens. Delphine got four — one of them from the famed Mistress Sincy the ribboner.

'Keep me in mind,' the dame said as Delphine hesitated over her indigo token.

The Forum took on a festival atmosphere as the afternoon lengthened, with more of the crowd there for sightseeing than official business. Velody sat with the remains of her pasty in her lap and her cider hidden beneath the trestle, watching the world go by.

She almost bit the neck off her bottle when she saw a tall young man with red-gold hair stroll through the Forum. He had one arm thrown carelessly around the shoulders of a dark-haired man, and he held hands with a demoiselle about Velody's age whose face was painted — as Aunt Agnet would say — like a trollop. The three of them wore bright, dandy clothes like musette costumes. It was the redhead who caught Velody's eye though. He was strangely familiar.

How can that be? she chided herself. *You've never been to this city before yesterday. You have met no one except the demmes and their chaperones.*

So why did this pretty boy make her head hurt and her chest ache, as if he reminded her of some colossal embarrassment?

The redhead leaned down and kissed his painted demme

— messily, with lips and tongue and teeth. Before Velody could even blush at the impropriety of it — kissing in the streets! — he turned his head and bestowed a similar kiss upon his male friend.

As the three of them passed Velody's little stall, the redhead winked saucily at her and she quite forgot how to breathe. She looked over at Delphine to see the other demoiselle fanning herself with a handful of ribbons.

'Things are quite different in the big city,' said Velody.

'You're telling me,' said Delphine, pretending to swoon. 'I plan to enjoy every minute that I get here.' She sat up straight all of a sudden. 'There! In the mauve shawl. That's Madame Mauris!'

'How can you tell?' Velody asked.

'I sent Letty to her boutique this morning, of course,' Delphine said, referring to her maid. 'She reported back with a very detailed description. There can't be two noses like that. Hush! She's coming this way!'

VELODY LEANED back on her stool in something like shock. Madame Mauris had examined the work of every young seamstress and needleworker at the fair, and placed her bronze token very purposely on Velody's table.

Once Velody recovered herself, she tore her eyes away from Madame Mauris's departing back to look apologetically at Delphine. She was not there.

When Delphine returned from the registration table with the indigo band of Mistress Sincy the ribboner around her wrist, Velody congratulated her. From that day forward, Delphine pretended that she had intended to take the ribboning apprenticeship all along, and neither Velody nor Rhian ever challenged her on it.

That was what friends did.

3
GARNET

o what do you want to know? We have all the time in the world. Ask your questions. I imagine everything you've heard about me is bad.

Ashiol? Why am I not surprised? Of course your first question is about him. My *friend*. We were like brothers, you know. Long before we came to the Creature Court. Long before we fought the sky, side by side.

When his mother and stepfather sent Ashiol to the city, to play dutiful grandson and almost-heir to the old Duc, he begged them to let me join him. I was nothing to them, the son of two servants, with no purpose but to replace my father when he grew too infirm to tend the grounds of the estate.

I talk like a gentleman, don't I? You wouldn't be the first to be fooled about what I am.

They allowed me to leave home, to walk a pace or two behind Ashiol, to pick up his clothes when he flung them on the floor, to (let me state this clearly) *ensure he got into no trouble in the big city.*

Are you laughing at that? I can wait until you are finished.

It did not matter what role I was supposed to play in the Duc's Palazzo. Ash and I found another world that wanted us both. A secret war, fought above the city in the nox sky. The Creature Court did not care whether we had been born on linen sheets or the kitchen table.

We were young, we were powerful, and we were finally equals.

I ran mad with it. For the first time in my life, I was somebody. Animor flowed hot in my veins. When the sky lit up with burning death, I was there to fight it back, to save the city, nox after nox. I took to drinking the fear away, and when the drink wasn't enough, I turned to potions and powders. The Creature Court was all about decadence, and I embraced that. Every time I fell down, Ashiol was there to catch me.

One kiss changed it all. That little brown mouse looked meek and young, but her animor was sweet. With her power inside me, mingling with my own, I didn't need anyone's help. I didn't need my high-and-mighty beloved Ashiol picking me up out of the gutter, time and time again.

I was stronger than him. Better. He didn't realise at first, but when he did... how could he not hate me for it?

We were Tasha's cubs, within the Creature Court. Five of us: Ashiol, me, Lysandor, Livilla, the boy. An unbreakable family. Tasha taught each of us the prime survival traits: selfishness, decadence, viciousness. We loved each other, but she made us hate too. Everything was a competition. If Ashiol was her darling, I was wounded. When she kissed Livilla, the rest of us felt the lack of that kiss on our own mouths.

Tasha taught us ambition. As a woman, she could never aspire to being a King, but she breathed power. She wanted to rule the Court through us. Once we were Lords, she expected we would let her keep pulling our tails. The hideous thing was, she was probably right. We adored her so very much.

It's for the best that I killed her.

When Tasha fell, the animor rocked through me, transforming me. I glowed from within. It tasted even better than that kiss I stole from the little brown mouse — how could it not? Tasha was our Lord and I quenched her, drinking deep from the power she had wielded during her lifetime. I was not the only one. But I was the closest, and the best.

'What have you done?' Livilla screamed, when they discovered us.

The boy stayed quiet, staring, like he always did then.

'What do you think?' Lysandor said in disgust, looking at our fallen Lord's body. 'He has done exactly as Tasha taught us all. Lived her lessons fully.'

I only had eyes for Ashiol. Part of me so desperately wanted him to be proud of me. The other part... I let my face settle into a satisfied smirk. 'I win.'

'Congratulations,' he said, dark eyes sweeping over her once, and then locking on mine. 'Lord.'

ASHIOL BECAME a Lord in his own right, and Lysandor not long after. We were friends, companions, brothers, everything. We fought the sky, defended the city, laughed, loved, danced, killed, frigged. We were untouchable.

When I was twenty-one, I quenched a fallen warrior in battle and my animor burst into new shapes, new powers. I became a King.

I had thought Ortheus — our Power and Majesty — would resent me, but he rather took me under his wing. Taught me what I needed to know. Our Court was to be rich in Kings, as it happened. Ashiol and Lysandor were raised up less than a year after I. The sky had no chance against us.

Then... ah, Ortheus fell. It happens even to the greatest of us. Suddenly we had a Court in turmoil — three young, healthy Kings to choose from. Who would rule? Who would take care of us all?

I was the most powerful. They knew that. The most ruthless too. I proved that again and again. I won.

It should have made them love me more.

There had always been a craven streak in Lysandor. He left the city soon after my rule began, declaring that he could not bear seeing what I had turned into, the lengths I was willing to go to in order to be Power and Majesty. A coward and a traitor, Lysandor. Waste of flesh.

Ashiol stayed. I saw the look in his eyes — that same look Lysandor had given me from time to time — but he stayed true. He stayed for me, as I always knew he would. My right hand. Most trusted, most beloved.

4

CHIEF DAY OF
SACRIFICE, LUDI SACRIS

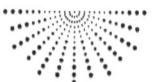

FOUR DAYS BEFORE
THE IDES OF FELICITAS

DAYLIGHT

Seven years ago, when Velody first came to Aufleur to become an apprentice, she had thought she would never get used to the place. Now she was twenty-one and this city was home. Aufleur was so much larger than Tierce, and grander. For every festival she thought she knew, there were dozens of extra traditions to learn. The month of Felicitas, for instance, in the middle of summer, had fifteen days entirely devoted to sacred games. Fifteen days! The city should screech to a halt with such frivolity, and yet everyone around her took it for granted.

It was a steaming hot morning when Velody climbed the Avleurine hill to the Temple of the Market Saints with her two friends, all of them wearing their apprentice collars.

'Spare a cake for a poor penitent, demoiselles?' begged a shabby man beside the path.

Delphine cradled her basket protectively. 'Are you mad? I sold my body for these.'

Velody and Rhian laughed.

'Really sold your body?' asked Rhian.

'I had to kiss Saul the baker's assistant,' said Delphine with a shudder. 'I'm traumatised by the entire matter, and every day in the future when someone says "Oh, Delphine can get the honey cakes," I will remind you of my pain.'

'Believe me,' said Velody. 'Everyone from the Verticordia to the Aurian Gate knows of your pain.'

'Are you implying that I complain a lot?' asked Delphine. She shoved the basket at Rhian. 'This is too heavy. You carry it.'

IT TOOK time for the three of them to become real friends. Delphine did not stop being a snooty cow straight away — if anything, she was unspeakably worse for the first few months in the Apprentice House, cutting down every friendly overture with an acidic remark.

Then the machine arrived. All the demmes gaped as it was delivered — a wrought-iron beauty with treadle and table, needles so sharp they hurt your heart. It was Delphine's fifteenth birthday present from her parents.

She stared at it, stricken. Later, Velody found her kicking the thing, and they had to call in Rhian to make a cold poultice for her foot.

'They don't understand,' Delphine muttered. 'I can't use it. Mistress Sincy makes sacred ribbons — for garlands and other state festivals. They have to be stitched by hand, that's what she's teaching me. It's what I want her to teach me. I'm not wasting seven years just to run up hair ornaments for the factory demmes.'

'It's a beautiful machine though,' Velody said enviously.

'You have it,' said Delphine in one of a long line of impulsive gestures.

'I couldn't,' said Velody, shocked at the thought. 'It's so valuable.'

'What do I care about that? You must take it. I'll only lose my temper and set fire to it, you know I will.'

Rhian spoke up, 'You can't burn metal.'

'I can find a way,' Delphine said grandly, and then the three of them laughed.

It all seemed so long ago.

THE TEMPLE of the Market Saints was crowded. Every citizen sacrificed to their saint of choice on this day, but with the biggest market week of the year so close, every merchant and craftsman in the city wished to do their duty by the Market Saints. It was nearly noon by the time Velody, Delphine and Rhian squeezed their way into a nook near one of the temple fires. Delphine shared out the honey cakes with due reverence, taking the best ones for herself.

Velody wrapped her cakes in a hemmed square of linen she had dyed a rich green. 'Take this offering with my grateful thanks for the year past and ahead,' she said to the saints. 'Be kind to me, if it please you, and guide Madame Mauris's hand to release me from my apprenticeship with full honours.'

Rhian laid out three stems of bright carmentines and stacked her cakes beside them. 'Keep my family well and safe back home, and may the year ahead be bright and fortunate,' she said, bowing her head as she spoke.

Delphine placed her cakes on the stone shelf and laid a violet silk ribbon atop them. 'I don't want to go home to Tierce when my apprenticeship is up,' she said firmly. 'I don't want to marry the fat old man my father has lined up for me, I don't want to leave my friends, and I don't want to spend the rest of my life sitting idle in a drawing room. I expect you to fix it for me.' She gave the offerings a sharp push and they burned with a hiss.

Velody was quite proud of herself for not laughing. 'We should be getting back to the Apprentice House,' she said instead.

'Well,' said Rhian as the three of them emerged into the hot summer sunshine, 'while Delphine was selling her body for honey cakes, I fetched our post from the Noces Gate — letters from Tierce.' She delved into her satchel. 'One from your family, Velody. And one for you from my brother,' she added, wrinkling her nose.

'Another letter from Cyniver,' Delphine crowed, snatching it from Rhian. 'I quite thought he'd forgotten about you this week. Of course, it must take him at least a week to produce the letter, what with the three rough drafts, and then the careful calligraphy, and the blotting, and the corrections, and the precise folding of the paper —'

Velody grabbed her letter and tucked it away to read later. 'Trust me,' she said. 'There's something to be said for a man who knows how to do a job thoroughly.'

'Have mercy on a sister's ears!' wailed Rhian. 'Honestly, why you had to take up with him!'

'She'd already smooched every redhead in this city,' said Delphine. 'Obviously she had to write home for reinforcements.'

Velody elbowed her and Delphine shrieked. 'Leave off, will you! I'm delicate. Anything for me?'

'Three,' said Rhian, handing them over.

Delphine stared at the seal of the first letter. 'Father.'

Velody pulled her off the path to sit on the grass. 'You told your family about our plans?' she asked.

'To work the markets until we've saved enough for our own premises?' Delphine looked hollow. 'Oh, yes.'

Rhian reached over. 'Shall I read it for you?'

'No! There's no point. It will say exactly the same as the others.' Delphine tore the envelope open and scanned the words on the thick, expensive paper. 'Well then,' she said and scrunched the letter in one hand.

'Are you disowned?' Velody couldn't help asking.

'Not yet. He's giving me one last chance to change my mind. If I come home by the Ides, leaving my apprenticeship incomplete, all will be forgiven.'

Rhian rested her chin on Delphine's shoulder. 'And if not?'

'He's writing to Mistress Sincy to withdraw his financial support.'

'That's not a problem,' said Velody, doing the sums in her head. 'We've less than a month to go. Rhian and I have enough savings to cover your board until then.'

'And what about the licence to trade, and the bond on the room we were to rent, and the silks I ordered from the Zafiran mercantile?' Delphine demanded. 'I'd pledged to cover all that with my inheritance from Grandmere, but Father won't release the funds. He says he'll have me declared incompetent if that's what it takes. Every banker in Tierce is in his club. I have nothing!'

Velody sighed and put her feet in Delphine's lap. 'Thimblehead. You have us. We'll sort something out.'

'There's always the Market Saints,' said Rhian, murmuring into Delphine's hair. 'I'm sure you've frightened them into submission and they're working on the problem even now.'

'Read us something from Cyniver,' Delphine commanded, toying with her other letters. 'Cheer me up.'

Velody blushed. 'No. It's private.'

Rhian rolled her eyes. 'I'll stick my fingers in my ears and sing if it's dirty. No reason why Delphine should miss out on the good stuff.'

'He wants to marry me.'

There was a long pause from the others. Then Rhian pounced, hugging Velody madly and squealing — Rhian, who had never squealed in her life.

Still a little stunned, Velody raised her eyes to meet Delphine's cool blue gaze.

'Well,' said her friend, a few moments later. 'That's you settled then.'

The thing was, Velody thought, she wasn't sure she wanted to be settled.

ONE DAY AFTER THE NONES OF CERIALIS

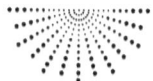

DAYLIGHT

*M*elody stared out the window of the rattling train all the way from Aufleur to Tierce, wishing she had brought some piecework to keep her hands busy. She kept going over and over the words in her head, trying to make sense of them.

There had to be an easy way to tell your young man that you loved him, but didn't want to marry him.

Her neck itched where the apprentice collar was removed yesterday. She was a qualified dressmaker, finally. Rhian and Delphine were released with honours as well. She should be with them, celebrating, finding somewhere to live, filing a claim for a market stall. Instead, she was going home.

She stepped off the train, the thick summer air blowing in her face along with steam and dust from the platform. The borrowed coat from Delphine was too warm for Tierce, which was further inland than Aufleur.

Velody searched the platform. The crowd bustled with

ladies in full-length gowns and gentlemen in those wide-brimmed hats she had almost forgotten about. Aufleur must be starting to feel like home, because the fashions there made more sense to her.

Finally she spotted a dark head of curls and waved frantically to her brother.

'Needles!' Sage announced, catching Velody up in a bear hug. 'Finally made it back, eh? Not too prissy for us? What are you wearing?' He eyed her skirt with a wariness that was only half put on.

'My knees are covered,' she said defensively.

'Only just, missy.'

'Sage, I hate to break it to you, but I'm not the only demme in the world who has ankles.'

'You're the only one in this city who's showing 'em,' he muttered, taking her canvas bag from her as they walked along the platform, Velody's smaller arm tucked into his larger one. He limped as he walked, but it was less noticeable than it had been the last time she came home for a visit.

'How are you?' Velody asked, checking him over. There was colour in his cheeks.

'Well enough,' he said, shying away from her questions. 'Got some work at the clock factory. No heavy lifting.'

'That's wonderful.' He was nearly thirty now, the eldest of them. She knew it drove him up the wall to be stuck in the family bakery, surrounded by flour and hot ovens, having to put up with Papa's way of doing everything, from turning the dough to stacking the shelves. 'You enjoy it?'

'It's a living,' Sage grunted. 'It's mine, anyway.'

'And you're not...'

'Naught stronger than ale,' he said in the heavy voice of a put-upon brother. 'Still.' Then he smirked out the side of his mouth at her. 'Megora wouldn't have it any other way.'

'Oh, Megora is it?'

Velody's mouth was still open from the teasing laugh when she saw another familiar figure, a slender man with spectacles and a formal suit, standing uncomfortably by the station door. 'Oh,' she said softly. Cyniver. She hadn't told him she was coming home, not wanting to give away any hint at what she had to say to him. Obviously someone couldn't keep a secret.

Sage jabbed her with an elbow, looking far too pleased with himself. 'I told Mam you were taking the later train. Reckon you've got an hour — and if she finds out, you tell her I was with you every step of the way. Sisters need chaperones, to keep their reputations nice.'

'You've done this sort of thing before,' Velody said dryly, now realising how it was her sisters managed to get away with what they did.

'Call me an old romantic,' said her brother.

CYNIVER AND VELODY walked along the docks slowly, getting closer and closer to Cheapside, listening to the cries of the boatmen as they steered their wares back and forth.

'Everything's so bright here,' she said softly. 'I'd forgotten.'

'It's the stone,' he said in the voice that meant he was about to start lecturing on something he had learned from a book. She had missed that about him. 'They don't have any sandstone mines near Aufleur, that's why all the buildings are so dark. Brown and grey and black.'

'I've been gone so long,' she said.

Cyniver said nothing for a few moments, and they just walked.

'You can say no,' he said finally. 'I won't be heartbroken. Well, I will. But I don't want you to say yes just to be nice.'

Velody did her best not to laugh at how earnest he was. 'I

want to say yes,' she said. 'Not to be nice; I really do. But I can't leave Aufleur. Not to get married. My life's just starting. I've worked so hard for it all. I want to live with Delphine and Rhian and make dresses.' She sighed, not wanting to make eye contact.

'So,' Cyniver said. 'You're choosing a city over me.'

Velody was a little startled at the dry note in his voice. 'Yes,' she said.

'It had better be the city, then.'

She blinked. He didn't seem overly upset. 'What do you mean?'

Cyniver took both her hands in his. Her palms were still sticky from the train, but his skin felt cool. 'I mean, there are bookbinders in Aufleur. I can get a good recommendation — I'm sure I could find work. Better than that... I don't want to bind books my whole life. I want to draw buildings. Design new buildings. They don't have to be made of sandstone. Grey bricks will do just as well.'

She had forgotten how sweet he was. How had she forgotten that?

'You're coming with me?' Velody whispered.

'Of course. And maybe... if you don't want to get married yet... then in a year or two...'

She flung her arms around him, face buried in his neck. 'Maybe,' she said in his ear. 'In a year or two. Yes.'

Dame Threedy from next door was walking past with a basket of fish and pretended not to see them, though she walked faster until she was around the corner and away. Mam would have heard about this before Velody got herself home.

'You'd better give me the ring,' she sighed. 'It will distract them nicely.'

6

IDES OF CERIALIS

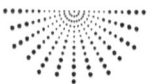

NOX

*T*hings came together surprisingly well. Delphine, it turned out, had an aunt who thoroughly disapproved of a demoiselle being disowned for daring to work for a living. Aunt Marcialle declared that her own first marriage had been 'an appalling exercise' and that as Delphine was the first Ingiers woman in three generations to show an ounce of gumption, she was going to support her bid for freedom. She gave Delphine a house.

It was a small house on Via Silviana, with two rooms below — the shop-workroom in front and kitchen at the back — and three above, with a wash-pump in the tiny yard behind. It was sandwiched into a street full of similar little shops and residences only two blocks from the Piazza Nautilia (with the best public baths in the city) and two streets away from the bustling merchant district of Giacosa. All this, and no rent to pay. It could be a shop one day, if they earned enough from the market to set it up.

Too good to be true, Velody found herself thinking one nox as she put the finishing touches on a brown and gold harvest tunic by lantern light. She squashed the thought almost as soon as she had it, but the damage was done.

If the saints tumbled this into our laps, what do they expect in return?

Cyniver was coming to Aufleur soon. Whenever Velody thought of him, her heart melted. He had already made inquiries about work with the best bookbinders in the city, and insisted their betrothal could be as long as she liked. Or he could move into the house straightaway if she would marry him now...

Velody had liked other boys here and there, nothing as serious as this. But she had never been able to imagine herself married. She could imagine being married to Cyniver.

On the few occasions they managed to spend the nox together, she did not dream.

Velody could never remember her dreams, except for brief impressions — herself, walking in a noxgown. Sometimes she was underground, in an odd ruined city. Sometimes she was running. Sometimes she was up high, staring at the sky, at the stars, at other colours...

There were mornings when she almost caught a real memory of her dream — a snatch of dialogue in a familiar voice. A laugh that made her shiver, or hardened her nipples for no sensible reason.

Yes. Marrying Cyniver would solve that too. With him at her side, the dreams would be gone.

THIS DREAM WAS DIFFERENT. Velody was not in Aufleur, for a start. She was barefoot, running through Tierce. She could not find any of the streets she knew. Where was Cheapside? Where were the docks? Where was her family's bakery? Bolts of light fell from the sky, smashing the boats and the canal walls to pieces. She looked up and saw shapes, like people only not, flailing against glowing tendrils of fire and ice. It was as if the sky itself was attacking the city. One by one, the figures in the sky vanished in bursts of light, until they were all gone.

No one left to defend us.

Defend us from what?

As Velody ran, the golden buildings peeled away from the cobblestones and were dragged into the sky. She stared in horror as the bridge broke into pieces, each of them sucked upwards with a hideous noise.

She could hear screaming, and it could be anyone, but her heart told her it was her brothers and sisters, being swallowed by the sky.

A body fell hard in front of her, a woman in black leathers who burst apart into a scattered heap of dead black rats.

VELODY WOKE WITH A START. She had fallen asleep in her chair. The harvest tunic slipped to the floor as she leaped up and ran to the kitchen door.

She was still in Aufleur. It was just a dream. She knew that. And yet when she unlatched the door and stepped outside in her bare feet, she expected to see... something. Some sign that a city had been torn up by its roots and destroyed.

I have to remember this dream, she told herself fiercely. *I have to remember, I have to remember.*

How could she forget the sight of Tierce — the city of her childhood — ripped apart like it was made of paper?

She stood there, shivering in the darkness, holding on to what she knew.

'Velody?' said a voice, some time later. Rhian came out, carrying a quilt with her. 'What are you doing out here? It's barely dawn.'

Dawn. The dreams always disappeared in daylight. Velody turned, opening her mouth to tell Rhian: *Tierce. Something has happened to Tierce. My family... your family... Cyniver...*

'Your brother,' Velody said finally. Yes, that. Focus on Cyniver, on his gentle hands and that smile he hid behind his spectacles when he was amused. *Remember.* She did not know why it was so important, only that it was.

Rhian looked confused. 'I don't have a brother.'

Velody stared at her as the courtyard lightened around them both. Rhian didn't have a brother. Of course she didn't. None of them had families — not Delphine, nor Rhian, nor Velody. It was one of the things that bound them together — they had no one else.

'I forgot,' she said in wonder.

'Were you dreaming?' Rhian asked with an odd look on her face. 'Whatever it was, Velody, it wasn't real. You're working too hard.'

'That must be it,' Velody agreed. She allowed Rhian to lead her inside.

Days later, when she found a collection of letters written to her by a man named Cyniver from a city called Tierce, Velody threw them away without hesitation. The words meant nothing to her.

7

GARNET AND ASHIOL

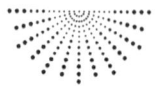

*T*ierce was not our fault. That was not our Court, not our city. We had our own battles to fight.

Ashiol came to find me after Tierce fell. He sat beside me on the wall, our legs swinging as if we were boys and courtesi again. As if we were friends. 'Quiet nox,' he said, the bastard. Waiting for me to say the true thing, to acknowledge what had happened.

'Aye,' I agreed. 'But if the sky wasn't quiet right after eating an entire frigging city, what hope would we have?'

He said nothing, for some time.

'It's not my fault,' I added viciously, when the silence started to gnaw at me.

'Never said it was.'

'Oh, no? And you haven't come to tell me that Livilla is in pieces, and Poet's drinking again, and half my sentinels are mourning their frigging families?'

'No,' said Ash. 'I came to see if you were all right.'

'I'm peachy.'

'Can see that.'

He tipped back his head, staring at those devil-damned

36

benign stars. I can see him now, the image of him. I could trace around him with a finger. I remember exactly his tone of voice. How careful he was not to accuse even as he said, 'Must have been something we could do. Heliora warned us weeks ago.'

I hated him in that moment. There had always been moments of hating him. For all I loved him, I could never forget that he was the aristocrat slumming it in the streets, while the Creature Court had given me more than the daylight world ever could.

'Our precious seer isn't always right,' I growled. 'Do you know what she told me the other day? She said, "Ashiol will be the death of you." What do you think she meant by that?'

He actually grinned, the bastard. As if somehow I had changed the topic to a more amusing one. 'Well, she's not always right.'

I wasn't smiling. 'This charming idea of yours, that we could have somehow done more to save Tierce from the sky even if it meant abandoning our own city. Have you shared that thought with anyone?'

'Of course not,' he said, sounding offended. 'You are Power and Majesty. I'm yours. You know that.'

'Good,' I said, wanting to hurt him. Wanting him to show some bloody respect instead of mouthing the words. 'If I ever hear you questioning my authority again — in public or private — I will bite your throat out.'

He was remarkably quiet. When he finally spoke, after such a careful, thoughtful pause, he said, 'If you can't trust me, you can't trust anyone.'

Exactly my thoughts.

Things tumbled differently after that. Tierce was the first real test of how much our Creature Court believed in me as Power and Majesty. Naturally, they were found wanting. You know the rest, I'm sure. You'll have heard all the grotesque details. How Garnet became a monster. How every day that he was in power brought a new wave of mistrust.

How I wrapped myself up in my own misery and suspicion, clinging to the few remaining people who were loyal to me.

Ashiol was not one of them.

I knew he worked against me, that he thought I was unworthy to lead the Court. After Tierce fell, he did not look at me the same way. None of them did. Conversations ended when I came near.

I was the fucking Power and Majesty and they treated me like a child to be indulged lest his madness prove contagious. Every single one of them. They did not respect me as they had Ortheus. They looked to Ashiol instead — seeking his approval; his confirmation that I was not a total madman. I saw the tiny nods, the acknowledgement that he supported me, this time. For now.

I burned with it. The authority should be mine, not his. They trusted him more, loved him more. If I was truly to be the Power and Majesty, I would have to bring him down. Prove to them once and for all that I was the master.

Is this what you want to hear? How I humbled him, humiliated him? That he stayed at my side even after I made him bleed? Too much pride, both of us. When he would not stand down, would not let his discomfort even show in his face, I took it further.

He became my prisoner. My toy. I hurt him and tortured him and it made sense at the time. *He gave me no choice.*

Ashiol awoke in the dark room. He braced himself for the pain that always came first. The burn of the skysilver net, threading scorchlines in patterns over his skin. The deep hollowing ache of a blade in his ribs. Garnet's fingerprints on his back or hands or feet, still glowing with light.

There was nothing. No pain. He bent his body forward, letting the chains take his weight. They should burn too — steel wrapped in skysilver — but they did not. Ashiol licked his lips, and tasted blood that was not his own.

'You were out of it,' said a familiar voice in the darkness. 'I only gave you a little.'

His senses were dulled. Normally he would know Kelpie by her scent as well as her voice. Ashiol could not feel animor pulsing through his veins. She had given him a taste of her own mortal blood and with it taken away both his power and whatever pain Garnet had inflicted upon him. He couldn't remember. Was it a bad sign that he couldn't even remember?

'You shouldn't be here,' he said. 'He knows you creep in here. He always knows. He'll punish you, or the others, and it's not worth it.'

'I stopped your pain,' Kelpie whispered angrily. As if he should feel gratitude. Thanks to the blood in his mouth, he couldn't feel anything. She had done him no favours.

'It won't last,' said Ashiol. 'He'll just hurt me again. Harder next time. Giving me a few hours of relief won't make a difference.'

'You sound like you've given up,' she accused. 'Like you expect him to keep torturing you forever. You're *letting* him do this.'

Ashiol managed a sound that was almost a laugh. His throat was red raw from screaming. 'What do you want me to do? Run?'

She came forward, and even with the mortal senses he was now limited to, he could smell her skin and her hair. The leathers she wore. The metal of the swords on her back. Familiar scents, all. 'He is the Power and Majesty,' she whispered. 'But you're a King too. You could take it from him. We'll support you...'

'Pretty words from a sentinel,' he said bitterly. 'Treason, in fact.'

She made a noise of disgust. 'You'd rather let him do this to you, over and over, than betray one oath to him?'

Ashiol smiled in the darkness. Odd to hear it spoken aloud. 'Yes,' he said simply.

Kelpie left, not even bothering to conceal the sounds as she slammed the door behind her. Ashiol stayed on his knees in the darkness, waiting.

Time passed, and then Garnet came, as he always did.

'Ting, tie, tan,' he said in a mocking voice, reciting an old nursery song. 'I smell the blood of a mortal man. You have to bless those sentinels, don't you? For persistence, if not loyalty.'

'They can't help it,' Ashiol said. He could still taste Kelpie in his mouth. 'You put them in a difficult position. They are supposed to serve and protect all the Kings, not just the Power and Majesty.'

'Aye, it must be so confusing for them,' Garnet said cynically. 'Imagine, two Kings at war. I'll bet that's never happened before.'

'Are we at war?' asked Ashiol. 'I thought we were on the same side.'

Garnet came nearer, one hand resting on a chain. 'You knew I was listening in.'

'I wouldn't have said anything different either way.'

It was true, sadly. Ashiol was loyal. Much good it did him.

It was possible that Kelpie was right. Ashiol could successfully beat Garnet and become Power and Majesty. But that would mean killing his friend, and ruling the Court as ruthlessly and viciously as Garnet did.

The price was too high. What was the point of over-throwing a monster only to become the monster in turn?

Garnet unfastened the cuffs with deliberation, letting Ashiol drop to the floor. 'You should tell them,' he said, 'that you hate being like them more than you hate the pain.'

Ashiol rubbed his wrists. His body felt numb all over. 'They don't believe me,' he said.

'They don't understand you.' Garnet reached out, touching Ashiol's face. It was all Ashiol could do not to flinch away. 'I'm the only one who knows how you think.'

'Of course you are,' said Ashiol, agreeing as he always did, smoothing things over. Letting Garnet think he was in control. *If you knew how I thought, you wouldn't keep expecting me to betray you.*

Garnet smiled once and then turned, leaving the door open as he walked out of the dark room. Ashiol waited for the trap, and when it did not come, he followed Garnet out into the light.

Maybe this time, they could get back what they'd once had. He had finally proved his loyalty... hadn't he?

It lasted so much longer than I had expected. Ashiol in chains. An example to them all. The sentinels helped him through it, traitors all — I never trusted them again after that.

It was not pain that broke him in the end, but love. I forgave him. Freed him of his chains. Took him in my arms and soothed his hurts. He forgave me too, so easily I almost wept.

Then I did to him what I did to the little brown mouse so many years earlier. But not with a kiss, and not with consent. I tore his powers from him while he fought and screamed.

Stole every pulse of animor in his body. Left him nothing but a daylight husk.

Finally, finally, he crawled away in exile. Left me. Proved what I had known all along — that he could be weak. He could be broken and shamed. I should have been satisfied. It was a proud, great moment. Everything I had been working for.

I remained in an empty Court, surrounded by people who hated and feared me. I had rid myself of the one person who had ever truly loved me. A victory indeed.

Do I disgust you? Do you think you can save me? Better people than you have tried. I broke them into pieces. What exactly do you think you can do to make a difference?

8

LUPERCALIA

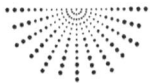

TWO DAYS AFTER THE IDES OF LUPERCAL

DAYLIGHT

'*A*re you asleep?' Delphine asked, from a long way away.

Velody mumbled and pushed at her friend. She had been working for two days flat out, turning and topstitching ceremonial baking aprons. The poxy things flew out of the shop as fast as she could make them, and there were still two days of the Fornacalia to go.

Rhian and Delphine had been similarly rushed off their feet producing garlands for the nine days of Parentalia, during which all citizens of Aufleur travelled to lay flowers and sweetmeats on their family tombs and grave markers. In the three years since they moved into this house, Delphine and Rhian had hit it big with a major garlanding contract for the City Council. The council often chose to distribute numbers of free garlands for particular festivals, and they paid their workers well.

Delphine was justifiably proud of their contracts, and

pushed Velody to work towards her own private commissions so that they could close the shop altogether. Turning their home into a place of business was not the grand dream they expected, but a hassle from beginning to end.

It was difficult, though, to acquire a reputation making gowns for the Great Families and other wealthy women in Aufleur when no one had heard of you. Velody kept applying for commissions, but had little success. Her only regular private work was providing pantomime costumes for the local musettes and penny opera stands.

Today was Lupercalia, a one-day festival stuck smack bang in between the two more substantial holidays. Considering that the streets would be filled with carousing men wearing goatskins, Velody had considered herself justified in closing the shop and snoozing in front of the fire.

'I'm awake,' she muttered now, almost falling out of her armchair. 'What's up?'

A vague shade of a dream still lingered with her (*'I miss Ashiol,'* said Garnet) but Velody shook it off as she stared up at Delphine. (*'Well then,'* said a sharp voice in an Islandser accent, *'you shouldn't have broken him, laddie. He's not coming back, and you'd do well to learn to manage without him.'*)

'Where's Rhian?' asked Delphine. 'I went out to get more white silk for the garlands, but the drunkards and goat-lovers have taken the streets. I only made it back in one piece because the butcher boy escorted me with his cudgel.'

'Is that what they're calling them now?' Velody replied dryly.

'Hush, I'm serious. It's mad out there. Goatskins and revelry, and where the saints is Rhian?'

Velody looked around the workroom. 'She was right here. Waiting for the courier to take that batch of Parentalia garlands to the Forum — he was late.'

'The garlands have gone,' said Delphine. 'The courier must have picked them up. I'll check upstairs.'

'What's the urgency anyway?' Velody called after her. 'I'll tell you together!' Delphine sang down.

There was a thump and rattle at the shop door. Velody answered it, and a bloodstained boy fell through to land on the floor.

'What happened to you?' she asked, recognising him as one of the council couriers.

'Sorry I'm late,' he gasped. 'Got caught in a riot on the Via Leondrine. Streets are frigging crazy on Lupercalia.'

'You're hours late,' said Velody, staring around the messy workroom. There were no Parentalia garlands anywhere.

'She's not in her room,' said Delphine, coming down the stairs. 'Shall I check the neighbours? Oh, hello. Who are you, and do you need bandaging? I'm rubbish at it, but Rhian's pretty good.'

'She's gone,' said Velody, trying not to panic. 'The courier was late —'

'There was a riot!' the boy protested. 'Three streets deep.'

'A riot,' repeated Velody. 'A riot, and the Lupercalia antics, and hordes of drunk men filling the streets. I think Rhian has gone to deliver the garlands to the Forum herself.'

'Poxing bollocks,' said Delphine. 'We'd better go look for her.'

THE STREETS WERE MAD, and full of men. Goat masks and flapping leather filled the Piazza Nautilia from edge to edge, and the air was contaminated by the sickly stench of honey wine and vomit. Velody and Delphine stayed close together, glaring at any of the revellers who dared come too close.

Delphine had armed herself with a rolling pin, and Velody had a solid darning mushroom concealed in her skirts.

'Curse it, she must have come this way,' said Delphine. 'I mean, it's madness out here, but she wouldn't have taken the backstreets, would she? Not on a day like today.'

'This is useless,' said Velody, leaping out of the way as two hairy men dragged a giggling flute-demme along with them in something that had probably started out as a ceremonial dance but was now on its way to becoming a threesome. 'We'll never find her in this.'

'Stupid frigging council,' said Delphine. 'They said they'd fine us if we were late again. She comes out in this because one of their couriers ballsed it up.' She threw her arms up in disgust. 'You're right, let's get back.'

They were one street away from home when a drunk in a goatskin and mask caught hold of Delphine's arm. 'Going my way, lovely?'

'Get off,' snapped Delphine, trying to shake him away from her.

He held on all the harder. 'You wouldn't be out here if you weren't after a taste of Lupercalia cock, demme.'

Velody came up behind him, pressing her darning mushroom hard against his neck, hoping it felt like a more threatening weapon. 'Leave her alone, you lech.'

Delphine took the opportunity to knee the old goat in the balls and twisted away from his grasp.

She and Velody ran for it, laughing and breathless, until they got to their yard and let themselves in the kitchen door.

'Rhian?' Delphine bellowed into the house. 'Are you hoooome?'

Velody's breath caught in her throat. She stared at the kitchen table, a solid block of oak on sturdy legs that Rhian had built herself before they could afford to buy furniture. A red braid of hair lay on the pale wood, surrounded by loose tufts and locks, tangled in Velody's embroidery scissors. She couldn't do anything but stare for a moment. It looked so out of place.

There was blood beside the hair on the table. Just a smear, but the sight of it made her stomach tighten. She stumbled to the inner doorway and found another splash of blood on the floorboards.

'Rhian?' she called.

Both demmes raced up the stairs to Rhian's room.

'Are you all right?' Delphine called through the door, which caught on the slight latch when she pushed at it. She darted a look at Velody, as if wanting her to... what? Reassure her that nothing bad had happened?

'Let us in,' said Velody, knocking sharply. She pressed her ear to the door and heard only quiet sounds, somewhere between breathing and sobbing.

It took them far too long to force open the door — in the end they resorted to hitting it with a bronze flower bucket until the latch snapped and let them through.

Rhian was a crumpled figure on the floor, back against the wall, knees tucked up to her stomach. She jolted in fright when the door slammed open. 'No no no no...'

Velody stared at her friend. Rhian's head was practically shorn, loose ends fraying down around her devastated face. Her arm... a deep gash dripped blood slowly into her lap.

Delphine let out a tiny sound.

Velody ran. She clattered downstairs and fetched clean muslin. Hot water, they should have hot water, but there wasn't time to boil it, not now. She returned to Rhian's room on unsteady feet to find that neither of the others had moved. Delphine still hovered in the doorway, unsure what to do.

'Rhian,' Velody said softly, approaching her with caution.

Her friend flinched, staring at her as if afraid to be touched. Oh, hells.

'Did you do that to yourself?' Delphine asked in a high, strained voice.

'I had to do something,' said Rhian. She sounded calm, almost normal, but she was shaking.

Velody leaned towards her, tearing strips of the muslin. 'You have to let me stop the bleeding.'

Rhian's eyes were terrible. 'Do I? Will that help?'

'It will help me,' said Velody, and her hands were shaking as well as she did her best to bandage her friend's arm.Rhian shied away at the first touch, but eventually submitted to being tended. She held herself awkwardly the whole time, and, as soon as Velody had fastened the bandage, she shuffled across the wall, putting distance between them.

'What happened?' Delphine blurted. 'What did those bastards do to you? Rhian!'

'Nothing happened,' said Rhian. Her voice didn't sound normal any more. It was vague and soft as if it might drift away at any moment.

'Horseshit,' Delphine snorted. 'Someone hurt you!'

'I don't want to —' Rhian's voice broke. 'Please. If you are my friends, don't ask me.'

Friends. They had been close for so long — ten years now since they'd first met. Being loyal to each other, looking after each other, these were things that Velody believed beyond question. They had all lost something, were all without family, and then there was that odd lack, the missing years before they set eyes on each other, which bound them together more strongly than most people.

'It might help if you tell us,' Velody began, not wanting to push, but not knowing how to leave this alone.

'No,' Rhian said sharply. 'I don't want to — I just want to forget. We've forgotten everything else. I don't remember my childhood, my parents. I don't know anything about myself before the day I set foot in the Apprentice Fair. Delphine doesn't remember the name of the aunt who gave her this damned house, you don't know who gave you the ring that always makes you so sad. If we can forget all those things, then I can forget today.'

'You think it will be that easy?' Delphine asked, bristling. She was the one who most hated any reference to their strange memory losses; the one who ran around dancing or drinking or screaming with laughter, anything to blot out the fact that she had those gaps in her memory — the same gaps as Velody and Rhian.

'It has to be,' said Rhian. She cradled her arm close to her chest. 'I want to be alone. Can you both... I promise I won't cut myself again. Just go.'

Velody knew a wall when she saw it. 'We'll be downstairs,' she said softly and rose to leave, taking Delphine's arm and all but dragging her away from the door.

'So, what?' Delphine demanded when they both reached the kitchen again, out of earshot of Rhian. 'Are we really going to let her pretend everything's bright and bonny? We don't even know what happened!'

'Don't we?' said Velody.

She swept Rhian's hacked hair from the table and tossed it into the cold grate of the cooking range.

'You think she was raped?'

'Don't you?'

'There are laws,' Delphine said sullenly. 'We should call the vigiles.'

'On Lupercalia, with the streets full of masked men with their cocks hanging out?' Velody said in disbelief. 'Even if she could bear witness — and she doesn't want to speak of it, evidently — who's to say she could identify her attacker?'

Attackers, perhaps. She couldn't help thinking of that

49

giggling flute-demme. Had she really wanted to go off with those goat-men? How much had she drunk to cause her to go along with it? Should Velody have tried to stop her?

'We have to let Rhian decide what to do for herself,' she said helplessly.

'And pretending things didn't happen is our speciality,' Delphine shot at her.

Well, yes. It was.

Velody lit the fire. Rhian's hair frizzled and crackled and began to burn up. 'If she wants to forget it, we should let her,' she said, her hand shaking on the taper.

Rhian would get through this. They had forgotten so many other things. What was one more missing piece?

They could go forward from here, and everything would be all right.

9

FOUR DAYS BEFORE THE KALENDS OF FLORALIS

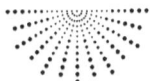

NOX

*T*he Arches. A world of broken buildings and disused tunnels, buried deep beneath the city of Aufleur. Macready hated this place. There was honour here, once. Now there was just dried blood.

He made his unsteady way through the darkness until a tunnel opened up into the wide concrete slab of the Haymarket. Oil lamps flickered everywhere. The Creature Court was in session. The Lords lay indolently on piles of cushions and rugs, their courtesi kneeling at their feet. Platters picked clean of food lay scattered around the floor.

In the centre of it all, a lean gattopardo body lay on a dais draped with a silken coverlet. The large spotted cat seemed to be asleep, his chest rising and falling. As drunk as he was, Macready still saw the half-lidded eye that watched them all.

Another game.

'Careful, oaf,' Livilla spat as Macready made his unsteady way to the dais.

'Begging your pardon, milady,' he said in his usual gabble, fast enough that she didn't catch the sarcasm that was always there, just under the surface, when he dealt with the Lords and Court.

Priest got in Macready's way next, his large velvet-clad body serving as a substantial barrier. 'You smell like a distillery, man,' he said in distaste.

'Fit right in here then, will I not?' Macready slurred, gesturing at the empty wine bottles that littered the floor. His Islandser accent grew stronger when he drank, even to his own ears. Odd, that. 'I'm here to see himself,' he added loudly. 'There isn't one of yez can stop me.'

That made them laugh — Lords and Court alike. 'Let him pass,' Warlord drawled. 'It should be entertaining, if nothing else.'

Priest moved aside with a smirk.

'That's better,' Macready declared, making his way forward. He had a plan. The drink might have him all fogged, but he could still follow through.

A short demme in a sentinel's uniform matching his own came forward next, to stop him getting near the dais. Kelpie. 'Macready, what are you doing? You'll get yourself killed,' she added in an undertone.

He leaned forward and gave her a smacking kiss on the nose. 'And wouldn't that be a fine, fine way to finish off the day, my lass?' He lurched around her. 'Awake, my son! We're all dying to hear from you, so we are.'

The gattopardo stood, stretching his body lazily. His limbs blurred together, creating a form that eventually shaped itself into a red-haired cove, naked as the day he was born. He sniffed and picked up a nearby robe, throwing it casually over his nakedness. 'I hope there's a good reason for this sudden lack of manners, sentinel,' said Garnet. Power and Majesty. Right bastard.

Macready fell to his knees in exaggerated obeisance. 'Always, Majesty,' he said roughly. 'I came to —' *Kill you, I came to kill you. Our swords might be gone but I've a knife here with your name on it, so I have...* '— tell you...'

He swallowed, tasting bile in his mouth. Either that or the booze had been nastier than he thought at the time. '... Ilsa's dead.'

Garnet gave a flicker of a smile, reseating himself on the silk. He beckoned with one hand and Livilla came to him willingly, curling her body against his and sneering at Macready.

'Remind me,' Garnet said. 'Which one was Ilsa again?'

Macready willed himself to stay steady, not to clench his hands into fists. He'd never get a knife near Garnet if he was that obvious about it. He opened his mouth to say something equally flippant, but nothing came out.

'She took a wound in the last battle,' Kelpie said, her voice only a little uneven. 'It went bad. We were hoping...'

Aye, lass, hope. Precious little of that around here.

'Goodness,' said Garnet, sounding amused. 'We are running low on sentinels, are we not?'

Macready's head spun. He'd drunk more than was healthy. 'You'll not be happy till we're all dead,' he said out loud. He didn't care any more about watching every word.

'I don't need you,' Garnet said, utterly delighted with himself. 'I never needed you. Ashiol might have relied upon the sentinels, but he was weak and now he's gone.'

Macready knew exactly where the knife was, hidden under his shirt at the small of his back. It was the Silver Captain's old dagger, may-he-rest-peaceful-enough, the only weapon that had been overlooked when Garnet took the blades away from the sentinels. It was made of skysilver, the one thing that could put Garnet in the ground. Macready could grab it, even drunk off his arse like he was. He could try. He could die trying. That option was looking pretty bloody good right now.

Garnet smiled, as if he knew exactly what Macready was thinking. As if he knew that Macready would never do it. Kelpie wasn't so sure, watching him with wide, wary eyes.

No, Macready couldn't use the knife. He smiled, acknowledging it to himself. The oath held him here. Kept him loyal. The sky could fall in and he still would serve Garnet.

'Have you heard the news about the Daylight Duc?' he asked instead. 'Old codger finally kicked off. The grand-daughter rules them now.'

Garnet's expression did not change, though his stillness spoke for itself. 'What makes you think I give a frig what the daylight folk do with themselves?'

Macready kept smiling. Knowing he couldn't use the knife made him feel oddly free. 'There's a rumour that she'll be bringing her cousin Ashiol back to the city, so she will. He's her heir now, until she weds and starts popping out the babbies.' He couldn't stab, but he could sting.

Garnet lashed out and Macready braced himself for the blow. Instead, the Power and Majesty grabbed him by the collar and pulled him in, close enough to smell spiced potions on his breath. 'I've known Ashiol Xandelian for longer than you have,' Garnet hissed. 'If you think he's going to march back in here and challenge me, you're wrong. I beat him and he crawled away. He won't be back.'

Macready gasped, unable to breathe until Garnet let go, allowing him to drop back to his knees. The world tilted sideways, blurring badly.

'Now,' announced Garnet pleasantly, 'what sort of punishment is suitable for a smart-mouthed sentinel who doesn't know his place? Anybody?'

Around him, Macready heard the Lords and Court laugh.

Vultures, the pack of them. 'As long as it's entertaining, my Power!' called out one sly voice. Poet, Macready thought, smarming up as usual. He braced himself, waiting for the pain.

When it came, a burning shock that ran up his arm, he lost control and hurled the contents of his stomach at the foot of the dais. He ended up flat on his back, shaking with pain, aware that something had happened to his hand, something bad.

The last thing he saw before he lost consciousness was Garnet, and it wasn't much consolation that the bastard looked rattled.

Should have just fecking knifed him.

10

NINTH DAY OF THE LUDI AUFLEURIS

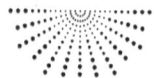

DAYLIGHT

'*A*sh, Ash, Ash!' The boys crashed into the librarion, two lanky teenagers falling over themselves to get their side of the story out — it wasn't Jemmen's fault, or Zade's, but somehow the statue in the west garden had broken and Keeper was going to mash them, but it was only an ear or two, maybe they could fix it, if only he helped them. That was what big brothers were supposed to do.

If the alternative was working on the estate accounts for his mother, Ashiol could live with that. He put the pen down. 'Explain it from the top,' he suggested, and the boys launched into their saga once again. They were so noisy that none of them heard their mother entering the room.

The Dowager Baronille Augusta Xandelian Lanouvre Diamagne, former Ducomtessa of Aufleur, was a woman born to be a matrona — more confident and beautiful in her late forties than in her demoiselle days. Widowed twice and a mother of six, she was oddly satisfied in this backwater estate and her life here.

'Dearlings,' she said in a firm voice. 'I need to talk with Ashiol alone.'

Her two younger sons made themselves scarce, obviously worried she had overheard their troubles.

Ashiol shook his head, feeling like an old man. At their age, he was in the city, dodging fussy ministers and public rituals by day and making his first steps into the Creature Court by nox. He had never been as young as those two, or fretted over problems as minor as a broken statue.

'What is it, Mother?'

Augusta had her careful face on. She sat on the far side of the ancient carved desk that had belonged to the Baronne di Diamagne, Ashiol's late stepfather. 'Another letter from Aufleur,' she said, and placed the heavy envelope on the desk between them. The Duchessa's seal was bright and waxy.

Ashiol eyed the letter, making no move to open it. It would be the same as the others. 'Don't worry,' he told his mother. 'I'm not going back.'

There was a chiming sound from the hallway, and then another. His mother's late husband had collected clocks, the kind with gears and levers and noise every hour. You never saw clockwork in Aufleur — another of the city's mad traditions — which meant Ashiol got an hourly reminder he was here and not there.

'Perhaps it would be good for you,' said Augusta once the chimes had died down. She did not sound overly convinced.

He didn't blame her mistrust. He had returned from the city half-dead and hollow-eyed, four years ago. His mother had no idea what had driven him into a black cloud of desperation, no knowledge of the Creature Court, or Garnet's betrayal, or the fact that he couldn't breathe in

Aufleur now that he had lost his power, his animor, everything that made him sane.

She didn't know he had been a hero once. All she knew were his failings. The potions and drink he had turned to when there was nothing else. The suicide attempts. But she had brought him home to heal, and he almost thought he had. Except when his damned cousin sent one of those letters.

'It's not like she hasn't been ruling the city for years,' he said sourly.

The Old Duc had succumbed to the 'family complaint' a long time ago. Their grandmother, the Old Duchessa, had served as his Regenta for years, then Isangell had taken over after her death. For an eighteen-year-old demoiselle, his cousin had plenty of practice at politics.

'If only she'd find herself a husband,' Augusta sighed. 'She needs an heir of her own...' She darted an apologetic look at her son.

He laughed. 'Believe me, I don't want to be Duc. Can you imagine it?' How would that be for irony? Cast out of the Creature Court, only to rule in the daylight. 'Isangell has some crazy idea that my presence will help her with the City Fathers. She's too young to remember why they don't have a lot of respect for me.'

Ashiol was not going back. Here in Diamagne he could survive his loss of power. The sky never opened here. He could feel almost whole. Nothing Isangell could write in a letter would change that.

Later, after his mother left him alone, he cracked open the seal and allowed the words to wash over him.

Need you... please, Ashiol, I need a show of strength... they want me married off, and I won't make that decision hastily... if not now, then at the end of my year of mourning: I need a consort to stand at my side for the Floralia, one without political implications...

It was the last paragraph that slayed him.

You were always so strong. I need to borrow that strength.

Apparently his little cousin didn't know him at all.

11

KALENDS OF VENTURIS

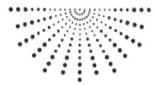

DAYLIGHT

*I*t was a new year, bright and cold, and the streets were streaked with slush. The snowfall had only lasted a few hours, and the perfect look of the frosted streets lasted even less.

Velody's boots were wet as she made her way to the Palazzo. She had an invitation to meet with some factotum or other to discuss a contract — livery, she expected. She had made uniforms for one of the Great Families last spring: boring work but good income.

The Palazzo was a grand old building sprawled over the Balisquine hill. The stone was dark, like everything else in Aufleur. Sometimes Velody imagined a brighter city with yellow, dusty stone buildings, but she didn't know where those thoughts came from. She had never lived anywhere but here.

Velody was taken to room after room, and finally waited in an eggshell-blue parlour for almost an hour, trying to keep her hands still. Finally the door opened and a demoiselle in a simple white mourning robe entered. She had a long braid of blonde hair and was awfully young to be in the position of ordering uniforms for the Palazzo.

'Thank you for waiting,' the demme said apologetically. 'Matters of state, you know.'

Oh, saints. Velody was an idiot. This was no factotum. This was the Duchessa d'Aufleur herself.

'No trouble at all, High and Brightness,' she said, relieved that she hadn't spoken her error aloud. 'How can I be of service?'

The Duchessa was pretty, though she had her grandfather's nose — it dominated her face and gave her a rather stern look, except when she smiled.

'I want a dress,' she said, and in that moment she sounded like any old merchant's daughter with a special dance coming up. Velody started to relax. One client was much like another, surely. 'I loved the costumes you made for the Saturnalia columbines,' the Duchessa added. 'The moonlight dress in particular. Such a stunning effect.'

'Bugle fringe,' said Velody. 'It creates a cascade of light and shimmer.' Those costumes had been worn by dancers at her local musette, the Argentia. Hardly the sort of place one would expect the city's ruler to frequent, even if the Duchessa did go out in public, which she had not since the death of the Old Duc. 'How did you happen to see them?'

The demoiselle blushed. Goodness, she was young. Velody had nearly a decade on her, and found it hard to take in how much power this near-child wielded from behind her walls.

'Sometimes I go out in disguise,' the Duchessa confessed, her eyes bright at the thought of it. 'I love the musette. Far more than the sacred games, or any of the performances they allow into the Palazzo.'

'And you want a dress,' Velody said, oddly disappointed.

'Oh, not for that,' the Duchessa assured her. 'My year of mourning ends just before the Floralia, and I'll be taking a public role in the festival. It's months away, but I need to look perfect.' She bit her lip. 'I know what they all think of me. The City Fathers talk over my head like I'm a child. I let them make far too many decisions for me when I first had to replace my grandmother as Regenta and they have grown used to such compliance. They will not take me seriously until I have the love and belief of the people to hold over their heads. That means I have to put on a show from the first day of my public career. A good one. I want a dress that no one will forget, and when I saw those columbines... I thought anyone who can make a dusty old theatre look like it's full of moonlight has to be the dressmaker I'm looking for. Will you do it?'

Velody was startled at the Duchessa confiding so openly in her. She thought fast. This was an astounding opportunity, and not just for herself. Rhian was working again, weaving flowers into garlands with Delphine's ribbons, but she still wouldn't set foot out of the house. They had closed the shop because she reacted badly whenever male customers visited.

'Something with fresh flowers,' Velody said. 'For the Floralia. I have some ideas — I may have to bring in a florister as well. And a ribboner.'

The Duchessa nodded, looking absurdly grateful considering that she was the customer. 'Anything you need.'

A dress that no one would forget. Velody could do that. And if this commission brought Rhian back to the real world at the same time, all the better.

12

APHRODAL

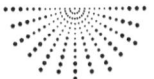

FOUR DAYS BEFORE THE
KALENDS OF FLORALIS

*T*he third letter did not convince Ashiol that he should ride to Isangell's rescue. Nor did the fourth, or the fifth. Each sweet entreaty worked like a drop of acid, reminding him what a coward he was.

He drank more, snapped at his younger siblings, and spent far too long staring at the blank, unthreatening sky.

His mother broke first. 'If you don't go back, you'll never face your fears. You're a grown man, and stronger than you think. Perhaps you should just go.'

Would she encourage him if she knew what he was really hiding from?

~

SO ASHIOL XANDELIAN entered the city of Aufleur for the first time in five years. His entrance was modest and uneventful, except that he spent the entire walk from the Aurian Gate Station to the Palazzo watching the sky and thinking *Garnet, Garnet, Garnet* with every step.

The sky told him nothing.

At the Palazzo, Ashiol was greeted with the usual flurry of servants and officials. He dodged the formal reception as soon as he could and made off in search of Isangell's private rooms. Halfway there, he realised that he was heading for the nursery, which wasn't right. The little Ducomtessa had become a ruling Duchessa; she would not be sleeping in a child's cubby with bars on the window. Gritting his teeth, he hailed a servant and was directed to an elegant suite in the Inner Sanctum, alongside the Old Duc's rose atrium.

The woman waiting for him was not the demoiselle he had left. A tall, slender creature sat on the Duc's favourite bench, her long fair hair hanging carelessly to her waist. Ashiol watched her for several minutes before she turned that tree-branch neck and saw him. Her wicked grin, at least, was much the same.

'Hello, Ash,' said the Duchessa d'Aufleur.

'Hello, Isangell.' He eyed the thin white shift that barely covered her to mid-thigh. 'Is that what you're wearing to the festival? The City Fathers might be overly aroused.'

She rolled her eyes at him. 'The festival is hours away. Besides, my gown hasn't been delivered yet.'

'Cutting it fine, aren't we?'

'You'll see why when it arrives. I have to wear it fresh.'

'You are aware that festival gowns aren't food?'

'Someone told me, but I don't believe a word of it.' She stared at him and laughed. 'You got old!'

Ashiol wasn't thirty yet. 'You too, gosling. Nineteen and not married? "Spinster" is such an ugly word.'

'I've missed you,' she said. 'Everyone else refuses to be mean to me. It's quite wretched of them.'

'I'm sure your mother more than makes up for it,' he said dryly.

'Yes, well. The less said about that, the better.' Isangell was serious for a moment. 'I'm glad you came. I need you here, in Aufleur.'

'Because that worked out so well last time.'

Ashiol barely remembered the last few months of his time here, except that he had sampled every mind-altering substance under the sun to blot out the pain of what Garnet had done to him. He certainly hadn't left the city on his own two feet.

'You look good,' said Isangell. 'I mean, better than before.'

'I worked out my demons.' Potions and powders were so difficult to purchase in the provinces. Easier to do without. 'I don't know why you want me here,' he said abruptly. 'I mean, I know why — I know the role you want me to play. But I have four strapping younger brothers, all with blood as fine and Aufleurine as my own. None of them have the history I have with this city.'

None of them were cut down from a rope in the deepest wine cellar, gibbering about the man who had destroyed him.

'I'm sure they're lovely boys and your mother raised them well,' said Isangell. 'But I don't know them, Ash. They never lived in the Palazzo. They never told me stories of saints and angels. They have no bad history with the city because it doesn't know them at all. I want you. I need you here, by my side.'

And there was that voice, the one their grandmother had used to such effect when she wanted a thing done.

'Well and fine,' Ashiol muttered. 'I'm here, aren't I?'

'You promised me a year.'

'I'll do my best to keep that promise.' Not likely to go running with the cats and wolves in the street this time around. Garnet made sure of that.

'Mother,' Isangell said, in a different voice.

Ashiol steeled himself for the dour glare of his least favourite Aufleur matrona. 'Aunt Eglantine,' he said politely.

'Nephew,' said Isangell's mother. 'Isangell, dear, you should be sleeping. You have only a few hours before we must prepare you for the festival.'

'I was greeting my cousin,' Isangell said impatiently. 'It's hardly worth sleeping now.'

'It won't do to look tired for the Floralia parade. Spring is about renewal.'

'And cosmetick is a marvellous thing,' said Isangell.

'We were expecting you yesterday,' Eglantine added, addressing Ashiol.

'I like to make an entrance,' he replied.

Eglantine gestured at the silent servant who had accompanied her into the atrium. 'Armand will escort you to your chambers. Your festival costume awaits you. We had to guess at the measurements.' She eyed his arms as if disapproving of the muscle he had put on in the last five years.

'Your kindness overwhelms me, madame, as ever,' said Ashiol. He dropped a wink at Isangell. 'See you in the parade, gosling.'

His chambers were spacious enough, and about as far from Isangell's rooms as one could get without actually being in the kitchens. Ashiol was amused by his aunt's work. Eglantine had always been terrified that her rakish nephew would seduce her daughter, but he was a greater threat now that Isangell was of age and had the power to choose her own husband.

Ashiol had no words to describe to Eglantine how unlikely it was that he would ever desire to climb under Isangell's skirts. He had read her bedtime stories when she was three years old. The thought that Isangell might want him as a husband had likely given Ashiol as many nox terrors as it had Eglantine.

The festival costume was as appalling as Ashiol had feared, but he was grateful at least that it was not pink. The

Floralia was one of those festivals designed to challenge one's masculinity.

He ate a few mouthfuls from the supper plate left out for him, and stretched out on a couch to have a snooze before the servants woke him for his first official engagement as the Spring Consort of the Duchessa d'Aufleur.

THE SKY CRACKED OPEN, raining blood across the city. Ashiol laughed aloud. 'At least it isn't any ordinary battle that's going to kill us.' He had missed the glory of this, *saints*, he had missed it.

They had been fighting all nox, and just as they thought they had beaten the damn sky into submission, it had this to throw at them. Shapes of darkness sizzled out of the wounds in its expanse. Spears of light and silver stabbed and pierced the city below. In the centre of it all, a screaming, pulsing rift tore the sky apart.

Livilla screamed as a hail of fire burst across the rooftop where she stood. It was Macready, the sentinel, who saved her from the flames, tackling her to the ground below.

Ashiol tried to go to them, but his body would not move. 'Not here, not really here,' he reminded himself. He ached for his animor, for the ability to transform himself into the clawing chimaera and feel the thrum of battle in his veins.

The Lords and Court streaked into the sky, throwing everything they had at that awful, tearing rift.

'If it's my dream,' Ashiol said, 'why can't I have my powers back?' He launched himself up through the clouds. As the cold air flooded over his skin, he shaped himself into his chimaera form. His arms lengthened and thickened. His body swelled with strength, new flesh and muscle. Claws descended from his knuckles with a nasty sound.

Someone was caught in the rift. He couldn't see who at first, there were too many Lords and Court struggling at the mouth of it. Ashiol batted away several of Priest's winged courtesi. Useless waste of skin and feathers.

Warlord was working so hard that sweat splashed off him. He diverted various screeching missiles of light and ice with his own bolts of power, shielding the others.

Poet was the closest in, his feet braced against the stiff edges of the rift as he tried to save the idiot who had been weak, stupid and careless enough to get himself caught.

As Ashiol soared past the crowd of glowing, defensive courtesi, he finally figured out that it wasn't a courteso that Poet was trying to save. Not a courteso, and sure as hell not a Lord.

It was a Creature King. The Power and Majesty. It was Garnet.

'MY LORD,' whispered a nervous voice. 'My Lord Ducomte? It's time to get dressed for the festival.'

Ashiol awoke with a grunt. It was still dark, an hour or so before dawn. *Garnet's alive.*

'Thank you,' he said, and rolled off the couch, fumbling for the ornate white tunic and trousers that Isangell's people had provided for him. Some of the servants tried to help, but he growled at them until they backed off.

Once he was clothed and tidy enough that he wouldn't disgrace his cousin, he allowed the servant to lead him to her.

She awaited him in a cloud of pink roses masquerading as a dress. 'What do you think?' she asked, evidently delighted with herself.

'I hope there isn't too strong a breeze as we cross the

Church Bridge,' he said, reaching out to pick at her petals. 'Or you'll be flashing your shift to the City Fathers anyway.'

Garnet's alive.

She slapped his hand. 'Don't even think it. Your job is to protect me from breezes, rain and well-dressed assassins.'

'Marvellous,' he said. 'And me armed only with a pair of lace cuffs. Mind you, they will serve as blunt weapons in an emergency.'

They were led out to a horse-drawn pavilion that looked like a bridescake. Even as he bantered back and forth with Isangell, Ashiol kept his eyes on the quiet nox sky. Had he been dreaming a real battle, one that went on at this very moment? Without his animor, he had no way of knowing. *Damn you, Garnet. Took my eyes as well as my power.*

The pavilion began its rocking progression down the avenue. Isangell reached out her hand, shivering a little in the cool air, and Ashiol wrapped his fingers around hers. *Garnet's still alive*, he chanted inwardly as the pavilion rattled along. *Alive, still Power and Majesty, still whole, still sane.*

Ashiol was going to break every promise he had made to Isangell. Nothing in this city was going to stop him seeing Garnet again.

King, my King, my King, my King.

VELODY DREAMED OF A BATTLE. Lords and ladies fought the sky, throwing lightning with their fingers and shaping themselves into all manner of fearsome creatures.

She had dreamed such things before. In particular, she had dreamed of the red-gold man who blazed at the centre of the battle, hurling balls of fire at the unseen enemy.

He was beautiful in his passion and his violence. She

could watch him for hours, dancing the sky with blood dripping down his face and hot light pouring from his fingers.

This time, the sky caught him and would not let him go.

'Velody.'

She awoke in darkness, gasping for air. He was caught, he was trapped... could they pull him free this time, or would the sky swallow him?

A hot cup was pushed into her hands and the aroma of mint and sage drowned out everything else, even the lingering memories of the dream.

'You do want to catch the parade, don't you?' asked Rhian.

Velody swallowed a mouthful of tisane. 'As if I'd miss our masterpiece.'

'Tell me everything about it when you get back,' the other demme said eagerly.

Velody drank deeper, burying her disappointment. *The dress is half your work, you should see it, why aren't you braver?* 'You know I will.'

'Veeeeelodeeeee,' sang Delphine from the door. She held a lantern, and was wrapped in just about every garment she owned. Her bobbed blonde hair was shoved under a knitted hat she had once claimed was so ugly that the creator of it should be forced to wear last year's fashions for a decade. 'Wrap up warm, don't want to get cooooold!'

'I think you'll be warm enough for both of us,' said Velody, putting down her cup. It was time to go to the Floralia parade.

13
GARNET

I thought of them both, when the sky swallowed me. It was the nox before Floralia — the warmth of spring just beginning to touch the air.

Twelve years earlier I kissed a demoiselle on a balcony and stole the powers that were beginning to awake within her skin.

Five years earlier I stole the powers of a King, my dearest friend, and made him crawl away into exile.

When I went into battle, I knew. I knew he had returned to the city that very nox. He was coming for me. To take back everything I had stolen. My head was full of him, and every time I forced him out of my thoughts to concentrate on the frigging battle in front of me, I saw the little brown mouse before my eyes instead.

It wasn't much of a kiss, but it changed my life, and his, and is it any wonder she was as tangled in my thoughts of Ashiol as her animor was tangled with his and my own?

The three of us, warring inside my skin. Maybe that's why it happened.

I was caught in a rift like some frigging first-year courteso. It had to be the two of them finally getting their revenge. I couldn't feel my legs. I would kill them both as soon as I got out of this.

The sky dragged me deeper and I started losing it completely. I thought I heard Ashiol's voice in my ear: 'Remember that day when you carved three scars into my skin, and I begged you to let me go because you needed me on your side, needed me to save your arse half a dozen times a nox, and I would still do it, because you were my Power and Majesty and the best friend I ever had? Looks like I was right.'

'If I'm seeing you,' I said with a gasp, 'does that mean I'm dead?'

I didn't feel dead, but how could I tell? I didn't feel anything.

'Not yet,' said Ash. A damned good hallucination. He even smelled right, as familiar as my ma's beef and apple soup. 'There's still time.'

'Time for what?'

'Time to give it back,' said the not-Ash, and he didn't look fifteen any more. There were scars along his arms, and on his neck, and on that face of his. My scars. I did that to him.

Then he was gone again, and it was Poet in my frigging face, his hands clawing at my ribs. 'I've got you,' he said. Stupid lamb never did know when to give up.

'What are you planning to do with me?' I demanded. 'The rift is closing.'

It wasn't just that I couldn't feel my legs. I didn't know if they existed any more. No one knew what lay beyond the sky, but I was damned sure it would do me no favours.

'Get him out of there!' yelled Warlord as he streaked past, wrestling tendrils of ice and light.

'I could amputate everything from the waist down,' snapped Poet. 'Do you think that would help?'

Priest was there too now, fat fucker, so bloody satisfied with himself. 'Burn him out if you have to. If he's going to die, we need him dead on this side of the rift.'

Aye, Priest, I frigging love you too.

'No one's going to die!' insisted Poet.

The sky swam around me. I was dizzy from their impressive levels of stupidity. When I opened my eyes, I was in bed with Tasha.

You never met her. I'm not going to waste time telling you how beautiful she was. As golden as the day I killed her.

'Promise me,' she said, arching her back against the warm pillows with a sleepy pure-sex smile.

I could hear the voices of Poet and the other Lords trying to free my body, but none of that mattered, not with Tasha here and warm and alive.

'I'll promise you anything,' I said.

'Stupid,' she said scornfully. 'Wait and see what I'm asking first. Have I taught you nothing?'

I felt fifteen years old again. How could I not?

Tasha was talking, expecting me to hang on her every word like we always did. 'We're getting weaker. Day by day, with every soul we lose to the sky, the Creature Court is diminishing.'

I remembered this lecture. She wanted us to promise that when we got ourselves killed, we'd be generous enough to do it in the gutter like real men, instead of wasting our animor by letting the sky swallow us whole. Death meant something if the ones left behind got to quench you, to suck you down and take your power into themselves.

'Screw that,' I said aloud, and, just like that, I was back in the rift. My lungs were tearing at me. I tried to push my body into gattopardo shape, but it didn't take. Too exhausted for chimaera, as well. Fuck. Out of options.

'You know what you have to do,' said the hallucination Ashiol, back to torment my last few moments.

I laughed into his scarred face. 'The real Ash wouldn't be pleading with me to "do the right thing". He'd know better than to ask.'

'You're right,' said the hallucination. 'I'm not him.' His dark, broad-shouldered figure shaped into a narrower body with sleek muscles, pale complexion and bright red hair. 'I'm you.'

'Is that supposed to impress me?' I sneered. Now I was torturing myself — there was a certain poetry in that.

'You're the Power and Majesty,' my other self said to me. 'Act like it. If the rift takes you, your animor and Ash's are both gone for good. He's the last King and you've crippled him. If you take his power with you, there will be no one left to lead the Creature Court. The whole fucking city will go up in smoke. Another forgotten relic, just like Tierce. Will you let that happen?'

I grinned. 'Apparently you don't know me very well, friend.'

My body slipped a little further into the rift.

'We're losing him,' said Poet.

'Blast his bloody head off and drink him dry,' said good old Priest. 'He'd do the same to you in a second.'

It was nearly dawn. The sky was lightening. If I could just hold on for another few minutes, the rift would leave me be. Wouldn't it? I'd never known a skybattle to end this close to daylight. Maybe it wasn't going to end at all.

The other Garnet leaned in close. 'Give him this,' he whispered. 'You loved him once. He's wandering around somewhere in the city below, powerless and miserable. You can give him back his place in the Creature Court. You can give him everything you stole from him. You can make him Power and fucking Majesty.'

Fire burned in my belly at the thought of it, of Ashiol flaunting the title I had worn proudly. 'Stupid prick. Serve him right if I did.'

The rift growled and rippled against my body. They were still there, why were they still there? They had to get clear.

'Get away from me,' I yelled at Poet. 'Let me go, you stupid bloody brat, I'm not worth it.'

'Make me!' Poet yelled back.

Warlord and Priest were already moving back, eyeing me uncomfortably. *That's right, lads. Save yourselves.*

It's how we work. Loyalty is for the living. I was a dead man already, and they knew it.

'I said, get away from me!' I lashed out at Poet, not with my hands but with animor. It flared up inside me, an uneasy mix of my power, Ash's power, her power... Ha. *That demme on the balcony*, I thought in that moment. *Isn't she in for a frigging surprise?*

Poet's hands lost their grip.

I let go. My skin screamed at me to hold on, to keep it together, to fight and spit my way out of the sky until my feet were on firm, solid ground. But I ignored all that and let the stolen animor go.

It tore its way out of my flesh in burning arcs that sprayed wildly across the sky. I didn't expect it to hurt like that, but what did it matter now?

'Take it, you bastards!' I screamed.

But not mine. I let the demme's go, and Ash's, but I held mine tight inside myself. I had no idea what hells were waiting for me on the other side, but I wasn't going to face them naked and alone.

I was still laughing as the rift closed over my face.

14
FIRST DAY OF THE FLORALIA (MAIDENS)

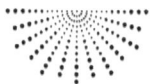

BEFORE DAWN

*I*t was still dark, for the most part. Velody hugged her thick wool shawl around her shoulders. Delphine kept up a steady stream of mutter in her ear about the cold wind and the shoving, restless crowd around them in the packed Forum, and most especially about how stupid spring festivals couldn't have parades starting in the middle of the day instead of an hour before sunrise.

Even above the noise of the crowd and the garland sellers, they could hear the distant tinny sounds of cymbals and springsong. The Floralia parade was getting closer.

'Let's just go home,' Velody said suddenly, losing her nerve. 'It's not like we'll see a thing in this mash.'

'Are you kidding me?' replied Delphine, grasping Velody's sleeve tightly with her painted nails. 'We're not leaving until we see the Duchessa's dress.'

Velody reached out and tweaked the pink flower garland that rested on Delphine's head. 'Well, if you insist...'

The Forum was awash with lopsided pink and white rose-crowns and trailing ribbons as the crowd gathered. There were people everywhere, a hungry mob spending a fortune on sweet fruit, candies and romantic tokens for each other while they hustled to get the best position to view the parade. Some of them had set up makeshift scaffoldings to clamber on, while others hung from balconies and upper windows of the churches and public buildings.

'My neck's cold,' Delphine complained.

'Shouldn't have cut your hair off then, should you?'

'You should try it. Such a liberating feeling to give up the snood and bobby pins forever.'

Velody touched her own dark hair defensively, and a shower of white petals from her festival garland scattered on the pavement. 'Shoddy workmanship.'

'I blame the garland-maker,' said Delphine.

'It was one of yours.'

The rosy tips of dawn edged over the hills of the city. Floralia was about to begin. Somewhere in the distance they could hear cymbals as the parade approached.

'Darlings!' shrieked a voice in the crowd. 'A toast for Floralia!'

Velody and Delphine rolled their eyes at each other.

'More of your grape juice, Guillaume?' Delphine asked wryly.

'None of that!' said the curly-haired cordialler as he pushed his way through the crowd towards them, his vials rattling on a tray around his neck. 'This is the finest cherry hot-drop, just right to warm the cockles.'

Delphine sniffed at the contents of the glass flasks. 'Sugar and cheap spirits, no thanks.' She whimpered at Velody, who gave in and opened her shawl so Delphine could share its warmth. 'I almost wish it was Saturnalia again. At least we could have hot cider and bean syrup.'

'Roasted chestnuts,' said Velody, her tastebuds melting at the thought of it.

'Yum!' Delphine turned her eyes on Guillaume. 'You don't have any roasted chestnuts, I suppose?'

'You should be so lucky, sweetheart. You won't get anything but rose dumplings and sugar violets from the vendors today. Don't you know it's Floralia?'

'As if I could forget!' Delphine leaned forward to tug at the lopsided garland Guillaume wore over his curls. She hated to see a ribbon wreath worn sloppily. 'Sugar makes my teeth itch.'

'No Rhian today?' Guillaume asked.

'She doesn't do well with crowds these days,' Velody said shortly.

'I don't blame her,' said Delphine, changing the subject. 'Too many festivals in this hellish city. If I didn't make my livelihood from them, I'd complain to the council.'

'Sick of Floralia already?' said Guillaume. 'Five days to go.'

'At least you can set aside the roses and pink ribbon after tomorrow,' Velody reminded Delphine.

Delphine huffed, taking more than her share of the shawl. 'Doesn't get any better. It's cords to wrap around hawthorn crowns next, with white and green silk for the Kalends, then deeper reds for Passion and Abundance. Then only a day or two to rest before it's time to start threading shade-garlands for the Lemuria.'

'You're just cold and tired,' said Velody. 'We can go home if you like. I'm sure we could squeeze through —'

'No!' Delphine said. 'You're going to watch this parade if it kills us both. Have you no sense of perspective?'

'I hate seeing people wearing my clothes,' Velody sighed. 'They never look as good as on the mannikin.'

She had a secret dread that the roses would all have fallen out, leaving her client in nothing but a beaded silken slip and a fine translucent net. What a thimbleheaded idea for a dress design — and for an outdoor parade! She should have done something safer, less troublesome. So many future commissions rested on the reception of this one garment.

'Aren't you a pair of grizzling wenches?' commented Guillaume. 'Is it too much to hope you're here to enjoy the parade like everyone else?'

'Parades!' mocked Delphine. 'There are three a week at this time of year. It's not going to be anything new.'

'This is the Duchessa's first public appearance as ruler of the city since her mourning period for the Old Duc ended,' Guillaume said in a gossipy voice. 'Aren't you interested to see who she's chosen as her Spring Consort?'

Delphine quirked an eyebrow up, slightly interested. 'One of the boys from the Great Families.'

'But which one? There will be a diplomatic incident whichever lad she chooses.'

The one thing Guillaume and Delphine had in common was a lust for Great Families gossip. It astounded Velody how a demme who couldn't name three historical battles or three great novels from the last century could rattle off aristocratic genealogies at a moment's notice.

The crowd oohed and ahhed as the head of the parade — a marching band in full regalia — finally appeared at the mouth the Forum. Velody watched them stomp with perfect choreography, and wondered exactly how the seams had been sewn on their costumes. That livery satin was so slippery to work with.

'But if the Gaugets are snubbed, the Paucini clan will be delighted,' Guillaume said to Delphine.

They were squabbling now. Another few minutes and they would be laying bets. Velody concentrated on the parade instead. The Irean Priestesses followed the marching band, each swathed in fluttering white garments and carrying a bundle of ceremonial scrolls bound with knotted cord. Behind them came the Silver Brethren, chanting and singing.

'I'll bet you a honey cake to Serenai that it's Atticus Aufrey,' Delphine said triumphantly. 'Their family dates back to the founding of the city. It's a conclusive way to establish precedence without making a commitment towards a betrothal.'

'I'll bet against that,' Guillaume said in a businesslike voice. They spat and shook hands on it. A woman in the crowd tried to purchase a flask of rosewater from him, but he waved her away as if she was annoying him. 'I'll bet you a chicken to the crossroads that our Duchessa chooses her consort from a family much closer to home. Does the name Xandelian mean anything to you?'

'The Duchessa's own clan?' Delphine frowned. 'But there isn't anyone except the cousins.' Her eyes widened. 'None of them have set foot in the city for years, unless you know something I don't.'

'I'm saying nothing more,' Guillaume said smugly. 'Will you take my bet?'

'No way! If I'm up for a honey cake I can't afford a chicken as well.' Her eyes narrowed. 'You took my bet on false pretences. If the Ducomte or one of his brothers is here and you knew it, that's not fair. Of course she'd choose them above the others. A Xandelian would be the only Spring Consort that no one could get offended about.'

There was the sound of clopping horse hooves. Velody felt cold. 'Delphine, can we go?'

'Of course not!' Delphine squeezed her hand. 'Here they come.' She shot a dirty look at Guillaume. 'We can't rely on him to tell us which way the bet turned out. Or to describe what your dress looked like.'

Velody moaned. 'I can't feel my feet.'

Was this stage fright? The whole city would be looking at the Duchessa today... would already have seen her, from Church Bridge to the Forum and along every main street in between. Velody's only consolation was that most of those watchers would have seen the thing in the half-light of lanterns and shadows.

'You've gone white,' Guillaume said at her elbow. 'Drink this.'

Velody found a flask of cordial in her hand and gulped the contents. Delphine was right. The stuff was sickly, but she could feel her toes again, even if she was probably about to throw up.

The horse-drawn pavilion was white, streaming ribbons in the breeze. Contrary to tradition, there were no pink flowers on the royal float, and it was immediately obvious why.

Duchessa Isangell Xandelian d'Aufleur was dressed in pink in honour of the Floralia and nothing would be allowed to upstage her. The most powerful woman in Aufleur stood waving to the crowds, her slim body clad in a simple fall of pink roses bound to a knee-high beaded dress in the latest fashion, with ribbons trailing down to her feet. The Duchessa's honey-coloured hair was pinned up in a garland of roses, and the sweet look on her face charmed the crowd, who screamed and threw flowers at her.

It had been timed perfectly. The last of the nox shadow faded from the sky as the Duchessa's pavilion began the descent into the lower Forum. The light of the sunrise gleamed off her gown and ribbons.

'Not a petal out of place!' Delphine crowed.

Velody breathed out. Everything was all right. The dress was perfect, and it wouldn't be long before word spread that Velody of the Vittorine, Via Silviana was responsible for it. She could already feel the pin calluses on her hands ache at the thought of all the new commissions. Maybe they would actually have a month or two without having to rely on Delphine's garlanding to pay the council taxes, licence fees and living expenses for three people.

'Beautiful,' said Guillaume. 'What a bloody picture.'

'I didn't think you fancied demmes or gowns,' said Delphine.

'I'm not talking about either — no offence, Velody. I'm talking about that peach of a man.'

'He is a stunner,' Delphine agreed.

'Ducomte Ashiol Xandelian d'Aufleur, grandson of old Duc Ynescho,' said Guillaume with a smirk. 'My brother saw him leave the Aurian Gate Station last nox.'

Delphine laughed. 'You rat. I owe you a honey cake for Serenai.'

They were talking about the Spring Consort. He was the dark and brooding type, at least ten years older than his radiant cousin, and looked as uncomfortable in his white festival suit as the young Duchessa was relaxed in her gown of roses. The man's collar was uneven, which suggested he had been slouching around and tugging at it before the parade. A decent tailor should have recognised his hatred of formal attire and put him in a low-necked shirt.

Velody frowned. She had seen him before, hadn't she? He looked familiar. But his hair was so short. It should be falling in his eyes...

'We're losing him,' said Poet.

'Blast his bloody head off and suck him dry,' said Priest. *'He'd do the same to you in a second.'*

Velody had a splitting headache. For a moment, as she watched the Ducomte on the pavilion, she thought she saw a web of scars crossing his face, neck and arms. But then she blinked and they were gone.

'Did you see that?' she asked.

'See what?' responded Delphine.

Guillaume, cheerfully abandoning them now that he had won his bet, raised his voice to the crowd. 'Floralia cordials? Toast the new spring? Get your rosewaters here, my lovelies!' Someone raised a hand and he nipped off in that direction. 'Yes, seigneur, and a drop for the demoiselle? Blessings of the day, seigneur.'

'Take it, you bastards!' screamed Garnet.

Velody staggered. The air tasted sweet, and heavy. 'I don't feel well.'

Delphine took her arm. 'No wonder, up every nox working on that damn dress. I'll get you home.'

'Can't breathe.' Velody clawed her shawl away. Her skin was hot and sweaty. Pain stabbed through the veins at her temples.

The sky — still not quite light — shivered, and for a moment it pressed down around her skin. When Velody looked up, she saw a sizzling bolt of gold light spinning towards her. She could not move away from it if she tried. Did anyone else see that, or was she the only one?

She opened her mouth to ask Delphine, then froze as the swirl of light slowed, only inches from her face. Waiting for something.

Crazy, that was definitely crazy. She opened her mouth to speak — to make her excuses and leave this place. The gold light lashed out towards her, even as another spiral shot into the crowd, in the direction of the Duchessa's pavilion.

Velody gasped, breathing the light into her body. For a moment, she thought she could see the stuff streaming out from under her fingernails.

Someone screamed. Not her, thank goodness. A long bellow of masculine pain and outrage that tore into a second scream, and then a third.

The crowd surged.

'Saints and devils!' exclaimed Guillaume a little way away, wrapping his arms protectively around his tray of cordials as a wave of people pushed past him.

Delphine grabbed Velody and the two of them hung on to each other, moving with the mob rather than trying to fight against it.

The Duchessa's pavilion had stopped up ahead. Velody slammed against a hitching post, and held on to it in the hope that she wouldn't be dragged along any further. Delphine was ripped away from her and vanished into the crowd. Velody was afraid that her friend had been crushed in the stampede, but the familiar blonde head surfaced a few minutes later, breathless and laughing.

Half the mob were fleeing the Forum, and the rest of them strained to see what had caused the excitement. Everyone who could craned their heads up at the bright white royal pavilion. Velody had an unexpectedly good view from where she stood. The Duchessa's lictors, the honour guard who had been marching behind the float at a discreet distance, were now cut off from the Duchessa and her consort by the milling crowd.

Ducomte Ashiol Xandelian d'Aufleur was screaming.

He knelt among the white ribbons and satin in a halo of scorching golden light, bellowing with pain. The crowd muttered and stared at him, but none went to his aid except his cousin the Duchessa, who hovered uncertainly over him as if he were a wounded child.

And yes, Velody was not imagining those scars now. They webbed his face and neck and arms in ugly streaks. She stared with morbid fascination at the screaming man with the ruined skin. The dark ridged lines that had sliced his face into a twisted mess were moving... wriggling. The scars fell off his face like rivulets of water, and he screamed as if they burned as they left his skin. The Ducomte's voice ran hoarse, and he gaped in silence as more scars dragged themselves from his hands and wrists, dripping off his fingers and leaving perfect, unmarked skin beneath. As he breathed, the golden light poured into his nose and mouth, glowing out of his eyes and from beneath his fingernails.

If I'm mad, Velody thought with a touch of hysteria, *he is too.* It wasn't a comforting thought.

The Duchessa reached out to her cousin and he pulled her to him, burying his face in her gown of beaded silk and roses. Pink petals fell to the floor of the white pavilion.

The lictors scrabbled towards the float with greater urgency, using their rods of state to bat people out of their way.

Up ahead, Delphine glanced at Velody across the heads of the onlookers that separated them and shrugged.

Velody was even more certain now that no one but herself — not even the Duchessa, currently cradling his face against her stomach — could see why the Ducomte was in such pain. As she thought this, she saw a brown-cloaked man crouching on the sloped rooftop of the council curia across the way. Even from such a distance, she could see his eyes boring down upon the figure of the damaged Ducomte.

He knows, Velody thought, then wondered why she was so sure. The cloaked man lifted his gaze to make eye contact with her. *He knows about me too.*

She didn't know why she was suddenly so afraid, or what the stranger could possibly know about her, except that she could see the scars when no one else could. She glanced at her hands, and was relieved to see no hint of the strange light that had entered her.

The crowd slackened around the float, many of the witnesses losing interest in the tableau of ruling Lady and mad Consort. The Ducomte drew away from the embrace with his cousin and stared at her with a fierce intensity.

Not at her, Velody thought, and this time panic rose fully within her. *He's looking at the dress.*

The Ducomte's hands lunged out, grasping the fragile fabric of the gown and tearing violently at it. The silk ripped and a cloud of petals exploded around him as he tore the Duchessa's dress away from her stomach. The crowd gasped with delicious horror. The Duchessa looked stunned as her cousin brandished a handful of torn pink silk, beads, ribbon and roses at her. 'What is this?' he bellowed in pure rage. 'What *are* you?'

The young Duchessa squealed as her cousin pushed her back on the pavilion, covering his body with hers, scrabbling his hands over her pale and perfect face.

'You're not a King!' he screamed at her, his voice breaking hoarsely. 'I can feel you're not a King, I can taste it. Who do you think you are?'

'Ash!' the Duchessa gasped with tears in her eyes. 'Ashiol, please —'

The lictors had finally made it aboard the pavilion and now threw themselves to their lady's defence, dragging the Ducomte from her and holding him fast between three of them while a fourth helped the Duchessa to her feet, shielding her torn gown from the populace with his black and scarlet cloak.

'You're not a King!' the mad Ducomte screamed at the Duchessa. 'Where did you get that dress? Whose hands knitted those roses, whose fingers trimmed those ribbons?'

Velody clung to the cold wood of the hitching post, feeling hollow inside. The dress was spoiled. It could only ever have been worn once, so it shouldn't matter, but somehow it mattered dreadfully. That, and it appeared to have driven a man mad.

'He got to you!' the Ducomte howled. 'Five years in exile,

and for what? New tortures, new games. What is this, Garnet?'

He's not making any sense, Velody thought light-headedly. *Why won't anyone stop him?*

'What have you done to my scars?' screamed the mad Ducomte.

'Scars?' muttered a seller of rose dumplings near Velody. 'What scars?'

'What have garnets got to do with anything?' agreed her friend. 'Boy's gone daft.'

'And that poor dress, Salle. I could weep.'

'They were mine!' screamed the Ducomte, struggling against the firm grip of the lictors. 'You're with them, Isangell. You've been consorting with Kings. Who gave you that dress?'

The lictors tried to manhandle him off the float and away from the Duchessa, but the Ducomte held his ground, not allowing them to budge him. One lictor made the mistake of drawing the sharp axe that was bound to his bundle of rods.

The Ducomte let out a bloodcurdling growl and started fighting for real. To the surprise — and evident enjoyment — of the mob, he turned out to be rather good at it. He flipped two lictors to the ground with great force, and slammed another against the side of the pavilion. The fourth was hurled back against the huddled, weeping figure of the Duchessa.

The crowd hissed as the Ducomte made an impossible leap towards the rooftop of the curia. His hands scrabbled wildly on the guttering, but he made it with a helpful hand from the man in brown, who hauled him upwards. The two of them ran up the slope of the roof and vanished over the other side, out of view of the crowd in the Forum.

And that was all. The crowd began to disperse. A few remained to watch the gulping Duchessa pull herself together. Some shouted out helpful advice to the lictors about how best to comfort a crying woman, but these soon descended into bawdy remarks.

Delphine made her way back to Velody, her eyes shining. 'What did you make of all that?'

'I don't know,' said Velody. She didn't want to explain about the scars or the golden light or the strange look that the man in brown had given her.

'Your poor dress!' Delphine said, giving her friend a hug. 'What a brute! Gorgeous man, but you can't respect a fellow who damages good frocks for no reason.'

'It doesn't matter,' Velody mumbled. 'Let's go home.'

'Last time something went wrong at a Floralia parade we had the worst summer harvest on record,' Delphine said chattily as she wound her arm into Velody's. 'It rained for three months, do you remember? And that was just because the sacrificial bull wasn't drugged heavily enough and sprayed blood on the Damascine Virgins. For a mad Spring Consort and a half-ravished Spring Queen, we'll probably have sleet from Lucina to Cerialis.'

Velody buried her face in her hands. She could not wipe away the image of the mad Ducomte screaming as the scars tore themselves from his hands and face. *Is he mad? I saw it too. Perhaps we're both mad.*

'Still, you have to look on the bright side,' said Delphine with relish. 'No one will forget what the Duchessa wore to this parade!'

PART II
POWER

FIRST DAY OF THE
FLORALIA (MAIDENS)

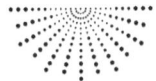

MORNING

*T*he battle was over, and Garnet was dead.

Macready rolled down the sloping roof of the Cathedral of Ires on the Octavian hill, landing with a thump on the reassuringly flat roof of the city librarion. He crawled from the shadows into a patch of morning sunshine. Nice. He closed his eyes and relished the warmth for a little while before checking his body for damage.

A long scorch mark tore his uniform from shoulder to sleeve, and he could see the ugly redness of skyburn on his exposed flesh. He prodded the burn with one finger to see if it hurt. 'Feck it!' he exclaimed at the burst of pain.

There was more pain, in his leg and lower back. General aches and scrapes and bruises. He vaguely remembered throwing himself at Livilla to save her life and cursed himself. It was Garnet he was supposed to have been protecting, and Garnet was dead. Macready hadn't been close enough to make a difference, even if it had been possible. Swords might have bloody helped.

A small, sturdy figure jumped down from the parapet. 'Ow,' she said as she landed, glaring at Macready as if her bruises were somehow his fault.

He found himself grinning. It was good to see Kelpie in one piece, even with a damaged foot and an extra scar or two for tomorrow. 'Eh, lass. You're a sight for sore eyes.'

'Sore is right,' said Kelpie, limping over to him. Her boot had split open around her foot and her red, blistered toes stuck through the hole.

'Come and sit in the sunshine with me,' he invited. 'A lovely afternoon, is it not?'

Kelpie gave him a dirty look, but lowered herself to the concrete near his feet. She was bedraggled. Her dark horse-tail of hair was a tangled mess. Her uniform was as torn and scorched as Macready's. She let out a lungful of air in one huge exhalation and closed her eyes. 'I saw Garnet... well, "fall" isn't exactly the right word, is it?'

'Swallowed by the sky,' said Macready. 'They won't like that, the Lords and Court. Denied their chance at cannibalism.'

'You haven't lost your sense of humour then.'

'Would it not be a tragedy if I had?' He thought he saw wetness in her eyes and deliberately looked away. Macready wasn't good at dealing with weeping females, and the prospect of tough-as-nails Kelpie bursting into tears filled him with great alarm.

'We lost him,' she said. 'I can't believe we lost him.'

'You're not mourning that bastard?'

'We were sworn to protect him —'

'And we failed. Get over it, lass, I already have.' It was an easy enough lie to tell while he sat in the sunshine, the horror of the nox's battle behind him. 'I seem to recall his

High and Mightiness, the King of Us, saying on more than one occasion that he could well look after himself. What was that phrase he used? "A true Power and Majesty needs no guard dogs yapping at his heels." Charming man he was, our Garnet, very gracious.'

Kelpie stared at Macready with a fierce rage. That was fine with him, so it was. If anger kept the tears at bay, then he was all for anger.

'Doesn't it bother you that he was the last Creature King?' she asked.

'Not at all. We could do with a holiday, the three of us. Young Crane could surely do with a few weeks of rest and relaxation somewhere warm — he's been looking a mite peaky.' Macready frowned. 'Where was our Crane last nox ? Not like him to miss a massacre.'

Kelpie hesitated, as if not sure whether to tell him or not. 'Garnet sent him on a spying mission yesterday.'

Macready swore. 'And that's what I'm talking about. We're sentinels, not ruddy spies. Our Power and Majesty has no respect for us; why the seven hells should we respect him?'

'Because he's dead?'

'All the more reason. Safe to hate him now.' Macready tried a reassuring smile, but somehow it didn't work out too well.

Kelpie rubbed her face. 'I can't help remembering the old days. He was such a sweet boy.'

Macready was tired. The sunshine wasn't so restful now that Kelpie was cluttering it up with her sentimental chatter, trying to turn Garnet into a fallen hero.

'That sweet boy grew into a bad man and an evil King,' he said. 'He was a monster and a lunatic and he hurt you more than the rest of us put together, so if you shed a tear for him, Kelpie, I may well have to punch you in the face.'

Her eyes flickered dangerously. 'Like to see you try, little man.'

That was more like it. This was the Kelpie he knew how to deal with. 'Is it nice to tease a cove about his height?'

'Big talk for a feller who hasn't got any.'

A dark cloud of birds fell out of the sky, transforming into a mass of feathers and wings and long black limbs. The air crackled around the creatures as they shaped themselves into a single figure, a hard-muscled naked teenager with blazing yellow eyes. 'I should kill you,' he snarled at Macready as soon as his bare feet slapped the roof.

Macready darted to his feet, moving away from the menacing figure. 'Eh, Janvier, and how is your sweet mistress? Is there any chance that you would be bearing thanksgiving tidings for the noble way I pushed her out of the path of that devastatingly lethal skybolt?'

'Must have missed that,' said Kelpie, grinning. 'Damaged her, did you?'

'Perhaps a bruise or two, but 'tis a small price to pay for her continuing life and good health, would you not think?'

'You broke her fucking leg,' said Janvier.

Macready hoped beyond all hope that the burst of laughter building up in his throat would not break free. The last thing he needed was to have his head pounded in by one of wolf-bitch Livilla's muscled thugs.

'Eh, I'm sorry to hear that,' he said, dancing back a step or two every time Janvier advanced on him. 'I've nothing but respect for the demoiselle, as you know, and I was only acting on instinct, protecting a lady from harm, as the gentleman I am.'

Janvier curled back his lip. If he were a wolf like his mistress, he might have uttered a howl, but instead it was a hoarse raven screech that tore out of his throat.

Macready backed up again, but he had miscalculated the

distance and was now dangerously close to the edge of the flat roof. Smart-mouthing the Lords and Court was reckless enough back when he and the other sentinels were armed. These days it was just plain daft. *Don't taunt the animals, my lad*, he reminded himself. Being Macready, he did it anyway. 'You do remember that rule about sentinels being sacrosanct, do you not? Courtesi are not allowed to do physical harm to sentinels.' Helpfully, he drew a circle around his body in the air. 'Invisible barrier of protection.'

Behind Janvier's menacing presence, Macready saw Kelpie slap herself in the forehead. He wasn't doing himself any favours.

'How is it without a King to protect you, little sentinel?' asked Janvier. 'Feeling your mortality?'

'Technically we protect the Kings,' Macready gabbled. 'But obviously you're not interested in our job description —'

'We won't be without a Creature King for long, Janvier!' Kelpie shouted from her side of the roof. 'You know how these things work. The courtesi kill each other, and the most ruthless survivors become Lords. The Creature Lords kill each other until one of them quenches enough to become a King. There will be blood and death, and at the end of it *we'll* be useful again. Where will you be? Your mistress can't be King, so what does that make her? Bait.'

Janvier whirled towards Kelpie with a threatening shriek.

Macready took advantage of the distraction to scamper back to the centre of the roof. 'The lass has a point. Is your mistress not the most vulnerable of Lords at the minute? While you're settling this score between us, there's only one courteso left to guard her, and her lyin' there with a broken leg.'

'Dhynar and his boys are the most dangerous,' Kelpie said helpfully. 'But I wouldn't underestimate Priest's ambition.'

'Poet is a dark horse, I've always thought that,' said

Macready. 'And as for that Warlord — sure, it wasn't tea and biscuits that earned him his name. It will be a grand old bloodbath, will it not?'

Anger and frustration crossed Janvier's face. 'I'll get you,' he promised Macready.

Macready smiled sweetly. 'Invisible circle of protection?'

Janvier moved so fast he was a blur, shaping himself into a cloud of ravens as he threw himself into the sky. Once they were three streets away, the dark birds dropped down out of sight.

Macready breathed out. 'That can be our good deed for the day, can it not? Warning the lad about his lady's safety.'

'Two good deeds for you,' said Kelpie. 'You broke Livilla's leg.'

'Only in the interests of her ongoing health and happiness,' Macready said in a lordly tone.

They broke then, hanging on to each other as they howled. Livilla's broken leg was the funniest thing either of them had heard in months. The fact that Mac hadn't meant to do it made it even funnier. 'Invisible circle of protection!' he wailed in between bouts of mad laughter.

Something furry brushed against their legs and both sentinels flinched back and away from each other. A cat stood between them, a patient little greymoon with short slick fur and green eyes. It opened its mouth and spoke a simple message in Crane's voice. 'I need you both now. The Crucible, Via Alysaundre.' Message discharged, the cat walked on dainty paws to the sunniest spot on the roof and licked itself.

Kelpie moved fast, crossing to the edge of the roof and checking the safest way to get from there to street level. When she realised Macready wasn't joining her, she looked back impatiently. 'You coming or what? Crane's the proudest of all of us — he never asks for help unless he's up to his eyeballs.'

Macready had not moved. He was still staring at the placid greymoon. 'I'm all for running to the rescue, lass. I just have one small question to ask about this situation of ours.'

'What?' she demanded.

'Since fecking when has Crane used *cats* to carry his messages?'

THE CRUCIBLE IN VIA ALYSAUNDRE, on the less respectable side of the Alexandrine hill, was actually The Crest and Crucible, a shabby-looking inn with a closed bar at the front and guest rooms on the upper floor. It was obvious that this was the place Crane had meant, because there were cats everywhere. Tabbies, greys, tortoiseshells, blacks and whites, short and long hairs, moggies, strays and elegantly preened house cats — every kind of feline imaginable swarmed around the inn, some clambering on the roof while others rubbed themselves up against the windows as if they could will themselves inside.

The innkeeper, his bald head decorated with a wilting Floralia garland, stood in the street and swatted the cats with a broom, trying to keep them away from his door. 'The damned weather, so it is,' he grunted as Kelpie and Macready approached him, his Islandser accent as thick as Macready's. 'As soon as Aphrodal rears its head and we get a day or two of sun, all the animals in this city go crazy.'

'Sure, there's crazier still to come,' said Macready.

'Eh, but you're a countryman,' the innkeeper said, a cordial smile breaking across his face even as he belted several cats across the nose with the flat of his broom. 'How long since you set foot on the Green Isles, son?'

'Far too long,' Macready said with a sigh. 'My mammy will be sore at me when I do make it home, right enough. I told her I was only going out for a jug of milk.'

They laughed together.

'We're looking for a youth,' Kelpie broke in, glaring at Macready as if to forestall a duet of Islandser drinking songs. 'He said to meet us here. He's this tall, and he looks, um...' She waved a hand vaguely across her face. 'How do I describe him, Mac?'

'Pretty,' said Macready.

'I wouldn't say pretty...'

'Do me a favour, Kelpie. The lad looks like something they paint on theatre ceilings. He might be wearing a brown cloak,' Macready added to the innkeeper.

'Him,' said the innkeeper. 'Aye, he's upstairs with the other cove. A little under the weather, if you ask me.'

'A scarred man?' Kelpie asked intently. 'Dark eyes, talks fast?'

'Talks fast, right enough,' the innkeeper agreed, blocking the path of one persistent moggy with his boot. 'No, you don't, old Tom. I'll set the rats on you, so I will. Didn't see any scars.'

Macready grabbed Kelpie's elbow. 'We'll be going up to see them, if you don't mind.'

'Eh, help yerself,' the innkeeper said with a shrug. 'Come down and have a drink afterwards, youngster. I'm sure we have kin in common.'

'More than likely, so it is.' Macready steered Kelpie through the inn doors.

'If any of those dratted felines have made their way inside, do us a favour and chuck them out the window?' the innkeeper called after them.

'Aye, I will!' Macready yelled back.

'I don't understand,' said Kelpie as they crossed into the

empty bar and went up the rickety stairs to the rooms above. 'If it's not Ash, who is it?'

'You're not thinking with your brain,' Macready scolded her. 'His scars don't show to the daylight folk. Eh, and it could as easily be a new cat in town.'

'Just when we need a Creature King?'

'Don't get your hopes up,' said Macready. 'If there's one thing our Ashiol isn't, it's a Power and Majesty. We learned that last time around.'

Crane waited in the corridor upstairs, his lanky frame folded against a door. Two ginger kittens were playing with his bootstraps.

'I don't think I want to know,' said Kelpie, hesitating.

Macready rolled his eyes in Crane's direction. 'Will you not put her out of her misery, laddie-buck, and tell us if it's our man in there driving every cat in this city to distraction just like the bad old days?'

'It's Ashiol,' Crane confirmed.

'Is he...' Kelpie trailed off as if she wasn't sure what question she wanted to ask first.

Macready could think of a few. *Is he in one piece, is he sane, is he likely to kill us where we stand?*

Crane looked haunted. His angelic face had aged a year or two since yesterday. 'A couple of hours ago, he was the same crippled mess we saw when he was exiled from Court,' he said. 'Didn't have enough juice in him to call a cat to dinner. Then dawn came.' Crane indicated the kittens frantically attempting to climb up his legs and scratch their way into the room beyond. 'Now he's a full-blooded Creature King with animor leaking out of every pore in his body. It hit him hard. He's half-drunk with it. I take it Garnet died at dawn?' Crane spoke casually, but Macready caught the hurt in the lad's voice.

'Don't you start,' Macready growled. 'He's not worth the mourning.'

'Didn't say he was,' Crane shot back, defensive.

'I need to see Ashiol,' said Kelpie. 'Is he... will he be all right?'

Crane shrugged. 'He started raving when the animor hit him. Tore the Duchessa's dress half off in the middle of the Floralia parade, accused her of being in league with the Creature Court.'

Macready grinned at the odd picture this conjured up. 'I'd have liked to see that.'

'The whole city thinks he's a madman.' Crane yawned, exhausted. 'Saints, he is a madman. Worse than ever. I've had nearly two hours of his ranting. I came out here to give my ears some peace.'

'Let me through to him,' said Kelpie. 'Now, Crane.'

'Fine.' The young man moved away from the door. 'Just prepare yourself, that's all. He's not at his best. He was tearing up the room, scratching the bedding to bits and flinging furniture around. We may have to pay the innkeeper extra.'

'All's quiet now,' said Macready. 'Mayhap he's knocked himself unconscious.'

'We can only hope,' muttered Crane.

Kelpie flung open the door. Macready and Crane peered around her, preparing to duck if anything large was flung their way.

The place was a wreck, not least because the window was open and four dozen cats of various breeds had let themselves into the room. The ripped mattress now served as a nest, while other cats crouched upon the flat spaces on and around the upturned chairs and table.

'Which ones are him then?' Macready asked, counting the black cats among the mass of many.

'None of them,' Kelpie said in disgust. 'Crane, you *idiot*.'

'You didn't hear him,' Crane complained. 'It was like being trapped in a room with three Islandsers who all want you to marry their ugly sister.'

'Charming cultural stereotype, but I take your point,' said Macready.

'Five years of animor all in one hit and you let him escape,' groaned Kelpie.

'What was I supposed to do — tie him to the bed?' asked Crane. 'If all three of us were in here sitting on top of him, he could still leave any time he wanted to.'

'You didn't have to make it so easy for him.'

Macready ignored their bickering. He spotted a fallen pink rose among a pile of leggy kittens and grabbed it. 'I wouldn't have picked our Ashiol for wearing a Floralia garland.'

'Are you kidding?' said Crane. 'You should have seen him primped up as the Spring Consort — all white satin and ribbons. That one's from the Duchessa's dress.'

'The one he ripped down the middle?'

'Aye. He was fixated on that gown of hers, kept saying that the dressmaker was a King, or in league with the Creature Court.' Crane looked at the rose. 'You don't think he was right?'

Macready pressed his lips together. 'I cannot see any of our Lords and Court going to the trouble to make up a frock for the daylight Duchessa, can you?'

'Did I mention that he was paranoid and raving?'

'We have to find him,' said Kelpie. 'The Arches isn't home to him any more. If he's been staying at the Palazzo, maybe he'd go back there.'

'Cousin or no cousin,' said Crane, 'the lictors are after him for assaulting the Duchessa. They'll have alerted the militia by now, and if they see him they'll arrest him or lock him up as a lunatic. He's not so far gone that he wouldn't know that.'

Macready held up the limp pink rose. 'I don't suppose he had more of these on his person?'

'He had a whole panel from the dress,' said Crane. 'Wouldn't let go of it — I'm surprised he let this one fall.'

'Our man Ashiol had a keen nose for tracking, did he not? With a handful of that dress in his paw, is it not likely he could track down the person who made it?'

'Kings,' Kelpie said in disgust. 'They always have to do things the hard way. It'll take him most of the day to track the source across the city.'

'So,' said Macready, 'that gives us most of the day to locate our man before he terrifies some poor dressmaker half to death. It's a while since we've had such a noble mission, is it not?'

16
FIRST DAY OF THE
FLORALIA (MAIDENS)

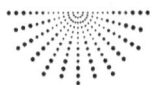

NOX

*I*t was late. Velody had been out of sorts all day, snappish and tired. Rhian was quiet and distant. Delphine was hells knew where in her best dancing dress, living the high life as hard as she could.

'I'm glad I wasn't there,' said Rhian, staring into the fireplace. 'At the parade,' she added, as if Velody might not know exactly what she was referring to.

'I'm glad of that too,' said Velody, setting aside a panel of embroidery. She had been trying very hard not to think about the events of that morning. 'Have you sent your order in for tomorrow's hawthorn blossom?' she asked, for something innocuous to say.

Rhian nodded. 'Sheelagh's a good worker, she's getting better at picking the good blooms from the bad.'

'It must be hard, making do with what she brings you.' Velody knew she was in dangerous territory, but couldn't help continuing. 'You used to be such a perfectionist, waiting for the boats to come up the river every day an hour before dawn. Choosing your flowers one by one, harassing the boatmen until they learned to keep their best stuff aside for you so they wouldn't have to surrender to your nagging and nitpicking.'

Rhian shrugged, trying to pretend she didn't care. 'I save time by sending one of the demmes instead. One flower's as good as another when they're falling off someone's bedraggled festival garland.'

'You don't mean that,' Velody blurted out. 'Sorry. I'll shut up.'

'You must be impatient with me.'

'No,' said Velody, furious with herself. She slid from her own armchair to kneel at Rhian's feet and took her hand, remembering how many months had passed before even such a simple gesture of affection had been possible.

Whatever had happened to Rhian that Lupercalia — and she had still never told them, not in words spoken aloud — it left its mark. She tried at first to act as if all was well, but it grew harder and harder for her to step outside the house... and soon Delphine and Velody got into the habit of making it easy for her to stay here, where she felt safe. They closed the shop. They did not allow men over their threshold. It seemed to help. Eventually Rhian no longer shied to their touch, though it still cost her considerable effort to allow that closeness.

'Don't listen to me,' said Velody now. 'I'm irritable. You know we'd do anything to protect you. We just wish you could be well again. Yourself.'

'I am well,' Rhian said. 'I'm content. I'm doing fine.'

Velody rocked back on her heels. 'I hate that they're still winning. Every time you want to go out of the house and can't, it means they're still hurting you. They shouldn't be allowed to do that. You're not getting better, and it's not fair.'

Rhian shrugged. 'Nothing's fair, not really. I don't have a bad life.'

You don't have a life at all, Velody thought, but she was restrained enough (finally, finally!) to drop the subject.

AFTER RHIAN WENT TO BED, barring her door and window with heavy bolts for the nox, Velody sat up for a while, straining her eyes under a candle lamp on the kitchen table as she read the latest chapter of a popular newspaper serial, *The Crimson Castellano*, by Evander X. The tale was a swashbuckler about a masked highwayman — a nobleman in disguise, of course — and his doomed love for a lesbian patrol sergeant named Harriet, who was determined to bring him down at all costs. It was a stupid story — Delphine adored this kind of trash — but Velody was trying to fill her brain with something, anything, other than the recurring image of the mad Ducomte screaming as his scars peeled off his face.

That was a gruesome enough scene to be worthy of *The Crimson Castellano*. Perhaps Velody should pen a few lurid tales about the double life of a scarred, mad Ducomte and make her fortune. It would have to be under a pseudonym, of course, so that the Duchessa never discovered that her new dressmaker was slandering her cousin in print.

How many days before the customary note of courtesy from the Duchessa arrived, remarking on how the dress had been received and — hope of all hopes! — ordering another? How diplomatically might it be phrased? *The rose gown was a great success until a hysterical family member ripped pieces off it before the crowd. Please consider making me another for the Lemuria.*

Velody's eyes were tired. She blew out the lamp and

checked that the kitchen door — unbarred against Delphine's return — was at least latched securely. Then she stepped into the workshop to quench the coals. With so many flammable fabrics around, they never let the contents of the workroom grate burn through the nox.

A man sat in Delphine's armchair, illuminated only by the gleaming coals in the hearth. Velody stared at the male shape, her heart speeding up. Her first thought was of Rhian.

'We don't receive men in this house. The shop is no longer open to the public,' she found herself saying in a stiff little voice.

He turned his head towards her, and her mouth went dry. It was the Ducomte, that insane Ashiol Xandelian who had ripped his cousin's dress open at a public parade, then escaped over the rooftops.

'So,' he said in low, rich tones, 'are you the dressmaker, or do I need to wait for your friends?'

Oh, Rhian, don't wake up. Velody's eyes flicked to the shop door, which was triple bolted and chained as always. They only ever used the kitchen door now, and Velody herself had been sitting beside that for an hour or more.

'How did you get in?' she rasped through her closed throat. Her voice didn't sound like it belonged to her.

There were shapes moving outside the wide shop windows — cats, rubbing up against the glass, purring and mewing and catting to get in. A lone ginger moggy — a neighbourhood tom that Velody vaguely remembered Delphine leaving scraps out for — was inside and rubbing at the intruder's ankles, purring like a steam engine.

The Ducomte uncurled from the chair, an imposing figure as he stood against the soft light of the dying fire. He held out something that Velody barely recognised at first, a scrap of silk and mesh and embroidered ribbon with a few glum petals and stalks still clinging to it. In the pale bronze light, it was hard to tell that it was supposed to be pink.

She stared at him, suddenly furious. 'Why did you have to ruin that dress?'

He laughed, and the sound of it hummed under her skin. 'Sit down,' he said, almost like the polite gentleman he was trained to be. 'We need to talk.'

It occurred to Velody — a strange, sourceless thought — that he had not stood to intimidate her, but because a lady had entered the room. He would sit again if she did. The thought of sinking into the other chair by the fire terrified her. She reached out to the shelves where she kept her tools in careful order and located a pair of sharp shears by touch alone.

The Ducomte lifted his brow a little at the weapon, but gestured to the seat opposite him. Velody climbed into the chair like a tense animal, her feet coiled under her to spring and flee at any moment, the shears tightly gripped in one hand. 'What do you want?'

'I want to know whose hands made the dress,' he said in a low, almost charming growl. 'I think it was you, but perhaps not only you?'

Velody was tempted to lie, to say that only her hands had touched the gown, but she had an awful feeling that perhaps he could smell a lie.

'There were three of us,' she said. 'I designed it and made the basic garment, the others stitched on the ribbons and wound in the roses.'

'Three of you,' he said with something like a smile. 'Only one of you is a King though. Which is male — the ribboner or the florister?'

Velody almost laughed in surprise, but the intensity of his gaze told her he was serious. 'None of us. We're all demoiselles. I don't think any male hands touched the dress except for the courier's. And yours.'

He tilted his head to one side. 'You saw my little show today.'

'Yes.'

He held out the sad little scrap of pink fabric. 'Did it pain you when I ripped this from her body?'

'Yes,' said Velody. She gripped the shears so hard that the little curved handles bit into the softest part of her palm.

'Where is the King you are hiding?'

'I don't know any Kings.'

The term made no sense to her — Aufleur had always been a city of Ducs and Duchessas. There were Kings and Queens in fairytales — particularly those of Islandser lore — and some of the festival rituals, but she had never heard the word used of actual people.

'He may not know he is a King. There have been sleepers before, who rose through the ranks without tasting the power they held, who quenched the dead without knowing what they did. It bleeds into everything he makes, everything he touches.' The Ducomte's eyes flicked around the room. 'Where are you hiding him, this King of yours?'

'There are no men here,' she said again. What if he tried to search the place? If he didn't believe her now, what could she possibly say to convince him that she told the truth? 'I told you, we don't allow men in the house. Rhian — my friend is afraid of them. You have to go.'

'A pretty story,' he said, dismissing it as irrelevant. 'Is your friend home? Perhaps I should ask her.'

'No!' Velody sat up angrily, glaring at him. 'You won't speak to her, you won't touch her. I won't allow it.'

The Ducomte moved like a cat in a long, sleek leap that had him on top of her, his body covering hers in the armchair. Velody jabbed the shears upwards, but he grabbed her hand and twisted it hard, removing the weapon and tossing it to the floor in a clatter. His face was close to hers, his body pressing her forcefully into the chair.

'You won't allow? I am a Creature King. I do what I like.' He was so close that he purred the words into her skin.

He smelled of cat fur and wood oil and tavern smoke. Velody willed herself not to panic, not to move, not to give him any reason to hurt her. *This is how Rhian felt*, she thought desperately. *This is how she feels all the time.*

'If you are a King,' Velody whispered, 'why do you need another?'

The Ducomte smiled down at her as if she had said something clever. 'Garnet's dead. If I can't find another King, they'll make me be the monster. I can't do it. I don't want to do it. I'll make a worse monster than he ever did. But the dress — the dress was made by a King, and I don't make dresses, so someone is lying to me.' He arched his back, leaning away from her even as his deep, dark eyes roamed her face. 'Do you want me to be the monster?'

Did he realise he was speaking gibberish, that his words meant nothing to her? 'I don't want anyone to be a monster,' said Velody. 'Why does anyone have to be the monster?'

The Ducomte crowed like a rooster, bouncing back and away from her. On his feet, he paced the room smartly, round and round, his boots slapping the floor. He spoke rapidly, as if the ideas were coming too fast for his mouth to keep up with.

'There's always a monster — lots of monsters, in truth, but the Power and Majesty has the sharpest teeth and the sharpest bite. Ortheus was the great serpent, thunder and fur and pain, and others came close — came close, but none of them were monster enough. Tasha wanted one of her boys to be King, but she over-reached herself there, and then — and then, and then — and then there was Garnet, the bright-eyed boy, the hardest, fastest monster of them all.' He whirled on Velody, a strange intensity in his face. 'I hope your King is a better monster than Garnet. For all of our sakes.'

It was making no sense, and his speech was such a tumble that Velody wasn't even sure she was getting all the words. *Garnets, he talked about garnets in the parade, and that does sound familiar, like something I dreamed once... is Garnet a person?*

'Where did your scars go?' she asked.

'Saw them, did you?' replied the Ducomte. 'What a spectacle — a whole parade to witness Garnet's last little joke. He carved them into me, and then he took them away when he gave me my soul back. Damned fool never could make up his mind.' He snapped his fingers so quickly that Velody jumped. 'Did he make anything else?'

'Who?'

'Your tailor King, the dressmaker boy you're hiding under your skirts.' The Ducomte flung open a cupboard and started rummaging inside. 'What else did he make?'

Velody said nothing, afraid of angering him further.

Truth wasn't helping — but what was the right kind of lie to make him leave?

'Aha!' The Ducomte found the chest in the corner and threw it open. It was full of clothing that she had never sold, a few half-made patterns jumbled up with fully finished garments. He leaned over and buried his arms in the chest, embracing the fabrics. 'Marvellous. I can feel him here in every stitch. A rare gift, something made by a King. You have such a wealth of it.' He turned and stared over his shoulder at Velody. 'He must love you, or trust you, very much.'

'I made them,' she said quietly. 'Those are mine.'

The Ducomte looked intently at her. 'You lie very well. I like you anyway. Can I have this?' He was holding a half-finished shirt of black cotton, the collar and cuffs not yet attached, the hem trailing threads.

'If you like,' said Velody. She hadn't finished that piece because Delphine dripped candlewax on it and left a mark. *Take anything in this house that you want as long as you do not set foot on those stairs.*

The Ducomte grinned at her with all his teeth and unpeeled his limp white festival tunic, buttoning on the black garment instead. It suited him, although the white trousers now looked even more hopelessly out of place.

'There are breeches of all sizes in that trunk,' she volunteered, pointing to her samples chest in the far corner of the workshop. She hadn't taken on a male client in the last year, preferring to work with female customers for Rhian's sake.

The mad Ducomte was quite delighted with this treasure trove, examining and dismissing a dozen pairs before he found the breeches he liked, black like the shirt and close enough to his size. Velody winced when she saw they were the one pair made of leather — expensive stuff from a failed experiment in theatrical costuming. She had planned to re-use the material. Still, if it kept him calm...

The Ducomte pulled off his boots and trousers without a hint of shame. Velody found herself looking away out of politeness. *He's a trespasser*, she scolded herself. *You should take this opportunity to wallop him over the head with a firedog, not sit here blushing about his state of undress*!

When he turned, clad entirely in black, the Ducomte was more poised and calm than before. 'These clothes are powerful. I can taste him in every stitch.'

Velody gazed at the proud figure that he made, so different to the tortured, broken man on the Floralia pavilion. 'I can't tell you anything else. I don't have the information you need.'

'Do you not?' The Ducomte padded barefoot towards her, ignoring the abandoned white boots that no longer matched his clothes.

Vain, Velody thought, wondering how she could use that against him. She straightened her back as he approached her, refusing to huddle in the chair like a victim. 'I want you to leave.'

He stood over her, his body tall and unyielding. 'You haven't yet told me what I want to know.'

'I don't know anything!' she exploded. 'None of this makes sense to me — it's just words, half of them in the wrong order, the other half fanciful. I don't know you and I don't know any Kings and you're *terrifying me* so will you please leave me alone?'

The Ducomte fell to his knees so quickly that she thought he was suffering another attack, but he just knelt there, gazing up at her. From this angle, he was less threatening. Anguish crossed his face. 'Am I already a monster?' he asked her.

I think you might be, and I'm sorry for it. 'It's not for me to say,' said Velody. 'I'm no expert on monsters.'

He knelt there silently for what seemed like a long time, staring into her eyes. 'I don't want to hurt people,' he said finally, in a voice that suggested *but I will if I have to.*

Velody moistened her lips, speaking carefully. 'So, don't. Don't hurt people.'

The Ducomte smiled a sad little smile. 'You make it sound easy, little dressmaker.'

He talks like someone I once knew. Doesn't he? Why can't I remember?

'It should be easy,' Velody said, recovering some of her fire. 'It shouldn't be difficult to not cause pain.'

The Ducomte reached out and found her right hand, lacing their fingers together. Velody shivered at his touch, but he was no longer paying any attention to her, only to her hand. He looked at it in wonder, turning it over to examine her pin calluses and torn cuticles as if they were rare and precious gems. *Or something good he is about to eat.*

Velody stared at the creases around his eyes and on his brow, wondering whether he had been crazy all his life, or if this was a new development.

At the sudden rush of sympathy, she chided herself. The man was dangerous, to her and her friends. He didn't need her to nursemaid him; he needed to be locked up somewhere with thick walls. *And stout bolts,* she thought suddenly, glancing back at the bolted front door and wondering again how he had found his way into the house. Had she left a window open somewhere upstairs? Rhian would never forgive her for such an oversight.

The Ducomte leaned forward, surprising her as he kissed her hand with his soft, warm mouth. 'I like you.'

Oh, help. Not too much, I hope.

'I wish I could make you stop lying to me.' He looked up at her with those dark eyes and smiled a devastating smile. 'I could eat out your throat and taste the truth in your blood. That might be nice.'

Velody thought her heart had stopped beating. The silence hummed in her ears and his face swam a little before hers. *Saints, he's going to kill me and I'm going to let him.*

'Ashiol!'

Another male voice. One of his gang? Velody dared to turn her head and saw a short, sandy-haired man in the doorway to the kitchen. He had a craggy, good-humoured face. His clothes were charred and torn like they had seen a battle or three. His left hand curled up, so you could almost ignore the missing ring finger.

What battle? There have been no wars for generations.

The Ducomte hissed between his teeth at the interruption.

The newcomer shook his head with a grin. 'Now is that a

nice way to greet an old friend?' he asked in a light Islandser brogue.

The Ducomte still gripped Velody's fingers in his, but his eyes were on the Islandser. 'Are you here for me, Macready, or the other King?'

'If there's another King in Aufleur, I know nothing of it,' said Macready in that same untroubled tone. 'You're our one and only, so put the nice dressmaker down, man, and come away with us.'

They're all crazy, Velody thought desperately. *A gang of madmen.*

The Ducomte was wary. 'It's a trick. Garnet's last trick. He wouldn't leave without setting a trap for me. She tastes of him.'

'No trick, no trap,' said another new voice, a female one. 'Just sentinels serving their Creature King. As it should be, Ash, always.'

The demme came down the staircase as she spoke, with a young man at her side. They both wore brown cloaks.

'How did you get up there?' Velody demanded, finding a voice in her anger. Saints and angels, had they walked right past Rhian's door?

The demme shrugged, her eyes on the Ducomte rather than Velody. 'Crawl space in the roof. Same way our friend here came in, I expect.'

Velody turned horrified eyes on the Ducomte, somehow feeling betrayed. 'You were upstairs?' Furious, she shoved at him, reclaiming her hand and knocking him off balance. He fell back, not moving or retaliating. 'How dare you, all of you? Do you have *any* idea what this will do to my friend?'

The Ducomte wasn't even looking at Velody any more. His eyes were on the brown-cloaked woman as she approached him, her hands outstretched. 'Kelpie,' he breathed.

Beneath the brown cloak, the woman wore a shirt and breeches, her clothes torn and charred like Macready's. She approached the Ducomte without hesitation. 'We're here for you now,' she said in a soothing voice.

'It's all coming too fast,' he said. 'I'm trying to spot the plan, to find the pattern, to see what Garnet is doing to us all, but the pattern doesn't fit together. It doesn't make sense yet!'

'We'll help,' said the woman — Kelpie. 'We'll help you find the pattern, Ash, but you have to rest now.'

'Rest?' he demanded, his voice rising again. 'Do you think I can sleep with the scars in my head? They're still here, you know.' He tapped his skull menacingly. 'I know there's a pattern if I look hard enough. There's a hidden King, and he can be the Power and Majesty if only she will tell me who he is. Where he is.' He stabbed a finger in Velody's direction.

Kelpie barely spared Velody another glance. 'She's not important, Ash. She has nothing to tell you. Garnet's dead. There is no other King, there's just you.'

'No.' Tears were running freely down his face now. He was so miserable that he was shaking with it, his body trembling wildly. 'It can't just be me. I can't do it by myself. He's my King. He can't be gone.'

Velody felt her own eyes pricking with sympathy. The Ducomte was in such a torment of confusion and pain that it was hard not to feel sorry for him.

Kelpie tugged him to his feet. He towered over her, but clung to her small frame as if she was the only thing keeping him upright. 'Come to my nest,' she said. 'You can be safe and warm and have as much time as you want to figure out the pattern. I'll look after you, heartling.'

The Ducomte stared across the room to Velody, his head tilted as if he couldn't quite recognise her. 'She doesn't fit.'

'Well, then,' said Kelpie, 'leave her alone. She's nothing to do with us.'

She led Ashiol out to the kitchen. The young brown-cloaked man went with them, shooting an apologetic look in Velody's direction. She stared after him, wondering if he had been the one on the roof above the parade.

Now only one of them remained, the Islandser called Macready. He grinned in a friendly manner at Velody. 'Sorry you were troubled. No harm meant and all that.'

'No harm?' she said incredulously, thinking of Rhian upstairs, lost in her terrors.

'He won't be bothering you again,' the man assured her, still smiling brightly. 'We'll see to that, don't be worrying yourself about it.'

Velody advanced on him, forcing him back into the kitchen. 'It can't be healthy for him, the way you feed his delusions.'

A strange expression crossed Macready's face. 'Ah, well. We've been looking after him a long time, and we have our own way of doing things. He's not usually this bad — it's not been the best of days is all.'

'Who are you people?' she asked.

It was all very well to pass off Ashiol Xandelian as some kind of escaped lunatic, but she knew he was more than that — and more than the Ducomte d'Aufleur. She had seen scars pouring off his body with her own eyes. Unless she shared his delusion. *Am I mad too?*

Macready's smile twisted a little and he looked more genuinely sorry than before. 'I hope you never have occasion to know more about us than you do now, lass. We're not part of this pretty world of yours, with the festivals and ribbons and honey cakes.'

Did this grinning loon with his mad friend think her life

was so frivolous and safe? Velody opened her mouth to rail at him, but could honestly think of nothing to say.

'I'd have someone look over that latch of yours,' Macready said helpfully, backing towards the open kitchen door. 'It's a bit dodgy, easy to pick if you know what I mean. Won't want intruders wandering in here after hours now.'

Velody picked up the nearest cooking pot and flung it at him with all her might. Macready jumped out of the way and fled. She shut the door after him with a bang, latching it firmly and then hitting the wooden frame with her open hands and then her fists. She wanted to scream.

How dare they, how dare they, how dare they?

Velody was so angry she couldn't think for a minute or two. Finally, she took a shaky breath and headed for the stairs.

There was no response when she knocked on Rhian's door. 'Are you in there?' She knocked again, and strained to hear inside. There was a soft sound, like whimpering. 'Rhee,' she called. 'What did you hear?'

There was another small sound that might have been her friend weeping.

'I'm sorry,' Velody said helplessly through the thick door. *I didn't let them in, it's not my fault* welled up in her throat, but she didn't dare say the words aloud. Would it be worse for Rhian to know that Velody had not been given a choice? That strangers had forced themselves inside her one safe place despite all their precautions?

'They were harmless really, but they wouldn't leave,' she tried, only to hear Rhian cry harder, gasping for breath. *What else do I say? I'm sorry I can't protect you from madmen and criminals?*

There was a crash from below, and a small scream came from within Rhian's room. Velody jumped, but guessed what it was at once.

'It's fine,' she said. 'It's Delphine coming home. I'll bolt everything up now. It will be all right.' *Lies, lies*, she thought as she fled back down to the kitchen. *I was more honest with the mad Ducomte.*

Delphine was on the kitchen floor, having tripped on the fallen cooking pot and brought the kitchen table down with her. She was still laughing helplessly when Velody marched past her to slam the bolts on the kitchen door. High on something, no doubt.

'Enjoy your evening?' asked Velody in a hard voice.

Delphine's giggles faded. She looked like an absurd child's doll with smeared cosmetick on her face, her golden bob of hair sticking up in all directions. 'Uh-oh,' she said, her voice lowered to an exaggerated hush, 'Velody's in her mother hen mood. Bad demmes beware.'

Velody glared at her friend, righting the table before she lowered a hand to pull Delphine to her feet. 'You're a mess, and you stink of gin.'

The smell was actually ansouisette, the latest cocktail, a heady mix of aniseed and lemon liqueur. Gin was more insulting.

'Cheap, like me,' said Delphine. She wore one of the new dresses Velody had made her for the season — sage green linen hung with white fringe. Someone had spilt a drink — clear, thankfully — over the hem and the fringe stuck out in clumps.

'I don't know why you bother to wear nice things,' said Velody. 'You always come home looking like trash.'

'Sign of a good nox,' hiccuped Delphine.

'And how do you think Rhian feels about you running around the city with your skirt over your head, swapping drunken gropes with anyone who'll buy you a glass?'

'Rhian knows I'm a tramp. She doesn't hold it against me. Unlike some people, I don't aspire to sainthood.'

Delphine turned on her heel, which broke. She stared down for a moment, as if trying to figure out why one foot was suddenly lower than the other. Then, with great dignity, she started limping towards the staircase.

'Even the Sweetheart Saints have a better social life than you, Velody,' she threw over her shoulder. 'And they only get laid once a year!'

Which was worse: letting Rhian down or taking it out on Delphine? Miserable at herself, Velody put the cooking pot away and quenched the last lantern, then padded through to the workroom and checked that the coals in the grate were dark enough to abandon for the nox. Upstairs, she slowed outside Rhian's door but heard nothing from within.

When she opened the door to her own bedroom, she found it full of mice.

The rodents were everywhere, covering the floorboards and also her bed, dressing table and shelves. Every possible surface in the room was a mess of little brown furry crawling creatures. Absurdly, Velody wondered what had happened to the tomcat who followed the Ducomte into the house. Couldn't he have stuck around to do something useful?

She cleared her throat, which was hardly necessary since every one of the thousands of mice in her bedchamber was looking directly at her. Saints, but they had beady little eyes.

'I'm going to get a broom,' she said in a steady voice. 'When I return, you are all going to be gone. Understand? Any mouse left behind gets a face full of bristles.'

Without waiting for them to respond — with what, Velody, a formal speech? — she spun around and went back downstairs. She took her time finding the broom. How long did it take to clear a room of several thousand mice? How many people in the world had ever in their lives needed to ask themselves such a question?

Finally, with the stout broom tucked under her arm,

119

Velody stomped back up to her bedchamber. The mice were gone, which was both a surprise and a relief. She swept her floor briskly, gathering the mouse pellets into a small pile that she put in the chamber pot to go outside with the refuse. She had to sweep more pellets from her shelves and table, and shake them from her bedding as well.

When that was done, she washed her hands thoroughly, changed her sheets, blankets, quilt and pillowcases, and finally undressed for the nox. She nestled down beneath the layers and layers of bedding, buried her face in the pillows and then screamed into their muffled depths for several minutes.

She felt better afterwards.

17
SECOND DAY OF THE
FLORALIA (SWEETHEARTS)

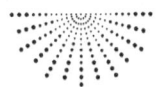

MORNING

*A*shiol woke up and the world was sane again. It was worth savouring — a mind that calmly dealt with one idea after another without jumbling them together in a mass of colour, noise and panic. And then there was the power — the taste of it, the glory and terror of animor in his skin, blood, brain.

I got it back, Garnet, you bastard. Took me forever but I got it back from you. I'm whole again, and I'm going to kick your arse all the way back to my mother's estate. Just you wait.

Ashiol inhaled, recognising where he was by the scent. This was Kelpie's nest — her crawl space, safest of safe houses. Without opening his eyes he rolled over, knowing which side she would be sleeping on, knowing the exact distance that would be between them on the firm, familiar mattress.

She was fully clothed, he noticed as his hand found her

hip. Disappointing, but hardly a surprise. She didn't trust him yet. He hardly trusted himself. What had happened yesterday? That question stirred up too many images — flashing memories of faces and axes and cats. The boundary between madness and the recollection of madness was a narrow one. Ashiol groaned, and Kelpie woke up.

She moved slowly against his hand and snuggled back into him. 'Good morning.'

Ashiol's only response was a grunt. He was sorting through some of the more prominent memories from yesterday's mess. Isangell's face stood out from the chaos, pink and scared. *Of me. Scared of me, damn it all.* He had been so determined to do right by his cousin, and he had frigged it up in less than half a day.

He remembered another frightened face, a woman he didn't know. Dark hair, pale skin, troubled grey eyes, beautiful hands torn to ribbons by a thousand tiny needles... The dressmaker. Ashiol's eyes flew open. He stared at the low, lopsided ceiling as the memories swamped him.

'What the hells did I do to her?'

'Do you want a list?' Kelpie asked dryly.

'Not particularly. How much danger are we in? Does Garnet know I'm back in the game?'

Kelpie turned towards him, spiking her fingers through her hair. 'What?'

'Don't mess me around, Kelps. Do we have enough sentinels on our side to get me out of the city before Garnet figures out I've got my animor back? If I can leave without facing him, I will.'

Though I could take him now, couldn't I? Send him whimpering into exile, see how he likes it.

'Garnet's dead,' she said in a clipped voice. 'Remember?'

Ashiol's ears hummed loudly as he processed the information. How had he forgotten something so important? 'Did

I kill him? Did I quench him? Is that how I got my powers back?'

The previous day and nox were a blur to him, wiped out by the shock and glory of tasting animor again. No, he hadn't quenched Garnet. The animor surging through his veins was his own, no one else's.

'No one quenched him,' Kelpie said in that stiff, impersonal voice she only used when she was really upset. 'He skyfell, Ash. He's gone, and he left nothing of himself for the rest of us.'

'Typical,' Ash said absently.

It hurt more than he had ever expected it to, knowing Garnet was dead. There was relief in there, an overwhelming surge of relief, but that only made it hurt all the harder. *He gave my animor back. Why?*

Kelpie continued to talk. 'When he fell, it all came unwound. You got five years of animor in one hit, which goes some way to explaining yesterday's madness —'

'So who's going to be Power and Majesty?' Ashiol interrupted. 'Who's the strongest candidate to take Garnet's place?'

Kelpie gave him the *I can't believe you're this stupid* look that reminded him painfully of another time, before anyone had ever bowed to him and called him a Creature King. 'You are.'

The world crashed in on him again, a mess of images and ideas and animor and panic. Ashiol was vaguely aware of fighting, screaming and letting power tear out of his skin in a long fierce howl. When he came to himself again, Kelpie was kneeling on his chest with her arms tightly braced against his.

'Sorry,' he said, noting a new swelling along her jawline. 'Did I do that?'

'Hard to tell,' she said, breathing hard. 'It might count as self-inflicted. You weren't ready to hear the truth.'

'I'm not ready for any of this,' Ashiol growled. 'Get off me.'

Kelpie slid off his body and crouched near the foot of the mattress.

Ashiol sat up, stretching. 'Takes a while to get used to. I haven't tasted animor for so long, and suddenly I'm a Creature King again. Screws with the head.'

There was something else, another source of power. Ash looked down at himself and plucked at the half-finished black shirt he wore, then ran his hands down both thighs to touch the leather breeches. There was energy in every stitch and thread, particularly concentrated along the seams.

'Where in the seven hells did I get these clothes?'

Kelpie snorted. 'The dressmaker. Perhaps she was offended by that godawful Floralia suit the Duchessa made you wear. White never was your colour.'

Ashiol pressed his palms into the leather of his new breeches, trying to remember some of what he had said to that dressmaker. He couldn't get past the thought that among the rantings and ravings had been the seed of something very, very important.

'How many Lords at Court?' he rapped out in his best businesslike voice.

'Five,' said Kelpie. 'Priest, Livilla —'

'No Kings other than Garnet?' He cut her off deliberately, not really caring to know which of his old companions still played the game of the Creature Court. He knew the worst of it. *Garnet is dead and Livilla's alive...*

'Just you,' said Kelpie.

There was trust in her eyes, and loyalty if he chose to see it. Ashiol shut that thought away. This was going to be hard enough.

'Good,' he said. There wasn't enough room to stand up in the space, so he crawled towards the trapdoor that led down and out. 'Then there will be no one strong enough to stop me from leaving.'

'Leaving the nest?' she asked as Ashiol released the blood seal on the trapdoor and shoved it open, lowering his legs into the narrow exit.

'Leaving Aufleur,' he said, and jumped.

'YOU CAN'T BE SERIOUS,' Kelpie yelled after him in the street.

It was early enough that there were few people around; in another hour or two the streets would be flocking with daylight folk making the pilgrimage to the Sweetheart Saints, exchanging paper hearts and sugarplums as if their lives depended on it.

'Watch me,' said Ashiol.

His bare feet smacked against the rough cobbles. *Where the saints and devils did I leave my boots?* The cat in him was more than happy to walk barefoot, but the man had to be aware of loose stones and blisters. In the country, he could go barefoot all day if he avoided his mother's disapproving stare; it was less than practical here in the city.

'I'm going to the Palazzo to apologise to Isangell,' he said, 'and then I'm out of here. This isn't my city any more, and I'm damned if I'm going to play the big chief monster over all the little monsters.'

That struck a chord with him even as the words spilled out of his mouth. He had raved about being a monster last nox. He must have known then that Garnet was dead — at least, a part of him had known. *I bet I confused seven hells out of that little dressmaker.*

They were in the Margarethe district, surrounded by

peeling paint and falling-down shops. Ashiol headed north, using the pinnacle of the Church of the Lares to guide him through Giacosa and towards Via Ciceline. If he had to walk barefoot back to the Palazzo, he was damned if he wasn't going to take the easiest route.

Kelpie kept up with him easily, her own sturdy boots keeping her feet protected. Ashiol tried not to resent her for it.

'You can't leave us,' she said.

'Can. Will.'

'But we need you!'

'You think I have an obligation to this city? To the Court? They chewed me up and spat me out.'

Her face went savage at that. 'Not fair. You know —'

'Aye, I know how it works. All Kings are equal, but the Power and Majesty is the most equal of them all.' Ashiol's words came out in quick, sharp slaps as he walked along. 'I wasn't even a King in the end, was I? Those last few months I was a tortured *pet*.' He glared at Kelpie. She kept pace with him but avoided his gaze. 'Do you have any idea of the pain and humiliation that bastard put me through?'

'We saw,' she said in a ragged voice. 'We all saw.'

'And felt sorry for me, no doubt. Perhaps even wept a tear or two in my name.' He grabbed her arm, pulled her close to him. 'After Garnet stripped my animor and threw me out that last time, they took me in at the Palazzo, but they couldn't help me. I was seriously crazy, not just Court crazy. After I tried to kill myself the second time, they sent me home, out of the city. It took me years to make it up to my family, to heal, but I damn well did. I only came back to this bloody place because of Isangell.' *Because my mother told me to face my fears.* 'But it was a mistake, and I am out of here. Right now.'

Ashiol tried not to dwell upon the Diamagne estate, of his

mother and brothers and sister. The home that had kept him safe these last five years. It seemed wrong to think of them here in the city that had nearly destroyed him.

'The daylight Duchessa?' Kelpie said scornfully. 'A pretty little noblette who thinks she has something to do with ensuring the safety of this city. What's so special about her that you'd come all this way to do her bidding?'

'She needs me,' said Ashiol. 'She thought I could help her, that I would stand by her side and be the brave big brother she never had.' His mouth twisted angrily. 'I ignored her pleas for months because I was afraid of Garnet. I finally got up the courage to come back and be a part of her life, and look what I've done to her!'

'A little public embarrassment, a ripped party dress. So what? It's hardly important.'

'If it isn't, what is?' Ashiol demanded. 'If we're not saving the city for the daylight folk, then what are we saving it for? Ourselves? This sorry, fucked-up mess of a Creature Court?' He released his hold on her and started walking again.

'And what about saving the city?' Kelpie demanded, racing after him. 'Aufleur will fall without a Creature King.'

'So find one.'

'There's you, Ash, there's only you!'

'Then maybe the city should fall. A failed King is worse than no King at all, Kelpie. I'll never be anything but a failed King to this Court. How can I command them when they remember the scars Garnet gave me, the whimpers and moans that came out of me when the lash fell and the claws tore and the knives bit?'

'You're afraid.'

'Not denying that.'

'What are we going to do without you?' It was a wail of desperation.

Never seen Kelpie humble before. Really doesn't suit her.

'Find the King that the little dressmaker is covering for,' he said. 'Find out why she's lying and you've got your man.'

'And if she's not lying?' Kelpie demanded.

Ashiol swayed. The lingering effects of being power-drunk on animor had blinded him to that one single, simple possibility. He staggered to the side of the street and sat on the pavement, his bare feet resting in the gutter. 'My scars,' he said softly. 'Kelpie, did you ever see my scars?'

She made a disgusted noise. 'Of course I saw them.' She knelt at his side. 'I've shared blood with you, Ash. The sentinels may not be of the Creature Court, but we're not daylight folk either. I've seen your scars.'

'So has she.'

'What?'

'At the parade, Kelpie. The dressmaker saw my scars when no one else did. She saw them as they ripped themselves off my face and body. She said so last nox. That makes her one of us.'

'A sleeper.' Kelpie's voice was disbelieving, but she hesitated before she said the words.

'What is she, mid-twenties?' he guessed. 'It's not unknown. Priest was near thirty when it came to him.'

'So he says anyway,' said Kelpie.

Ashiol ran his fingers along the seams of his shirt, feeling the delicious tingle of power from the tiny, perfect stitches. 'I was off my face with the animor last nox — I could have been in the same room as another Creature King and not known it. But women can't be Kings. Damn it all!' He exploded to his feet, mind speeding up. 'How stupid am I? I should know by now that you can never trust the rules.'

'What do you need?' Kelpie asked.

'Heliora.' Ashiol turned to her, breathing fast. *Slow your thoughts, damn it, don't lose it again. You need to be sane.* 'Tell me she's still alive.'

'I haven't heard otherwise.'

'Well then.' The possibilities surged through Ashiol's mind. If the dressmaker made the clothes he now wore, had she also made Isangell's dress? Saints, if that was possible, what else was?

'Still the Basilica?' he asked.

'Yes.'

Ashiol said nothing more, saving his breath as he strode past the Church of the Lares and on into Via Ciceline. This was part of the affluent Centrini district. There were more people on the streets here, already tipsy with the wine offerings for the Sweetheart Saints. It was a bright new day, and shopfronts unfurled their signs to welcome eager customers inside.

'Do you have any money?' Ashiol asked as they passed a stretch of quality cobblers.

'Not enough to buy boots.'

'Damn.'

No cabriolets were allowed in the city during the day. Walking was the only option. Ashiol could do nothing but offer silent thanks to the city planners two hundred years earlier. At least they had designed the main streets of Aufleur to flow around the hills. He walked faster.

The streets were busier along Via Ciceline as the good citizens of Aufleur jostled each other to buy sweetheart tokens and religious offerings as well as their usual purchases. After his battered feet were trodden on for the third time by a little old dame with laden shopping baskets, Ashiol veered off into one of the side streets. These were only marginally better, but at least he was near the Gardens of Trajus Alysaundre now, with the possibility of walking on soft grass — assuming the raw skin of his soles didn't find broken wine jugs and thorny rose garlands scattered across the lawns.

Cats didn't care about such things. It was five years since he'd thought like a cat.

With Kelpie still trailing him, Ashiol headed up the narrow stone steps to the first grassy bank of the gardens that had once held the decadent public baths set up in honour of the third Duc d'Aufleur, Trajus Alysaundre. The gardens were now shabby curves of greenery punctuated by ruined stone walls and the broken remains of skeletal pools, the marble tiles long since scraped away and — most likely — sold at a profit.

'Ash...' Kelpie said in a warning voice as they passed the first of the ruins.

He nodded and kept walking, eyes ahead. The scent of ferax was familiar, and telling. 'Dhynar made Lord?'

'Two years ago.'

'Courtesi?'

'Four.'

Ashiol's eyebrows went up. 'Interesting.'

A moment later they were on him, hard and fast. A pack of hounds, black mixed with white, had him on the ground, paws scrabbling and teeth snapping. He twisted under them, punching dog bodies with his fists even as he summoned the animor within him.

I remember how to do this. Really, I do. It goes like this.

Ashiol exploded out from within the mass of darkhounds and brighthounds, escaping his clothes by shaping himself into a dozen street cats. When he was free of the confines of cotton and leather he changed again, burning the hounds as he shaped his feline bodies into something else — something dark and menacing, with teeth and claws and wings and the taste of power on the back of his skin. Chimaera.

Two ferocious golden stripecats joined the brawl, half the size again of the dogs, and three lean and silver slashcats.

They tore at him with claws and teeth, but he rose above them as if they were nothing. *I am King. I am more than you.*

He didn't need to strike them with his power, to burn them with flashes of light and pain. He didn't need to reach inside them and twist their lesser animor with his own until they gasped voicelessly for mercy from their King. He didn't need to leave them as a pile of bloodied, barely breathing bodies heaped up against the ruined stone baths. He did it anyway.

When it was over, there was only the ferax. Its lithe red body balanced on one of the crumbling stone walls. Its eyes glittered as it surveyed its fallen servants and the creature who had defeated them. It was more powerful than the hounds and cats combined, and it was barely as long as a human's right arm.

'Where's the rest of you?' growled the chimaera creature that was Ashiol.

A second ferax, slightly redder of coat, joined the first. After a moment, more jumped up to join them. The eight, smaller than all of them, slunk up last.

Ashiol breathed out, and unwound from the chimaera to become himself again — the taller, harder, sharper Lord version of himself whose every skin cell sang with darkness and power and animor, but himself nevertheless.

The five feraxes fell forwards from the wall, blurring together to form a single human shape. He was small, narrow of body and of face, his reddish-brown hair pulled back in a tail reminiscent of the bushy red tail of the ferax.

Like Ashiol, he was more than human, eyes glowing and narrow, ears pointed, claws clenched and ready for action. 'Welcome home,' he said in a polite voice.

'Dhynar,' said Ashiol. 'Is this a challenge?'

The young man — frighteningly young — gave him a smirk. 'If it was a challenge, surely I would have brought more power to the field?' He motioned towards his pile of moaning, whining creatures. 'They hardly made a mark on you.'

There was sweat on Ashiol's brow, and a line of blood dripped from a deep scratch on his left arm. 'If this isn't a challenge, Dhynar Lord Ferax, what the seven hells is it?'

Dhynar was still grinning, as if this was nothing but a game. *I remember feeling like that*, Ashiol thought. *I remember feeling immortal. But I was younger than him when I learned this life is more than power trips and pissing contests.*

'I heard a rumour,' said Dhynar, 'that you were home, but planning to skip out on your responsibility to replace Garnet as Power and Majesty. That you were going to leave our Court without a leader. How do you plead, Ashiol Creature King?'

Ashiol offered no reaction. 'How did you hear such a rumour, Dhynar?' *How stupid was I not to guess I was being spied on?*

'The streets have ears,' said the young man. The grin peeled off his face. 'You didn't think we would let you leave, now, did you?'

'This is not the way things are done,' said Ashiol. 'Lords do not make demands of Kings. Kings twist Lords into cringing pets until they agree to everything we want, everything we decide.'

'So give some orders,' said Dhynar. 'Smash me into the wall, Ashiol. Make me bleed and make me obey you. Take your rightful place as the Power and Majesty. Just don't leave us to fend for ourselves.'

Ashiol moved, only dimly aware that Kelpie was crying out for him to stop. He seized Dhynar's throat with his hands and flexed his claws into the flesh. He let his animor pour into the other man, burning as it tore his face from the inside out. When Dhynar started screaming, Ashiol pulled away. He diminished into his human form, shaking as he pushed the animor down into the deepest part of himself.

Dhynar sagged to the grass, still conscious. The gashes in his face, neck and arms began to heal themselves, but the process was painfully slow. He twisted his face into a grimace, still able to manage a grin. 'Don't let our city fall into the sky,' he said between cracked and bleeding lips.

Ashiol picked up his fallen clothes and walked away. Kelpie stood at some distance, staring at him.

'This is what you want me to stay for,' he said angrily. 'This is what you are happy for me to become. Garnet's gone, so let me be the monster.'

'We're all monsters,' she said.

'And where was my sentinel when the fighting started?' he blazed at her.

'You didn't seem to need my help.'

'Not the point. Where were those Sisters and Nieces of yours, Kelpie? Are you saving your strength and your blades until you know whether or not I'm worth defending?'

She looked at him as if he were crazy. 'Have you noticed anything odd about me, Ash? Anything unusual?'

He stared back at her. She was just Kelpie. Straggly hair pulled back into a horsetail, pissed-off expression, battered combat clothes, sturdy boots. 'Where's your cloak?' he asked finally. 'You always wear it in daylight, even in the height of summer.'

'Clever man,' said Kelpie. 'Anything else?' Deliberately, she turned her back to him.

How had he not noticed this earlier? Too wrapped up in myself, that's how. 'Kelpie, where are your swords?'

She swung back to face him. 'Our beloved Power and Majesty decided that it made him look weak having armed sentinels at his back. Either that, or he was worried one of us would stick a knife in him. Garnet took our blades off us years ago.'

Ashiol was finding it hard to take this in. 'But you were in a skybattle yesterday.'

'Yes,' said Kelpie. 'We were.'

'Doing what — serving refreshments?'

'Mainly we were dodging skybolts and staying out of the way, when we could. Macready managed to break Livilla's leg, saving her life. We make ourselves useful from time to time.'

'Where are the blades? He can't have destroyed them.'

'Mounted in the Haymarket, as trophies,' said Kelpie. 'He liked to have the sentinels handy in case he needed blood, or messages sent, but that's all we were good for.'

Ashiol shook his head. 'Garnet always did think he was indestructible. How did you protect yourselves from the Court?'

'We didn't,' she said, still in that unemotional voice. Her eyes flicked to the fallen figure of Dhynar and she shuddered visibly. 'Garnet declared us sacrosanct, but he never demanded a blood oath. Most of the Lords chose to interpret the rule fairly loosely.'

Ashiol was so angry he couldn't see straight. He grabbed Kelpie's arm, pulling her further along through the park. Let the ferax and his courtesi make their retreat without witnesses. He walked Kelpie halfway across the curved lawn until they came to a carved bench near the statue of Duc Trajus. He pushed her onto the bench and then dressed himself silently. The garments had held up well. When he was clothed, he sat beside Kelpie on the bench so they could both gaze ahead at the creeper-covered ruins and neither of them would have to meet the other's gaze. That, and he could finally give his feet a rest.

'How many sentinels survived this madness?'

'I thought you realised,' Kelpie said. 'There are only three left. Me, Crane and Macready.'

Names and faces flashed through Ash's mind. Beautiful Ilsa, laughing Zyler, quiet Tobin. Andronicus, Rory and Nathanial the Silver Captain. The last he had seen of any of them was their blank faces as he left the Court for the last time, powerless and alone. It still hurt that they were gone.

'All dead?'

Kelpie said nothing.

'No new blood?'

'Since we weren't armed, there wasn't much point in bringing in more of us. There have been a few potential candidates since the Captain died, but Garnet forbade us from adding to our numbers.'

Ashiol stared at the statue of the daylight Duc, willing himself not to turn chimaera and start smashing things for the hell of it. 'Garnet's been dead since yesterday. I know I've provided something of a distraction, but what's stopping you from marching down into the Arches and taking what's yours?'

'A Creature King — the Power and Majesty — ordered us to give up our blades,' she said. 'His death doesn't countermand that order.'

'Well, I'm a Creature King and I'm countermanding it,' he snapped. 'Fucking arm yourselves. Where are Crane and Mac?'

'You told them to keep watch on the dressmaker's shop — to take note of any men who visit the house.'

'Glad to know I was even slightly lucid before you put me to bed. Get all the blades and get yourself over to Via Silviana. I'll meet you there after I've spoken to Hel.'

'All right.'

'Don't look at me like that,' he said irritably. 'This doesn't

135

mean I'm staying and it doesn't mean I'm the Power and Majesty.'

'Can I be grateful anyway?' she shot at him.

Ashiol stood up fast and started striding in the direction of the Forum, ignoring the screams of his feet. 'I don't want your gratitude, Kelpie. I'm not doing this out of friendship or loyalty or compassion. I just want your fucking swords at my back.'

18

SECOND DAY OF THE FLORALIA (SWEETHEARTS)

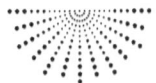

MORNING

*V*ia Silviana was a narrow street that ran down the affluent Vittorine hill and ended up in the shabby, bustling Giacosa district. The west end of the street classed itself as Vittorine, with lavish shopfronts and vendors who regularly made an effort to sluice detritus from the cobbles in front of their place of business. The east end was like any other street in Giacosa, carefree and colourful but worn around the edges.

At the halfway point between the two, beneath the Sign of the Rose and Needle, stood a cheerful-looking little shop. A wide glass frontage displayed a few elegant festival gowns that might appeal equally to a rich Vittorine debutante looking to slum it, or an upwardly mobile merchant's daughter from Giacosa looking to splash out. Most of the window was taken up with flower arrangements and a rainbow of hand-stitched ribbons in a simple but effective display. The window was so packed with produce that you couldn't see inside unless you were unreasonably tall — or high on a rooftop overlooking the large window.

A sign on the window said, *By Appointment Only.*

'Funny kind of shop,' muttered Crane. 'Never open for business.'

Macready grunted as a sharp piece of tile dug into his knee. 'Tell me, my lad, is there a reason why we cannot be watching this dressmaker from the comfortable hot food bar below, instead of sharing a roof with every fecking pigeon the city has to offer?'

'After we broke into her house?' replied Crane. 'She'll recognise us.'

'I don't think she was paying much attention to either one of us last nox with our man spouting madness into her ear and gazing soulfully into her eyes,' said Macready.

'Can't risk it.'

Macready shot the youngster a dirty look. 'You get off on this spying lark, if I'm not much mistaken.'

Crane grinned a little. 'Makes a change from ducking and dodging for our lives, or opening a vein to please our precious Power and Majesty.'

'Eh, there'll be plenty of that before long,' said Macready. 'Don't be hoping for anything original from our Ashiol. He's cut of the same cloth as Garnet, mark my words.'

'Can't be,' said Crane. 'If he was anything like Garnet, he wouldn't have been beaten by him.'

Macready barked with laughter. 'Ashiol's weaker than Garnet, so he might make a finer King? You're a rare lad, Crane, to have so much hope in you.'

Crane made a face, as he always did when Mac played the 'wise old cove' routine. It was fair enough. Macready was only thirty-six and he had already taken on the cynical persona of their dear departed Captain, who made it his life's work to spoil everyone's fun.

'Will he be himself this morning, do you think?' Crane asked after a while. There was no need to specify whom he was talking about. There was nothing but Ashiol on their minds.

'Eh, the gabble should have run out by now.'

'He seemed calmer when he gave us our orders last nox, before Kelpie hauled him away.'

'That's you being hopeful again,' said Macready. 'I reckon the first thing he'll do when he recovers his senses is to tell us that this thing with the dressmaker was one of his delusions and we've been wasting our time.'

'Could be worse. He might not think to tell us for a day or two.'

Macready growled.

Crane leaned forward, his eyes alert. 'Something's happening down there.'

'Saints be praised, do we have action at last?'

Crane was disappointed. 'A fellow looked in the window, but he kept walking.'

'A shop with the door still bolted at an hour to the noon bell. I can't be imagining how it is they have so few customers.'

'You're twitchy. Go for another walk.'

'I've been for three. I know this district inside out now, and I'm likely to be arrested for loitering if I do another round before lunchtime. How can you be so fecking serene?'

Crane wriggled closer to the edge of the roof to get the best observation angle. 'Lucky.'

'Humph.' Macready shook his head. 'Three lasses living together and not a gentleman caller between them. It's not natural.'

'Perhaps they're nuns.'

'Perhaps they're only interested in each other.'

Both men shared a dirty cackle at that one.

'Having fun, lads?' Kelpie climbed up onto the roof. Crane waved a hand in greeting, but didn't move from his observation of the shop below. Good little spy. Macready, pleased by the distraction, settled himself with his back to the street view so as to watch Kelpie approach.

There was something different about her. Her hair was scraped back into a businesslike knot, and instead of her sentinel's cloak, she wore a long leather coat that Mac hadn't seen for years. She looked unaccustomedly... what? Pleased with herself, he decided. *Saints and devils, don't tell me she took him to her bed again. That's all we need.*

'What have you found out?' Kelpie asked.

'Macready makes a rotten spy,' said Crane without turning around. 'No patience.'

'Crane's an excellent spy,' broke in Macready. 'The lad must have been practising as a peeping tom in his spare time.'

Kelpie swaggered across to them, her feet neatly finding footholds among the tiles. 'Too much to hope for any news on Ash's dressmaker?'

Macready sighed. 'Go on, laddie. You know you're dying to make your report.'

Crane shot Macready a look, but didn't protest. 'There are three of them,' he said. 'A blonde with bobbed hair — all lip paint and flouncing, that one. Then there's our dressmaker, and another demme, a tall redhead, called Ree or Rhian.'

'Any men?' asked Kelpie.

'Not in the house,' said Crane.

'Eh, it's not even lunchtime yet,' Macready said lazily. 'Perhaps their gentlemen callers only come after sunset.'

'A few messengers have been and gone,' said Crane, giving Macready a dirty look. 'A delivery boy came with a crate of fabrics about an hour ago. Here's the thing though. Whenever anyone comes to the door, the redhead vanishes. Goes upstairs, or retreats to the kitchen.'

'Not everyone,' said Macready. 'Some lassie came to the kitchen door with a basketload of hawthorn blossom and the one called Rhian talked to her for about a quarter of an hour.'

Kelpie raised an eyebrow. 'You can see and hear all that from up here?'

'I went prowling around the back a time or two,' said Macready.

'You really can't sit still for long, can you?'

'Sitting still's for dead people. It's not in my job description. I'm more interested in why you're all bouncy. Don't tell me someone broke Livilla's other leg?'

Kelpie's eyes gleamed with something Macready hadn't seen in her for a long time. Happiness?

'I've got a surprise for you,' she said.

'It had better be a fecking good one, lass.'

Kelpie spread her coat open a little, allowing them to see the twin hilts on her hips. Steel and silver gleamed beneath the dark leather. A pair of daggers.

Macready's throat went dry. He swallowed, and it hurt. 'Kelpie, have I mentioned what a bonny woman you are?'

'Not lately.'

Crane had a hungry expression. 'Tell me it's not just you.'

Kelpie strutted back across the roof to scoop up a flat box from behind the gable. Macready could see the lines of two swords sheathed against her back, under the soft leather of the coat.

'Saints and devils, it's a beautiful day,' he breathed.

Kelpie returned to them and flipped the box open. There they were, his lasses, sheathed in leather and waiting for him. Two knives, long and green-hilted. Two swords, one slightly lighter than the other. Macready lifted one and then the other, weighing them in his hands. The balance was off, but that was hardly surprising. He'd had all his fingers, last time he held them.

Crane was cooing over his knives, pulling them into a heap in his lap, examining them both.

Macready eased his steel sword — Alicity — out of her sheath. She was perfect, of course. The swords had not been built to rust. The soft sound of her emerging into the sunlight made him grin so hard that his teeth almost fell out of his face. He resheathed her and reached for Tarea, the skysilver sword still waiting for him. His hand shook just a little as he pulled her free of the leather coffin.

Kelpie shook her head, looking superior. 'Macready, you're way too excited about this. You need a woman.'

'Wouldn't want my ladies getting jealous, now would I?' He slid both daggers — Jeunille and Phoebe — out of their sheaths. 'Are you telling me you're not jumping over the stars and moon to have your Sisters and Nieces back in their rightful?'

Kelpie reached behind to check that the twin swords were still safely strapped to her back.

'We're sentinels again,' said Crane, half in a daze. He shot an alarmed look at Kelpie. 'This is permanent, right? He's not going to take them off us again?'

'Ash is not Garnet,' Kelpie snapped back.

'Pray to the saints he never is,' Macready said without thinking.

Kelpie glared at him. 'His exact words were "fucking arm yourselves". He's not stupid enough to think he won't need us.'

'Is he not?' Macready responded slowly. 'He'll be our Creature King then, a true Power and Majesty. He'll heal the ills of the world and rule us wisely and we'll all live happily ever after. Aye, what times we'll have.'

Kelpie flushed and looked away. 'He can do this, I know he can. He can be what we need him to be.'

'He couldn't beat Garnet,' said Crane.

'Nobody could fight Garnet,' Kelpie said crossly. 'We loved him too much in the beginning. Then we were too scared of him.'

'And how much do you love Ashiol?' Macready asked, unfairly.

'Frig off,' said Kelpie. 'We have to believe in Ash because he's all we've got. Otherwise we might as well sit back and wait for the sky to fall.'

Macready shrugged, allowing her the victory. 'Aye, well. I never was good at sitting around.'

We have to believe in Ash because he's all we've got. Saints and devils help us all.

19

SECOND DAY OF THE
FLORALIA (SWEETHEARTS)

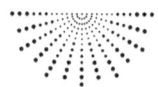

DAYLIGHT

*A*shiol left the soft grass of the park, his bare feet hitting cobbles again. He walked towards the maze of spring pavilions that had been erected around the Lake of Follies. The area was already packed with vendors and merchants, all hoping to catch the trade of passers-by on their way to the Sweetheart Saints further up the Alexandrine hill. Crowds trickled across from the Forum and the Duchessa's Avenue. Most folk cheerfully sported their wilted garlands from the day before, and many of them carried offerings for the saints.

Ashiol, halfway now between the Lake of Follies and the arch that marked the entrance to the Forum, was suddenly tempted to just start for the Aurian Gate Station and keep going. It might be hours before Kelpie looked for him, and by then he could be on a train going south. *Forget Heliora, forget Isangell, forget the sentinels. Never look back.*

He wheeled abruptly at the arch and headed up the

Alexandrine, avoiding the well-trodden path of the pilgrims. He pushed through thick trees and shrubs until he found what he was looking for: a broken and overgrown set of stone steps leading up to a garden that had once been the pride of one of the Great Families, but had been abandoned and closed off after the death of a beloved daughter. It was one of many forgotten places scattered around Aufleur — places that none of the daylight folk knew or cared about.

The garden, tangled and unkempt, smelled as sweet as ever. Ashiol climbed the steps to a stone balcony overlooking the Forum. Strange to be alone and hidden so near to the bustle and chaos of the market centre of the city. You could see everything from up here; not only the Forum and Basilica and the gleaming Lake of Follies surrounded by pink and white pavilions, but all the curves and lines of the city. Ashiol sat on a wall in front of a hidden grotto and stared out at Aufleur. *When did this stop being my home?*

He wasn't alone, of course. That was the trouble with the forgotten places — everyone in the Creature Court knew about them.

The first warning was a playful hum that tickled the back of his neck. Ashiol tilted his head back and listened. The tune was familiar, but only just. He couldn't quite remember where he had heard it before. The one thing he could be certain of was that the melodic humming was getting closer with every muffled note.

A perfect male voice broke into song, just overhead.

> 'She was the sweetest flower-demme
> And — oh! — I loved her well.
> I cut her flesh to pieces, son
> And buried her bones in the dell.
> La la la la la la la la ...'

'Charming,' said Ashiol. He tilted his head up and saw two slender legs sticking out from the overhang of greenery that swamped what had once been another tier of the forgotten garden.

'Don't you just love those old country folk songs?' laughed the perfect voice.

'How are you, Poet?'

A head swung into view, haloed by a short blond fuzz of hair. Sunlight gleamed from wire-rimmed spectacles. 'Welcome home, kitten. How are those claws of yours?'

'Sharp,' said Ashiol, hoping it was at least partly true.

'Glad to hear it.'

There was a movement in the tangled bushes nearby.

Ashiol looked hard in that direction, making out a large, steady figure among the leaves and vines. The skysilver axe on his back was what gave him away. A second, childlike figure crouched further back, attempting to conceal the shine of his small knife.

Ashiol turned his eyes back up to Poet. 'Times have changed.'

'They tend to do that,' said Poet with a smile. 'I'd introduce you to my boys, but they're ever so shy.'

'I remember a time when you refused to take courtesi into your service. What was it you said? "Nothing more pathetic than a Creature Lord who needs toadying slaves to primp his ego and fetch his slippers." What happened to those high ideals of yours?'

'You've been gone a long time, kitten. If you're here to stay, better catch up fast.'

'I don't know if I am here to stay,' said Ashiol.

The mocking smile vanished from Poet's face. 'Don't even hint that to anyone else, Ash,' he said firmly. 'They'll tear you apart.'

'And you're on my side, are you?'

The foolish grin was back, complete with vacant eyes and swinging feet. 'Of course not, kitten. I'm on my side. Always have been.'

'I suppose loyalty was too much to hope for.'

'Around here? Breathing in and out is too much to hope for.' Poet waved a careless gesture at the two courtesi in the shadows and they melted back out of sight. 'A word of advice for you, Your Kingliness.'

'I'm listening.'

It was no good trying to bully Poet. He had a history of enjoying pain. Better to hear his advice and judge later whether it was anything more than word games.

'Dhynar's the one to watch out for.'

Ashiol laughed at that. 'Too late for that warning. I left him and his pets in a bleeding heap a few minutes ago. I wouldn't call him a threat — just a boy with big ideas.'

Poet wasn't laughing. 'Careful, old man. Your prejudice is showing. Remember me as a boy? Remember Garnet? I even heard a rumour that you were a boy once, a right little sweet-heart by all accounts. Dhynar is the worst of us right now. He's been sucking up power left, right and centre, and he's ambitious enough to stick a blade in your back if you let him. He doesn't know any better. That's what makes him dangerous.'

'Thanks,' Ashiol said.

What had Dhynar done to Poet to make him so keen to mark him out? *Don't get involved. You don't care about these people. You're going to find your escape route and leave them all to their petty duels and grand heroics.*

'Don't thank me, kitten,' said Poet. 'Just don't leave us. We need a strong King right now.'

'If not a good one?'

Poet's smile widened and he drew up his feet. 'Can't have everything.'

Ashiol shook his head and headed back to the broken stone steps. *The sooner I hear the truth from Heliora, the sooner I can get out of this place.*

Behind him, Poet started singing again, the cheerful tune following Ashiol as he left the forgotten garden.

> '*She was the prettiest shepherdess*
> *And oh, her kiss was sweet.*
> *I bruised her mouth and tore her dress*
> *And ravished her there in the sleet.*
> *La la la la la la la la ...*'

THE FORUM WAS the same as it had been for three hundred years: a space of majestic public buildings and stately temples, surrounded by a shambles of ramshackle stalls and tents belonging to merchants, food vendors and public hecklers. Ashiol cut across the Forum, heading up to the Basilica.

The Alexandrine Basilica had once been the largest church in the known world, a tremendous work constructed by the fourth Duc d'Aufleur, mad old Ilexandros. His successor, Duc Giulio Gauget, declared the Basilica to be an unholy abomination and stripped its rich furnishings to ornament his own decadent Palazzo. Aufleur was not a city to let such valuable public space go to waste. Hollowed out and falling down, the Basilica was converted into a marketplace. A merchant's lot here was worth a small fortune — people had died in the riots fought over square inches of this valuable property. Heliora had never told anyone how she acquired her coveted space in the very centre of the Basilica.

There was the usual gang of lovelorn females outside Heliora's tent, waiting their turn to have their fortune told by the exotic and romantic figure within. Madama Fortuna's

Pavilion of Mystery was a gorgeous piece of work. It started out as a basic carnivale tent, but was primped and prettied up with so much purple satin, gold voile and beaded gauze that you would swear it had been imported directly from one of the glamorous Zafiran cities that featured heavily in the djinn-and-princessa cabaret shows that were popular this year.

The demmes in the queue entertained themselves by swapping snatches of gossip they had heard about the woman inside the pavilion, who called herself Madama Fortuna. Most of them believed that she was a genuine Ultana, thrown out of her harem when her husband discovered her mystical powers. She had nearly been burned as a witch in Zafir, but was spirited to the western lands by helpful spirits, or, in an alternative version of the story, handsome grain pirates.

Ashiol smirked as he listened to the chatter. The snot-nosed kid pickpocket who had stumbled into the world of the Creature Court fifteen years ago was a born-and-bred Aufleur brat, a street baby with the ability to reinvent herself at any opportunity. Hel had never even been as far east as Diamagne. Last time he was here, her tent was Carlotta's Grotto: bright with scarlet cotton, sprigs of heather, painted flowers and iron luck-charms. The rumours then were of a carnivale queen kidnapped from her tribe and sold into slavery. That was the year that Romani musettes were the theatrical fashion. Before that, she was an Islandser princessa with waist-length red hair and seventeen dead warrior brothers who whispered secrets to her from the spirit world.

Ashiol circled around the tent and unpegged a silky back panel, letting himself inside.

As with all decent carnivale tents, there was a compartment at the back, veiled from the customer, where the merchant could hide all of their possessions that didn't fit in with the image they wished to present. Heliora's storage space was crammed with costumes of all kinds, an assortment of wigs, and bundles of the coloured candles and incense sticks she used to set the mood for her clients. There was also a narrow pallet made up as a bed and a few sturdy trunks stacked beside it. Saints and devils, was she living here? Ashiol didn't blame her for keeping her distance from the Creature Court, but it seemed excessive to set up house in the back of a fortune-telling tent.

Incense was burning in the main pavilion. Sandalwood and cinnamon scratched at his throat, making him want to cough and splutter. He hated scented smoke.

'You have been lost,' said a throaty female voice, so calm and familiar that the hairs stood up on Ashiol's arms. 'But you are finding your way now, and you are on the right path to the future you should have had.'

He touched the shimmering curtain of dyed blue gauze. On the other side, which glowed with the light of far too many candles, two women sat at a small round table. A large domed crystal lay on the table between them.

'But is there love in that future?' asked the client. She was a painfully thin demoiselle in an expensive festival gown. Even through the veil of coloured gauze, Ashiol could read desperation in her eyes.

'When you least expect it,' said the fortune-teller. 'A stranger will show you the way.'

Ashiol pushed the curtain aside. 'I hope he's going to be tall, dark and handsome.'

The client turned, her prim face wavering between embarrassment and outrage at the interruption.

Heliora tilted her head to gaze at Ashiol for a long moment. 'I'm sorry, demoiselle,' she said finally. 'I will have to end this session.'

'I paid for the full hour,' protested the client.

Heliora produced a shining gold coin and moved the demoiselle to the tent flap with practised poise. 'Sadly, even one such as I, in touch with all the Spirits of Fortune, cannot always know where the day will take me.'

She secured a 'Closed for Religious Observances' sign to the outside of her silken door. A chorus of disappointed moans rose up from the waiting women as Heliora ducked back inside the tent, breathless.

Despite the ridiculous outfit of purple satin, beaded breast-cups and jangling bells, not to mention the shiny black wig and gilded cosmetick lines on her eyes and mouth, this was still his Hel. For the first time since he had returned to this saints-forsaken city, Ashiol truly felt like smiling.

'How dare you be back for two days and not come and see me until now!' she said in a rush, her bright eyes roaming over him as if she had to check that every inch was intact.

'Word travels fast.'

'It does when you attend public parades.' There was an edge to Hel's voice.

How bad had it been for her, these last five years? Ashiol wasn't sure he wanted to know.

'You never did have much patience,' he said, trying to lighten the tone of their banter. *The longer I stay here, the more people I'll have to fight, Hel. Don't make me fight you.*

Heliora pulled off the shiny black wig, revealing a shaven scalp. She strolled to the back of her tent, playing the hostess. 'Something to drink? Tea's too expensive this season what with the river raids, and I can't heat water very well in here, but I've a cool lemon posset that's very refreshing.'

Ashiol reached out and touched her arm as she passed him. 'Brat.'

She turned and hugged him quickly. She smelled of smoke and rose oils. 'You're here because you need something, not because you missed me,' she said, the words muffled against his chest.

'I missed you,' said Ashiol. He rubbed the stubble of her hair under his thumb, remembering the texture. 'But this isn't a holiday. I don't have time to run around catching up with old friends for the sake of it.'

'I know that.' Heliora pulled away and sat at her table, motioning for him to do the same. She calmly wiped emotion from her face. 'Business, then. You don't want to be the Power and Majesty.'

Ashiol sat opposite her and pinched out the stem of incense that was sending out curls of pungent smoke. 'Not if I can help it. What have you seen lately?'

Heliora raised one knee and rested her chin on it. 'I didn't see Garnet fall until the sky swallowed him. There were no warnings he was going to be lost. I don't think it was supposed to happen.'

'Then how do you explain me happening to be in the city within a day of his death?' Ashiol challenged.

She grinned like a kid at him. 'Are you asking me if you're destined to take his place? That's not the Ash I know.'

'Me neither. To be honest, I want you to guarantee me that I'm not destined for the top spot.'

'Can't do that.'

'I know. But I'll take what I can get.'

Heliora made a face at him. She wasn't much younger than Ashiol, but when her eyes were open and sparkling, she looked like the urchin he remembered. 'I didn't see you coming back,' she said after a moment. 'I haven't seen much of anything lately, except mice.'

That was of interest. Ashiol leaned forward. 'Mice. Not rats?'

'If it was Poet, I'd say so,' said Heliora, irritated. 'Little brown mice. There are no mice in the Creature Court, so that means someone new. I've seen the sentinels bladed again.'

'I've done that.'

'About frigging time.' She looked hard at him. 'We needed you years ago.'

'I was here years ago. Remember how that turned out?'

'Hmm.' Heliora was unconvinced. 'Roses,' she said. 'I've been dreaming of roses.'

'On a dress?'

'Aye, I heard about the show you put on at the Floralia parade,' she said dryly. 'Ripping the Duchessa's new frock to threads and petals — all very symbolic. No, not a dress. Just roses. But I don't think they have anything to do with you. Maybe more to do with me.'

'Nothing about another Creature King?'

'You don't get out of it that easily, old man.'

'I'm serious, Hel.'

'So am I! You want there to be another Creature King so you can duck out on your responsibility, just like you did when you left us to Garnet's mercy.'

'I've felt it,' he said angrily. 'Felt the traces of another King, somewhere in this city. We can't afford to ignore that. Especially since...'

'What?'

'I think it's a woman,' admitted Ashiol. 'I think there's a female Creature King in the city.' Heliora didn't respond to that. He pressed on. 'I know it's impossible and stupid and crazy; I know there's never been one before. But if it's true, then it's different. It's something new. Maybe... maybe she can be a different kind of Power and Majesty. Maybe she won't become another Garnet.'

'Maybe you won't,' Heliora shot back. 'You're a good man, Ashiol, why won't you believe that?'

'Garnet was a good man. He was the best of men — better than me. And then he became Power and Majesty.'

'You haven't grieved for him yet,' Heliora said softly.

The incense stem was still puffing out smoke. Ashiol wrapped his fist around it, letting its spark sting his palm. 'I grieved for Garnet the first time he killed a courteso to show them all who was boss. I grieved every time I saw him torture a friend.' He drew a finger across his cheekbone, up past his ear. 'And the first time he scarred me, I stopped grieving. Don't tell me it's in my future to take his place as the ringmaster to a twisted menagerie of monsters and clowns. Don't do that to me, Hel.'

'I haven't dreamed your future.'

'You could. You're the seer.'

Her eyes were troubled. 'You want me to look?'

As the seer of the Creature Court, Heliora received glimpses and visions of the futures on a daily basis, but searching for a specific future was far more difficult and dangerous.

'I need to know which reign holds the most hope — mine or hers.'

'And you're prepared to deal with the consequences?'

Ashiol's mouth twisted a little. 'It's not exactly a hardship for me, Hel. I'll bring you back if you get lost. I've done it before.'

'A Creature King could order me to do this, not ask.'

'I'm not going to do that.' He paused. 'But you will, won't you? For the Court, for Aufleur.' No orders here, just emotional blackmail, served raw and cold.

Hel gave him a withering look. Her face told him that she knew exactly what he thought of the Court and Aufleur. 'Oh no, Ashiol Creature King. You don't get to know what I'm doing it for.'

Heliora folded the table away to give herself floor space.

She extinguished every candle, and lit a lantern instead. She sat in the centre of her florid purple and gold carpet, and motioned Ashiol to sit opposite her. It was a long time since they had done this together.

'No candles?' he asked.

'You might remember how inconvenient they can be.'

He recalled the burning sensation of hot wax biting into his back as he rolled across the cold concrete floor of the Arches. 'Good point.'

She closed her eyes. 'It's a long time since I've summoned the futures.'

'Garnet never asked you to?'

'He asked.'

Not for the first time, Ashiol was profoundly glad that he was one of Heliora's favourite people. 'You don't have to —'

'Shut up, Ash.'

She breathed deeply for a while, then reached out and found his hands. Her palms were soft and warm. After that, she was silent and still for a long time. Ashiol's foot began to cramp, but he didn't move, afraid to disturb her. Did it usually take this long?

Hel's eyes snapped open suddenly, her pupils darting back and forth around the room. This was the hardest part for her to manage — she wasn't looking at the future but the futures, so many that she could barely control the thousands, millions of visions that assaulted her.

'Help me narrow it down, Ash.'

'Futures where I am the next Power and Majesty,' he commanded.

She nodded, her eyes still darting around. 'It's going to be a bad year.'

'I could have told you that.'

'There are some possibilities here. Positive futures. The city is still in one piece in most of them.'

'Good to know. What about the bad futures?'

'You know the worst of it. You wake up screaming over the worst possibilities. Death, torture, abuse of power, and you on the wrong side of all of it. That's there, in spades. Shovels too.'

'What are my chances of making it work?' he asked urgently.

Heliora laughed, a hollow laugh not quite her own. 'You want numbers? Statistics? I'm not going to count them, pet. Some futures work out and some don't. There's no perfect path.'

'You must be able to tell me more than that.'

'Just one thing.' She squeezed his hands tightly in her own. 'Your chances are better of making it — of being a good Power and Majesty — if she's with you.'

Ashiol sucked in air. 'So she is a Creature King.'

'Oh, that and more. You were right: she's different. She'll make a difference, standing at your side.'

'What about if I'm standing at her side? If she is the Power and Majesty?'

Heliora's pupils flickered faster and faster. Her body twitched a little, a sign that it was getting too much for her. 'That's another thing entirely.'

'Well? What kind of Power and Majesty does she make?' Ashiol knew he was being too pushy, but they were running out of time.

Heliora sighed. 'She doesn't know how the Court works. It's hard enough for a sleeper courteso to adapt, or a Lord, anyone who comes late to their animor. There's a reason most of us join this world young. She loses the battle, loses the city, loses herself... it's crazy to expect her to go in blind like this. It's unfair.'

'I don't want your opinion, I want the future,' he growled.

'They'll eat her alive.'

'Apart from that?'

'That's if she makes it at all. Her body's not built for this kind of power. Remember the story of Samara? This demme has that fate in her futures too: blown apart from the inside by the animor.'

'What else?'

Heliora tilted her head, as if she couldn't quite believe what she was seeing in the many futures. 'It's different.'

'The Court, or the city?'

'Both. She makes it different somehow...'

'Different good, or different dead?'

'Both. Oh!' Heliora pulled her hands away from his, holding her head. 'Frig, it hurts.'

'Come back, brat. That's enough.'

Heliora's pupils slowed. 'She will be a better Power and Majesty than you could ever imagine,' she said in a hoarse voice, the one that meant she was channelling a direct vision. 'Not just strong, but... there's a chance that she'll make the Creature Court what it should have been, what it always should have been. She's worth the risk, Ash. But whichever way it falls, you won't have her for long.' She slumped forward into his arms.

'Hel, wake up. Come back to me.' He touched his bare hands to hers, then to her face. She felt cold. 'What's wrong with you?' Her body shuddered against him and he realised that she was crying. 'Heliora?'

'Ash,' she said in a small voice, choking on tears. 'Ash, I can't see past Saturnalia.'

'What do you mean?'

'Those futures. You and she — I couldn't see past this winter coming. Sometimes the blackness sets in earlier, around autumn. Sometimes as soon as Lucina. But Saturnalia is the last I saw. I can only see the futures within my own life span — if I can't see it, that means I'm going to die.'

'In which future?' he demanded.

'All of them. It doesn't matter who the Power is, or whether the city falls or not. Something's coming for me, and I can't see it. Can't see anything else either.'

Ashiol was holding her so tightly that his hands were numb. 'I'll always save you, Hel, you know I will. Tell me how.'

'You don't,' she said. 'In all of those futures — every single one of them — you don't save me.'

He couldn't breathe.

Heliora's body was shuddering more violently, and not from her tears. She clung to him as the shakes got worse. Her pupils were snapping back and forth. 'Too fast,' she gasped. 'I see her and you, so many of you!'

'Come back, Hel. The futures are closing in on you.'

There was no easy way to turn off the flow of visions. Sometimes the seer would keep receiving image after image, future after future, in a stormy rush until she lost her mind completely. Unless someone broke her connection.

'So many S-s-saturnalias,' she stuttered. 'So many bad things. So many skyfalls, so many battles, one after another... the sacrifice of the King... so much pain!' Her eyes were wide but she didn't see him any more. Her body twitched madly as the futures collapsed in on her. 'So much everything!'

Ashiol kissed her, forcing his mouth hard on hers. She struggled against him for a moment and then surrendered to the kiss, devouring him hungrily, her hands clawing for the warmth at his face and neck.

'Make it stop,' she begged him as their mouths came apart for a moment.

'I will,' he promised, and pushed her back onto the floor, his body hard on top of hers.

Heliora's eyes rolled back in her head. 'Bring me —'

Ashiol's hands were under the purple gauze now, stroking

up and inside her thighs until his fingers curled into the hot, wet heat of her.

Heliora started babbling — this was the good stuff, the meat of the futures that she would never tell him when she was in her right mind. Details of Ashiol the monster, of the deaths of people he loved, even Heliora's own death, when it was lingering enough for her to know what was happening to her. Ashiol could have held off, listened to her spill out her visions until he knew exactly which course was the best for all of them, but he had a promise to keep. He covered her cunt with his mouth and drowned out the futures with long sweeps of his tongue until she howled into incomprehensible sounds.

It wasn't just sex — but then, it never had been between Ashiol and Heliora. At the age of thirteen, as soon as she developed something resembling a woman's body, she had staked out Ash as her man, the one who would make her a woman in all senses of the word. He, sixteen and not a complete idiot, knew better. Their uneasy friendship turned into an elaborate game of cat and mouse that went on for years, thoroughly amusing the rest of the Creature Court.

Then Hel the sentinel found a new calling as the seer, and the rules changed.

Ashiol moved positions now, kissing her mouth and letting her taste herself on his lips even as he pulled at the lacings of his leather trews. This was familiar, and he pushed his cock inside her with a fierce rhythm. Most of Heliora was still wrapped up in the millions of futures that warred inside her head, but part of her was here in the present with him. She gasped and moaned as her body responded to him.

The first time Ashiol made love to Heliora had been a desperate attempt to bring her back from the futures, grinding her against a wall in a bizarre form of chivalry. If he hadn't done it, Ortheus — the Power and Majesty at the time

— would have ordered someone else to do the job. Someone Heliora didn't like nearly as much. Hard to go back to being just friends with a woman when you had screwed her in front of the entire Court.

In the end it was Hel, obsessed by the new power she wielded, who broke off the chance of anything serious between them.

She was back with him now, entirely in the present as her body flexed hard against his. Her eyes showed a different kind of urgency, and Ashiol was there himself, spilling over and into her as she cried aloud.

Catching her breath afterwards, half-collapsed under him on the itchy Zafiran rugs, she laughed. 'One of these days we'll have to find out what it's like to take it slow!'

Ashiol was still numb from his release, absorbed with the scent of her skin. 'Why mess with a system that already works?'

Hel tilted her head at him, a cynical expression taking over. 'Same old Ash, always in a rush. Any minute now you'll button up your breeches and run off to stop some invasion or catastrophe, to save the world or a damsel, and I won't see you for months unless you need my help.'

He was a little light-headed, but he honestly couldn't think of anywhere he needed to be for the foreseeable future. He scooped her up in his arms and dragged her into bed. 'Hells with that. Let's see what it's like when we take it slow.'

20

SECOND DAY OF THE FLORALIA (SWEETHEARTS)

DAYLIGHT

*I*t was warm, up on the roof. This spring had been a cold one, but the sun was working a little harder as they moved towards summer, and the year was picking up.

Macready soaked up the sunshine, nestled against the tiles of the sloping roof. Kelpie could be trusted to keep an eye on things, and to nudge him awake a second or two before Crane returned so he could pretend to have been awake and alert the whole time the lad was gone.

Kelpie took over Crane's observation post so that they could send him for luncheon supplies. It was a long-held tradition that younger sentinels performed such tasks for the elder ones, and there was no reason to change it just because there were only three of them left.

While Crane was gone, Kelpie and Macready settled into their usual habit of companionable silence. There was no reason to fill the air up with banter and one-upmanship, as they did when the lad was around.

A musky, familiar scent woke Macready from his doze. He glanced across to Kelpie, whose troubled eyes told him that she had caught it too. Ferax.

'And a pleasant morning to yourself, Lord Dhynar!' Macready called out in a singsong voice, not moving from his comfortable position.

Kelpie squinted along the roof, and Macready could guess by the angle of her gaze exactly where the young Ferax Lord was standing. Good to know.

'I thought you'd still be licking your wounds,' said Kelpie. 'A little early to invite a second helping, wouldn't you say?'

Dhynar's light, supple footsteps moved towards them. 'And where's that King of yours now to defend your honour?' the young Lord asked in a teasing voice. His foot hit the tile closest to Macready's head. He made no move of aggression, but he smelled of threat.

Macready rolled into a defensive stance, sliding Tarea — the skysilver sword, his favourite lass — out from where she had been hidden at his side. Kelpie moved too, stepping forth as she drew one of her Sisters, so that Dhynar was faced with two sentinels and two long, sharp skysilver blades. The sword tips danced close to his throat.

The young Lord swallowed. 'Ashiol gave your swords back.'

Macready smiled pleasantly. 'And fine pieces of work they are, these lovely blades of ours. Not a speck of rust on them, would you believe, after all this time?' His left hand was free to unsheathe Jeunille, the skysilver dagger that was a pair with Tarea. 'Not just the swords,' he added helpfully.

Dhynar stepped back.

Kelpie's smile was fierce. 'Did you have something to say, my Lord? A message to pass on to our Power and Majesty perhaps, or something important to discuss with his loyal sentinels?'

Dhynar moved another step or two out of range of the blades. 'He is our Power and Majesty? I'd heard otherwise.'

Macready saw Kelpie's knuckles whiten a little on the hilt of her sword. He nudged her with his hip and she nodded, lowering her blade as he did. All very well to pose in dramatic fashion, but standing in attack stance for more than a minute took its wear and tear on the shoulders.

'Did he give you any reason to think he wasn't up for it?' Kelpie demanded.

Dhynar had his grin back, though it was less cocky than it had been earlier. 'Not me, demoiselle. His performance was very impressive. But if our Ashiol is so keen to lead us, where is he? Why hasn't he marched into the Arches and declared his intentions? If he is so certain about staying, why is he consulting the seer right at this moment?'

Now that was funny. Macready smirked. 'Have you been scrabbling about in the gutters and alleys, following our boy about his morning chores? I would have thought it beneath your dignity, my Lord.'

This was how to get the young coves. Attack them in the ego.

'I have people to do that for me,' Dhynar said defensively.

'I shouldn't think your courtesi were up to much after that beating Ashiol gave them,' said Kelpie.

'Think what you like,' said Dhynar, recovering his composure. 'Interesting things have been overheard this morning. A word here, a sentence there. Your precious Ashiol is scrabbling to find some alternative to getting stuck here as our Power and Majesty. A menagerie, he called us. Monsters and clowns. I'm not saying he's wrong...'

'Sounds like a fair assessment to me,' said Macready. And my, it was fine to have the freedom to be rude to Lords of the Court again.

Dhynar backed up slowly until he reached the ladder. 'Ask

163

yourself, if Ashiol Creature King is ready and willing to be our Power and Majesty, why does he have his most valuable servants on a roof in the middle of nowhere spying on some shabby little dressmaker?'

It was a valid point, and one Macready had been trying not to think about. 'Spit your poison somewhere else, my Lord. We have no time for you here.'

Dhynar's face twisted into something ugly. 'We know what he's doing, this King of yours. If you think we'll let him get away with it, you're more stupid and loyal than I ever thought possible.'

Macready let out a long breath after Dhynar was gone. Then, very solemnly, he kissed the blade of his sword, then his dagger. 'Nice to have you back, my lovelies.'

'I've had a nasty thought,' said Kelpie.

'Just the one?'

'When Dhynar says "we", who does he mean?'

'Feck! An alliance?'

'That's what it sounds like.'

'How could we have missed that?'

'We've been preoccupied since yesterday.'

'You think it's that recent?'

'Dhynar's scum, and he's a child. None of the other Lords gave him the time of day before now, even when he took on his fourth courteso. He wasn't worth anything when Garnet was Power and Majesty, but the landscape of the Court changed yesterday.'

Macready shook his head. 'They think he's a maggot. Not one of the Lords would lower themselves to ally with him.'

'Unless he suddenly has something that's valuable,' said Kelpie, thinking it out. 'Dhynar joined the Court only a year before Ash's exile, right? Ash was spending less and less time at Court then, and when he did he was tied up with Garnet's power games.'

Macready nodded. It was all horribly clear now. 'Dhynar is the only one of the current Lords who's had few dealings with our boy. Poet, Priest, Livilla, Warlord — Ashiol knows them all too well, inside and out.'

'Dhynar's the only Lord that Ash doesn't know exactly how to handle. That's worth something to whichever of the Lords is smart enough to see it.'

'As if the little pip wasn't powerful enough already. An alliance will make things messy, so it will.'

'If all they want is for Ash to take his place as Power and Majesty, we shouldn't have too much of a problem,' Kelpie said hopefully.

Macready just looked at her.

The ladder creaked behind them as Crane bounded up, carrying a parcel of food. 'Who was it?' he asked breathlessly. The other two looked at him. 'Who was what?' Macready asked.

'The man who came to the dressmaker's door with flowers and sweetheart tokens.' Crane's face changed as he took in Kelpie's and Macready's blank expressions. 'Weren't you watching?' He pushed past them both and practically threw himself over the parapet. 'He's gone!'

'We were a mite busy,' said Macready.

Crane glared at them both. 'We've been sitting here for fourteen hours waiting for some evidence of a man linked to this household, and you missed it?'

'Lucky you caught a glance of the cove, is it not?'

'I turned my head away so the dressmaker wouldn't recognise me,' Crane said between gritted teeth. 'I thought you'd be up here getting a good look and preparing to follow him. Too much to hope that you could pay attention to a job for ten minutes straight...'

'Getting a little full of yerself, are you not, master spy that you are?'

'At least I take our work seriously!'

'Will you both shut up,' Kelpie snapped. 'Crane, it doesn't matter about the man.'

'But Ashiol wanted —'

'I said it doesn't matter.'

Macready was watching her face. 'And now we've gotten over the joy of those shiny distractions you brought us, my lovely, and our blades are settled back in their rightful places, will you tell us exactly what it is you know that we don't?'

Kelpie looked uncomfortable, but motioned for them both to sit down. 'Ash wanted to know if there was a man attached to the household, yes? Last nox, he thought the dressmaker was in league with a hidden King, one that came into his powers late, or has been hiding his powers. He might have been her brother, lover, whatever. Someone close to her. But this morning, Ash realised he had been looking at things the wrong way. The reason we're still up here, keeping an eye on that shop across the road, is that Ash thinks *she* is the hidden King.'

Macready blinked. 'That bit of a lassie?'

'One of the three demoiselles in the house, yes. Most likely the dressmaker herself. Ash felt the King's animor in the rose dress and the clothes in the workshop.'

'A lass as a Creature King,' said Macready, thinking it over. 'Thought it wasn't possible.'

'Just because it's never happened before doesn't mean it's not possible,' said Kelpie. 'Ash went to the seer to find out for certain. But from what Dhynar said — I think she must be. Somehow, Dhynar knows about it. Probably whichever Lord he's allied with knows it as well.'

'Why is Ashiol so interested in this demme?' interjected Crane. 'She's not a threat to him. If she's belonged to the daylight world this long, it's unlikely that she'll suddenly rise up out of nowhere and challenge him.'

Macready rolled his eyes. 'Will you explain it to our inno-cent here, Kelpie my love, or shall I do the honours?'

'Be my guest.'

'Laddie-buck, our man Ashiol isn't worried that the dressmaker will rise up out of the daylight to challenge him as Power and Majesty. He's worried that she won't.'

Crane's face fell. 'He really wants to leave us.'

'That's his plan,' said Macready. 'Can you blame the man? I'd leave us if I could.'

'And the question is,' Kelpie said. 'If Dhynar and the other Lords are planning to force Ash into staying, do we help or hinder them?'

Macready tilted his head at her. 'Lass of mine, that's not even a question.'

Kelpie sighed in agreement. 'Our loyalty's not to the city or the Court. It's to the Creature Kings.'

'Both of them,' said Crane, looking back across the parapet and, down at the little dressmaker's shop.

THE DELIVERY WAS FOR DELPHINE, of course. Velody didn't know why she bothered opening the door on sweetheart days.

'Is she in by any chance?' asked the suitor in a hopeful voice, hanging on to his armful of flowers, sweetmeats and love poems.

Velody slid her eyes sideways to the kitchen door, where Delphine stood shaking her head wildly.

'Apparently not,' Velody said to the suitor, relieving him of his bundles.

'They're not all from me,' he said with a sigh. 'Some other lads put a few tokens in — they were too bashful to come themselves.'

Velody grinned at him. 'And you thought being the only one brave enough to come to her door might earn you an extra point or two?'

He smiled back, unconsciously charming and oh, so young. 'You'd think.'

'I'll tell her which are yours,' she promised him.

'The poppy posy and the sugared almonds,' he said all in a rush. 'And that note there, on the peach-coloured paper. I'm Simeon of the Alexandrine, Via LaChette.'

'I'll tell her,' said Velody, stepping back so she could close the door in his face.

She carted the armful of sweetheart tokens into the kitchen and let them fall onto the table. She and Delphine hadn't spoken to each other all day and this was as good an excuse as any to make amends. 'How do you do it, Dee? There's a whole army of Aufleur men madly in love with you, and not one of them knows a thing about you apart from your address and your favourite hem-length.'

'If they did know me, they wouldn't be in love with me,' drawled Delphine.

'Is it my imagination, or do these swains of yours get younger every year? I swear that one didn't have his beard grown in yet.'

'They always look older by lantern light...'

Their eyes met for a moment and they exchanged wordless apologies.

'Is Rhian down yet?' Velody asked, when the moment was over.

'I took up breakfast,' said Delphine. 'She says she's fine and she'll be down later.'

'She always says she's fine.'

'Doesn't mean it's always a lie. What on earth happened the previous nox — I can't have given her that big a scare with the table, can I?'

'It wasn't you. We had an intruder. He was either drunk or mad, and his friends turned up to haul him away.' Velody had spent most of the morning wondering how to explain the strange events of last nox. It was surprisingly easy, in the end, and not even too much of a lie.

'That's all we need,' said Delphine. 'Did he get upstairs?'

'It's how he got in.'

Velody rose early this morning to investigate the crawl space in the roof. She nailed a few boards here and there to make things difficult next time the mad Ducomte or his friends planned an uninvited visit. She also scattered around a few nasty surprises up there — improvised caltrops made from needles and other spiky sewing implements. Next time she went by a smithy, she would invest in a few of the steel variety.

'No wonder she's a mess,' said Delphine. 'Should we send for the midwife?'

The only women in Aufleur allowed to practise as dottores were those registered as midwives, although many of them covertly dispensed other forms of medical advice on the side. Their local midwife had regularly visited Rhian over the last year, advising on various potions and powders to calm the worst of her anxiety attacks. A male dottore was not an option.

'I sent a note to her already,' admitted Velody.

Sorting through her sweetheart gifts, Delphine held up a powder blue envelope. 'You sly witch. You didn't tell me you had a man on your string.'

'I don't even have a string. What are you talking about?'

Delphine handed over the elegant envelope. 'This one's for you.'

The envelope was expensive, with the thinnest line of gold leaf around the rim. The name Velody was calligraphed in flamboyant purple ink. It certainly looked like a sweet-heart note.

'I haven't met any men in months,' Velody started to say, then hesitated, remembering the dark eyes of the Ducomte as he knelt before her, holding her hand between his.

'Aha!' said Delphine triumphantly. 'There is someone!'

'Not at all.'

Velody opened the envelope. A blue card fell out, embossed with curlicues and gilded images of cupids. Delphine leaned forward with a whoop and snatched it out of Velody's hand. 'Oh, this is grand. This is better than grand, it's downright elegant. This is the Vittorina Royale!'

'The musette?' said Velody. 'It's a theatre ticket?'

The only tickets she had seen before were the thin paper tokens you bought at two centi each for the pit, or the slightly more upmarket shillein tokens that got you a half-decent seat in the stalls on variety evenings. There was no note in this envelope. Nothing to suggest from whom this unexpected gift had arrived.

'It's a box theatre ticket!' crowed Delphine. 'This is better than all my baubles put together, sweetie-my-sweet.' She waved the card back and forth in front of Velody's face. 'The Mermaid Revue this evening — and, best of all, you can bring a friend!'

21

SECOND DAY OF THE
FLORALIA (SWEETHEARTS)

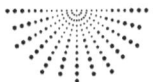

NOX

*V*elody knew that using the tickets wasn't a good idea, but she was not given much choice in the matter. Rhian was her only valid excuse for staying home, and Rhian had been in a firm state of denial all day, refusing to admit that the previous nox's antics had bothered her at all. She accepted a potion from the midwife, and insisted that Delphine and Velody not give up their chance to sit in a musette box on her account.

Sometimes Velody couldn't help wishing that Rhian was a little less selfless.

So Delphine and Velody raided their wardrobes for the most elegant finery they possessed — only Velody's original designs, of course. More than a chance to watch a revue in luxury, this was a rare chance to advertise for potential clients by being seen and noticed by Society.

Velody wore a lavender gown that fell to just below her knees. The hem was beaded, and she wore a matching headband over her long dark hair. It was the fabric that would catch the eye of fashion hounds — hopefully — as it was imported and unusual, a crumpled crepe that was not readily available anywhere south of Atulia.

Delphine's frock — sky blue shot with silver — was cut in a more daring fashion. It not only revealed her bare arms and the upper swell of her small breasts, but it had a diagonal hemline that would guarantee she was noticed. On her right side, the hemline reached three inches below her knee, more than a respectable length; but on her left side it was at least three inches above the most racy of the current fashions.

The more conventional set, who had declared it the end of the world when hemlines began brushing the knee recently, might well faint at the sight of Delphine's dimpled thigh. Velody could only cross her fingers and hope no one prevented them from entering the theatre on the grounds of indecency.

Delphine had thought of that, teaming her frock with a long fringed stole that elegantly covered her left side as the Master of the House accepted the ticket and escorted the two young demoiselles to their private box seat. Only once he had left them alone with a bottle of Orcadian bubbled wine, a platter of sugared apricots and a box of ciocolate fondants wrapped in silver tissue, did Delphine drop the stole and stand up so that the theatre crowd could see exactly what she was wearing. She arched her neck and turned slightly to reveal the dress from several angles.

Velody sat near the gilded railing, noting which faces tilted upwards to see Delphine's dress and which gossiped to their neighbour. The centi crowds in the pit and shilleins in the stalls were of little interest, but there were plenty of stares — and the occasional admiring glance — from the more affluent dress circle.

After less than a minute, Delphine sat beside Velody,

covering her knees with the stole again. 'Always leave them wanting more,' she said in a sly whisper. 'Those who didn't see me will probably hear about it between now and the first intervale.'

Velody grinned. 'I imagine you'll want to take a little walk to stretch your legs about then?'

Delphine smirked back at her. 'You know, I just might.'

The costumes in the show were more lavish than those at the Argentia, the little musette in Giacosa that sometimes gave Velody costume contracts, but the content of the revue was the usual frivolous mash. There were comic songs, most of them lusty, and the occasional drag or animal act. Classical scenes were enacted as an excuse for an actress or songstress to remove parts of her clothing — or for her historically re-created garments to be ripped off as if by accident. Tumblers and mimes ran on between the more substantial acts, to perform in front of the curtain and enable sets to be changed.

The first intervale came and went. Delphine walked up and down the theatre, allowing several gentlemen to buy her oranges and cups of rosewater. She managed to whisper the name and address of her dressmaker into the ears of several curious ladies.

With that job done, the two of them could get on with enjoying the show. The wine was excellent, the fruit and fondants a welcome treat, and the entertainment could not be faulted for being a little stale — there wasn't much that was original on the stage these days. The glorious painted eaves and mirrored ceiling were far better appreciated from these lofty heights. None of that explained why Velody couldn't relax and enjoy the decadent experience.

The obvious explanation was guilt — how could she be out at the theatre with Rhian at home, incapable of joining them? But this didn't feel like guilt. It was more like dread.

Velody's skin prickled in the stuffy heat of the theatre as two clowns exchanged bawdy jokes behind gilt cosmetick and striped satin pyjamas. What was wrong with her? Why did she feel as if a storm was coming, or an army of bailiffs, or a pack of wild animals? Her hands were shaking, and she hid them in the meagre folds of her dress before Delphine noticed.

The clowns made grandiose bows and somersaulted into the wings, to great applause and catcalling from the stalls.

'And now, my lords and ladies,' bellowed the thickly moustached ceremonial, striding across the stage in crimson and gold livery for all the world like a toy soldier at Saturnalia. 'It is my great pleasure to present for you the star of our little revue, the one and only Mermaid's Fancy, the Pearl Beyond Price, the Golden Voice, the favourite son of the Vittorina Royale, his humble highness — the Orphan Princel!'

The crowd went mad, whooping and slamming their feet against the creaking floorboards in rapturous applause.

'Never heard of him!' said Delphine. 'Must be good though.'

Chords began, a simple melody from the stage organ, played by an invisible figure in the orchestra pit. As the crowd subsided, the music swelled. The ceremonial smartly removed himself, leaving that rarest of things, a completely empty stage. The set was simple — a backdrop suggesting an anonymous back alley. Velody had never before heard the tune that was playing, but it was strangely compelling.

'I want to go home,' she hissed in Delphine's ear, but her friend swatted her as if she were an annoying insect.

A new, perfect note broke into the rising orchestral music, and Velody was distracted for a moment as she tried to work out what kind of instrument it belonged to. Then the Orphan Princel strolled across the stage and she realised that the sound was his voice, still held in that perfect note, unwavering.

Didn't he need to breathe?

Even as Velody thought that, the figure on stage snapped out of his single note, danced a quick four-step jig and barrelled into his song.

It wasn't anything special, as a song. It was a fairly standard musette act. He was a grown man dressed as an urchin boy in short, ragged trousers, capering across the stage. The song told of how he was really a princel who had been kidnapped from his Palazzo and ended up on the street in a strange city, begging for crumbs and half-starving to death. It was an odd mix of pathos and comedy. He drew tears out of the audience with a verse about his misfortunes, then winked merrily to assure you not to believe a word of it.

Standard stuff, yes — almost as hackneyed as the tale of a common orange-seller (or florister, or streetwalker) with a heart of gold who dreamed of being whisked away from her life of cheerful poverty. The difference was that this performer — this Orphan Princel — was mesmerisingly good. His voice was as hypnotic as the bright blue eyes that stuck out of his funny-looking face. The audience was riveted to his every canter and twirl.

Velody sweated as she watched him. She could feel moisture pricking her skin as the Orphan Princel carolled his tune to the dress circle. At one point, he turned and doffed his shabby hat in the direction of their box, and she almost stopped breathing.

There was something familiar about all of this, but she couldn't for the life of her think what it was. All she could do was watch in amazement as this ordinary, silly little performer sang in his angelic voice and danced his perfect steps. Then, when it was over, she applauded and cheered

along with everyone else, clapping her hands so hard that
they hurt.

The Orphan Princel's next number called for assistance
from the chorus line. Here, he was a clownish figure desperately trying to paint the portraits of a group of snooty
columbines, who ignored him and turned elegant pirouettes
in the background while he sang of his troubles and strife.
The third number was a serious solo, the old musette
favourite 'Lonely Boy', which he performed with such
sadness and perfection that Velody found herself crying, and
wasn't the only audience member to be so affected.
Delphine was rubbing her eyes on her fringed stole by the
end of it.

Finally, by popular acclaim, he returned for one last
encore as the Orphan Princel, cheeky and charming all over
again, singing about how he and the rest of the lovable,
chirpy street characters celebrated the various city festivals,
from Lupercalia to Saturnalia.

When the Orphan Princel was gone, bowing and teasing
his way off stage as the audience hollered for more, Velody
felt quite empty.

Delphine breathed a deep sigh and reached for her wine
glass while a herd of mimes and acrobats tumbled across the
stage. 'It's going to be a bit of an anticlimax after that, don't
you think?'

'How long does it go on?' Velody asked.

'Oh, goodness knows. Hours. I think I heard someone say
there were six intervales in all.'

'Six?' said Velody. 'I don't think I can stand it. I mean, it's
good...'

'I know,' said Delphine. 'Too much of a good thing can
make your stomach ache.' She tilted her empty glass. 'Besides,
we've finished all this.'

Relieved, Velody folded the last of the fondants into a

piece of tissue to take home to Rhian. The improvised parcel fitted perfectly into her satin purse. 'Let's go.'

As they turned towards the curtain that hung across their exit, it swished suddenly aside. A large usher stood there, so muscled around the shoulders that he barely fit into his formal suit. 'May I help mesdames?'

'Demoiselles,' corrected Delphine.

'We're just leaving,' said Velody.

She had hoped to slip out without making it obvious to the performers on stage. Too late, she realised as she looked back. The mimes had spotted Velody and Delphine making their escape and promptly launched into a spot of improvisation in which two haughty ladies made their distaste of the show clear by walking out of the theatre between intervales. The audience were laughing, sharing the joke as they too eyed the demoiselles trying to escape the private box.

Blushing, Velody dived for the curtain, sliding around the large usher and out of view. Delphine giggled and lowered her stole, giving a little turn to show off her scandalous dress one last time. Several wolf-whistles followed her out, at least one from a mime on stage.

Velody was not cut out for these publicity stunts. Her heart was beating fast just from being the centre of attention for half a minute.

'If the demoiselles would follow me,' said the usher, 'one of our performers wishes to present his compliments. He hopes you gained pleasure from the tickets he sent you.'

Velody hesitated, but Delphine lunged forward, smiling her prettiest smile at the usher. 'Not the Orphan Prince! He's adorable,' she added back over her shoulder at Velody.

'Is he?' asked Velody, trying to ignore the shiver that ran through her body at the sound of his name. What was wrong with her? Since when was she attracted to skinny, funny-looking men with angelic singing voices? Every instinct told her to run, to go home and bolt herself into her bedroom as Rhian did every nox. But this theatre was a maze, and they were already being led into unfamiliar territory, back and behind the stage.

Surely it wasn't usual for audience members to be taken backstage during the show? Afterwards, yes, but not during. Velody had been invited backstage at the Argentia once so that the Peacock Queen, a well-known opera singer, could compliment her on the dress she had made for the final number — stitching in extra panels at the last moment to accommodate the singer's rapidly increasing girth from an unexpected pregnancy.

Behind the scenes at the Vittorina Royale, the performers were on edge, snapping at each other and running around like mad things, hissing about the wrong shade of cosmetick or repairing torn costumes with desperate haste. On their way through, Delphine and Velody witnessed several tantrums, two lovers' tiffs and a horde of half-naked clowns climbing into animal costumes.

Finally they were in a quiet corridor underneath the main stage. A large, tacky gold star was fixed to the door, with the name 'The Princel' inscribed on the rough wood in chalk, and then below, in a different colour, the words 'and don't you forget it!' in a rough scrawl.

Part of Velody wanted to turn and run, to crash her way through the scenery and costumes until she was out on the street and away from this place. But another part of her was desperately curious to meet the man who sang 'Lonely Boy' with such sadness and longing.

The usher knocked on the door.

'Enter,' said a light voice.

It was an ordinary dressing room, as much as Velody had ever seen such a thing. A large mirror and dressing table, various sprawling boxes of cosmetick, half a hundred assorted costumes. A narrow bed.

Their host sat on a straight-backed chair, devoid of make-up. He appeared quite ordinary — skinnier and more funny-looking in person, to tell the truth. He looked older than he had on stage.

Delphine stepped forward in full flirtatious flight. 'How darling of you to invite us.'

'Not at all,' said the performer graciously. 'I hope you enjoyed the show.'

'Oh, we did, didn't we, Velody?'

'Yes.' Velody's eyes were drawn to an old theatre poster stuck to the corner of the mirror. It depicted a sketch of two laughing, bawdy demoiselles in feathers and sequins under a banner: Visit the Mermaid and See the Pearls Beyond Price!

'I'm so glad,' said the Orphan Princel. Now Velody's eyes were drawn to him and his very blue eyes.

'Why did you send the tickets?' she blurted out.

'Vee!' Delphine elbowed her. 'It's not polite to question gifts.'

Velody rolled her eyes at her friend. 'Just because you smile and flirt if someone gives you so much as a glass of water doesn't mean I have to, and I want to know why someone I've never met before sent me such an expensive present.'

Their host laughed. 'You're right to be suspicious, demoiselle. There is no need to worry. I sent the tickets at the request of a mutual friend.'

Velody frowned. 'Who?'

The Orphan Princel reached out and sipped from a glass of water. 'He likes cats,' was all he said.

Oh, *hellfire*. It was the mad Ducomte after all. 'Is he stalking me?' Velody demanded. 'Are you part of his weird little games?'

The Princel smiled a sad smile. 'Hardly that, my sweet. He was afraid he had upset you, and asked me to make amends on his behalf.'

'Why can't he make his own amends?'

'Perhaps he thought you would not accept them from him?'

'Perhaps I won't accept them from you.'

'Perhaps, perhaps. A world of perhaps. Has anyone ever told you that you're awfully suspicious? No wonder my friend was so worried about offending you... I'm rather frightened myself.'

'I doubt that,' said Velody, glaring at him.

Delphine was looking from one to the other. 'Are you two sure you don't know each other?'

'Positive,' said Velody.

'You give me little credit, demoiselle dressmaker,' said the Princel in his light, musical voice. 'I know many things about you.' He stood, walking three steps past Delphine so that he could lean towards Velody's ear. 'I know that you dream of brown mice.'

Velody stared at him.

He gave another of those sad smiles. 'Mine was white rats. If you ever have any questions, I want you to know you can come to me. I remember what it is to be young and afraid and new to the game.'

Velody didn't want to ask what game he was talking about. 'I have one question for you, seigneur Princel. If we try to leave now, will you stop us?'

'I don't want you to leave yet,' he said with a shrug of his bony shoulders. 'But I will not stand in your way.'

Velody reached out her hand to take Delphine's. 'Time to go.'

'I wish you'd tell me what's going on,' Delphine

complained as they headed for the door. 'You're both scaring me.'

'Me too,' Velody said in an undertone.

The door was locked. Somehow, Velody was not surprised. 'Let us out of here,' she demanded.

The Princel wasn't smiling now. 'Only after I have shown you the truth, demoiselle dressmaker. This is your future.'

He changed before their eyes, his body dissolving down into something... else.

Delphine started screaming.

22

SECOND DAY OF THE
FLORALIA (SWEETHEARTS)

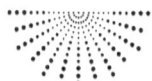

NOX

*a*shiol only intended to close his eyes for a minute.
When he awoke, his body precariously balanced
beside Hel in her bed, the tent was almost completely dark.

'Damn,' he said aloud. 'What time is it?'

Heliora yawned and shifted against him without opening
her eyes. 'I'm sure the Ducomte d'Aufleur can afford a water-
clock for every room in his house, but we peasants have to
rely on the good old sun. I don't have one handy right now.'

Ashiol sprang out of bed and pulled back the gauze
curtain to search for his clothes in the main section of the
tent.

Hel pulled the covers more tightly around her. 'On the
other hand, if that lantern of mine burned down to the nub,
it must be past sundown.'

'I suppose it's too much to hope that any stalls selling
boots will still be open for business?'

'Unlikely. Most of the vendors pack up around dusk,

except the ones trading in food, booze, religious artefacts and loose women.' Heliora pushed herself up on one elbow. 'Where do you have to go that's so important, Ash?'

He padded back across the tent floor to drop a kiss on the top of her head. 'To save the city, of course.'

'Again?'

'Job's never done.'

'And when will you be back? Six months? Another five years?'

'Something like that.'

'At least Garnet used to bring me presents when he wanted me to see things.'

'I thought you never gave him visions of the future.'

'He still brought presents.'

'I'll buy you a giltfish in a glass next time I'm passing.' Ashiol made to move away from the bed, but Hel slid her arms around his neck.

'Don't go. You're exhausted, and your feet hurt. What will one nox of sleep hurt?'

'With the rest of the Court up and about between dusk and dawn? I hate to think.'

Heliora's arms tightened. 'An hour then. I'm cold, Ash. Come to bed.'

Ashiol tapped her on the nose. 'You're seven hells of a woman, Hel. If I was the settling-down kind...'

That did the trick. She slammed her arms away from him so quickly that the bed almost spun. 'Get lost.'

'I knew you'd see it my way.'

'Next time, send Macready to beg for a vision of the futures!' she yelled as Ashiol made for the tent flap. 'He's cuter than you anyway!'

'And is she not a sweet lass for saying so?' broke in a cheerful brogue from outside the tent.

Ashiol almost jumped into the air. 'Mac?'

'Out here, my King.'

'How long have you been there?'

'How long is a piece of string, or a sweetheart's smile, or a sunset?' Macready's tousled head pushed through the tent flap. 'Long enough to hear the demoiselle compliment my charms in those dulcet tones of hers.' He waved a hand at Heliora. 'Hello, my lovely.'

'Piss off,' she said, throwing the blankets over her head.

'I wouldn't have interrupted such a tender moment,' said Macready. 'We only thought you'd want to know about this dressmaker of yours.'

Ashiol pushed his way out of the tent. It was definitely nox. The Basilica was all but closed down, although, as Heliora had predicted, the food stalls at the far end were still bustling. 'What has the dressmaker done now?'

'She's taking in a show at the Vittorina Royale,' Macready said apologetically.

Ashiol stared at him. 'Oh, fuck.'

'Isn't that just what I thought you'd say?'

THERE WERE RATS EVERYWHERE, and Delphine wouldn't stop screaming. Velody beat on the door with her fists, but there was no response to her yells and thumps. Rats clawed at her back and her neck and her hair. Tiny teeth sank into her left shoulder. She swatted at the horrible creatures and kept yelling for help, scraping her useless fists against the solid wood of the door.

There was a crash, and Delphine's screams turned into broken, muffled sobs.

Velody whirled around. The white rats were gone, replaced by a single, powerful creature, upright like a man and glowing, clawed and sharp-toothed like the rat and only barely recognisable as the Orphan Princel. He grabbed her by the upper arms and flung her across the room so that she crashed into the weeping, huddled figure of Delphine.

I can fight him, she found herself thinking. *He's afraid of me, and I don't know why. If I did, maybe I could fight back.*

But then the tall rat-man melted and shaped himself back into the gang of red-eyed, white-furred rats, and they poured across the floor towards the two huddled women.

I am not going to cower and scream like some helpless centi opera heroine, Velody said sternly to herself, but when the creatures started swarming over her again, it was too hard to be brave and her screams rivalled Delphine's.

BACKSTAGE AT THE VITTORINA ROYALE, Ashiol and Macready found Kelpie confronting a huge slab of a man outside the star's dressing room. He smelled of the Creature Court, and it didn't take a genius to work out whose courteso he might be.

Come to think of it, Ashiol had caught sight of this one earlier that day, though they hadn't been introduced.

'You don't want to do this, Halberk,' Kelpie warned, her steel Sister hovering at the big man's throat. 'One last time, where's the damned key?'

Halberk grinned widely. 'Zero has it,' he said in a thick Inglirren accent.

Kelpie hissed between her teeth. 'And where is Zero?'

'Running errands. Could be anywhere, little blighter that he is. Very untrustworthy.'

'Fine,' she said. 'Stand aside, or I'll start slicing things off.'

Halberk was unconcerned. 'You've got a shiny sword and suddenly you're a killer, little sentinel? Don't see it somehow.'

Kelpie growled. 'I didn't say I'd kill you, meat sack. I said I'd slice bits off. Small bits. Many small bits.' She glanced back over her shoulder and saw Ashiol. 'Or failing that, I'll just let him do it.'

'Hello, Halberk,' said Ashiol in a friendly voice. 'Haven't met officially, have we? I'm your Lord and master. Bow down before me.'

The big man looked him up and down, then snorted. 'I've got a Lord and master, matey, and he ain't you.'

Screaming started inside the room. A woman's scream. Another, not-quite-so-helpless woman was yelling her head off and banging on the door. Ashiol was strangely pleased.

'Do I have to remind you what a Creature King is, Halberk? Didn't Garnet teach you that important little lesson?'

'Garnet?' Halberk spat at the ground. 'Limp-wristed pansy. I wasn't impressed by him, sonny boy, and I'm not impressed by you.'

'Interesting.' Ashiol brushed aside Kelpie's blade so that he could stand nose to nose with Halberk. The effect was slightly marred by the fact that Halberk was half a head taller. 'Obviously none of your Lord's charm and diplomacy has rubbed off on you.'

Halberk smirked. 'I've heard of you, Ashiol Creature King. I heard how loud you screamed and whimpered when our last Power and Majesty scratched a few scars into your pretty cheeks. I don't think you've got anything to scare me with.'

Ashiol smiled his friendliest smile. 'Why are the big ones always stupid?' he remarked to no one in particular, and then sank his teeth into Halberk's throat.

It was a hard snap of a bite, teeth grinding into flesh and blood. Halberk dropped to his knees and Ashiol went with him, his jaw slamming harder into the powerful grip. He could taste the courteso's history in the thick skin of his neck, knew by the taste of his animor that he was bear, and forty-seven years old, and had quite a few unsavoury sexual practices. And yes, Ashiol could taste Halberk's Lord and master in the bloody flesh, but there were no surprises there.

Halberk went limp, and Ashiol punched him to the floor, then leaped to his feet. Kelpie and Macready were trying to shoulder the heavy door, but it held well under their assault. Calmly, Ashiol moved them both aside.

'The screaming stopped,' said Kelpie, sweat dripping down her face. Even as she said it, the screams started up again — both women this time, high and shrill and in absolute screeching terror.

Ashiol could have gone chimaera and made the door crumble under his weight, but with Halberk's blood still dripping from his mouth he was in a mood to be civilised. He rapped on the door. 'Poet, if you don't let us in, I'm going to start taking mouthfuls out of your large friend here, and when he's run out of arms and legs I'm going to start on you.'

The screaming stopped again. A few moments later, a key turned in the lock and the door opened. Poet shrugged a silken dressing gown over his naked body, and drew a pair of his round spectacles from the pocket to place on his face. 'Lucky I keep a spare key in here,' he said in a friendly voice. 'I never know when my boys are going to take it upon themselves to lock me inside.' He glanced past Ashiol to the crumpled, damaged mess that was Halberk. 'Glad you didn't kill him.'

Ashiol smiled with his blood-smeared mouth. 'They never taste as good when they die.'

A glint of humour appeared in Poet's eyes. 'And isn't that a shame?'

Ashiol pushed Poet aside, striding into the dressing room. The two women were backed into the far corner beside the dressing table, hands clutching at each other for comfort. Without a word, Ashiol walked towards them. He reached for the nearest — the blonde — and scooped her into his arms. She sagged like a broken doll.

With a hesitant look at Poet, Macready followed Ashiol, but the dressmaker gave him a dirty look as he approached her. 'I can walk by myself.'

'I'm sure you can, demoiselle,' said Ashiol. 'Let's take it outside, shall we?'

The blonde in his arms closed her eyes and moaned. She smelled of champagne, ciocolate and artificial roses.

'Velody,' said Poet in a clear voice. 'The dressmaker's name is Velody.' He gave Ashiol a scornful look. 'You didn't even know that.'

Ashiol carried the blonde out of the dressing room, and out of the theatre. He didn't have to look to know that the dressmaker — Velody — was following, Macready at her side whether she wanted him there or not. Kelpie fell in behind them.

The performers and backstage crew barely gave a second look to this strange, grim procession. Perhaps demoiselles were carried half-unconscious out of the Orphan Princel's dressing room every day. Ashiol didn't particularly want to think about that.

Poet followed them all, at a distance.

The cool nox air hit Ash hard after the muggy atmosphere of the theatre. Away from the thick scents of greasy cosmetick and sweat, it was like stepping out of the shadows into the light.

'Put her down,' said Velody.

'She's not heavy,' said Ashiol. 'We'll see you safely home.'

'I said, put her down.'

Power rolled off the fierce dressmaker and it wasn't the kind of power he was used to tasting. Ashiol lowered the blonde to the cobblestones, allowing her to find her own feet. She grabbed at Velody, and the two of them held each other.

'Now,' said Velody in a calm voice, 'I'm afraid I don't have any threats left in me, so you'll just have to imagine them. We are going home alone right now, the two of us. I don't imagine there is anything on the streets that is nearly as much of a threat to us as you people.' Her gaze took in Poet, shivering in his thin robe, but also Kelpie, Macready and Ashiol himself. 'I don't know what this game is,' she added, her voice shaking only a little. 'But our part in it ends now. You will not approach me or follow me, you will not come near my house, and you will not touch my friends. Is that understood?'

After a moment, Poet bowed his head in a polite acknowledgement.

Ashiol hesitated, then nodded. 'I think that is the least we owe you.'

'Yes,' Velody said in a terrible voice. 'It is.' She turned her shaking friend and guided her away from the theatre, heading towards the Vittorine.

Ashiol watched them until they were almost at the end of the street, then nodded at Kelpie and Macready. 'Follow them discreetly. I'll be along later, when I've had a word with our friend here.'

The sentinels nodded and set off, moving swiftly and silently.

Standing side by side, Ashiol and Poet stood and watched until the brave little dressmaker had turned a corner and moved out of sight, unaware of her two shadows.

'I like her,' Poet said eventually. 'She's going to be fun.'

Ashiol stared at the Rat Lord's feet. They were about the right size. 'Got any boots I can borrow?'

23

SECOND DAY OF THE
FLORALIA (SWEETHEARTS)

NOX

*T*here were no nox cabs, of course. The horse-drawn cabriolets that were only allowed in the city between twilight and dawn tended to congregate near the Forum, and there was never one around when you wanted it. Velody and Delphine stuck to the main streets, not even stopping at the Piazza Nautilia to hire a lampboy. Neither of them spoke until they reached the slender alley that ran behind Via Silviana.

'Who were they?' Delphine finally rasped.

'I don't know,' said Velody. 'I don't want to know. Let's just get home to Rhian.'

'They were the ones who broke in last nox.'

'Some of them, yes.'

Velody was furious at herself. Delphine might be stupid enough to accept an anonymous, extravagant gift, but Velody should have been more wary.

'What do they want from us?' Delphine asked.

'I don't know that either.'

Delphine took a deep breath. 'That was the Ducomte d'Aufleur who carried me out of the theatre, right? The one with blood all over his chin?'

'Uh-huh.'

They were almost at their kitchen door now. Velody had never been so pleased to see it in her life. Twenty more steps, now fifteen...

'Fine,' said Delphine. 'Just so long as I know. Oh, help!' She tumbled forward without a scream. Neither of them had any scream left in them.

Velody looked down, squinting in the low light to see what Delphine had tripped over. It was a body.

'A tramp,' Delphine said. 'Is he dead?'

Velody reached out to touch the shoulder, her hand encountering rough wool. 'He doesn't smell like a tramp.' The fallen figure was warm, though he didn't stir at her touch. Certain that nothing more could frighten her this nox, she rolled him slowly onto his back.

His face was bloody and battered, so bad that it was a miracle he still breathed. Velody touched his pale hair, certain now that she didn't have to see an unmarked face to know who he was. He was the brown-cloaked young man whose face — before this brutal battering — had resembled that of a stained-glass saint. He groaned softly at her touch, but didn't open his eyes.

'I don't know who they are,' Velody muttered. 'I don't know which of them are protecting me and which are attacking. I'm not sure if they know themselves. But it's not good that he's out here.'

'Why not?' Delphine asked, her eyes wide with fright.

'Because it means that whoever did this to him is probably in there.' Velody looked up at their kitchen door.

She didn't even realise that she had got to her feet and

was running until she was inside the kitchen, the door having crashed open at her touch. That was wrong too. It should have been latched — it was always latched. 'Rhian?' she yelled hoarsely into the house, and heard nothing.

Delphine was close behind her. 'They couldn't have got here first. We came straight here.'

'Not them,' said Velody. 'Maybe someone worse than them.'

There was no one in the workshop, not even a glowing coal in the grate. There had been no point in setting a fire with both of them out for the evening, as Rhian would be upstairs behind her bolts and locks.

They ran up the stairs together. Seeing Rhian's door torn off its hinges was a punch to the stomach.

Delphine made it to the doorway first. Half a step behind, Velody had to look around Delphine to see the scene within the room.

Rhian sat on the bed, stiff and terrified. A man sat behind her, cradling her hard against his chest, a fierce smile on his face. He wore festival clothes, bright and merry, a lopsided white garland on his reddish-brown hair and sweetheart embroideries on his cuffs.

'Hello, Velody,' he said. 'I'm so pleased to meet you at last. I just know we're going to be good friends.'

Velody did not move, relieved that Rhian was, at least, alive. The sight of a man in her private sanctum though, the chill horror in her eyes as he held her body to his, was unbearable.

Delphine was not thinking so clearly — or, perhaps, was thinking more clearly than Velody. 'Monster!' she screamed, throwing herself at him with her nails outstretched, her eyes blazing with rage. He flicked a hand in her direction and she flew back, as if a solid blow had connected, crashing into the wall.

Velody could not move to Rhian's defence. She could barely speak. 'Which animal are you?' she asked, and was only half-aware of how together she sounded.

'Ferax,' he said, naming the urban fox that plagued parts of the city. Almost as bad as rats, they say, she found herself thinking, and resisted the urge to laugh. 'Which animal are you, Velody?'

Little brown mouse, she thought, and wondered why. 'I'm a dressmaker,' she said, and there were silk shears in her hand. Had she picked them up in the workshop? She couldn't remember. 'Step away from her, ferax, or I will cut out your heart and eat it while you watch.'

The awful thing was, she meant it. She had seen the bloodstains around the Ducomte's mouth as he carried Delphine out of the dressing room, and something deep inside her had said, *I could do that*.

The ferax grinned as if this little exchange meant that — somehow — they were friends. 'So you are one of us.'

'I'm not one of anything.'

'You must know you belong with the beasts. You must have felt it.'

'I don't belong anywhere but here.' Velody winced as he tightened his grip around the shuddering Rhian. 'I belong to this house, to her and her.' She pointed first at Rhian, then at Delphine. 'Why will none of you leave us alone?'

She was so very exhausted, but she had to be alert now. She had to save Rhian. She had to make their house a fortress again. But how could they ever trust locks and bolts after this?

The ferax opened his arms and Rhian fell free of him in a desperate tumble, her elbows pushing away from him as she rolled, sprawled on the floor. Slowly, she scrabbled her way towards Delphine. Velody could not help but notice the painful way in which Rhian moved.

'What did you do?' she demanded in a fury.

The ferax stood up in a smooth movement, walking towards Velody. She gripped the silk shears, but something about his golden eyes made her hand relax. He was able to hold out his hand and take them from her. He touched her chin, gazing into her eyes with something almost — but not quite — like parental concern. 'So,' he said. 'This is the one they would have as our King. Weak.'

'Why is everyone always talking about Kings?' Velody asked. She was so tired of not understanding the strange things that these people said. What kind of world did they belong to, that all this made sense to them? 'There are Ducs and Duchessas and Ducomtes, Comtes and Baronnes and a hundred different kinds of noblemen up to the rank of Princel and Princessa, but we just don't have any Kings. No one has had Kings for a hundred years, not even the Inglirrens or Islandsers.'

The ferax moved in closer. 'Wishful thinking if ever I heard it,' he said, and then he kissed her. His hands held her arms fast, and his grip was so pinchingly tight that she couldn't struggle. The experience was entirely unpleasant, although she couldn't help wishing he would put his wet tongue a little further into her mouth so that she could bite it off.

He flew away from her with a sudden yelp of pain, slamming to the floor, his whole body twitching. Velody looked with calm detachment at the knife in his shoulder. The hilt was quite ordinary, wrapped in strips of green leather. The blade was something else again — at least, the inch or two of metal that wasn't buried in the ferax's shoulder. It gleamed and shone, more fiercely silver than anything she had seen before. Tiny motes of light danced across the surface, although it wasn't tilted at the right angle to catch the reflection of the single lantern in the room.

'Took something of a liberty there, I'm afraid,' said an apologetic voice from the doorway, in Islandser brogue. Macready offered a shamefaced grin as Velody glared at him. 'You wouldn't have been enjoying that at all?' he asked.

'No,' she said in a hard voice.

'Well, that's all right, so. I'd have hated to interrupt such a tender moment if the pleasure was mutual.'

The ferax was curled in a ball, moaning.

Velody walked on unsteady feet past Macready to her friends. Delphine was conscious but huddled in on herself. Rhian sat with her back to the wall, her arms and legs as stiff as they had been when the ferax was holding her captive. Velody took Rhian's hands between hers. 'What did he do to you?' she asked, and couldn't help but think of that horrible day over a year ago, of begging Rhian to tell them what had been done to her and that awful silence, worse than if they'd heard the grisly details.

'Hit,' said Rhian in a distant voice. Her face was swollen on one side. Velody hadn't noticed that before. 'Here... here... here.' Her hand passed over her body, marking where the ferax had hit her. She managed a wan smile, being brave. 'Nothing worse.'

'That's bad enough,' Velody said. She wrapped her arms around Rhian's trembling body, offering what little comfort she could.

After a long moment, Rhian hugged her back. 'I thought it would happen again.' Rhian started sobbing, her whole body convulsing against Velody's. Delphine crawled towards them, adding her body to the awkward embrace.

There was no time for this, necessary though it was. Velody eased away from Rhian, allowing her to wrap her arms around Delphine instead. Only then did she look back up at Macready.

The light-hearted banter was gone. The sight of Rhian

weeping — the sheer devastation wrought by the ferax — had affected him. His face was hollow. 'How can I help, lass?'

It was vaguely reassuring to see that these people were not all monsters. Velody looked at the crumpled ferax, then back at Macready. 'You can leave, and tell me that none of you will ever be back again.'

Macready hesitated, and she knew he was deciding which lie to tell her.

The woman — Kelpie — appeared in the doorway beside Macready, bright-eyed and breathing hard, a sword in one hand that glittered with the same shimmering intensity as Macready's knife blade.

'Crane will live, if you're interested,' she said, mainly to Macready. 'I found Dhynar's hounds skulking around in the shadows. Made them whimper.'

'Not now,' said Macready, his eyes on Velody.

Velody stood over the ferax. Slowly, she reached down and pulled the knife out of his shoulder. It was jammed hard against bone and cartilage, and it took great strength to pull it free. The ferax moaned, still cowering from the weapon. Blood gushed out of his wound.

'Don't touch the blade,' warned Macready. 'It will burn you.'

Velody nodded slightly, indicating that she had heard him. She wiped blood from the shimmering metal on the ferax's bright tunic and then touched the flat of the blade to his face. He howled and cowered from her. She pressed it harder against his skin. 'Get up.'

Slowly, the ferax got to his feet. She ran the flat of the blade down his face, resting the edge finally against his throat. 'Walk,' she ordered.

Kelpie and Macready moved aside from the door to let them past, but Velody shook her head. 'You two go first. I don't trust any of you.'

'Crane almost died protecting your house,' Kelpie flared.

'Is that supposed to make me feel better? You've been watching our home, following us in the street. These... creatures didn't start taking an interest in us until your pet Ducomte did. What exactly did he tell them about me and my friends to make us such interesting targets?'

Kelpie was prepared to argue the point, but Macready took hold of her elbow and steered her out of the room. Velody, still pressing the blade to the ferax's neck, followed them.

Kelpie and Macready were halfway down the stairs, Velody and the ferax only a little way behind them, when the Ducomte Ashiol Xandelian d'Aufleur swept in from the kitchen as if he owned the place, high black boots ringing on the wooden floor and a long black coat swirling around his body. He took in the little tableau with a frown. 'What happened here?'

Velody gave the ferax a sudden push with the knife. He cringed away from it so wildly that he fell, tumbling down the stairs. Macready and Kelpie both pressed themselves to the sides so that he fell without taking them with him. As he hit the wooden floorboards at the bottom, his body split open into five or six red-gold furry creatures that darted around the Ducomte's ankles and fled towards the open kitchen door.

Velody met the Ducomte's eyes. She held up the shimmering knife by its green leather-wrapped hilt, noticing again the fascinating way it gleamed even in semi-darkness. 'Will this knife do to you what it did to him?' she asked.

He inclined his head slowly. 'Yes, it will.'

'Good. Then you won't come back.'

'You can't keep it!' protested Kelpie, genuinely shocked.

Velody weighed the knife. 'Try and stop me.'

The other woman's eyes narrowed. 'I could take it off you

in a heartbeat,' she said. 'Skysilver doesn't burn humans; that blade won't even scratch me.'

Velody hesitated, a question forming in her mind if not yet on her tongue. *Why did Macready warn me not to touch the blade if it has no effect on humans?*

'She can keep the knife,' Macready said quickly. 'She'll need it more than I will.' He glanced up at Velody, tipping an imaginary cap to her. 'Her name is Jeunille. Take care of her, my lovely, and she'll do right by you.'

'You only just got them back!' Kelpie wailed.

Macready shook his head. 'Let it go, lass. You've no idea what we've done to these demmes.'

Without another look at Velody, he headed for the kitchen. Kelpie followed him.

Now it was just Velody and Ashiol. It was silly to keep thinking of him as the Ducomte, no matter how regally he might behave. She came down a step or two, pointing the knife at him. 'You're not ranting and raving quite as much as you were last nox. You seem relatively normal.' *And you've washed the blood from your face. All very civilised.*

Ashiol winced. 'I wasn't having a good day. I'm not usually a raving lunatic.'

'I see.' Hard to forget the sight of him crashing into the dressing room, blood dripping from his teeth and tongue, swooping Delphine up into his arms as if she were a fainting damsel in a romantic play. 'So this is you on a good day?'

'Pretty much.' He eyed the knife, and backed up to the kitchen as Velody advanced on him. 'We need to talk.'

'Talk.' She almost laughed at that. 'What do you think we have to talk about, my Lord Ducomte? The state of politics today? The sociological significance of fertility festivals? Or perhaps you'd like to tell me exactly why those creatures came after me and my friends?'

They were in the kitchen now.

'I don't know how they found out,' Ashiol said, almost at the open back door. 'They weren't supposed to know about you — not yet anyway.'

'Weren't supposed to know what?' she snapped as Ashiol stepped backwards through the door, stumbling a little on the first step before finding his feet. She kept him moving until they were in the alley beyond the backyard. 'Weren't supposed to know what about us?' she repeated.

Macready and Kelpie waited further up the alley. Their friend Crane was between them, on his feet despite the nasty injuries, his face swollen. Velody tried not to remember how damned pretty he had been before the assault, tried not to feel guilty about what the ferax had done to him. *This is their fault, not mine.*

Ashiol stopped moving, his dark eyes almost daring her to advance on him further. 'I didn't know for sure,' he said calmly, a far cry from the manic explosion of words he had thrown at her the nox before. 'I needed to be certain.'

'Certain of what? Why are you all so interested in a florister, a ribboner and a dressmaker?' There was something in Ashiol's face that brought Velody closer to the truth. 'It's not Delphine or Rhian. It's me you're all after. What is it you think you know about me, seigneur Ducomte, that I don't know myself?'

Ashiol's eyes flickered.

Velody squeezed the leather-wrapped hilt of the knife and touched the shimmering silver blade to the skin of her left hand. The pain was unbelievable, a fierce burn that brought her to her knees before she was able to pull the thing away. She gasped, trying to regain a halfway normal breathing pattern so she could find her voice.

'If this knife doesn't work on humans, what am I?'

She could see — damn it, could smell — that he was about to lie to her, to say something vague and uninformative, that he was trying like anything to avoid telling her the truth. With a scream, she launched at him, the knife still in her hand.

Ashiol's watchdogs were good, she had to give them that. When it was over, the knife was on the ground and Velody was pinned to the wall by all three of them. Kelpie was the first to peel off, checking that Ashiol was all right. Crane was the next to go, muttering about how many ribs he thought he had broken before that little scuffle, let alone after.

'You may not believe me, but I am sorry about this,' Macready gabbled in her ear, still holding her fast. 'I know you've been through a lot this nox, but we couldn't let you kill him, so. It's our job to protect him. He belongs to us in the same way that your Rhian and your Delphine belong to you.' He relaxed his hold on her a little, leaning back so that their bodies were not quite so close. 'The funny thing is, lass, if you are what he thinks you are, we'll have to protect you too.'

Velody looked past Macready to Ashiol, who was dabbing blood from his cheek. She had got in one cut, at least, in her wild and slashing attack. 'What am I?' she asked him.

Ashiol looked at the blood on his fingers, and licked it. 'I don't know,' he said, and this time it wasn't a lie. 'I want to find out.'

Rage surged through her, a burning anger. 'No more games,' she said as heat prickled across her skin. 'No more games, Ducomte! Tell me what I am!'

Velody felt her body shifting explosively within her skin, as if it was not quite hers any more. She was breaking apart, tearing into a thousand separate pieces.

Macready threw himself aside, shielding his eyes as Velody burst open, her body flying apart and finding new, small shapes to climb into. Suddenly she was everywhere, inside hundreds of tiny warm bodies with tiny unblinking eyes.

Little brown mice, she thought hysterically. *Saints and angels. I'm little brown mice.*

2 4
SECOND DAY OF THE FLORALIA (SWEETHEARTS)

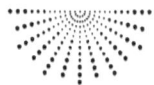

NOX

*I*t was a long time since Heliora had visited the Arches. As the seer of the Creature Court, she occupied a strange in-between status, one foot in the nox and another in the daylight.

When Ortheus was still the Power and Majesty, the seer had been expected to stay at his right hand, offering advice and opinions at every given opportunity. Heliora was presented with jewels and fine clothes and installed in living quarters in the Haymarket, Ortheus's own territory.

His successor offered no such incentives to stay nearby. Garnet had embraced the idea of a pet fortune-teller only until he realised that her interpretations of the cards and crystals were not always going to be the ones that he wanted. The seer's grand rooms in the Haymarket were soon appropriated for Garnet's lover Livilla, while Ashiol gave Heliora living quarters in his own territory.

After Ashiol went into exile, there was even less of a

reason for Heliora to stay in the underground sanctum. Garnet did not object to her spending more of her waking — and, eventually, her sleeping — hours in the Basilica, as long as she made time for any member of the Court who wished to consult her.

It was several years now since Hel had last set foot inside the Arches, and nothing had changed. She found her way in by the Lock at the foot of the Lucretine, holding her long skirts out of the water as she skipped nimbly across to the concealed path that led down to the cobbled and concreted streets of Old Aufleur.

Most of the area was uninhabitable, ruined by neglect and rockfalls. Other parts had been demolished to make way for a sewer and water-pipe system more than a century ago. But the heart of the old city was still intact: an underground canal running south off the Verticordia, the remains of a small but stately cathedral, several warehouses, a few shambling alleys lined with old abandoned shops. The museion was still in one piece, and some rooms in the fallen Palazzo were habitable. There was even an ornate bridge that had been erected in honour of the very first Mayor of Aufleur in the days before the Ducs and Duchessas, when the people of the city huddled underground in the hope of escaping the horrors that came from the sky.

There was no reason for any of the daylight folk to return to this place. For the Lords and Court, who still battled the sky, it was the only place they could feel remotely safe — at least long enough to sleep when sleep was needed.

Heliora avoided the tunnel that led past the cathedral to the Haymarket, making her way instead to the Shambles. It was too much to hope her presence would pass unnoticed among the Lords and Court, but with any luck they would ignore her. It was nox, in any case. Most of them were awake now and roaming the city above.

The only light down here was what you brought with you. Heliora had a long lantern hanging from a hooked cane that she had hired for two shilleins from a lampboy in the Forum.

The Shambles wasn't completely dark. Lamplight glowed from the upper storey of a shop that still had the name of its original proprietor — a grocer — painted in peeling letters above the door. Heliora set down her lantern cane at the door, and pushed it open. The old shop was full of shadows and little else. No one moved, but she knew she was not alone in here. 'I'm a friend,' she said aloud.

'Are you?' replied the voice of a boy. He was nearer to her than she had guessed. Heliora leaned into the darkness of the room.

'They call you Zero,' she said. 'Not your real name though. Your real name is —'

'Hey!' The boy jumped forward, and she could just see the outline of his outraged face from the light of her own lantern streaming in through the open front door. 'No need for that, demme! I didn't do anything bad to you, now did I?'

'I'm the seer,' she said. 'Has your Lord mentioned me at all?'

The boy's face grew sulky. 'You better go up.'

'Thank you.'

Heliora made for the stairs she could see, heading up towards the crack of light that illuminated a closed door. As she pushed the door open, heat hit her full in the face.

An elderly cooking range was the main feature of the upstairs room, belting out hot air as it churned wood into flame. It must have been purloined from an abandoned baking shop and installed up here by the current occupant. No one sensible would design a house to hold a stove on an upper storey.

'I like this,' she said, moving towards it and holding her hands out to take the last cold edge from them.

'Only way to get warm down here in the Arches,' said her host. 'Even in the height of summer everything is cold and damp.'

'I remember that.' Another reason to stay in the upper world. Having come to terms with the devastation possibility that the sky might fall at any moment, Heliora preferred to live in the sunshine while she could. 'How are you, Poet?'

'Not wounded, demoiselle, nor dead.'

He was relaxed here, wrapped in a dressing gown and surrounded by what could only be described as opulence. Strange to see so many antique paintings and rich furnishings crammed into a room that had once housed a humble grocer's family.

The boy Zero came up the stairs and lifted a bubbling pot from the range, pouring some of its contents into a large clay tankard. "S for Halberk,' he muttered.

Poet nodded, and the boy scampered up another staircase to what must be an attic room, carefully balancing the mug.

'Your other courteso is feeling under the weather?' Heliora said politely.

'Something like that,' said Poet. 'Our Ash bit his throat out this evening.'

'Did he deserve it?'

'Oh, yes. I'm lucky he didn't start biting pieces out of me. What are you here for, Hel?' Poet's voice was hard, but only slightly suspicious.

Heliora sighed deeply. 'I want a cup of tea.'

Caught off guard, he chuckled.

'I'm serious. I know you have the stuff. You're rolling in money from those theatricals you take such delight in. It's as rare as a virgin in a brothel up in the daylight.'

Shrugging into a comfortable armchair, Poet waved

towards a large wooden chest at the far end of the room. It was about the size of a packing crate, but far more ornately carved. 'Help yourself.'

She opened the lid to discover that the chest was packed almost to the rim with finest Camoiserian leaf. 'Poet, this is a Duc's ransom. This is three Duc's ransoms.'

'What else am I going to spend my money on?' he asked lazily. 'If I bought jewels, Livilla would just sneak in and steal them all. The only threat to my tea supply is Priest, and at least he's polite about it.'

Heliora found a worn copper kettle and a barrel of water to fill it from. While the kettle was heating on the range, she scooped a healthy helping of dried leaves into an elegant porcelain teapot. 'You live well, for a rat in a hole.'

Poet smiled at her. 'And you have refined tastes for a card-sharking whore.'

The niceties over, they sat in companionable silence and waited for the kettle to boil.

As the tea brewed in its pot, Heliora busied herself with cups, sugar and fresh cream that Zero had reluctantly fetched from the cellar at Poet's yell. Only when the ritual was almost complete did Poet finally bring up the subject that was on both their minds.

'So, my sweetness, what's in the cards for the Creature Court? What does our future hold?'

Heliora poured the tea, slowly and precisely. 'All manner of interesting things, half of them false.'

'Do those interesting things include a demoiselle King?'

'You know about that?'

'Seven hells, Hel, every creature from Church Bridge to the Alexandrine has heard it by now. What's Ashiol playing at?'

She finished pouring the second cup, and handed the first to him. 'I don't think even he knows what game it is.'

'So you can't tell me anything.'

Heliora clambered to her feet and found an armchair of her own. 'What do I know? I didn't even know you could have female kings.'

'You can't,' said Poet, cradling the absurdly delicate china cup in his hands. 'Tasha used to tell the story about a demoiselle Lord called Samara, mistress to the Power and Majesty who ruled before Ortheus. Samara killed the Power and quenched him whole, but the animor did terrible things to her. She was barely alive when they found her, a piece of wreckage with eyes and skin. There are other stories too, further back. No woman of the Creature Court has ever reached a rank above Lord — and those who tried died instantly.'

'I saw it in the futures,' Heliora said. 'In some of them, this woman doesn't come into her power at all. In others, she does, but... as you say, with the story of Samara. She is melted by the chimaera form, or simply crumbles from holding too much animor within her skin.'

'Did you tell Ashiol about that?'

'I tried. He only wanted to know about the futures where it worked, where she stood as Power and Majesty and he was able to escape the Creature Court once and for all.'

Poet took a deep swallow of his tea. 'The question is, would we be better off with Ashiol gone?'

'I suppose that depends on whether this dressmaker survives the future Ashiol wants for her.'

'It's a shame,' sighed Poet. 'I really was getting to like her.'

VELODY HAD EYES EVERYWHERE. She was scattered across the cobblestones, over the doorstep, up the walls. She could smell everything, from the sweat on the skins of the humans and Ashiol to the emotional pheromones that spilled out of them all. She wasn't even sure that she was Velody any more.

That panicked thought made her pull herself together, literally. She formed a desperate image of her own body, her own skin, and poured herself into that shape. It wasn't quite right. She was Velody, standing on two legs, but she was stronger, sharper, taller than ever before. She was powerful.

She still had the senses of the creeping creatures, could tell by the scents in the air that Macready, Crane and Kelpie were friends, they would not hurt her, they would protect her with their lives. At the same time she knew that Ashiol was not a friend. He was a rival. An equal. He could only be trusted up to a point. Everything about him felt *threat* as Velody faced him down, and he too shaped into a harder, more dangerous version of himself even as he pulled off his boots, shirt and trews, appearing naked and glowing before her.

Naked. Yes, she was naked too. Her garments had fallen away when she shaped herself into the little crawling things. For some reason, in this hard and powerful version of herself, she did not mind that she was clad only in her skin.

Velody buzzed with thoughts and ideas, many of them belonging to Ashiol rather than herself. In his mind, she could see the next stage, the shape he would have to throw himself into if she attacked him. In her own mind, she saw that she had one of those shapes too. She changed a second before he did.

Now they were in the air, huge and black and bursting with a blazing inner light that Velody recognised as raw power. Was this what they meant when they talked about animor? Whatever it was, it tasted sweet. She was winged and clawed and mighty. With this, she could protect Rhian and Delphine from anything.

It occurred to her that she had become a monster and she didn't care.

Thoughts tumbled in and around her, making a strange kind of sense. Velody wanted to fly screaming over the city, to show them all what she could do and what she could be. The scent of ferax still hung in the air, and she realised with ravenous glee that she could hunt the miserable creature down and tear him into shreds of blood and bone.

It was getting hard to stay in the air. Her wings hurt from the strain, and she had to lower herself to the cobblestones again. Ashiol descended nearby, his fiery red eyes watching her with a predatory gaze. He had not attacked, but held ready in case she did. She liked that he was being so cautious around her. She was a threat to *him*.

Once her feet hit the ground, Velody sagged. The monstrous parts of her body peeled away into nothing, and she didn't even have the energy to retain that stronger, glowing version of herself. She fell to the cobblestones in her ordinary body, breathing in long gasps as if this was the last time she would ever suck air into her lungs.

Something warm and scratchy covered her. She knew without looking that it was Crane's brown cloak. When she recovered enough to wrap the thing around her and pick herself up off the ground, Ashiol was there with a steady hand to help her.

He, at least, had found time to dress himself again. How long had she been shivering and shuddering on those cold stones? Clutching the cloak more tightly around her body, she looked for the others. Crane, Macready and Kelpie were on their knees, heads lowered solemnly. To her.

'What's with all the bowing and scraping?' she asked, leaning down to pick up her fallen dress, shoes and under-garments.

'They're on their knees because they've never seen

anything quite like you,' said Ashiol, pulling on his long
leather coat. Where had he got that from — the musette? The
boots weren't his either. They smelled of Poet. 'Are you
hungry?' he asked.

Velody was about to say that she wanted nothing but to
be left alone to sleep, but it wasn't true. The exhaustion was
gone, leaving her with an alert mind and, yes — an empty
stomach. 'Starving,' she admitted, still waiting for Macready
and the others to meet her eyes or start acting normal again.
This prostrate humility wasn't like them at all.

'Good,' said Ashiol. 'Go get dressed. I'll take you to dinner,
and make some attempt at explaining what in the seven hells
is going on.'

VELODY WENT inside the house to dress, and the sentinels
exchanged meaningful looks. Macready moved first. He
resheathed his skysilver dagger Jeunille, feeling strange about
taking her back so soon after he had given her away. He
turned to Ashiol. 'Are you sure you've done the lass any
favours, man? Her life will never be her own again.'

Ashiol barely glanced at him. 'You saw what happened.
She came into her powers. I have a responsibility to show her
how to use them.'

'And you didn't help those powers along at all?'

Ashiol showed no interest in what Macready implied. 'It
was her time.'

'Awfully convenient for you, so it is.'

That was one comment too many. Ashiol turned dark
eyes on all three of the sentinels, daring them to question
him further. 'And your point is?'

Macready smiled a sick little grin. 'Oh, nothing at all, high and brightness. Were you wanting us to join yourself and the lass at dinner?'

Ashiol gave him a disdainful look. 'The place I'm thinking of, you couldn't afford.'

VELODY COULDN'T BRING herself to put her theatre dress back on. When she looked at it, she remembered being trapped in that dressing room with hundreds of white rats. Still clutching Crane's scratchy woollen cloak around her bare body, she hurried upstairs to splash water on her face and arms, and to find another dress. She chose one of her favourites — a comfort frock made of soft grey wool.

It felt wrong to be dressing to go out without the usual argument with Delphine about which extravagant perfume she should dab behind her ears, or which shade of cosmetick she should paint on her eyelids and lips. Velody hated artificial scents and powders. After a moment's thought, she rummaged in her wardrobe for a long, silky coat that she had put away this season because it didn't match the new hemlines. If she went through any more strange transformations this nox, she didn't want to rely on the chivalry of others to cover her nakedness in a hurry.

That was the first time she had let herself think about it all. She had to sit on the bed for a few minutes, controlling her breathing. *What's happening to me? What am I turning into?*

Ashiol had the answers. He had promised her an explanation, and dinner. She wasn't sure which of the two she was more desperate for. Her stomach felt scrapingly bare.

On her way downstairs, she saw that Rhian's room with its broken bolts had been abandoned. Delphine's door was slightly ajar and the two were inside, sitting on Dee's bed and talking in low voices. Velody hesitated, then pushed the door a little further open. 'I'm going out,' she told them.

Both looked at her in surprise. She wanted to tell them what was happening to her, but how could she? She didn't understand it herself. *Those men who attacked us this nox, I'm just like them.*

'The Ducomte has promised to explain all this to me, or as much as he can. I need those answers.' It seemed wrong to call him by name, Ashiol, as if he were just an ordinary person. The title seemed safer.

'Be careful,' said Rhian.

Delphine didn't say anything, but her eyes were reproachful.

Velody nodded, and closed the door behind her. With Crane's cloak tucked under her arm to return to him, she went downstairs to go to dinner with the Ducomte d'Aufleur.

25

SECOND DAY OF THE
FLORALIA (SWEETHEARTS)

NOX

*T*here weren't that many hot food places open for
dinner this late. Ashiol took Velody to a quiet
bistro near the crest of the Vittorine, which still had its
lanterns lit. It looked like one of those cheap nox cafés that
appeared near theatres and musettes, down to the grimy
walls and the melodic strains of a piano player messing
around. There were a few clues to the fact that this place was
not cheap: the smooth and expert politeness of the waiter,
the pristine cleanliness of the white paper tablecloths, and
the fact that there was no menu.

'Beef,' Ashiol ordered, his fingers measuring the size of
the steak he wanted. He nodded to Velody. 'Both.'

The waiter nodded and whisked away so fast that he
made Velody dizzy. The brisk walk up the hill had sapped
her of energy. 'I don't get to order for myself?' The thought
of red meat — such a rare and expensive luxury — made her
stomach uncurl with anticipation.

Ashiol tilted his head towards her. 'What would you like to drink, Velody?'

She was half-tempted to ask for an ansouisette, but it probably wasn't a good idea to drink anything that could make her head feel any stranger than it already did. 'Water,' she said.

'Red wine is more traditional with beef,' said Ashiol, and she had a suspicion that he was making fun of her.

'You asked what I wanted.'

'So I did.' He waved over another waiter to order jugs of water and red wine. 'And now,' he said, when they were both settled with a glass and there were no hovering waiters within earshot, 'what do you want to ask me?'

Velody took a deep breath. 'Everything.'

'I can't promise everything.'

'Start with something simple. Who are you people?'

Ashiol savoured his wine for a moment, then set the glass down. 'We are the Creature Court.'

'Which means?'

Ashiol sighed. 'It's complicated, but I'll do my best.' He was silent for a while, as if arranging it all in his head. Then he nodded and began. 'Poet and Dhynar — that is, the Orphan Princel and the ferax — are both Creature Lords. There are five Lords in the city now, so I'm told. I've been away a few years and I'm a little out of touch. Each Lord is served by a number of courtesi. The Lords themselves are supposed to serve the Creature Kings.'

'And that's you,' Velody said.

Ashiol nodded, though there was a hesitation as if this was not entirely the truth.

'Poet and Dhynar are your creatures.'

'No... no,' he protested. 'It's not like that.'

'What is it like, seigneur Ducomte? If they serve you, then they attacked us in your name.'

'I don't have any control over what they do!' He almost knocked over his wine glass with his fist.

The waiters were sending alarmed looks in their direction. Velody could see why, even if there were no other customers to be disturbed. When Ashiol was angry, his whole body spoke of violence. She shrank back into her chair.

Ashiol brought himself under control. 'You have to understand,' he said. 'The Lords answer to the Kings — if we give them an order and back it up with threats, or take a blood oath, they usually obey us. But they are their own creatures and they follow their own rules. They are dangerous, even to me.'

Velody shivered, remembering the Orphan Princel — Poet — as he advanced on her, and the look in Dhynar's eyes as he held Rhian in his arms. 'You're gangs, then? No control over each other, no real hierarchy?'

'The Kings are supposed to be the masters of the Lords, but the Lords grant little in the way of allegiance,' said Ashiol. 'That's why the Kings have the sentinels to serve and protect us. That's Macready, Kelpie and Crane. The sentinels are not of the Court, but they're not quite daylight folk either. In between. One of the Kings is chosen to rule over us all, by right of challenge. He keeps the Lords in line. We call him the Power and Majesty.'

'And that's you?'

'No!' He was awfully quick to deny it. 'Garnet was the last Power and Majesty. He died recently, at the same time as the Floralia parade. He... took my powers from me years ago, and they all came crashing back when he died.' He smiled, but without humour. 'Have you ever seen anyone hopped up on hot ice or sainthood?'

Velody had been to enough bad clubs with Delphine to

recognise the names of the party drugs he referred to. 'More than I'd like.'

'Well, a major dose of animor after a five-year drought had a similar effect on me. Hence the babbling lunatic who tore the Duchessa's dress and came after you in the middle of the nox. I'm sorry about that, by the way.'

Velody drained the last of her water. She was unbelievably thirsty. Garnet. Something in that word, that name — it meant something to her. She had thought as much the previous nox when Ashiol was rambling at her.

An image flitted through her mind briefly, a laughing youth falling naked from the sky, but then it was gone.

Ashiol leaned forward and refilled Velody's glass from the jug.

'You are going to be the Power and Majesty now, aren't you?' she asked. 'You can take control of the Creature Lords, keep them away from us?' This was really what she wanted to know.

'I'm not the only Creature King in this city. There's one other, who might be more suited to be Power and Majesty.' He was watching her carefully.

'What happened to me in the alley?' she asked, switching the subject to make him think she was satisfied with his answers so far.

'You came into your power. Unusually late, but stronger for it.'

Velody thought of the Floralia parade, of the light that had invaded her, and the colours in the sky, and the Ducomte screaming as scars poured off him, scars that no one but she could see...

'Why didn't I start babbling like a lunatic?'

The steak arrived, sizzling on large skillets. Velody stared at it. The meat was rare, oozing with blood. 'I can't eat that,' she said, her stomach turning over.

'Would the demoiselle prefer something else?' asked the waiter.

'No, the demoiselle would not,' said Ash.

Velody glared at him as the waiter moved docilely away. 'I've been out with men like you before,' she accused. 'Like to be in charge, don't you?'

Ashiol looked amused. 'This isn't a date.'

She picked up a knife and fork to cover her embarrassment. 'Forgive me if I got the impression I was being seduced.'

Ashiol began sawing into his steak. Blood spurted from it, splashing the bright white paper tablecloth. 'I was being generous. Answering all your questions.'

'You still haven't told me why Poet and Dhynar attacked me and my friends.'

He crammed a slice of meat into his mouth and licked his lips. 'That isn't one of the questions you asked me.'

'Did you send them after us?'

'No.'

'How can I believe you? I don't know anything about you except you're a mad, rich aristocrat who likes eating meat with a pulse!'

Ashiol chewed and swallowed the rare flesh with evident enjoyment. 'If you don't believe anything I say to you, Velody, what is the point of asking questions?'

She glared at him, and then at the revolting mess on her plate.

'It isn't compulsory,' said Ashiol.

'Eating steak?'

'Turning into a babbling lunatic. You asked me why you didn't, in the alley. Or even at the Floralia parade. It's not a common response. You don't have to worry about going mad.'

'That's something, I suppose.' Velody cut a slice from her

steak, but the welling blood made her feel faint. She laid the utensils down again. 'So I'm one of you. Your Court. I'm like you.'

'I don't think you're quite like anybody.'

'Do I have to be part of this? Can't I make it go away?'

'No, you can't.'

'I've lived twenty-six years without turning into a pack of little brown mice. Why can't I go back to how things were yesterday?'

'I've never known anyone who could go back. Once the nox is under your skin, it's with you forever.'

The savoury smells from her plate were driving Velody to distraction. Without looking, she speared a piece of meat into her mouth. It was hot but still raw in the centre and released a warm gush of blood over her tongue. The scent and taste of it flooded through her body and she was shocked by how good it felt. She cut off another small piece and ate it, forcing herself not to gobble.

'What was it like for you?' she asked, to distract Ashiol from extending his patronising smile into a comment that might force her to stab him with her fork.

'What was what like?'

'Coming into your power. For the first time.'

'Oh, that.' Ash gulped down another mouthful of meat with a swallow of wine, and started slicing more. 'I was eleven, nearly twelve.'

'So young?' The meat was so warm and moist that it tasted alive in her mouth.

'It usually happens between eleven and fourteen, when we start growing into our adult body. I was living in Diamagne at the time.' Velody allowed her confusion to cross her face and he grinned at her. 'Don't you know your royal history?'

'That's Delphine's hobby.'

'Ah. Well, my mother was the Old Duc's second child, and I was born into one of those appalling arranged marriages that royals like to inflict upon each other. My mother was widowed young and found herself a nice country Baronne as her second husband. I was brought up on the Diamagne estate, with an ever-growing number of half-siblings.'

Velody was slicing her steak into larger and larger pieces, for the pleasure of tearing them up with her teeth. How had she never known before how good meat tasted when it was red and bleeding?

'I can't imagine you in the country,' she said. 'You seem so citified.'

'I can hurl a hay bale with the best of them. My childhood was all very rural and idyllic, so naturally I was bored out of my skull. Garnet too.'

'Garnet the Power and Majesty?' Velody faltered as another memory invaded her. Hands holding her wrist, on a balcony, a kiss...

'That came later. When we were growing up he was just the son of the cook and the groundskeeper, my best friend. We did everything together — hunting, fishing, setting fire to things. We were like brothers.'

'How... idyllic.'

Velody was paying far more attention to the steak than to Ashiol. The pool of blood no longer repulsed her — on the contrary, she was quite happy to wipe her slices of meat into the warm red juices before putting them in her mouth.

'We didn't know what he was at the time, of course,' said Ashiol, and Velody had a feeling she had missed part of the story, but didn't like to ask him to repeat himself. 'Some elderly tramp who made his way to the estate to die. We didn't even know his name. Later, when we knew all about the Creature Court, we tried to find out who he had been, but no one had heard of an old Creature Lord in Aufleur. He must have come from one of the other cities.'

Velody was trying to eat at a leisurely, ladylike pace. The urge to cram the lumps of flesh into her mouth was terrifying. She had lost the taste for water and started on the wine. That was wonderful too, warm and red and spicy. Everything had taken on a rosy glow.

'My mother insisted on bringing him in and giving him a bed,' Ashiol went on, lost in his own story. 'Garnet and I were being punished for something —'

'Setting fire to something kind of something?' Velody asked, to show she was paying attention.

'Something like that. She set us to watch over him while she sent for the local dottore. While she was gone, the old man died.'

Velody paused in her chewing. 'Of what?'

'I don't know. Being old? When they cleaned him for burial later they found so many scars on him it was surprising he was still in one piece. Anyway, he died, and something happened to Garnet and me. A power of some kind ran through us both — so strong that we crashed into the wall. When we woke up, we were different.'

Velody realised to her horror that she was already two-thirds through the enormous steak, while Ash was less than halfway through his. She really was going to have to slow down. She drank some more wine, then carved another piece. You only live once.

'Different how?' This was what she wanted to know, the real story of what they were.

'Cats,' said Ashiol succinctly. 'They followed me everywhere after that. The estate filled up with all the local strays. They couldn't get enough of me. I didn't know why, until one day I got angry and turned into them.'

'Into the cats?'

'Not those cats, just into cats. I wasn't all that tall then, so I became about eight or nine moggies, mostly black. These days it's closer to fourteen, or fifteen if I've had a big dinner. I didn't tell anyone at the time, not even Garnet. I discovered that in cat form, I could spread out, go to half a dozen different places at once.'

'Let me guess — you used your new skill to eavesdrop on conversations and to spy on the upstairs maids?'

Ashiol grinned. 'Well, I was twelve. Then the gattopardo arrived, and I found out that it wasn't just me.'

Velody used a slice of meat to mop up some of the blood that was congealing on the plate. 'What's a gattopardo?'

'Mountain cat, gold with white spots. No one had heard of them in our region. They're only native to the far southern mountains in Camoise. We worked out that it must have been travelling for three months to get to us — or, to be precise, to get to Garnet. A month later, two more showed up, fawning over him the way the stray tabbies fawned over me. I told him the truth then, about being able to shape myself. I showed him how to do the same.' His face went distant, troubled.

'Wishing you hadn't taught him?'

'Wouldn't have made any difference. Comes out sooner or later. Look at you.'

'Mmm.' A sudden thought struck her. She laid her knife down. 'So I should have come into my power more than a decade ago. Why didn't it happen before now?'

'You got angry. That's how it usually happens the first time.' Ashiol frowned. 'I don't know why it didn't happen earlier. There's something strange about it.'

Velody reached for her knife again, only to realise that her skillet was empty except for a cool puddle of red moisture. 'Oh, help. How did that happen?'

Ashiol laughed. 'You were hungry. I told you so.'

'I've never been that hungry before.'

'Shaping takes a lot out of you, particularly the first time. If you hadn't dosed up on meat and blood, you would have been flat on the floor inside an hour, probably for days.'

She narrowed her eyes at him. 'And you knew that.'

'Aye.'

'What does the red wine do?'

'Tastes good. And it helps you relax.'

'Why do I need to relax?'

Ashiol finished his glass, smacking his lips. 'Because I'm going to tell you some things later that will make you feel very stressed. Do you want dessert?'

'What essential nutrients will that provide?'

'None, but it might keep you from gnawing your way through the table while I finish my dinner.'

Velody sighed, and suppressed the urge to lick her skillet clean. 'I'll stick to the wine.'

26

SECOND DAY OF THE
FLORALIA (SWEETHEARTS)

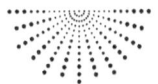

NOX

*J*n the alley outside the bistro, Macready argued with Crane. 'You should be at home, laddie-buck. Your face looks like my mam's best minced lamb porridge.'

'Thanks,' said Crane, pulling his cloak tightly around him. It was nearly summer, but the nox air was still chill on the skin.

'You don't need to be here.'

'Yes, I do.' Beneath the bruising and swelling that turned the young man's face into something both horrible and unrecognisable, his expression was resolute. 'I couldn't leave her alone with him. We don't know how stable he is.'

'And what am I, chopped kidneys?'

'You know what I mean. It's not like that episode last nox was the first time he's gone crazy on us.'

'And if he does it will take at least two of us to hold him back,' sighed Macready. 'Aye, lad. I know what you mean.'

He also knew that if Ashiol was really trying, he could kill them both in a heartbeat. Crane knew that too.

'I can sleep later,' Crane said stubbornly. 'Right now, I want to be near her.'

Macready gave his younger partner a quick look. 'Choosing sides already?'

'She doesn't know anything, and he's throwing her into a scorpions' nest. She needs us more than he does.'

'Is that so?'

'We have to learn how to balance our loyalties again. It's a long time since we've had more than one King in the city.'

'A few days ago, our Ashiol entered the city and Garnet sent you to spy on him,' said Macready, who had certainly not forgotten that particular detail. 'Not so long ago, it seems to me.'

Crane looked uncomfortable. 'I didn't say it was easy. The balancing.'

Macready clapped his hands together to warm them up. 'Saints and angels, how long does it take to gnaw your way through a side of beef?' He cast a dirty look at the bistro.

'Jealous?'

'Last bit of steak I got my teeth into, lad, was boiled and sliced and baked in wet pastry. Of course I'm fecking jealous.'

There was movement in the bistro. From their position, they could just see Ashiol getting to his feet, helping Velody on with her long coat. 'Cosy,' Crane said. 'Just like any other couple honouring the Sweetheart Saints.'

Macready looked at the lad. 'You wouldn't be interested in the demoiselle yourself at all?'

'I'm worried about her. She doesn't know what she's getting herself into.'

'Neh, she's strong, that one. Even before she went monster on us, she was the self-reliant type. If you're feeling protective, look to those lasses of hers.' Macready had not forgotten the sight of Delphine crumpled and white against the wall, nor the torment on Rhian's face as she crawled into Velody's arms. Those were the ones who needed looking after. Damaged, both. *And not your responsibility, Mac.*

'Kelpie's keeping an eye on them,' Crane said, his gaze on Velody as she left the bistro, her arm tucked awkwardly into Ashiol's.

'Not exactly what I meant,' said Macready.

They waited a pace or two after the Kings had passed their alley, then set off after them. There was no place for chat now, not if they were to stay unnoticed by Ashiol. He had told them to go home, to curl up in their nests and rest, leaving Kelpie — the only one who had slept in the last two days — to play sentry in Via Silviana.

Despite the distance, Macready and Crane could hear something of what was being said up ahead in the quiet street.

'I have another question,' Velody said, her voice a little muffled as she pulled up the collar of her coat to keep out the cold.

'Go ahead,' said Ashiol. He sounded almost chirpy, Macready thought. Must have been one hell of a steak.

'Why?'

'Why what?'

'Why Creature Lords and Creature Kings and Powers and Majesties and courtesi and sentinels? Why rats and mice and feraxes and cats and perfectly ordinary people turning into big black flapping monsters? What's the point of it all?'

There was a long pause, during which Macready had to stop himself from sniggering.

'Good question,' said Ashiol.

'Can you answer it?'

'Give me a minute.' Ashiol changed direction, his leather

coat — Poet's coat — swishing as he dragged Velody into a side street. 'Better yet, I'll show you.'

'Show me what?'

The lass was half-laughing, which had to be a good sign, Macready thought. He never again wanted to see that terrible look on her face when she had lunged at Ashiol with murder in her eyes and Jeunille in her hand. Perhaps she was starting to see the man as an ally rather than an enemy. It was the worst mistake she could make, but the lass wasn't to know that.

Crane surged ahead after them, too hasty. Macready grabbed the lad's sleeve and together — gently, my lad — they both peered around the corner.

Velody was all the way laughing now. 'You can't be serious.'

She and Ashiol stood at the corner of a solid-looking building with expensive copper piping up one side of it. Macready assessed the climbing potential of the wall and the roof, then grinned to himself. To think his mammy had wanted him to take up a respectable trade, like carpentry or butchery.

'An easy climb,' Ashiol protested.

'I can't go around climbing onto people's roofs! I'm wearing a dress. And it's... undignified!'

'Trust me,' said Ashiol, cupping his hands for her to put her foot into. 'If you're going to understand our world, you have to spend some time on rooftops. I promise not to look up your skirt.'

Looking dubious about the whole situation, Velody placed her boot in Ash's hands and launched herself upwards, hands grasping at the piping.

Macready covered his face with his hands. 'I can't watch. Did she fall?'

'She's doing fine,' said Crane, a note of wonder in his voice. 'Not bad at all.'

Macready removed his hands from his eyes and stared at Crane's bloodied and swollen face. 'Don't you topple for her,' he warned, trying to ignore the feeling in his stomach that told him this was all, already, inevitable. 'She's so far above you that you can't touch her shoes. There'll be tears before bedtime, and during, and after.'

'Sorry,' said Crane, as Velody made it safely to the roof. 'What did you say? I missed it.' He smiled proudly. 'Did you see how easily she got over that tricky bit of guttering?'

Macready briefly considered beating his own brains out on the nearest wall, but settled for a nearly inaudible groan.

IT WAS cold on the rooftops, but the view was amazing. Velody could see down the side of the Vittorine, clear across to the other hills of Aufleur and all the dimly lit houses, shops, temples and public buildings in between. There were hardly any lanterns burning at this time of nox, just a flicker here and there of someone working into the small hours, larger glows in the late theatres and drinking clubs, and the occasional tiny bob of a lampboy leading a customer home along the darkened streets.

Her silk coat wasn't much protection up here and she shivered.

'You asked me why we exist,' said Ashiol, his gaze on the view below and around them. 'What we're here for.'

'I thought you were avoiding that question.'

'I asked someone else that same thing once. I came to the city when I was thirteen. My Uncle Artorio was the heir of Aufleur, but his only child — our Duchessa now — was young and sickly. That put me squarely in the frame as the backup heir, so the Old Duc hauled me out of my mother's estate in Diamagne and brought me to the city to learn my duty as a scion of the house of Xandelian.' A thin smile. 'I think he regretted that action for the rest of his life, my grandfather.'

'What happened?'

'Garnet came with me — it was the only condition I had asked for, that my friend join me. So there we were, two country boys in the big city with one big secret. What we weren't prepared for was how different it was for us here. Animor is stronger in cities, and we almost drowned in our own power. Tasha found us within two days. Smelled us coming a mile off, and put everything she had into luring us out of the Palazzo and into her world, under the city. It didn't take much. She was... an enthralling woman. We were more than happy to be seduced.'

'Was she the Power and Majesty at the time?'

'No woman has ever risen above the rank of Lord. Tasha was the closest thing the Court ever had to a female leader, but only because she had our then Power and Majesty twisted around her little finger and half the other Lords on a leash. Garnet and I were hers, body and soul. Her courtesi.' He was distant for a moment. 'A few weeks after we joined her, on a roof like this one, I asked Tasha what was the point of us? Why did we have these strange powers? She just grinned her lioness grin at me and pointed at the sky.'

Velody shivered. 'The skywar? That was so long ago, if it happened at all.'

'That's what I thought. Blistering fire raining from the sky, explosions and devils and stabbing shards of ice. A city of people sheltering underground, rebuilding their lives despite the horrors that screamed down from above. It was the stuff of legends, ancient history, stories that had grown bigger in the telling. But the truth, Velody, is that the skywar never stopped. It's hidden from the daylight folk, but we of the nox are still fighting that war. It's our job to protect the city that can't protect itself.'

'How can there be a war?' asked Velody. 'How can we not know?'

'Two days ago, just before dawn, while you and your friends were watching the Floralia parade, the Creature Court were fighting a war on the rooftops. Garnet died. I got my powers back, and you — you got yours too. You don't believe me?'

'How can I? I live in this city. Surely I would have noticed it being blown down around me on a regular basis!'

'You belonged to the daylight then.' He shrugged. 'I did too. For the last five years... Garnet stripped me of my animor and I've been living as a daylight drone. Difference is, I knew about the secret world going on over my head and under my feet, even if I couldn't see it or touch it.'

Velody shook her head, feeling like an idiot. 'Here was me thinking you were starting to make sense. What do you want with me?'

'I want you to learn how to use your powers,' he said simply. 'How do you feel?'

'Suspicious.'

He rolled his eyes. 'I mean in your body. How do you feel?'

'Like I could run forever,' she admitted reluctantly. 'I think I'm drunk on red meat.'

His grin lit up his whole face, making him look almost boyish. 'Excellent. Let's play.'

Shaping herself into a few thousand small brown mice, it turned out, was not as easy as it had seemed in that alley. When not furious, Velody needed time and effort to coax her body to take on those little creature forms. It didn't help that Ashiol kept switching into his own gang of creatures. It was just wrong for cats and mice to be intermingling on the rooftops of the city.

Once she had the knack, Velody felt dizzy with the possibilities. As an army of mice, she could leap and crawl and perform all kinds of strange acrobatics. She loved the challenge of coordinating so many bodies at once. It was like an elaborate form of patchwork.

They rested finally, several rooftops further down the hill from where they had begun, breathless and laughing, surrounded by animals. All the local cats had come to be close to Ashiol, and what seemed like millions of mice had scampered up walls and pipes in the hopes of catching a glimpse of Velody.

More than a glimpse, she realised as her brain settled back to being human rather than mouse. 'Um, can we go back for our clothes?'

Ashiol was entirely comfortable in his skin, splayed out on the tiles as the cats nudged and rubbed up against him. 'Let's try the Lord form first. Then you won't care about being naked.'

Velody tucked her knees up and covered her breasts with her hands, giving him a dirty look. 'Is the Lord form the black one with the flappy wings and teeth and claws?'

He stretched out to scratch at the chin of a ginger tabby. 'No, that's the chimaera. The Lord form is the stronger, harder version of you. The one that glows with power and doesn't care about being naked.'

'Oh.' A thought struck her. 'If I can take Lord shape, does that make me a Creature Lord?'

He rolled over and stared at her. She wriggled uncomfortably until she realised that he really was only staring at her face.

'The courtesi can only take Court form — turning into

their creature,' Ashiol said slowly. 'The Lords can do that as well as taking Lord form. The Kings can do more.'

He hadn't answered her question.

'I just assumed everyone started as one of the courtesi and worked their way up,' she said.

'Not always.' He was still looking at her strangely. She longed for the security of her long silk coat — hells, she would settle for a breastband and knickers right now. Anything to place between her bare flesh and his eyes. 'You got your powers late, Velody. You passed the point of courtesa a long time ago.'

'I suppose I'm glad about that.' She shuddered. 'From what I've seen of Creature Lords, I don't particularly want to be in service to one of them.'

'No.' Ashiol still looked as if there was something he was waiting for her to figure out.

'So are you going to show me Lord form?' Velody asked finally. 'I don't think I can remember how to do it without you.'

'Yes.' He pushed the cats away and stood up. 'You're right. We haven't got much of the nox left.'

27

SECOND DAY OF THE FLORALIA (SWEETHEARTS)

NOX

*E*ventually, they found their way back to their discarded clothes on the first rooftop. The sky was beginning to lighten and Velody was finally tired.

'Is Tasha still around?' she asked as she fastened her undergarments and slid her dress over her head. Strange, how quickly she had learned to cope with being naked in front of Ashiol, even in her ordinary body, without dying of embarrassment. Perhaps it was because he had the courtesy to pretend he didn't notice any difference between her clothed and unclothed body, or even a difference between her body and a brick chimney. Perhaps he had been in the Creature Court so long that it really did make no difference.

'Garnet killed her,' Ashiol said, as he pulled on his breeches.

Velody stared at him. 'Was that when you started hating him?'

He looked genuinely surprised that she might think so.

'She was a cold-hearted, murdering bitch who deserved what she got.'

Velody pulled on her coat and looked around for her shoes. 'You were glad she was dead?' It was hard to understand how these people worked. As soon as she started thinking of Ashiol as normal, he threw something new and alien at her.

'I wouldn't have killed her myself, but I understood why he did it. I certainly didn't cry over her body. The problem was that Garnet was above us after that, a proper Lord while we were still courtesi. That changed everything.'

Velody found one shoe wedged in a gutter and pulled it out. She couldn't see the other one anywhere. 'So killing Tasha made Garnet worthy of promotion? I don't understand you people.'

'No, you really don't,' said Ashiol. 'Being a Lord isn't something that the Court chooses to bestow on you. Garnet became a Creature Lord in the instant he quenched Tasha, just as he and I unwittingly quenched the old man back home. When one of the Court dies, their source of animor leaves the body to find a new host. If a member of the Court is near, they get the biggest boost. Sometimes it expands their own source so greatly that it pushes them to the next level of abilities.'

'Even if they've murdered someone to get it?'

'We don't think that way in the Creature Court. We're not like you. We eat, fight, frig, survive. We value loyalty and the keeping of oaths, but sometimes you have to kill. It's better than dying.'

She thought it over. 'I suppose it makes sense, in a horrible sort of way. People live and die but the power levels in the city stay the same, shared out in different ways. Does that mean that if there are fewer members of the Court, they are more powerful than when there are many?'

'In the usual course of things. But there isn't as much animor around as there used to be. We've lost courtesi, Lords and even a few Kings over the years. Once they leave the city, they're gone from us. That's what happened to Lysandor, one of my brother courtesi under Tasha. When Garnet's reign got too hot for him, he left. Took Celeste with him, one of our more powerful Lords. We suffered from their loss. Not long after, they lost me, until now. And the sky swallows its share.'

Velody had quite forgotten about her other shoe. She was mesmerised by him as he spoke of this strange, dark world.

'When one of us is taken in battle — truly taken by the sky — then their body is obliterated. Every trace of their source of animor is destroyed instead of being shared around the Court. That's what happened to Garnet. Only — the powers he stole from me were released.' Ashiol looked at Velody strangely, his head tipped to one side as if an odd thought had occurred to him.

'So,' Velody said in a small voice, 'whom did I quench to become a Creature Lord?'

Ashiol swung on his leather coat. He had a surprisingly gentle look on his face. 'You didn't kill anyone, if that's what you're worried about. There have been sleepers before, who pick up motes of animor here and there without realising it. If no one is close enough to fully quench the power, it gets spread all around the city. It comes to us as naturally as breathing air.' He leaned down and unwedged something from the gutter nearest him, then handed it to her. A little worse for wear, it was her other shoe. 'You're wrong about what you are, Velody. You're not a Creature Lord.'

'But you said I wasn't a courteso.'

'Courtesa, if you're female. Courteso is male. And no, you're not. You took three forms in that alley, remember? Creature, Lord and chimaera.'

She pushed her bare foot into the shoe, wincing as it

squished a little. She hated to think of what else had been stuck in that gutter. 'You didn't tell me what chimaera meant.'

'No, I didn't.'

'What does it mean, Ash?'

He sighed, sounding genuinely regretful. 'It means you're a King.'

IT SEEMED an unnecessary civility to walk a demoiselle home when she had the power to transform herself into a monstrous form that could save the city from destruction, but Ashiol had never managed to shake the habits of chivalry. It was perhaps the last remaining trace of his life as a son of the ducal house of Aufleur.

That, and they still had things to talk about.

Velody's hands were shoved deep into the pockets of her long coat. 'Really a King?' she repeated, as if things might have changed in the five minutes or so since they had climbed down from the rooftops.

She had torn the hem of her coat a little on a jutting piece of copper pipe. He wondered if she had noticed. 'How often do you want me to say it?'

'But you said there were no female Kings. You sounded very sure about it.'

'It's never happened before. There were stories of women who tried to reach that level and destroyed themselves, and every female Lord since has restrained herself from quenching. You can do it if you concentrate hard enough. But you are what you are, and you are definitely a Creature King.'

'I have the same power as you?'

'You might be more powerful,' he admitted. 'We wouldn't know that without duelling.'

She looked so small in that coat. 'I'm not going to fight you, Ash.'

When had she started calling him Ash instead of the more formal Ashiol? He liked it from her. The easy camaraderie that grew between them on the rooftop was attractive and familiar. The first time he became a King, Garnet got there ahead of him, and Lysandor followed soon after. They were equals, brothers in matched power for three glorious seasons, until Ortheus died and they had to decide which of the three of them would be the new Power and Majesty.

'You might have to,' he said.

Velody looked at him warily. 'You said there were only two Kings in Aufleur.'

'Glad to know you were listening. Yes, just two. You and me.'

'So you are going to be the Power and Majesty.'

'What makes you think that?'

She laughed. 'Well, it can't be me.'

'Why not?'

'Are you serious? I've known about my powers less than a day. I don't know the history, the ways of your people. I haven't the faintest idea how to rule a court full of monsters and psychopaths.'

'I know,' said Ashiol. 'That's why I think you'll be better at it than me.' *I can't do it, Velody. It has to be you. This is the future Heliora saw. The good future. The hopeful future.*

'I can't take it in.'

Velody sounded near breaking point. Time to take some of the pressure off. Ashiol didn't want to ruin this by pushing too hard.

'It's a lot to understand. I wouldn't have forced it on you so soon, but we're running out of time. The Creature Court knows about you, and they're not happy.'

That was true enough, except for the part about not

forcing it on her. Was he so desperate to avoid Garnet's fate that he would sacrifice this demme to it? Yes, he was. Whatever kind of monster she became, it had to be better than what he knew he was capable of.

'I can't think,' she said, hands clenching and unclenching within her deep pockets. 'I need time, Ash. Space. I need to be left alone. For a while, at least.'

'I'll get you as much time as I can,' he promised, and realised to his surprise that he meant it. Right now, he would walk into the mouths of the seven hells to give her a day or two of peace.

They were nearly at Velody's door.

'Can you do that?' she asked distractedly, and he could tell that he had already lost her, that her mind was turning away from their nox of roofplay as she neared the house. She was worried about her friends.

'I think I owe you that much.'

They were being followed, but he had expected that. Ashiol turned to the shadows and made a summoning noise. A lithe figure emerged on all fours, purring.

'Oh!' Velody was surprised, which bothered him a little. Was she so out of tune with the nox that she thought all the cats had stayed up on the rooftops? 'Where did he come from?'

'I called him.' Ashiol lifted the heavy ginger tom into his arms, holding him out to her. 'I want you to keep him in the house.'

'Will he stay?' Reluctantly, she accepted the armful of cat.

'He will if I tell him to,' said Ashiol, staring into the creature's large yellow eyes.

Tom turned away, shamelessly snuggling against his new mistress. 'This is instead of the sentinels?' asked Velody. She sounded amused.

'He won't do much to protect you, but if you're in trouble, tell him and I'll hear you.'

'We can do that?'

'Try it yourself. You must have a local gang of mice competing to be your favourites?'

She looked embarrassed. 'I thought they were figments of my imagination.'

Ashiol leaned in to scratch the ginger tom's ears. 'He's the world's worst mouser. I thought that made him an appropriate choice.'

For a moment, her eyes were fully on him, not distracted by any other concerns. 'Thank you, Ash. I appreciate you showing me what I can do. It makes me feel a little safer.' She turned to go inside.

'The sentinels are yours as well as mine,' he called after her. 'I won't be able to keep them away from you altogether.'

She waved a hand, resigned. 'No men in the house.'

'We can work with that.'

At the door, she turned and said, all in a rush, 'I can't do this. I can't be whatever it is you want. I don't have the stomach for it.'

'You're stronger than you think,' he said.

Velody hugged the ginger tom closer to her. 'I'm not. It may look like I'm the strong one, but it's not true.' She turned and went inside.

Ashiol continued to watch the house after she had latched the door, long enough at least for Macready and Crane to catch up with him. 'I recall telling you two to get some sleep.'

'Aye, well,' said Macready. 'Our lad here had a sudden attack of duty. It'll pass, I'm sure.'

'Don't bet on it,' said Crane.

'All quiet here,' broke in Kelpie's cheerful voice from behind Ashiol. 'No more Lordly visitations.'

'They're learning,' said Ashiol. 'It's a start.' He regarded the three sentinels. 'Right. I'll nest out the day so none of you have to worry about me. That leaves Kelpie and Macready to take shifts over the Rose and Needle, assuming that's what you want to do.'

'You know the answer to that,' said Macready.

'Fine. I'm not expecting much during daylight hours, so make sure you take time to sleep. I'll pick you both up at sunset to come with me down to the Court. I'm hoping what I say will be interesting enough that there won't be anyone up here to threaten the house while I say it.'

'What about me?' Crane asked.

Ashiol turned his attention to the sentinel with the swollen face. Crane still carried himself like everything hurt, though he would never admit it. It was easy to forget how damn young he was. 'What I want is for you to take a week's rest. What are my chances?'

'Minimal.'

'Give me your knife then.'

There was a pause, as if Crane couldn't quite figure out what Ashiol was offering. From the look on Macready's and Kelpie's faces, they knew. They remembered what it was like to have a Creature King who gave as much as he received.

Crane drew his skysilver knife and held it hilt-out to his King.

Ashiol turned the point of the blade into his left wrist, cutting into the vein. The metal burned into his flesh, a moment of hard pain. As his blood welled up, he drew out the knife and held his wrist out to Crane.

The young sentinel didn't need to be told now. They were built for this — the instinct was there. He took Ashiol's bleeding arm in his hands and brought his mouth to it, sucking greedily at the wound.

Ashiol held out the skysilver knife in his right hand, allowing Kelpie or Macready to take it away from him. This was an old sensation: a sentinel's mouth on his vein, the rising pleasure from the sharing of blood. *I drank yours often enough*, he thought to Crane, remembering those last few months when the sentinels had taken turns to sneak into the dark room Garnet used as his prison, offering him a taste of their mortal blood so that the pain of the sky-wrought chains or wounds would be lessened for a few precious hours. Crane had only been a boy then, but he made the sacrifice as readily as the others.

The pleasure faded, replaced with a throbbing pain. Just as Ashiol was wondering if he would have to force the sentinel from his vein, Crane drew away. The brutal swelling of his face had reduced, revealing his usual angelic features darkened only by a few hints of bruising. His eyes gleamed fiercely in the dim light of the early morning.

Ashiol leaned forward to kiss the younger man's blood-stained mouth. 'Get some sleep,' he said, then walked away from them all.

Time to find a nest, and sleep. A little oblivion would be just fine right about now.

IN THE LAST minutes before he slept, curled inside a nest belonging to one of the dead-and-gone sentinels, Ashiol let himself miss Garnet. Not the Power and Majesty who had wounded and scarred and used him, but the Garnet he had spoken of to Velody this nox — the friend who was more than a friend, more than a brother, everything.

'Miss you,' he muttered in a whisper. 'Miss you, you colossal arse. Wait for me. One of these days, I'm coming to find you.'

THIRD DAY OF THE
FLORALIA (BRIDES)

*T*hank the saints neither Delphine nor Rhian was up yet. Velody clambered up the stairs and fell into bed without taking off her dress or shoes. She bundled herself into the pile of blankets and quilts and fell almost immediately into a deep, fierce sleep.

She dreamed of Garnet.

Velody didn't know who he was at first. She was swamped by the usual images from old, sensual dreams — a red-haired youth, laughing; cruel fingers digging into her wrist; a kiss...

This time, it was more than a kiss.

The beautiful boy pushed his tongue hard against hers, claiming her mouth even as his hands slid and rucked against the light fabric of her noxgown.

Velody drew him in, hard against her body, and it was definitely not her fourteen-year-old self in this dream. This was Velody the woman now, with curves and an aching cunt, Velody who knew what to do with a man's body.

'Garnet,' she moaned as his mouth travelled down the tender flesh of her throat. 'Saints, devils, oh.'

His fingers were inside her now, and she twisted and bucked against him to feel them deeper — further in, further in...

A different memory, a real one: *Cyniver (another redhead — how had she never spotted this pattern before?) lay on the bed in the hired room, thoroughly mussed and somewhat embarrassed, his spectacles abandoned on the floor. 'Was it... all right?' he asked.*

Velody leaned into him, her breasts still tingling, a sticky ache between her thighs. 'Perfect,' she said, kissing that mouth of his. 'Lovely. And we have so much time to get even better at it...'

Cyniver. How had she forgotten him so easily? Where had he gone? She didn't have time to work that part out before...

She was back on the balcony with Garnet — not really, this never happened — and her back was shoved up against the railings, and he was fucking her so hard she didn't even have the breath to gasp his name.

When she came, Velody's cry turned the sky pink and gold, and transformed the city into ash.

Velody woke up and remembered everything. Tierce unfolded into her mind like a paper crown: her home with its smells and sounds, her family, her brothers and sisters. She remembered Rhian's brother, the young man she had loved. Cyniver. Memories of him, of the life they had planned together, hit her until she could barely breathe. So long ago, but the loss was new.

She remembered a naked boy who fell from the sky, kissed her on a balcony and stole her animor. Garnet. That was *Garnet*. He took her power before she even knew what it was, and he kept it as his own for... twelve years? At the moment of his death, it all came flying back to her. And then some.

Ashiol isn't the only one he crippled.

For a moment though, just for a moment, her cheek

rubbing against the thick cotton of her pillowcase, Velody could not be angry with the boy who had taken her animor. He was dead, and Cyniver was dead, and everyone who... Saints and devils, *Tierce*.

What in the name of all that was sacred had happened to the city of Tierce?

Velody's room was flooded by sunlight, promising summer just around the corner. When had she last allowed herself to sleep so late?

Tomorrow was the Kalends of Floralis, the first day of the third month of spring and the festival day for duty to household gods, but today was the day dedicated to brides. Rhian and Delphine would be up to their elbows in hawthorn sprigs and satin ribbons.

Velody threw herself out of bed, washing quickly in her basin and putting on her blue workdress. It was a relief to feel normal after so much madness and confusion. *If I am a Creature King, I'll deal with it after dark. For now, I could do with some serious daylight.*

Velody rattled downstairs. The workroom was suspiciously tidy. Delphine and Rhian were in the kitchen, drinking mint tea.

'And she's alive,' said Delphine.

Rhian smiled with a little more warmth. 'We thought you were never going to wake up! You even slept through Marie's visit.'

Velody was glad to hear that Marie, the only female carpenter and locksmith in the city, had been. 'She came to fix new bolts?'

'On the kitchen door,' said Delphine. 'Not on Rhian's room.'

That was a surprise. 'You weren't trying to keep the noise down for my sake?' Velody asked.

'No,' said Rhian. 'It's just... that man tore through the house as if the locks and bolts weren't even there. So I thought it was time I learned to do without them.'

'That won't happen again,' said Velody, wishing she believed it.

Rhian looked resolute if far from happy. 'If I can't feel safe, I might as well be brave.'

Velody shot an anxious look at her friend. The beginning of things getting better, or more false hope? 'I'm glad for you, Rhian.'

Delphine poured Velody a cup of mint tea. 'Did you get things sorted last nox?'

'In a way.' What on earth could she tell them? 'We won't be bothered for a while.' *I hope, I hope.*

'That's something, I suppose.'

'So what have I missed?' Velody asked. 'The workroom looks spotless. Don't you have garlands to ship out for Brides?'

'You missed that too,' said Delphine. 'We had the hawthorn and silks bundled up for the courier an hour before noon, and it's well past that now.'

'I'm sorry,' said Velody. 'I meant to help you both. It's not like I'm swamped with commissions this month.'

Delphine and Rhian shared glances.

'Very kind of you, I'm sure,' said Delphine with mock civility. 'But before you break out your ribboning needles to slum it with us, perhaps you should examine your post. It's been quite busy here today while you slumbered away upstairs like a fairytale princessa.'

Velody's eyes fell on a pile of notes and cards in the centre of the table. The one on top had a Great Families seal on it. 'Are they for me?'

Delphine grinned. 'In case you've forgotten, you staged a major publicity stunt at the theatre last nox, *and* you were the creator of the Duchessa's show-stopping rose garment at a public parade the day before. Velody of the Vittorine, Via Silviana is in high demand.'

Velody reached out a shaking hand to touch the pile of messages. This was as good as dancing down a hillside of rooftops with Ashiol at her side, charged with animor and wild energy. This was better than rare steak and red wine.

'Really for me?' she asked in a small voice. Then, getting her breath back: 'Well, what are we waiting for? Let's rip them open!'

In the workroom, Delphine laid out a bolt of scarlet silk for the fertility ribbons they would need for the day after the Kalends, while Velody curled up in her armchair and read out the notes of commission. Rhian and Delphine chimed in from time to time, telling her which orders she should take and which she should politely decline (with encouraging notes to suggest that they request orders for festivals later in the year).

Neither of her friends commented on the ginger tom who joined them, purring as he cuddled up to Velody's feet, except when he dribbled on a patronising missive from a lesser merchant's daughter and Delphine commented that 'the moggy has good taste'.

After that, Velody and Rhian cut ribbon lengths for Delphine, while she put her perfect copperplate handwriting to good use, writing out the notes of acceptance and rejection under the heading 'Velody of the Vittorine, Sign of the Rose and Needle, Via Silviana', confirming appointment times.

By suppertime, they had the makings of eight dozen fertility garlands laid out to be finished tomorrow. Velody had accepted six dress commissions — two for the Shadows Ball of Lemuria in the middle of Floralis, one for the Ambervalia at the dying days of Floralis, and three for the Vestalia, the first major festival of Lucina. Velody's new clients included three titled ladies, two wives of very rich councillors, and an up-and-coming actress who had written with such enthusiastic praise for the daring gown Delphine had sported at the Vittorina Royale that they could not resist her.

Velody was a little disappointed that there was no word from the Duchessa, but promptly laughed at herself. How could she blame the ruler of the city for not wanting to be reminded of the rose dress that had been the centre of such an embarrassing spectacle?

Strange to recall that Ashiol had been part of that — that he was the Ducomte and the Duchessa's cousin as well as being a King of the Creature Court. Stranger still that it was the shadowy Creature Court of the nox that seemed so much more real now than the daylight aristocracy surrounding the 'daylight' Duchessa, when Velody had never belonged to either of them.

The three demoiselles ate a quiet supper. Velody watched the last of the light fade from the sky with some apprehension, wondering what this nox would bring.

Delphine caught her looking. 'Somewhere to be?' she asked, that sharp tone edging back into her voice.

'No,' said Velody. Ash promised her a few days at least. 'Nowhere else.'

'Good,' Delphine said with a grin. 'The council commissioned eight dozen garlands for the Kalends, but promised a bonus for every dozen above that. I reckon we can line our purses well if we work into the nox, and order more flowers tomorrow.'

'Don't you have somewhere else to be?' Velody asked, knowing Delphine's preference for partying madly after a hard day's work.

'Are you kidding?' replied Delphine. 'I can drink and dance for five days solid between the Floralia and the

246

Lemuria. Right now I want to earn the shilleins to pay for all that. Let's get stitching!'

Velody grinned back tiredly. She was glad for the chance to work her fingers to the bone. With any luck, she would be so exhausted after a long evening of ribbon stitching that she would sleep soundly, and forget the fact that she had stuck her fingers over and over with ribbon needles this afternoon without drawing a drop of blood.

Indeed, when she realised this and deliberately stuck a needle into the fleshy part of her hand, it passed right through her as if it — or she — did not exist. It was enough to make a demme wonder if there was still a place for her in the daylight world.

I T WAS one thing to be back in Aufleur, surrounded by the familiar dark walls and ornate architecture of the city. Returning to the Arches was something else altogether.

Ashiol tried to resist the dread that swamped him as he entered the Lock, following the canal path down into the undercity. He had to keep reminding himself that he was not walking into imprisonment and pain.

I am the master here. Let them fear me.

That made it worse though. Becoming Garnet was a greater horror than being conquered by him. He knew at least that he could survive the latter.

Ashiol walked through the echoing passages and tunnels. It was dark and damp down here, but early enough in the evening that most of the Creature Court would only just be coming out of their day slumber and readying themselves for the nox. Already he had picked up followers — creeping courtesi and crawling creatures that flickered in and out of the range of his senses, tracking him as he moved through the old city.

Macready and Kelpie trailed him as well, a reasonable distance behind, their blades on full display.

Ashiol was half-tempted to call the Court to him now, to lay down the rule and law, let them know exactly who was in charge around here. But, no. Better to give them some time to wonder what he was going to do. Besides, there was one reunion he would prefer to conduct in private before he dealt with the Creature Court as a whole.

This tunnel had been a main thoroughfare in the old days when this really was a city. The canal ran through the centre of it, all the way to the Haymarket, connecting up with the river Verticordia beyond. It had once been used for transporting boatloads of produce back and forth from the outside world to the city below.

The tunnel opened out into the familiar series of arches that gave the undercity its name. Each arch was carved with a story of old Aufleur, a chiselled triumph or a drilled battle anecdote. Beyond the arches was a wide buttressed gallery.

Mayor's Bridge was up ahead, and the cathedral. Ashiol was half-tempted to stop and exchange banter with Priest, but that would only be putting off the inevitable. In any case, who was to say that Priest would be an ally this time around? Poet had taken courtesi of his own and allied himself with Dhynar. The world was already upside down. Five years of Garnet had changed everything, and Ashiol wasn't quite ready to deal with an altered Priest.

Bad enough that he was about to face what those five years had done to Livilla.

Still, as he walked past the cathedral on the far side of the canal, Ashiol couldn't help glancing at the elaborate spires to see if there were pigeons up there, watching him with their beady little eyes. The domed roof was bare.

Ashiol lengthened his stride. Time to establish himself down here, to give Velody the space she needed to come to terms with all this. And the one thing he had to do before everything else was to see Livilla with his own eyes. Then maybe a few of his ghosts could be laid to rest.

The forecourt of the Haymarket was shockingly familiar, a giant concrete warehouse stripped clean by past members of the Court. The area was bleak and bare — there was little anyone could do to make this enormous, cold space look anything less than stark. The canal ran right through it. The forecourt was good for duels, at least — what with the high ceilings and the convenience of being able to sluice blood so easily from the floor.

Past the forecourt was another matter. These inner rooms, once devoted to packing and storage, simply dripped with stolen luxury. Carpets, curtains and other draperies swamped the space, all heavily perfumed to disguise their mustiness of age. It was Ortheus's taste in furnishings, but Garnet inherited it and made it even more so. He kidnapped a dozen fresco painters from the daylight and forced them to cover the walls with glistening gold and ivory paintwork depicting every animal of the world at play and at war. When it was over, he lined the artists up and called his favoured members of the Court to rip them to pieces.

The artists' blood was mixed with resin, and Garnet himself gleefully added splashes of it here and there across the walls, to make the fight scenes between lions and eagles and bears 'more realistic'. That was the day Ashiol had lost hope that his Garnet would be a different, better Power and Majesty than his predecessors.

Garnet's madness came as a surprise to no one else. The entire Court had seen it as... inevitable, really.

Stairways and ladders led up and around in all directions, to the various galleries and balconies that lined the walls and upper levels of the Haymarket. Ashiol hesitated. Would Livilla be in her old rooms, or had she already taken over Garnet's quarters? There were no other Lords to challenge her for the space — or were there?

He realised now that he was so wrapped up in self-pity and his desire to get out of the city that he never asked Kelpie to complete her report on who was still around. She was nearby with Macready, but so were half a dozen unfamiliar courtesi, watching Ashiol with the eyes of cautious animals. He couldn't call her forward here and ask for more details within earshot of them all. It would make him look weak.

Five Lords, Kelpie had said. Ashiol knew about Poet, Priest, Livilla and Dhynar. Who was the fifth? There was Lief, of course. He was still alive when Ashiol left the Court. But Lief's hounds ran with Dhynar now — Ashiol recognised them when they attacked him in the Gardens of Trajus. That almost certainly meant that Lief was dead. The fifth Lord must be newer, one of the courtesi who had risen in the ranks since Ashiol was last in the Court.

There were Lords nearby. He could feel Livilla's presence, above him in Garnet's old rooms. He could practically hear the thud of her heart beating beneath her skin. But there was another Lord too, here in the heart of Garnet's territory. A familiar scent, and Ashiol's heart turned over as he realised the truth.

He knew who the fifth Lord was.

Wrapping his enhanced Lord form around him like a shield, Ashiol made for the main staircase. As he did so, a dark figure appeared at the top of it, gazing down with unfriendly eyes.

'Mars,' said Ashiol.

'They call me Warlord now,' said the fifth Lord of the Court in his rich, deep voice. 'Welcome home, Ash.' As his

foot hit the second step, he shaped himself into a panther
and leaped into empty space.

MOST OF THE Creature Court started their lives out low,
street brats like Hel and Livilla, orphans and wanderers like
Priest and Poet. Ashiol was a rare exception: a nobleman
with a real home and a family who had watched his descent
into the darkness with fear in their eyes. They thought he
was running with street gangs, rebelling against the restric-
tive life of the Palazzo. They thought he was into knives and
drugs and crime. They thought he was a bad seed, in with a
bad crowd. *Seven hells, it's not like they were wrong.*

Ashiol rose to Lord less than a year after Garnet killed
Tasha. Once they were equal in status again, they returned to
being close as they had always been — friends, brothers. But
Garnet wasn't Ashiol's brother. He came from a family of
peasants and servants, and although he knew the price of
family disappointment, it was nothing like the weight Ashiol
had to live with every day.

The Creature Court was full of Lords and Kings, but
none of them were born noble. They were all in love with
their hierarchy and power games, and not one of them had
the blood of an aristocrat. Then Mars came along, and finally
Ashiol had someone who understood.

Ashiol had been in the Creature Court for six years and
he felt like he owned the world. Nine-year-old Comtessilla
Isangell had recovered from her early childhood illnesses
that so frightened the family, and it was looking less and less
likely that he would face the horrific fate of ruling the damn
city some day. But while Ashiol spent every nox with the
Creature Court, he was still expected to make appearances at
the Palazzo among the daylight folk. He gained a reputation

among his grandfather's court for being disreputable and possibly mad, which had the strange effect of drawing young noblewomen to him like moths to a candle flame.

Every time he went back to the daylight to attend one of his uncle's salons under the watchful eyes of the Old Duc and Duchessa, Ashiol promised himself that this would be the last time. He would disappear into the nox once and for all and bury himself in the Creature Court, leaving behind the disapproving glares of his family.

When he thought he couldn't stand it any longer, there was Mars. Maziz dal Sara was fifteen, the son of the new Zafiran ambassador who was a princel in his own land. Mars was flirtatious and handsome, confident for one so young. The keen young noblewomen who usually worried their mothers by flocking around Ashiol smiled and winked at the newcomer instead.

Ashiol watched the ambassador's son all that first nox, his eyes on the dark boy as he turned about the dance floor and escorted lady after lady to the supper table. Maziz dal Sara made easy pleasantries with the Duc and Duchessa, and skilfully evaded the flirtatious gaze of the Ducomte Artorio as well as that of his neglected wife, the Ducomtessa Eglantine.

Ashiol watched until he was absolutely certain. It was in the way the boy walked and held himself, in the gleam in his eye and bite of his teeth as he ate slices of smoked ham and raw fish — never the vegetable florets or sugared fruits.

Finally their paths crossed, and a tipsy Baronissa introduced them.

'So, my Lord Comte,' laughed young Maziz dal Sara. 'What do you think of me?'

'I can't quite decide,' said Ashiol.

'Now don't be jealous, Ashie, you know I adore you most of all,' hiccuped the Baronissa, amused at the thought that the two men might fight over her.

Ashiol couldn't remember her name then, let alone now.

'Can't decide what?' challenged the Zafiran ambassador's son.

'Whether it's gattopardo or tigris. Some kind of cat, I know that much.' Ashiol smiled too, a disconcerting sight rarely seen in the daylight. 'It's my business to know.'

The boy's eyes faltered for a moment, then he grinned and resumed his relaxed composure. 'Panther,' he said. 'As it happens. *Khatri zaba* in my own language.'

Later that nox, after both young men had made excuses to their respective guardians, they ran together on the roofs of Aufleur. By morning, Ashiol had his first courteso.

ASHIOL BUCKED against the heaviness of the Panther Lord, twisting so as not to be pinned to the ground by his weight. He could fight this battle in two-leg form — hells, he could shape himself into his collection of tom cats and still beat the bastard into submission. But that wasn't what today was about. Today was about demonstrating how easily he could take power.

Ashiol went chimaera and tore the panther to pieces.

When it was over, Mars lay bleeding, too wrecked to be anything other than himself. 'I'd forgotten,' he gasped. Blood bubbled up through his lips.

There wasn't a mark on Ashiol as he stood above the other man. His long black coat was barely damaged, but the transformation had ripped his shirt into shreds down the front and back. Amazingly, the breeches were still in one piece — the blazing power of the chimaera had split holes in the leather here and there, but Velody's seams held true. The boots were ruined, the soles having half- exploded with the force of the change. 'Forgotten what?'

'How frigging good you are.' There was a long pause. 'Majesty.'

Ashiol stared down at the Lord who had once been his friend, who had laughed with him and stood at his side for so long. They had fucked women together — hells, they had fucked each other on a few very memorable occasions. Mars was *his*. A thrill and shiver passed through Ashiol's body as the title was acknowledged. Part of him was screaming, *Velody, save me from this.* The other part was saying, *Why the hells not?*

He nodded to the shadows, where he could smell Mars's courtesi hovering anxiously. 'Do what you can with him.'

A striped brock crawled towards his master, shaping into a short, muscled young man as he did so. He was followed by an elegant greymoon cat with lustrous eyes. When the cat reached Mars's struggling, bloodied body, it became a dark-eyed woman who nodded respectfully at Ashiol before she bent over her master. They had a choice now — to huddle close and let him die in order to quench his power, or to make him whole again.

The woman — she was familiar, Ashiol thought, perhaps she had been a courtesa in the old days, under Lief or Lysandor or Celeste — drew a line of blood in her own throat with a sharpened fingernail and held herself over Mars so that he could drink. With loyalty like that, he would heal and recover.

Ashiol kicked off the remains of his latest pair of ruined boots and continued up the stairs unchallenged. At the top, he turned without thinking towards where he knew Livilla was.

A courteso stood in his way, fierce and uncompromising.

He was so young it made Ashiol's teeth ache. This lad couldn't be halfway through his teens and here he was, dressed like a warrior in hard brown leathers with a silver wolf tattooed on his bare left shoulder. He was probably sleeping with Livilla, would probably kill for her.

Ashiol had wondered what Livilla turned into during his absence, and now he knew the truth. She had turned into Tasha.

'She's busy,' said the lad in a clipped voice, like he meant business, like he didn't care that the man before him was a Creature King and had taken out the Panther Lord without even blinking.

Ashiol remembered sounding this tough, feeling this brave. He knew how easy it was to twist that confidence into something ugly. He stared at the lad for a full minute, watching impatience and stupid bravado flicker through his brown eyes.

The lad moved first, an attack blow, and Ashiol moved second. Within another minute he was holding the lad to the floor, arms bent up in a painful manner, knee inserted in his back, half his weight pressed hard into the limp, beaten body. 'I am your Power and Majesty, boy,' he said in a low voice, near the lad's ear. 'What am I?'

Livilla's lad let out a whine that might have had the words 'power' and 'majesty' in it.

'Say it again. Say it better.'

'Power an' Majesty.'

'Good.'

The lad hadn't even thought to shape into the wolf that Ashiol could feel lurking under his skin. It should have been instinctual, but he was in too much pain to let instinct set in.

Livilla's taste in pretty boys was going to get her killed. They weren't much use in a fight.

'Stay down,' said Ashiol, and pushed open the door to Garnet's bedchamber.

Two long bodies lay on top of the silken covers of the bed. Livilla's pale limbs showed up beautifully beside her dark lover, her second courteso. Ashiol looked the young man over — late teens, not as young as the other — and saw the ghost of raven feathers in his black hair.

'And here I thought I was giving you a chance to tidy up before I came in,' Ashiol drawled.

Livilla's pale face was made harder by the severe style of her dark hair, cut to her chin in the new fashion. Her lips were plum red and her eyes glittered. She didn't say anything.

It was the dark courteso who moved, rolling to his feet and staring Ashiol down. 'Get out,' he said in a snarl so full of self-importance that Ashiol almost laughed in his face.

'Livilla, which bit of him do you like best? I'd be happy to bite it off as a keepsake for you to remember him by.'

She tilted her head a little and licked her dark lips.

Ashiol eyed the raven courteso up and down. 'Go and see to your brother courteso,' he suggested in a low voice. 'He's hurt out there.'

'I won't leave her,' said the raven.

'Nice sentiment, if I was a Creature Lord looking to slice her in two and suck out her animor. That's not what I am, and that's not why I'm here.'

'Janvier,' said Livilla in her clear, childish voice, 'go and look after Seonard. My Ash won't hurt me.'

Ashiol was interested to hear that. 'Confident, aren't you?'

She reached for a black robe and draped it over her naked paleness, not hurrying. 'Confident, yes.' She lifted a fancy cigarette-holder from her bedside table and held it out for Ashiol to light like the nobleman he was.

Janvier hesitated, evidently torn between the threat he thought that Ashiol posed to his mistress and the cosy exchange that was now taking place between them. He must be trained not to interfere between Livilla and her lovers, particularly when one of them was a Creature King.

Ashiol lifted the gold lighter from the table and flicked it, lighting Livilla's cigarette. Janvier left.

Livilla sucked on the end of her cigarette-holder and smiled.

Ashiol had thought of a hundred things he wanted to say to her, but now he couldn't remember a single one. This wasn't the demoiselle he knew. It was a parody of her. A parody of all the women who had been touched by the Creature Court.

This is what Velody would turn into, if I had my way.

That made his mind up for him. If he was going to be a monster, then fine. Let him be the monster. He would do it the good old-fashioned way instead of corrupting a sensible woman for his own selfish needs.

'On your feet,' he said, making it an order.

Livilla's eyes flashed a moment of defiance, and then she relaxed against her pillows and inhaled a slow curl of perfumed smoke. The scent of it made Ash want to claw his own throat out.

'One of those useless sentinels broke my leg in the last skybattle,' she said. 'I can't stand up.'

Ashiol eyed her bare legs. A thin, lacy bandage was strategically tied around her left ankle. 'Are you telling me that with two juicy boys at your disposal, you haven't been able to suck enough bodily fluids in two days to heal that?'

She pouted her painted lips around the stem of the cigarette-holder. 'It's mostly healed. It still hurts when I stand on it.'

Ashiol reached out and pulled the cigarette from the holder, pinching it out and hurling it aside. She looked faintly ridiculous now, with the holder hanging from her mouth. He pulled that out too and tossed it to the floor. He took her throat in his right hand and squeezed. 'Show me how much it hurts.'

She laughed at him, a hard and mocking laugh. 'Think you're him now? Think you can walk back in here and play the Power? We saw you bleed and whimper under Garnet's fingers, Ash. You're nothing to him.'

'And what am I to you, Livilla?' He squeezed her throat a little harder. 'On your feet.'

She did it, lowering her feet to the floor and composing her face as she stood up. She trembled with the pain of it, but did not stumble. To her credit, she did not try to lessen the pain by putting all her weight on the undamaged ankle. She knew the danger of obeying the shape of a King's order without fulfilling the intent.

Ashiol released her. 'Very good. Now put on something pretty and come to the square in the Shambles. We're going to have a gathering of the Creature Court, and I want you to look your best.'

'Why the square?' she asked sullenly. 'Why not here in the Haymarket?'

'Because,' said Ashiol, 'if I have to spend another minute in this stinking hole of Garnet's, I'm going to have to bite out somebody's throat to get the taste from my mouth.'

He left her, and strode out the door.

'You don't want these rooms then?' she asked in a plaintive voice. 'I can stay here?'

Ashiol turned back, steeling himself not to look for the demme he had loved in this broken doll of a woman. 'If I don't kill you in the next day or so, sure. You can keep the rooms.'

Janvier was waiting, holding the trembling lad, Seonard, upright. As Ashiol came out of Livilla's room, the two courtesi went straight to her side, ducking their heads to avoid meeting his eyes.

Macready and Kelpie waited a little further along the balcony.

'Hell of a job you performed on Warlord down there, so you did,' said Macready, his lilting voice indicating neither approval nor disapproval.

'How do you feel?' asked Kelpie.

Ashiol contemplated the question. 'I can do this,' he said. 'It's getting easier.'

'What's next?' asked Macready.

'Call the Creature Court together,' said Ashiol. 'I think it's time they swore allegiance to their new Power and Majesty.'

29

THIRD DAY OF THE FLORALIA (BRIDES)

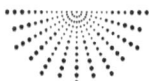

DUSK

*H*eliora awoke with the wrenching thought that she didn't know where she was. She slitted her eyes open, hoping to get some clue through a thin, eyelashed line of sight. The first thing she saw was chintz, and as she opened her eyes a little wider she recognised the armchair directly opposite.

She was still in Poet's den.

'I didn't like to wake you,' he said in an amused voice. 'You looked so peaceful.'

Heliora lifted herself up on her elbows, wincing at the cracked feeling around her eyes and mouth and the sour taste on her tongue. She was stretched out on one of Poet's lush couches, her body tight and hot inside yesterday's costume. 'How long was I asleep?'

Poet was at the window, his back to her. 'Would you believe all day? It's nearly nox.'

'Cack.'

He shrugged. 'We slept too. I assumed you'd wake when you were ready and make yourself scarce long before we were up and about. But you didn't.'

She felt like an intruder. It was a long time since she and Poet had been at all friendly, and their friendship had never extended to sleepovers. 'Sorry. Looking into the futures yesterday must have exhausted me more than I thought. I haven't slept so solidly in months.'

In the back cubicle of her flimsy tent in the Basilica, there were always noises to be wary of. Heliora slept light, an hour or two at a time. She hadn't realised how long it was since she felt truly safe.

But why the seven hells was she feeling safe around Poet? That made an entire lack of sense.

Someone had left a china washbasin and jug of water for her use. They looked a little silly on Poet's mahogany tea table, but Heliora was grateful for them. She poured water into the basin and washed her face and hands, rinsing out her mouth several times and massaging her wet fingers through the short stubble of her hair. Her black wig was hooked on to the end of the couch, but she didn't touch it.

'Must be an interesting view out there,' she said, noticing that Poet still stood at the window.

'Maybe I'm turning my back to be a gentleman,' said Poet.

'You?' The sarcasm came out before she could stop it.

He turned his head and grinned at her. 'First time for everything. Come and see the show, my lovely.'

She joined him at the window. From here, you could see across into the small town square — more of a lopsided triangle really — that rested in the heart of the Shambles. People were beginning to gather there — courtesi for the most part, but Heliora recognised Priest among his gaudy retinue, the ferax cub, and a subdued-looking Warlord.

'Clan gathering,' said Poet, sounding light about it. 'Conveniently near my threshold.'

'Is this the first time since...'

'Garnet died? Oh, yes. Someone's making a claim.'

His voice was low with a dangerous thrum to it. Heliora shivered at it, though she wasn't entirely sure that it was a bad shiver.

'Are you joining them?'

'Oh, sooner or later. Why give up the advantage of being able to watch them from up here?' He looked at her. 'Do you want to borrow some clothes?'

Heliora jingled her limp Zafiran garb self-consciously. 'Do I look that bad?'

'Never that. Just thought you might like to dress up. Everyone else is in their festival best.'

Below the window, two dark boys in leathers and lace carried a litter on which Livilla reclined, pouting in a glamorous ensemble of silver studs and soft black satin.

'Ouch,' said Hel dryly. 'Have you got anything to compete with that?' She eyed Poet up and down. She wasn't quite as narrow around the body as he was, but they were a similar size. 'Although drag isn't really my thing.'

'There are some dresses and so forth in the attic,' he said offhandedly. At her quizzical look, he added, 'Women do stay over from time to time, you know.'

'And leave their clothes behind? How quaint. I thought you only liked boys.'

'I like everyone, Heliora.'

And there was that shiver again, only it was going to places she didn't want to think about. 'I'll take a look at those dresses.'

It was ridiculous how important it was to dress up for these occasions. Most members of the Creature Court were quite happy to wander around naked for most of the time, but there was something about glamour and warpaint that provided a form of armour against the rest of them.

For Heliora, it was perhaps most important of all. As the seer, she wasn't quite one of them.

In the attic, Poet's two courtesi — the small Zero and the large Halberk — were in quiet conversation. At her appearance, they left without saying a word. Either they were being polite, or she had just been snubbed.

A chest in the far corner was filled with various female fripperies. Costumes, she realised, and that made sense considering Poet's theatrical hobby. For the first time, she wondered what kind of lovers he pursued, and who he would trust enough to bring down here.

She shivered, wondering why the women who had owned these clothes hadn't needed them to go home in. There were stories about Poet. He played the gentleman most of the time, but weren't gentlemen the most dangerous men of all? All those pretty manners, but you could never tell what they were thinking behind them all.

It was no worse than a thousand other things she had witnessed as part of the Creature Court. They might be lunatics, but they were her lunatics.

Maybe that's how I die, she thought suddenly. *Maybe Poet takes a fancy to me and slices me up in a back alley somewhere.*

Slumbering the day away, Heliora had briefly forgotten that she was going to die soon, but now it was back, clear as a musical note. She wasn't going to see Saturnalia, so what the hells did it matter what she wore?

It always mattered what you wore.

Heliora stripped off the jangling mass of Zafiran gauze that was part of her Madama Fortuna wardrobe, and sifted through the clothes to find something suitable for the seer of the Creature Court. She bypassed the black leather and satin ensembles with ease — everyone down there would be wearing that kind of trash. The seer should look different, if only to remind them all that she didn't pose a physical threat, that she was the only one who wasn't worth duelling.

She was too slender for most of these costumes. Finally she found a white lace petticoat that she could wear like a dress if she knotted a sash around her waist, and a wide green shawl that might possibly keep her warm.

A long red-blonde wig caught her eye, and she shucked it on without thinking about who had worn it before her.

Feminine was good, because it made her unthreatening. That was why she chose white and green in contrast to their usual bold blacks, silvers and scarlets; bare feet to their spike-heeled boots. Still, she felt an inner longing to dress as Kelpie did, as Hel herself had in the old days when she ran with the sentinels. Combat breeches and jacket, her stubble-short hair bared to the sky. She missed the blades that had once been hers.

Slowly, Hel took off the wig. The dress and shawl could stay, but why shouldn't she look like herself for once?

With all this attention to her wardrobe, she hadn't noticed much of anything else about the attic room — there were two narrow beds that must belong to his courtesi, but no hint of where Poet slept the days away.

As she turned to leave, Heliora saw the cage. It was tall and sturdy, wide enough to house four men of Halberk's size. Inside, a light mattress piled with pillows and coverlets suggested someone made a nest there on a regular basis. The cage was built of iron, but the most interesting feature was the wire that was wrapped tightly in a coiling sheath up and down every bar. Even if the glow of the stuff hadn't warned her, the fact that Heliora could only feel smooth iron when she laid her hand against it told her that the bars of the cage were wrapped in skysilver wire.

Skysilver was rare. Collecting so much and drawing it

into wire would have taken years — decades. It looked old, and she wondered who had owned it before Poet. Which Creature Lord had been crazy and clever enough to come up with a cage that would imprison one of the Creature Court as well as anyone who belonged to the daylight?

More than that, she couldn't help wondering why Poet was sleeping in here. Was it to protect him from assassination attempts from the other Lords, or was it to protect someone from him?

Poet was still at the window when Heliora came down from the attic — but he had taken the time to swathe himself in an over-sized tailored jacket with rich embroidery. It made him look like the Orphan Princel in borrowed finery.

'Ready to go down?' she asked.

He eyed her bare head with a slight smile, but made no comment about her appearance. 'You might prefer us to arrive separately. Imagine the fuss if they think the seer has attached herself to the retinue of one of the Lords.'

'It's not like I could play favourites if I wanted to,' Hel said lightly. 'We're all doomed, as ever.'

Something in Poet's face told her that he didn't see the humour. He gestured at the window. 'He's down there.'

'Ash?'

Poet sighed. 'I was so damned desperate to keep him in this city, to stop him running out on us. Now I'm not sure it was such a good idea.'

Heliora moved to the window. 'What do you mean?'

She could see Ashiol standing in the square, remote from the rest of them, flanked by Kelpie and Macready.

'See the look on his face?' said Poet.

'Garnet,' she breathed. 'That expression, those eyes, it's Garnet all the way. He must have made up his mind to stay and be the Power and Majesty.'

Poet's voice cracked a little. 'He won't be our Ash any more.'

Heliora gave him a fierce look. 'Did you only just figure that out? I've seen the futures, Poet. We don't have many options here. This is one of the better ones.'

'Is it?' he asked. 'Is it really?'

No, she thought, remembering the countless futures that had screamed through her head. *This isn't one of the better ones. This is how most of the worst ones start out.*

'Yes,' she lied firmly, looking him in the eye. 'Now let's get down there before he has us executed for being late.'

30

THIRD DAY OF THE
FLORALIA (BRIDES)

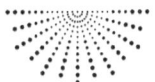

NOX

*V*elody couldn't sleep. Her fingers ached from the needlework she had devoted herself to all after-noon and all evening, and her mind simply would not shut off. She stared at the ceiling, thinking of needles and knives.

Most of all, she was resisting the urge to throw off her noxgown and run naked on the rooftops. Saints and angels, what was she turning into? What had Ashiol Xandelian done to her?

Somehow, the idea of him, just the intrusion of his name into her thoughts, was enough to get her on her feet and to the window. She ran her eyes over the crested roof, judging how easy it would be to leap from here to the neighbour's guttering and along the skyline.

One nox playing on the rooftops with a rebellious royal and you're already thinking like a cat-burglar from the newspaper serials.

Velody rummaged in her wardrobe for the right clothes.

Her workdress was tempting because of its ability to stand up to a bit of tile scrapeage, but she had to choose clothes that she was prepared to abandon if danger came and the little brown mice were the best escape route. Hard-wearing or not, her workdress was her most indispensable item of clothing.

She found a shapeless black frock near the back of the wardrobe. It had been an impulse buy (she usually only wore dresses she'd made herself) and never fitted her as well as she hoped; she had kept it because it was ridiculously expensive. She wouldn't mourn if it was lost, but it was loose enough that it wouldn't encumber her movements, and dressy enough to prevent embarrassment if she ran into any of the Creature Court.

Why was she thinking like this? She had spent too much time listening to Ashiol. Appearance meant so much to his people.

Our people. Oh, saints.

Velody's doubts vanished when her sandalled feet landed lightly on the edge of the roof outside her window. By the time she had taken a few running jumps to warm her stride along the length of Via Silviana, the blood was pumping joyously through her veins and she was half-flying with it.

No wonder they said that Aufleur was a fire trap, with so many terraced houses and shops and even the freeholds jammed up tight against each other. From Via Silviana Velody could leap and clamber halfway to the Piazza Giulia and the Church of the Lares without once descending to street level. She steadied herself for a moment and then started the real climb — layer after layer of welcoming roof tiles as she leaped and danced her way up the Lucretine hill.

The real Velody had been left behind. She was well and truly in Lord form now, her skin glowing white on the dimly lit hillside. She was larger and stronger, the dress clinging more successfully to this form than it ever had to her own. There was hardly any moonlight — the new moon was barely a sliver in the sky — but she could see like a cat, and it seemed impossible to put a paw wrong as she threw herself from roof to roof.

Mouse, not cat. I've got the eyesight of several hundred mice. No wonder I can see so far.

The view from the crest of the Lucretine was breathtaking, and Velody found herself laughing in long, half-hysterical sobs. It wasn't much from there to start crying for real, hard crying, her whole body shuddering with it.

The roof she ended up on was flat and smooth — a church, she realised belatedly — with ridged edges and an ornate cupola in the centre.

'Velody,' said a soft voice.

She jumped at the intrusion, only just restraining herself from screaming aloud. Even with her newly heightened eyesight, she couldn't see whom the voice belonged to until he lifted himself up onto the roof and made himself known.

Crane. Sentinel. Friend.

The tears started again, quietly this time. He came closer, dropping near her in a crouch, but not touching her. 'You were enjoying yourself,' he said, sounding confused. Nothing more uncomfortable than a young man faced with a crying woman.

'That's why I'm miserable,' she flung at him. 'I don't know who I am any more, what I am. Velody of the Vittorine at the Sign of the Rose and Needle, Via Silviana isn't the kind of demme to get her kicks out of dancing up and down drainpipes in the middle of the nox.'

Crane shrugged. 'You never know if you like something until the first time you try it.'

Velody wasn't crying any more. She looked more closely at Crane. 'What happened to you?'

'I got my face beat in last nox, don't you remember?'

'I remember,' she said. 'I remember that you looked like something out of a butcher's shop window, all scraped and swollen.' His jaw was slightly reddish, and there was some swelling around his eyes the colour of old bruises, but he had healed at a startling rate. 'I thought the sentinels were ordinary humans.'

'We are.'

'So how did you heal so fast?'

He paused as if he was trying to think up a lie, then shrugged a shoulder. 'Ashiol did it.'

'He can do that?'

'He's a Creature King. He can do anything.'

She wasn't sure how to feel about that particular remark.

'Why did you become a sentinel?' she asked finally. 'It seems like a thankless job.'

'Entirely thankless,' he assured her. 'Especially back when Garnet was in charge.'

'So why do you do it?'

'It's all I've ever wanted. What they do — the Creature Court and the Kings — it's more important than anything else that happens in this city. It's an honour to serve them.'

'I haven't done anything yet,' she said lightly. 'Is it an honour to serve me?'

His eyes darkened for a moment. 'Oh, yes.'

The pause after that became uncomfortable.

'I should go back,' said Velody. 'Rhian has bad dreams. If she wakes and finds me gone...'

'Stay a little longer,' Crane suggested. 'It's a beautiful clear nox. Why not enjoy it?'

Velody looked sideways at him. 'What, are you flirting with me now?'

'Maybe. How am I doing?'

She leaned forward and patted his shoulder. It was hard

not to like this one — the darkness and danger didn't seem to touch his general enthusiasm for life. 'You could improve your timing.'

A long silver dollop of something dripped out of the sky and hit the surface of the roof. It bubbled, eating a small hole into the stone.

Velody stared at it. 'What is that?'

Crane got to his feet, the teasing note gone from his voice. 'Slow rain. Don't let it touch you!'

DELPHINE WOKE to the sound of Rhian screaming. She ran half-naked across the little landing to throw herself into Rhian's room and her bed. It was strange to be able to simply open the door and scramble inside. Usually Delphine and Velody had to stand shivering outside Rhian's door, calling out reassurances until Rhian recovered enough from her dreams to pad across the floor and unbolt her fortress.

This was better. Delphine hadn't even lost the warmth from her own bed by the time she was under Rhian's covers. 'I'm here, honey. Don't be afraid.'

Rhian clung to her friend in a desperate embrace. 'I... oh...'

'Don't talk about it. You don't have to say anything.'

'I thought it was over,' Rhian whispered, shaking with frustration as well as another kind of shock. 'I thought I was getting better!'

Delphine had hoped much the same — that Rhian's decision to leave her door unbarred was a sign that she was finally healing. Now they were back where they had started, with Rhian a quivering wreck after another hideous dream.

We should be safe in our beds. Not too much to ask, is it?

'Where's Velody?' Rhian asked when she had calmed down enough to think clearly.

Delphine had been wondering that herself. They were usually both quick to wake when they heard Rhian's screams. 'She was so tired, perhaps she didn't hear you.' It was lame, she knew. Velody had the best hearing of them all, and though she slept as deep as a buried dog she was always up and alert at any sign of trouble.

Rhian pushed Delphine away and reached for her dressing gown, belting it tightly around her. She left her room like a sleepwalker.

Delphine grabbed a blanket off the bed to take with her, and winced at the cold feel of the floorboards under her bare feet.

Rhian pushed Velody's door open and stared at the rumpled remains of the bed, then at the window. 'She left it open,' she said.

Delphine looked at the telltale crack of the window where it had been hastily pulled down. The negligence of it numbed her. She was the irresponsible one, the addled bint who stayed out late drowning herself in men and booze, so the door had to be left unlocked if not unlatched. Delphine was the one who came in at all hours, drunken and exuberant, the one who made Rhian so unhappy with her antics.

Velody would have scratched Delphine's eyes out for forgetting to close a window properly, especially on the first nox that Rhian was brave enough to forgo her usual bolts and locks on her own bedroom door.

'Is she with them?' Rhian asked in a small voice.

Delphine shook her head, not trusting herself to say anything. She shut the window with a crunch.

'What do they have that keeps dragging her back to them?' asked Rhian.

'I don't know,' answered Delphine. 'Whatever it is, it's not good for her.'

She had her suspicions — the tall, dark and magnetic

figure of Ducomte Ashiol Xandelian was one hell of a start —
but since when had Velody been the kind of woman to lose
her head over a pretty man? She had been almost as much of
a hermit nun as Rhian this last year.

'Can I sleep with you?' asked Rhian.

'Sure.' Delphine would agree to anything if it meant she
could return to her cosy blankets and pillows.

They went to Delphine's room together.

'I'd like to send a message to Marie in the morning, to fix
the bolts on my door,' said Rhian.

'I don't blame you,' said Delphine. 'I might ask for a bolt
or two myself.'

THIRD DAY OF THE
FLORALIA (BRIDES)

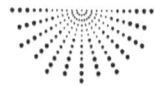

NOX

*M*acready held steady, two paces behind Ashiol. Kelpie was at his side, looking grim. When Garnet stripped them of their weapons, the sentinels became everyone's meat, easy prey, relying on Garnet to protect them rather than the other way around — and he only protected them when it suited him. They were now used to hiding in corners, staying out of the way during gatherings of the Creature Court. They had learned to fade into the background. It felt alien for them to be standing at their King's back, blades out, ready to take on all comers. For the sentinels to be part of a King's show of strength rather than his weakness.

Ashiol walked to the centre of the Shambles square, every inch a Creature King. He had discarded Poet's coat to stand in the ripped remains of the black clothes from Velody's shop. On anyone else it would look ridiculous, but his lean muscles gleamed where not covered by shredded shirt and breeches. His eyes glowed with power.

Dangerous, thought Macready. *I hope they're all paying attention. That's not the wreck of a King who left us.*

Obviously, Dhynar had an ear close to the ground. He and his entourage were already lounging in the square when Ashiol and the sentinels arrived. The Ferax Lord wore red, his favourite formal colour. His leathers shone like blood. His four courtesi — Shade and Lennoc the hounds, Grago and Farrier the cats — were dressed identically, each glaring and flexing his muscles.

In the old days, when there were more sentinels than any single Lord's pack of courtesi, it might have been funny. Now, Macready felt his shoulder blades itch. Even with the blades, even with Kelpie at his side, he was damned vulnerable.

There was no sign of Poet yet. They were within spitting distance of his territory, so he must be deliberately biding his time. Perhaps he didn't want to signal his alliance with Dhynar to the others? Assuming that alliance was still alive and well.

Priest was the next to arrive. His courtesi walked ahead of him, all female, garbed in versions of the outfits he himself preferred — finely tailored seigneur's suits, bright in peacock colours. Each courtesa carried a basket laden with wine, fruit and honey cakes, which they laid at Ashiol's feet with solemn precision. Above and beyond fighting skills, Priest demanded that his courtesi be able to cook and serve food with lavish skill.

Priest himself, fat and self-satisfied as ever, wandered in a few minutes later, his belly swathed in a waistcoat embroidered in purple, green and gold. He ambled up to Ashiol as if this were some innocuous social occasion, and nodded his head to him. 'Good to see you back, dear boy. You've done well for yourself.'

'I know,' said Ashiol. 'I'd make you kneel to me, old man, but I'd hate to hear the grinding of tired cartilage as you hauled yourself up again.'

Macready watched the exchange with interest. These two had never been enemies, though neither would lift a finger to help the other unless it was strictly in his own best interest.

'I hope you enjoy my gifts,' said Priest, making it sound like a challenge.

'I trust that I will,' said Ashiol, making it sound like an insult.

Priest backed away, joining his women at the edge of the square.

Warlord limped in next, doing his best at a show of strength — anything less would be an insult. He wore Zafiran silks. His torso, usually bared to display his bulky muscle, was sheathed in a dark tunic to hide the wounds of his recent battle with Ashiol.

Clara, the greymoon courtesa, walked at Warlord's side in veil and harem pants. It was obvious to Macready that she watched her Lord warily, prepared to catch him if he fell. Warlord's male courtesi walked behind them, also garbed in Zafiran finery.

Warlord passed Ashiol and bowed his head to him before taking up border territory in the square, equally spaced between Dhynar's leather-clad thugs and Priest's elegant women.

They were all cautious. Even Dhynar was playing it straight. This didn't surprise Macready in the least. Their choice for Power and Majesty was between a known King and an untried lass (assuming they all knew about Velody by now), so it was no wonder they were rolling over to accept Ash's rule. Poet and Dhynar only rebelled because they suspected Ashiol would try to leave; now they had what they wanted, why shouldn't they kneel and obey him?

But Macready's mammy had raised a suspicious son, not a stupid one. He glanced around the square, wondering when the trouble would start and who would start it.

If the Lords banded together, they could take Ashiol down between them, each hoping to quench enough animor to make it to the next stage of evolution. Poet and Dhynar in alliance had been a worrying enough turn of events, but the possibility of the Creature Lords uniting was bloody terrifying.

It had never happened before in the history of the Creature Court. *First time for everything? I bloody hope not.*

Livilla came next, on a litter carried by her two boys, Seonard and Janvier. The miracle was that young Seonard could take his share of the weight, with the beating evident on his face and body. Livilla must have shared blood with him to repair the worst of the damage — and that would have weakened her further.

She couldn't know about Velody, Macready decided. None of the other Lords would be fool enough to tell her. The story of Samara had kept female Lords repressed for generations, self-limiting their power. When Livilla found out that women could safely become Kings, all seven hells might very well break loose.

They should all be very, very grateful that Tasha was not alive to make use of this new and disturbing information.

Livilla's boys lowered her litter to the ground, and she rose to her feet without assistance. Her face was tight from suppressed pain, but she managed to bow gracefully to Ashiol and retreat to a place of safety without physical support.

It wasn't a shock that Livilla and her courtesi went straight to Warlord's side. When a Lord became King, he lost his courtesi. Ashiol's Kingmaking had set his courteso Mars free, and Livilla snatched him up with glee. When Mars in turn became a Lord — the Warlord — they retained the bond between them, and had been allies and lovers even throughout her tortured relationship with Garnet.

Warlord glared at Livilla as she approached, perhaps holding a grudge for the easy way she had capitulated to Ashiol when he himself attacked. He did not move away from her though. Alliances in the Court were rare, and not lightly discarded.

'And where is our Poet?' Ashiol asked aloud. His eyes went to Priest, who shrugged, and then to Dhynar, who scowled at the ground.

Macready had been trying to work out which of these bloodsucking bastards was the greatest threat to Ashiol's safety, and to Velody's. Even with the attack made on Velody and Delphine at the theatre, it had not occurred to him until right now that Poet might be the wild card. Dhynar was the Lord Ashiol knew least, but no one had ever quite got inside Poet's head.

Where the saints and devils is he, now?

Macready risked a glance at Kelpie, who looked uncomfortable. This little gathering could seal Ashiol's position as Power and Majesty, or it could turn into an almighty cacking bloodbath.

Finally, there were footsteps. Poet strolled into the square and rocked back on his heels as he saw them all, pretending surprise. 'Sorry, did I miss an announcement?'

Priest rumbled a laugh.

Macready was too far back to see Ashiol's eyes, but he had no doubt what would be there. Garnet had never tolerated Poet's easy lack of respect, and if the last few days had reminded Macready of anything, it was the similarity between Ashiol and Garnet.

'Glad you could join us,' Ashiol said in the mildest of voices. 'Where are your courtesi, Poet?'

Poet glanced behind him, as if he almost expected Halberk and Zero to be there. 'Sorry, I seem to have mislaid them. Halberk's feeling a little under the weather, you know.' He ran his eye around the square. 'But then, I see you've left your mark on a few of us, kitten.'

It was a test, Macready realised. Poet was testing Ashiol to see how traditional a Power and Majesty he was going to be. Garnet would have made Poet bleed by now. Ortheus would have sent the sentinels to take a blood price out on Poet's courtesi. What would Ashiol do?

'Where are your boys, Poet?' growled the Creature King.

'Oh, somewhere safe, I imagine,' said the Creature Lord. 'They're not anywhere near Via Silviana, tormenting those favourite demmes of yours, if that's what you're worried about.'

'And I should take your word for that?'

'Why not?' replied Poet. 'My word's never steered you wrong before.'

'Take my word, if you prefer,' said a silvery female voice.

Macready's head jerked around in surprise as the seer walked into the square, urchin-like in a white petticoat and shawl, her hair cropped close to her scalp. Macready hardly recognised her.

They had been sentinels together, he and Heliora, before she was called to her higher purpose. Growing up in the Creature Court was a hard ride, and she had started earlier than most. Was it really fifteen years ago? She still looked like a teenager, while Macready was feeling his years.

'Interesting,' said Ashiol. 'An unexpected alliance.'

Heliora gave him a withering look. 'You know better than that, Ash. The seer has no loyalties, no allies. That's why her word is worth so much.' She moved towards him, drawing his gaze away from Poet.

This was certainly interesting. Macready had never been aware of any particular friendship between Poet and the seer before.

'So what words of wisdom do you have for your new Power and Majesty?' asked Ashiol, anger evident in his tone.

Heliora looked him up and down. 'Is that what you are? You keep saying that you want things to be different. That you don't want to repeat the mistakes of Garnet or Orpheus. Would either of them have failed to notice that the sky started falling two minutes ago?'

There was a long, heavy pause. Macready's senses in these matters were limited, but if he strained he could just catch the metallic hint in the air. From the look of them, the Lords and Court (who should have tasted it coming ten leagues away, every damned one of them) were all realising that the seer spoke the truth.

'Slow rain,' said Heliora in the silence. 'Followed by scratchlight, and if that isn't dealt with fast enough you'll have a full-blown skybattle on your hands.'

No one of the Court moved, waiting for Ashiol's command.

'Go,' he snarled in the deepest part of his throat. 'Get out there and save the city. It's what we do.'

'We haven't sworn allegiance,' said Dhynar.

'I will take your allegiance at the appropriate time,' said Ashiol. 'Right now, I want your obedience. Assuming you have that capacity?'

Dhynar fell apart, shaping himself into his gang of feraxes. His hounds and cats followed suit, and they tore off into the side streets of the Shambles.

Priest and his retinue shaped at the same time, their tailored suits falling empty to the ground as dozens of birds took flight out of their bodies. Pigeons, gulls, plovers and sparrows flocked together in the air before taking off up the tunnels.

Livilla went wolf and vanished into another side street, her courtesi following close behind in wolf and raven form. Warlord went with her in panther form, followed by a motley assortment of brocks, greymoon cats and flying bats.

The sentinels had not moved from where they stood at Ashiol's back.

Ashiol looked at Poet. 'Waiting for something?'

'I hate to see them leave, but like to watch them go,' said Poet with a smile. 'Such a pretty sight, don't you think?' He exploded into white rats and scattered, scampering in various directions until the last of him vanished into cracks and holes that led to the world outside and above.

Heliora glared at Ashiol. 'You made yourself look like a fool.' Ashiol took two steps and seized her throat in his hand.

Macready steeled himself not to move in her defence. Ashiol was his King. He owed no allegiance to Heliora. His blade twitched involuntarily, not liking this. Glancing aside, he saw that Kelpie's face was calm, not bothered. She had never liked Hel that much.

'So,' snarled Ashiol, squeezing the seer's throat until she gasped. 'All those times you die between now and Saturnalia, my Hel. Who gets to kill you?'

Heliora gazed at him, eyes wide and calm in her childlike face. 'Sometimes it's you, lover.'

ONCE ASHIOL JOINED the rest of the Court in the sky, Heliora turned her back on the Sentinels and returned to Poet's grocer shop. It didn't feel right to keep the clothes she had borrowed — it felt too much like owing him a favour.

In the attic, she stared at the glowing cage of skysilver and iron. Poet's two courtesi were imprisoned inside it, looking furious.

'What does he think he's doing?' she asked.

'Don't ask us,' grunted Halberk.

'He thinks the new Power and Majesty will make an example of someone this nox,' said Zero with an angry flicker in his eyes. 'Reckons it might be one of us.'

Halberk thumped the bars furiously, then leaped back as the skysilver sizzled against his hand. 'We should be protecting him! This is just stupid!'

'I can't let you out,' Heliora said, and not only because her throat still hurt from Ashiol's hand. Skysilver was nothing much to her, but she couldn't bend iron, and there was no sign of the key. 'For what it's worth, I don't think Poet put you in here to protect you.'

That, at least, got through Halberk's humiliation. 'What are you talking about?'

'She's the seer,' said Zero. 'She knows all sorts of stuff. What have you seen, demme?' he asked eagerly.

'Not a thing,' Heliora admitted. 'This isn't based on any vision of the futures. But from what I know about Poet and Ashiol... this is about provocation, not protection.'

Halberk blew out his lips, making a noise of disgust. 'Stupid skinny bastard's going to get himself killed.'

'Yes,' said Heliora, not liking this at all. Losing Poet now would unbalance all the futures she had seen. 'I rather think he will.'

3 2
THIRD DAY OF THE
FLORALIA (BRIDES)

NOX

*V*elody watched the city melt.

Every time a long silver dollop of 'slow rain' hit the cobbles or a building, it hissed and ate away at the stone. Metal was worse — when one silver drip hit a nearby gutter, it buckled and all but dissolved. The huge Basilica sagged under the weight of the rain. Several thin tiles fell from the dome's roof to shatter below.

'Does this happen often?' Velody demanded.

She and Crane took shelter under the overhang of the little church. Here, on the far crest of the Lucretine, they could see the whole north half of the city, from the Forum and the Lake of Follies all the way north-east to the rich residences that surrounded the Palazzo on the Balisquine hill.

'A couple of times a month,' said Crane, his eyes on the sky. 'Shouldn't last longer than half an hour, if we're lucky.'

'Half an hour? Half the city will be gone by then!'

'It's not as bad as you think.'

TANSY RAYNER ROBERTS

'And that's why we're cowering up here, because it's not as bad as I think? What would happen to us if we tried to walk 'You're Court, so it would burn a hole in you. Most humans could walk right through it and not feel a thing.'

'So, you're not trapped here. You're human, you could just...' She waved her hand expectantly.

'It's not that simple. Sentinels have some Creature Court in them. Comes from hanging around you lot. That stuff out there — well, it wouldn't kill us, but on a normal nox it would give us a nasty case of skyburn.'

'Sounds painful. But if it's not fatal, you can still save yourself.'

'That's the other thing,' Crane said, shifting uncomfortably.

Velody couldn't help wondering how old he was. He was so confident most of the time, like the rest of them, but his body language was downright boyish. 'What's the other thing?'

'Ashiol shared his blood with me,' he confessed in a rush. 'Last nox, to help me heal. That means there's more than a bit of Court in me right now, and the slow rain would comfortably slice me up like butter on a hot plate.'

'Oh,' said Velody. 'So we're both stuck here.'

'Aye.'

She paused for a long moment, thinking over what he had just said. 'When you say Ashiol shared his blood with you, what exactly do you mean?'

Crane opened his mouth, then closed it again. 'Look at that! Riding to the rescue.'

Annoyed that he was avoiding the question, Velody only glanced briefly out into the nox. What she saw captured her attention fully. The Creature Court. Before now it was an idea, a concept she could barely get her head around. But this was the Court in all its glory. They were quite a sight.

A flock of birds — pigeons, gulls, a host of other flying things she could not identify — burst out from somewhere near the Alexandrine hill, taking to the nox sky in a mad spiral. They dodged and dived around the drips of slow rain, never allowing the acid to touch them.

Birds weren't the only creatures in the air. Velody gasped as a series of dark shadows soared over the Avleurine — familiar shapes: hounds and cats and feraxes.

'They can fly,' she said in wonder. 'They can all fly.'

Crane laughed. 'A lot of use they'd be up there if they couldn't.'

Somewhere, wolves were howling. There was a cloud of ravens in the air above the Forum, and something like bats. Cats, of course, leaping from rooftops into the sky.

'But what are they doing?' asked Velody. 'If this slow rain can hurt them, why don't they go to ground until it's over?'

Crane looked at her strangely. 'They're the Creature Court. Their job is to stop the destruction that falls out of the sky. We're at war here.'

'But why? Why don't they leave? If it only affects the Court, why fight it?'

'You have heard of the Silent Sleep, haven't you?' asked Crane. 'Didn't you ever think it was strange — a disease that doesn't spread from person to person, or follow any known pattern, but flashes like lightning on random victims? Children mostly, or the elderly. The vulnerable and the weak.'

Velody had her mouth open. 'That... it comes from the sky?'

Crane turned back to the battle. 'If it wasn't for the Court, half of Aufleur would be Silent by now.' He inhaled, and looked troubled. 'There's something nasty in the air this nox. We shouldn't have another massacre for months yet, not after the show that took Garnet.'

'What do you mean, massacre?' The very word sent shivers through Velody's body.

'You'll see.'

The sky cracked open. Thin streaks of violent pink and amber shot through the darkness in wild, random patterns.

'Scratchlight,' said Crane, his breath catching in his throat.

'Is that bad?'

'It can be, if it catches them by surprise. Let's hope that the slow rain was enough of a warning.'

A thin bolt of light and fire slammed out of the sky, crashing into a house only a few streets below where Velody and Crane were standing. The roof exploded with the impact and the windows shattered.

Velody rocked back against the church wall, fear and horror pounding in her skull. 'That house, those people! You say this happens *all the time?*'

Crane gripped her arm, squeezing reassurance. 'Whoever is inside, they'll probably be fine. Scratchlight's pretty shallow stuff, it only kills one in fifty or so. They'll wake up tomorrow morning as if nothing has happened. For them, nothing has happened. Now, if it was shadowstreak or gleamspray, that's another matter. They're rarer though.'

'But the explosion, their house...' Velody longed to under-stand, but it was so hard to put it together in her mind. 'How could anyone survive that blast?'

'The city will heal itself, like it always does. That house will be back to normal by the first light of day. Even if it wasn't, the daylight folk wouldn't be able to tell the differ-ence. Skybattle isn't part of their world, Velody. It belongs to the nox.'

In the Gardens of Trajus Alysaundre below them, a rumbling bolt of scratchlight reduced several statues to rubble.

'So the nox is the world of the Creature Court,' said Velody.

'Exactly. Scratchlight's mild stuff for daylight folk — mostly survivable — but it's like liquid fire to the flesh of one of our lot.'

'Then what are they doing out here? Why does the first sign of a sky attack bring the Court out here where they could get hurt or killed? How do they save the city, nox after nox?'

'Don't you get it?' asked Crane. 'They're not helpless when they use their powers. Animor provides some defence, and seven hells of offence. They're fighting the sky.'

Was that what they were doing? To Velody it looked like a wild dance, birds and mammals alike weaving in and out of the danger, a bizarre mixed menagerie putting themselves in the line of fire for no good reason.

As she watched, though, a huge black cat — a panther? — leaped directly at a stabbing thread of amber light, his jaws outstretched as if to bite it firmly between his sharp teeth. The impact hit him hard, flung him down near the Lake of Follies and out of sight, but a few minutes later he was in the sky again, and he had the wriggling amber thread caught firmly in his mouth.

Velody squeezed Crane's arm as the panther spat the amber thread back into the sky. It struck close to the wide fissure that was the source of the threads, and there was a light so blinding that Velody had to close her eyes.

'Excellent!' crowed Crane. 'They don't call him Warlord for nothing!'

The sky seemed aware that this man was a particular danger and several bolts of pink and amber spat in his direction. The panther shaped himself into a glowing man and stretched out his hands in readiness.

By the time the bolts reached him, he had help. Nine or

ten greymoon cats, a medley of flapping bats and several furry mammals Velody didn't recognise gathered around their Lord, supporting him with their presence. They all hit out at the storm of scratchlight, batting the bolts back into the sky. There was a louder, brighter explosion than the first.

These little battles were happening all over the city skyline. Turning one way and then another, trying to see everything all at once, Velody was eventually able to tell which were the Lords and which were their courtesi by the way they flocked together and the deference they showed each other. There were four Lords at work, in the centre of it all — panther, wolves, pigeons and feraxes. The rest were courtesi.

A new fissure opened, to the east above the Balisquine. Blue and green scratchbolts shimmered forth, fast and flickering. Before any of the Court could get there, a blazing white figure emerged from below, shooting upwards and into battle against the new threat. A fifth Lord.

'The Orphan Princel,' said Velody, somehow not surprised. 'Poet. Where are his courtesi?'

'Who knows? He's in trouble without them though.'

The glowing white figure of Poet was buried in a wriggling, tangled mass of scratchlight.

'Isn't someone going to help him?' Velody demanded.

Crane gave her a strange look. 'Isn't he the one who attacked you and your friends?'

Velody had half-forgotten, she was so wrapped up in watching this battle. 'Someone should still help him,' she muttered.

The Lord of Pigeons evidently agreed. He formed himself into Lord form — a large, round shape glowing with power — and flew to extract Poet from the scratchlight.

Another building crumbled — the Cathedral of Lucipher in the Portico Lattorio. Velody saw the outline of the

Duchessa's Palazzo on the Balisquine shudder as a bolt of scratchlight destroyed one of its ornamental towers, then a second.

Can they really sleep through all this? she thought. *Then, How many noxes like this have I slept through?*

Not everyone was sleeping. It was Aufleur, after all, the city of lanterns and late nox revels.

Below Velody, in the Gardens of Trajus Alysaundre, a small party made their lopsided way home from a nox on the town, led by a pair of lampboys. Several tipsy demoiselles dressed in the latest fashions lurched along with their bare arms hooked around each other. There were a few young men with them, staggeringly drunk. None of them seemed to notice the damage from the scratchlight — the broken statues and charred ground.

A crackle of flaming green energy slashed the grass only a few feet from them and the party didn't flinch. A bolt of scratchlight struck one of the demoiselles, exploding so fiercely that Velody expected her bobbed hair to burst into flames at the very least. The demme didn't notice a thing. The group continued to giggle and flirt with each other, in their own little world.

What world am I in? Velody couldn't help wondering. Theirs made more sense than the one she currently inhabited.

Across the city, near the Balisquine, birds flocked to their Pigeon Lord. He and Poet were in trouble. The blue and green scratchlight poured harder and faster down onto them. One of the gulls was hit by a stray bolt and vaporised with a shriek. The other gulls fell back as if they felt its pain.

'I should be out there,' Velody whispered, only just realising that. 'I should be fighting alongside them, shouldn't I?'

'You wouldn't last a minute,' said Crane.

A faint glow was coming from him. Velody realised that

he was holding his skysilver knife at the ready. In the darkness, it shone as if it held its own source of light.

'What's that for?' she asked.

'Deflection, defence. In case we need it.'

'We're not the ones who need help,' she said, staring at the battle between the Creature Court and the sky.

'They already have a King who should be defending them,' said Crane. 'Ask yourself where he is.'

A howling, tearing sound came up from underneath the city. The church behind them trembled, as did every building in Aufleur.

'He's coming,' said Velody, and didn't even question how she knew.

Ashiol roared up out of the smashed towers on the Balisquine. He was in chimaera form, a black and deadly shape of fur and feathers and claws, and pure, blinding rage. A monster in the truest sense of the word.

Velody had never been so glad to see anyone in her life.

Ashiol tore through the scratchlight as if it were spun sugar. He bit and clawed and fought his way to the wriggling threads of light that had overwhelmed Poet and the Pigeon Lord. When he threw stray fragments at the blue fissure above the Balisquine, it shrieked with pain and began to seal closed.

Above the Lake of Follies, Warlord fought the first fissure with renewed energy. He was supported by the Ferax Lord and a female Wolf Lord, along with their combined mob of courtesi.

With a last gasp of an explosion, the first scratchlight fissure closed up, leaving the sky around it blank and clean. A moment or two later, Ashiol hurled the last of the flaming fragments into the Balisquine fissure and it, too, disappeared into the sky.

There was a long moment of silence. It was almost calm.

Velody turned her eyes up to the bleak nox sky. What further horrors were lurking up there? Did each of the twinkling stars conceal a new enemy, a terrible threat or burning weapon to bring danger down upon them?

She had never thought much about the sky before. Now she knew how much she had to fear from it.

Ashiol, Poet and the Pigeon Lord descended to the sloping gardens of the Balisquine. The bird courtesi followed, shaping themselves into young women. When the surviving gulls came together, the woman who emerged from them looked wan and sickly. She fell to the grass, her body heaving and shaking. After a moment, her body broke apart into gulls again.

'She's lost part of herself,' said Velody. 'What will happen to her?'

'Usually if an animal is killed it can still be reabsorbed,' said Crane. 'Her gull was obliterated, though. She has to shape her body with less mass than she's used to — give up a hand, or some body weight, even some bone marrow. It will be a while before she recovers.'

Velody couldn't help thinking of the thousands of mice she could transform herself into. It would be so easy to lose one or two. She shuddered as she imagined mouse-shaped holes punched into her human flesh. 'Is it over then? For the nox?'

'Hard to say. The air still feels... I don't know. I'm not used to having such strong Court senses.'

In the Balisquine gardens, the Pigeon Lord carried several of the gulls, allowing them to perch on his bulky shoulders and hands. His other two courtesi took the remaining gulls onto their own bodies. They walked in solemn procession down into the city streets and Velody lost sight of them.

'What happens now?' she asked.

'Might be the danger is just beginning.'

Before she could ask Crane what he meant by that, Velody saw Ashiol. Still in his black chimaera form, he flew a slow, leisurely lap around the northern heights of the city, then another. When his circles brought him for a third time over the Gardens of Trajus Alysaundre, he descended to the grass and reverted to his human form, waiting.

The Panther, Ferax and Wolf Lords all gathered their courtesi and flew to him, each landing a respectful distance away and also reverting to human form. After several more minutes, Poet Lord Rat joined them, putting more distance than most between himself and Ashiol. He did not lose his Lord form, continuing to glow fiercely white.

A longer while passed, and the Pigeon Lord arrived on the wing, surrounded by his flying retinue. This time, his gull courtesa managed to pull herself back into human form and stay there. Pale and shaking, she was supported by the other two women who had been sparrows and plovers.

Velody couldn't help wondering, if that tipsy mob of revellers were to stagger through the Gardens of Trajus Alysaundre now, would they notice that it was full of naked people?

The Creature Court stood among the rubble of the statues that had been destroyed by scratchlight. As Velody watched, the fallen shards of marble shifted and moved as if they were autumn leaves twisting in the breeze. She was amazed to see the statues slowly reconstituting themselves, the broken pieces and marble dust floating back together as if reversing the damage that the sky had hurled down on them.

'Is Ash doing that?' she asked.

'No,' said Crane, a note of pride in his voice. 'Aufleur does it all by itself. Look.'

He gestured to the nearby house that had been obliterated by a blast from the sky. The roof tiles were coming together, crumbs and broken pieces snapping back until they were as good as new, then flying up to take their proper place. The whole house was healing, bricks and mortar crunching back into position. It happened all over the city. Even the gutters of the porch they stood under were unmelting, straightening, the marks of slow rain being erased from them.

'As if it never happened,' Velody said. 'Was it all some kind of hallucination?'

'Oh, it was real enough,' said Crane. 'Damson will take a long time to recover from losing one of her gulls. If any of them had lost their battle, they would have been killed for good.'

'But none of the damage is permanent,' said Velody, trying to understand.

Crane hunched up against the wall of the church. 'Ever heard of a city called Tierce?'

Velody felt as if she had been stabbed. *Tierce*. All afternoon and evening, working with Delphine and Rhian, she had fought the urge to test their memories, to see if it was really true that they did not remember a single detail about their friends and families and the city all three of them had grown up in. She knew it was true though. Until today, she had not remembered Tierce herself.

'Tell me about it,' she said softly.

'It was our nearest neighbour — the capital of the duchy of Reyenna.'

Velody frowned. 'Isn't Reyenna one of the northern baronies? It shouldn't even have a city.'

She had two sets of memories overlapping each other — the Velody who remembered nothing before she came to Aufleur, and the Velody who had written to her family every week, and loved Rhian's brother Cyniver. A rush of memories came back to her — his hands, the smell of his hair...

'You're going to have to trust me on this,' said Crane.

'Ammoria had three duchies once, each with a capital city. Bazeppe of Silano, Aufleur of Lattorio and Tierce of Reyenna. But the Creature Court of Tierce lost their fight. The last of them died, and there was no one to battle against the sky.'

'I've never heard of Tierce before today,' said Velody, choosing her words carefully. 'How long ago was this?'

'Five years ago,' said Crane. 'It was only two hours from Aufleur by rail, Velody. And no one of the daylight remembers that it ever existed. Tierce wasn't just wiped from the land, it was wiped from history.' He laughed bitterly. 'I was nine years old when I was sent to the workhouse here in Aufleur. I was lucky — our village was halfway between here and Reyenna. It could just as easily have been Tierce that I was sent to. That's where my brothers went. If it wasn't for the Court, I wouldn't remember them at all. My father died last year thinking I had always been his only son.'

'I'm sorry,' said Velody, knowing that it was inadequate. Her mind was racing. Five years ago, she and Delphine and Rhian had completed their apprenticeships, and Delphine was given a house, but couldn't remember the aunt who had given it to her.

Crane shrugged, as if it were an old wound that didn't hurt much any more. 'There are people walking around Aufleur who were born in Tierce and they don't remember anything about it. They have blanks where their history should be. That's why the Creature Court fights the sky. That's why I serve them. It could happen to Aufleur if they fail.'

'They don't strike me as the heroic type,' said Velody.

Down in the Gardens of Trajus, the Court began some kind of ritual. Ashiol approached each of the Lords and courtesi in turn, touching his lips to their foreheads.

Macready and Kelpie stood behind him, the only ones who were clothed.

'Oh, it's self-interest all the way,' said Crane. 'They like this city. It's theirs. Their powers are all tangled up in having a city to defend. There's no point to them without their mission.'

'Can we get closer?' Velody asked, to stop herself telling him, *I was born in Tierce. Garnet stole that memory from me along with everything else.* 'I want to hear what he's saying.'

33

THIRD DAY OF THE
FLORALIA (BRIDES)

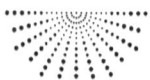

NOX

*a*fter a battle, it was the task of the Power and
Majesty to examine each member of the Creature
Court for damage and bestow his kiss of approval. Ashiol
had never done it before, but he managed the ceremony
smoothly enough. When Mars, Livilla, Priest, Dhynar and all
of their courtesi had been cleansed, Ashiol finally turned to
Poet. Poet still wore his Lord form, flouting convention. He
had always been expert at casual insolence.

'And you, Poet,' said Ashiol. 'Where were your courtesi in
this skybattle?'

'Sorry about that, kitten,' said Poet. 'I'm a little wary of
letting my boys near you since you bit one of their throats
out. You understand.'

'Are you saying that you deliberately withheld them from
battle?'

Poet smiled.

'It's a question of loyalty,' said Ashiol. 'Where is your loyalty, Lord of Rats?'

'My loyalty is with the Power and Majesty, always, unquestioning,' said Poet, his voice rising. 'Who are you to ask me that? You have taken no oaths, and neither have we. Are we expected to follow you into battle without the blindest knowledge of what you are to us? Where is your loyalty, Creature King?'

Ashiol stared at the younger man, genuinely surprised at his heat. When had Poet started caring? He was always the one most likely to mock their higher purpose, puncturing the ego of anyone who took the world too seriously.

Poet's voice was ragged as he addressed the whole Court. 'Ashiol didn't come back to lead us into battle! He happened to be here. Every spare moment since Garnet died, this so-called Creature King of ours has been hunting the streets for someone else to rule in his place, a demoiselle with less sky experience than the youngest of our courtesi!'

This was evidently no surprise to Dhynar, Priest or Mars, but no one had passed the intelligence on to Livilla. 'A demoiselle?' she repeated.

'A female King,' agreed Poet. 'And did our Ash bring this miracle, this marvel, to us to decide what to do with her? No, he hid her away so that he could train her in secret to be the Power and Majesty he knows he can never be!'

'You go too far, Poet,' said Ashiol. His control of the situation was slipping. Could he get through this without tearing Poet's throat out?

'And what are you going to do to me, Majesty?'

It was a challenge that had to be answered.

Ashiol rolled his power over the Creature Lord, crushing Poet's animor with the immense weight of his own. Poet fell to his knees with the pressure, eyes and mouth wide. A blood vessel burst in the white of his left eye, and he made a noise

that was half-gasp and half-laugh. 'Oh, that felt good, sweetling. Do it again.'

With a growl, Ashiol seized Poet by the throat and lifted
him high into the air. Poet was shorter, and he dangled from
the Creature King's hand like a broken puppet.

'I didn't want you to be the one that I made an example
of,' said Ashiol, gritting his teeth. 'But I am here to stay, Poet.
My moment of weakness is over. I will be the Power and
Majesty, and you will regret challenging me.'

It was better, at least, than the 'this will hurt me more
than it hurts you' line that he had once heard Garnet deliver
with only a faint trace of irony.

Something crossed Poet's face, an expression that Ashiol
didn't have time to decipher because he was busy forming his
free hand into a long black claw that gleamed with the dark
light of the chimaera.

'That's more like it,' Poet managed to rasp. 'Scare the shit
out of them, kitten.'

Ashiol drove the claw into Poet's stomach and twisted
hard. Poet screamed, his body twitching wildly.

It was hard, to keep the claw inside and twisting, to
deliver heat and pain into a horribly responsive body. It was
the hardest thing Ashiol had ever done in his life. Sweat
dripped into his eyes and, when he looked again, it was not
the Poet of now that he saw but the defensive, wide-eyed
child who had first been brought into Tasha's household. The
noise coming from the young man now was not even a
scream, but the moan of an animal in pain.

'Stop it!'

For a moment, Ashiol thought he was hallucinating. What
was Velody doing here? It couldn't actually be her standing
in the midst of the Creature Court.

She wasn't in Lord form. She was just herself, in a shapeless black gown and sandals, dark hair tangled around her face, large grey eyes wide and streaked with tears.

'Stop it, Ash,' she said again, so forcefully that he felt her animor uncurl within her body.

The other Lords felt it too. They stared at her as she approached.

Ashiol let go of Poet's throat and lowered his claw, letting the Creature Lord's body slide wetly to the grass with a thump. There was blood everywhere. Without Poet's courtesi to assist him, he might die of this. *Am I monster enough to let him? If not, why the frig not?*

'This is the way we do things,' he said aloud to Velody. 'This is what the Creature Court is.'

'Who is this demme, Ash?' asked Livilla, piercing as ever. 'What right does she have to speak to you like this?'

'If you had been listening, my dear,' said Priest, 'you would know exactly who she is.'

Velody had eyes and ears only for Ashiol. 'Why is this the way you do things?' she asked, her face raw and filled with horror. 'How do you even know this is the right way? Have you ever tried anything else?'

'Think you could do it better?' Ashiol challenged, seeing his chance.

That stopped her. 'No.'

He flung out an arm and threw a thread of animor at the nearest courtesa, who happened to be Priest's gull. The energy struck the demme on the left side and she screamed as it exploded in her face, throwing her to the ground. The smell of charred flesh filled the air. Priest and his other courtesi went to her side, holding her close and keeping her alive. *Where the hells are Poet's courtesi? Will they let him bleed to death? No one else here can raise a hand to help him without looking weak.*

'Now do you think you can do it better?' Ashiol asked in a steady voice.

'That's what you want me to say,' said Velody. 'I won't let you bully me into this.'

'Why not? Bullying is what we do.' Ashiol smiled, a genuine smile. He was wrong from the start. She wasn't the one to take Garnet's place as Power and Majesty. How could she? 'You were right, Velody. You don't have the stomach for this.'

Her grey eyes blazed, and she moved her hand as if to slap him.

Ashiol didn't see it coming. There was a fierce burst of light and then he was on his back, coughing. The scent of her animor overwhelmed him as he struggled to recover from the blast, and he tried not to think about how long it took him to master the trick that she had copied from him in a matter of seconds.

A new weight pressed on his chest as Velody set a sandalled foot over his ribcage. 'Ashiol Xandelian,' she said in a cold voice, 'you don't know me at all.'

He saw it, in that moment. Overlaying her sweet, angry face, he saw the truth of it. He wasn't the one that the Creature Court needed to be afraid of. Velody could be the monster after all. She might be frigging good at it.

IT WAS EASY. Velody was horrified at seeing Ashiol dispense pain so casually upon another person, and yet a cold part of her brain noted exactly how he drew the animor from within himself — only a little, not enough that he would miss it — and formed it into a destructive missile. It was a manoeuvre, that was all, something as simple as casting on a stitch or fitting a patchwork piece into place. Having seen him put it into practice, it was easy to turn his move against him and strike him down with this dark, sizzling power she was only beginning to recognise inside herself.

Then he was on the ground, and Velody stood over him. She was in Lord form, glowing with the strength of her own inner power. 'Ashiol Xandelian, you don't know me at all.'

'None of us know you,' broke in a refined voice — the Pigeon Lord, she thought. 'Who are you, demoiselle?'

She turned and looked at them. Poet was crumpled on the grass, coughing blood from his mouth even as more bubbled up from the gaping wound in his stomach. The other Lords glowed with the spirit of their animor and their creature. The Wolf Lord had pointed teeth behind her dark red lipstick, and she stood in a mannikin pose as if she was aware of exactly how good she looked naked. Like Delphine, she probably half-starved herself to mould her body into the new slender fashion for women. Her hair was certainly in line with the current mode — black and sharply bobbed.

The Panther Lord bristled with dark hair down his arms and stomach. His stance was defensive, perhaps because of the nasty scars and raw skin across his body. It looked as if his stomach had recently been ripped apart and put back together. *Ash did that*, Velody realised, scenting a trace of Ashiol's animor on the Panther Lord's skin. The Pigeon Lord stood as if unaware of his nakedness, unself- conscious of his large, bulging stomach and drooping penis. His arms were bulky too, but there was firm muscle there beneath the fat. He raised an eyebrow at Velody, as if waiting for a polite answer to his polite question.

'My name is Priest,' he said. 'Whom is it that we are honoured to address this nox?'

Kelpie and Macready stood at the back of the crowd of naked courtesi. Crane joined them now. All three sentinels had their skysilver blades at the ready, and Velody knew they would defend her if she needed them to.

But this was her fight.

'I'm Velody,' she said, and couldn't think of anything else to add.

An intense sensation like a headache rolled over the top of her scalp, and she looked up a few seconds before everyone else. Something boiled out of the sky, a dark red cloud that did not look as though it belonged there.

Dealing with this crisis was suddenly more tempting than thinking of something witty or threatening or conciliatory to say to the Creature Court. Velody pulled her dress off over her head and kicked her sandals to the grass before turning chimaera and leaping headfirst up into the sky.

She had barely practised this form, but it felt like an old skill. She knew exactly how to push her animor against the firm gravity of the earth to launch herself impossibly high, catching the slightest eddies and breezes with her powerful, expert wings to propel herself higher and faster. The impossibility of it dizzied her, but there was little point in worrying about that now. *The word 'impossible' is for daylight, apparently. Not nox.*

The red cloud pulled Velody towards it like a lantern in the fog. She spun and danced higher into the air. Reaching the danger was not a problem. *What the saints do I do when I get there?*

She wasn't alone. A second black figure swooped at her side, a chimaera who throbbed with familiar power. *Unless you'd like to handle this yourself?* a thought-voice suggested.

Are you kidding? she shot back. I have no idea what I'm doing!

It's simple enough, sent Ashiol. *The red cloud is the seed of a deathstorm. If we stop it now, we can save ourselves having to battle devils, angels and flaming hail all nox.*

Real angels and devils?

Let's concentrate on the current threat, shall we? Deal with philosophy later. There's one tried and true method to vanquishing a skyseed. The theory is something like lancing a boil.

Velody winced at the thought of it. *As long as I don't end up covered in pus.*

She couldn't see any facial expressions in his black and shapeless chimaera form, but she felt him smile. *Maybe you'd better wait for me on the ground.*

Oh hells.

Not today, I hope. Can you form a couple of long, sharp claws?

Velody thought of the claw that Ashiol had formed to gut Poet with. *I think so.*

Right. We aim for the centre of the cloud. As much force as you can manage. Throw everything you have into the blow.

Everything? Won't we need some animor left to fly down?

This is a tricky thing to try — best not hold anything back. With any luck, the Creature Lords will catch us if we completely drain ourselves.

She thought of Poet bleeding on the grass, the outrage on Priest's face as his gull courtesa was hurt, and the arrogant expressions of the Wolf and Panther Lords. *We're relying on that lot to save our lives?*

They're surprisingly good at that sort of thing.

They were close to the red cloud now. Its boiling, swirling substance was beginning to fold a second colour into its dark centre, an odd purplish shade.

Now, before it's too late! sent Ashiol. *One, two... three!*

In that instant, as they drove long clawed limbs into the centre of the dark cloud, it was as if their minds were connected, as if they had merged bodies and spirits. Velody could feel herself inside Ashiol's skin, taste the blood in his arteries.

He didn't say whether we were going on three or after three, she thought stupidly. *I knew anyway. This is all a little too close for comfort.*

You're telling me, sent Ashiol as their claws tore harder into the core of the skyseed.

There was a loud squelching sound, and Velody was back in her body again — her real body, wet and vulnerable. *Wet?* There was a sticky, gluey substance all over her skin, her face and hair, but that was less disturbing than the fact that she was falling out of the sky like an acorn in autumn.

A shockwave jolted through her body. Her arm screamed with pain so fierce that she thought it had been pulled clear off. But, no. Ashiol had caught her by the hand. She hung limply from him as he hovered in the air, his Lord form still intact.

She tried to think a response to him, but that didn't seem to work without their chimaera bodies to interpret. 'Well,' she gasped, after coughing to clear her throat of the sticky sky fluid. 'Now we know.'

'Know what?' he asked, unsmiling, making no attempt to catch hold of her by anything other than her single hand.

'Which of us is more powerful. That skyseed wiped me out, and you still have enough in you to hold on to your Lord form.'

'No,' said Ashiol. 'You're wrong, Velody. I didn't drain all my powers into the cloud because *you didn't give me the chance*. You poured yourself so damn fast into that claw of yours, I couldn't keep up.'

She stared up at him. 'What does that mean?'

It was hard to see facial expressions while dangling in midair, but she thought she saw a twist of a grin cross Ashiol's mouth. 'Means you're better than me, demoiselle dressmaker.'

Before she could respond to that piece of abject nonsense, Ashiol hauled her up into his arms and held her tightly around the ribcage as he lowered them both slowly to the ground.

For the first time, Velody was very much aware of the fact that they were both naked. It was hard to miss when you were holding each other this tightly. As soon as their feet touched the grass of the Gardens of Trajus Alysaundre, Ashiol opened his arms and released her so quickly that she almost fell over.

All eyes were on them. No, all eyes were on Velody. She stared defiantly back at the open curiosity of the Lords and Court, wishing her nipples were not so obviously hard.

Crane came to her rescue, holding out the crumpled black dress that she had cast aside. She pulled it on over her head, not caring about the effect that the sky mucus would have on the garment, only wanting to be clothed.

Macready came forward with her sandals and gave her a little smirk. She rolled her eyes at him, but was glad to pull her gaze away from the leering Creature Court long enough to slip the shoes onto her feet. Her wet, sticky hair slapped her back as she straightened up.

Were they waiting for her to say something? Her attention was caught by the fallen figure of Poet. He made no sound, but his wide eyes showed that he was still, painfully, alive. The grass around him was soaked with his blood.

Velody cleared her throat. 'I appreciate that I am of a great deal of interest, but did any of you consider helping him?'

As one, the Lords' gaze switched to Ashiol.

'They didn't want to displease me,' he said. 'I caused the wounds and they don't want to anger me by healing him. Even Dhynar, whom Poet called ally, didn't dare make a move without my consent.' He shot a mocking look at the Ferax Lord, who looked away. 'The protocol in these instances is for the Lord's courtesi to keep him alive until the

King decides what to do with him, but Poet deliberately kept his courtesi away this nox. Bad luck for him.'

Velody turned on Ashiol. 'You could heal him. You healed Crane. Why are you even hesitating?'

'Crane received his injuries defending innocents — defending the home of a Creature King,' said Ashiol.

'Poet received his injuries from you!' she said angrily. 'You should fix this.'

'Then what would be the point of making an example of him?'

Furious, Velody raised her hand to slap him, but he caught it quickly, squeezing her wrist so hard that it hurt.

'If you won't help him, then I will!' she said. 'It's all about sharing blood, right? I'll give him some of mine.'

Ashiol squeezed her wrist even harder. 'You can't. After draining yourself in the sky, you can't afford to lose any blood. You're vulnerable, Velody. There's barely a whisper of active animor left in you right now.'

Velody threw her other hand at him, trying to prise herself loose. He held fast, but she snapped her teeth at him and he opened his hand in reflex. She skipped back out of range. 'I'm still a Creature King, right? My blood will help him heal.'

'Yes,' Ashiol said reluctantly.

'So don't stop me helping him!'

'This is the Lord who attacked you and your friend in the theatre. He allied with Dhynar Lord Ferax, who beat Crane to a pulp and scared your other friend half to death. Why would you want to help him?'

'If I don't, he might die,' said Velody. She was half-expecting Ashiol to make another try at physically stopping her, but he watched with a strange look on his face as she knelt down beside Poet, pulling him into her arms. 'I'm not entirely sure how to do this,' she confessed, holding her wrist near his mouth. 'I don't have a knife.'

She glanced over her shoulder at the sentinels. Crane looked ashamed. Kelpie crossed her arms. Macready just slowly shook his head.

Velody took a deep breath. 'You'll have to bite,' she said. 'You can do that, can't you?'

Poet was staring at her. A little blood ran from the corner of his mouth. His chin was stained with it. Slowly, as if every movement caused agony, he nodded his head. He was not strong enough to go all the way into Lord form, but his eyes gleamed red and his incisors slowly lengthened to points.

Velody pressed her wrist to his mouth, preparing herself for a moment of pain. 'Well, then.'

Poet stopped glowing. His eyes and teeth faded to normal. He moved his head slightly from side to side.

'Why not?' she demanded.

Gently, he leaned into her wrist and kissed it. Mumbled words came from his mouth so quietly that she could barely hear them.

'I swear oath and allegiance to Velody as Power and Majesty, master of the Creature Court, King of Kings, over-lord of all.'

'Drink!' she said in frustration, but Poet closed his eyes and once again shook his head slightly.

'Stay close, sweetling,' he whispered. 'You're going to need all the juice you can get.'

She could feel his animor building inside him, like a spirit preparing to flee a dead body. *I don't want this*, she thought. *I don't want this.*

Poet was dragged roughly away from her. Velody gazed upwards, too exhausted to fight as Ashiol, glowing in Lord form, lifted Poet into his arms. With a growl, he extended his fingernail into a sharp, glowing white point and sliced at his own throat, holding Poet's slack mouth to the welling blood.

Poet drank, his mouth coming greedily alive, sucking and biting hard into the wound, his skinny body clinging to Ashiol's large muscular form like a spider.

Velody felt her whole body heave in revulsion. *What am I doing?* she thought desperately. *I was going to let him do that to me!* It was as if this whole crazy nox of battles and animor and excessive nudity, had finally driven her crazy. *I have to get out of here!*

She crawled backwards on the grass, trying to put some distance between herself and the horrible sight of Ashiol feeding Poet his blood. As she moved, Ashiol's eyes blazed down at her and she found herself caught in his gaze. He was saying something, but Velody was too dizzy and sickened to realise what until she recognised that the words were familiar.

'I swear oath and allegiance to Velody as Power and Majesty, master of the Creature Court, King of Kings, over-lord of all.'

Ashiol came down to Velody's level, falling to his knees. He batted Poet away as if he were an annoying moth, and Poet rolled free on the grass, his face now sticky with Ash's blood as well as his own. Poet's torso was still a mess, blood-stained and bulging with scar tissue, but the stomach wound was no longer open.

Still thinking of escape, Velody pushed her unsteady way to her feet, only to find that everyone — every Lord and all the courtesi of the Creature Court as well as the three sentinels — was on their knees. 'What are you all doing?' she demanded. Her voice sounded unfamiliar to her.

'They await their turn to pledge allegiance to the new Power and Majesty,' said Ashiol, thumbing blood from his neck. 'And that would be you.'

'You planned this!' Velody yelled at him.

Ashiol laughed, an honest laugh that recognised the absurdity of the situation. 'How in the seven hells could I possibly have planned *this*?'

She whirled on the rest of them, glaring equally at the four standing Creature Lords and their servile courtesi. 'I know I'm not welcome here, but guess what? I don't want to be part of your crazy little gang with all the blood and the skybattles and the handbook of bloodthirsty etiquette. I just want to go home and be left alone.'

She shot a disgusted look over her shoulder at Ashiol. 'You know what I'm capable of. I know their faces now. If I see any of them within a hundred paces of my home, I will kill them. It probably won't hurt, but it will be very, very fast.'

'Let's try her out,' said an unexpected voice.

Velody whirled around, to meet the calm gaze of Priest, the Pigeon Lord. 'What?' she demanded.

'To my mind, my dear, not wanting to be Power and Majesty makes you the sanest of all of us.'

'That's what I've been saying,' said Ashiol.

'You keep out of this,' Velody threatened.

Priest turned to the others. 'Livilla, Warlord, young Dhynar — you've all expressed doubts about our Ashiol being able to take up the mantle of dear, departed Garnet. Perhaps it's time we tried something new. Something different.'

'Is she up to it?' asked the Wolf Lord, Livilla.

'We've seen how powerful she is,' said Priest, pointing to the sky. 'No doubt she'd be an asset up there. She's equally new to us all, which gives us an even chance of finding favour. And there's a hint of self-sacrifice in the mix, very touching. I think we could do worse.' He lowered his head and started speaking the words. 'I swear oath and allegiance to Velody as Power and Majesty...'

Before he had reached the end, Dhynar was speaking the words, and the Panther Lord, and even — after a longer, more sullen pause — Livilla. Their courtesi chimed in at different times, making a rattling orchestral hum of words that Velody did not want to hear. She held her hands over her ears, hoping to block it all out.

Cool hands encircled her wrists, pulling her hands away. Her first thought was that it was Ashiol, but the scent told her differently. Poet was on his feet, standing behind her, forcing her to hear the chaotic chorus of allegiance. 'Listen to them,' he said, his breath tickling in her ear. 'These may well be the most important words you ever hear.'

Velody stood there, shivering in her black dress, waiting until the last of the Creature Court had finished saying the words that made them hers, and made her belong irretrievably to them. Poet's arms were cool, but they offered a breath of comfort, something slightly real to hang on to.

'This is a truly bad idea,' she said, when there was silence.

'Don't worry about it,' said Ashiol, sounding a long way away. 'This is the easy part. Tomorrow is when it gets difficult.'

PART III
MAJESTY

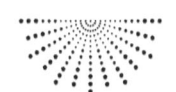

FOURTH DAY OF THE FLORALIA
(DUTY TO HOUSEHOLD GODS)

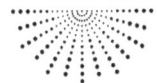

DAYLIGHT

*I*sangell, First Lady of the Silver Seal and Duchessa d'Aufleur, loved her mother very much. At moments like these it was important to remember that fact, to prevent her from fulfilling the urge to pick up a steel fruit slice and stab her mother in the neck.

'And then there's the Leorgette boy,' continued Eglantine, former Ducomtessa d'Aufleur. 'Very young, of course, but they say he's promising enough, and it would be easier for you to maintain control of a younger husband.'

'Mama, he's fourteen.'

'Exactly. He'll be so grateful to you for choosing him over all the others, he won't interfere with the running of the city.'

Isangell sat as she always did, the tea table pulled close to her pretty floral settee so she could sit in comfort with her feet tucked under her. Her mother, in contrast, sat primly on a straight-backed chair in order to demonstrate how a well-brought-up lady should behave. It was morning, the first sunlit hour of the fourth day of Floralia, the day devoted to the household gods. Tomorrow, marriages would be consummated all across the city and passion celebrated in all its forms.

'I want a proclamation made,' Isangell said, buttering a thin triangle of toast.

Choosing to breakfast privately in her room instead of the ducal family dining hall was her first decision as Duchessa. The most unhappy times of her childhood had been the meals in that large draughty room. Unfortunately, her mother never took the hint that Isangell preferred to spend the first hour of the day on her own.

'A proclamation?' repeated Eglantine, her teacup halting just short of her lips. 'Oh, darling, you mean about Jordan Leorgette?'

'No,' Isangell said, shuddering at the thought of that lanky youth putting his hands on her. 'About my marriage. I would like to formally announce that I will not choose my husband until I am twenty-one.'

Her mother blinked. 'But that's two years away.'

'I know. It's only sensible, Mama. It gives me the breathing space to make the right decision.' Isangell had been thinking about this for a while now. 'Take the upcoming Shadows Ball. If the Great Families think I might decide on a husband any day now, whomever I choose as my escort will be of huge political significance. If they know the decision is two years away, they're less likely to create a civil war over who gets to be my dance partner.'

Eglantine looked dubious. 'My darling, do you really think —'

'In fact,' Isangell said brightly, 'I should send a letter to each Head of Family asking them to propose one candidate to be my husband. That immediately cuts the possibilities down to eleven. With two years at my disposal, I can give each of them equal time for escort duty to major festivals, to be seen with me and for me to get to know them. No one can say I haven't been fair when I make my final decision, and I can be sure of making the best possible choice.'

Eglantine was staring at her daughter as if she had suddenly grown two heads and bobbed the hair of both. 'That all seems very... rational, darling.'

'You mean cold. What did you expect, Mama? I was raised in this household.'

'That's cruel.'

'Is it? You taught me about being a lady and how that mostly means flattering men. You taught me to be polite at all times, and to be seen to be modest and unthreatening. While you were doing that, Grandmama taught me how to rule.' Isangell felt suddenly very sad. 'When Grandpapa fell sick, she took on the role of Regenta like she was born to it. A woman can do things differently to a man because people expect less of her. They expect her to follow her heart and be sentimental and to let things like love and family and wistful little dreams affect her ability to make the tough choices. Between the two of you, you taught me that if a woman is polite and apologetic and ladylike at all times, she can get away with just about anything. I intend to make the Great Families damn well wait to find out which of their sons will be brought into this family, *and* I intend to choose the husband least likely to get in my way while I do my job.'

Isangell took a deep breath and sipped her cup of tea.

'I see,' said Eglantine in a stiff voice. 'Well, my dearling, it seems as if you know what you are doing.'

'Yes, Mama, I think I do.'

'Have you thought about your heir in the meantime?'

Isangell was surprised. 'Is that necessary?'

'People die, Isangell,' said her mother. 'You are young and healthy and you probably imagine you will live forever, but

TANSY RAYNER ROBERTS

accidents happen. Have you given any thought as to who would inherit if an accident or sudden illness took you from us?'

Once again, Isangell had to remind herself that she loved her mother and that she did not want to hit her over the head with a tea tray. She had been working on that speech for days and it barely raised an eyebrow.

'Mother, you know the line of succession as well as anyone. Aunt Augusta may have given up her claim to Aufleur when she remarried, but she has a surfeit of sons who are either adults or closer to coming of age than any babe I might conceive in the next two years.'

'Minor nobility from a rural barony,' Eglantine said through thin lips.

'Descended directly from the last Duc d'Aufleur,' Isangell shot back. 'And this isn't the point you're getting at, so why waste time? You would be quite happy for any of my country cousins to be my heir if it meant that I had disinherited their elder half-brother.'

Eglantine did not deny it. 'The man is mad, dearling. After that display at the Floralia parade, how can you possibly think otherwise?'

'I don't know what happened that day, Mama, and neither do you. Perhaps he does suffer from Grandpapa's complaint. Believe me, I do not intend to inflict another mad Duc on this city. But I will not make hasty decisions about Ashiol's future without at least speaking to him.'

'If the decision were taken out of your hands...'

'You wish me to declare you as my executor,' Isangell said in a quiet voice. 'I'm sorry, Mama, I won't do it. I know you believe that you know what is best for Aufleur, but you were not even born in Ammoria. Believe me when I say that I have made adequate provisions for the future of Aufleur in the event of my sudden death. The clerks have the name of my executor.'

'Augusta,' said Eglantine sourly.

Isangell smiled a little sadly. 'I thought my aunt was the best person to decide which of her children would make the best Duc d'Aufleur. Or Duchessa even — we mustn't forget little Pip.'

'Your mind can't be changed on this,' said Eglantine, not bothering to make it a question. She was beaten and she knew it.

'I have ensured that Ashiol will be kept from the line of succession if he is not well enough to rule. Don't you think a mother is best placed to judge the sanity of her son?'

'But the world still believes he is your direct heir,' protested Eglantine. 'And after Floralia, they all think him beyond salvation.'

'Actually, they don't.' Isangell was quite pleased with how she had managed this part. 'I sent out an announcement after the parade that the Ducomte suffers from extreme head pains, and that the bright sunlight brought on an attack. Our physicians are hard at work to find a cure.' She set her teacup down. 'Oh, and Mama? I would appreciate it if you asked me first next time before instructing my lictors to hunt my cousin down like a dog in the streets. I countermanded your order, of course. Ashiol will come to me when he is ready.'

Eglantine gave her daughter a look of blank hatred. 'He doesn't deserve to be protected by you, Isangell.'

'I'm the Duchessa,' her daughter said simply. 'Protecting people is exactly what I am here to do.'

That, at least, was enough to make Eglantine leave the room, rustling her old-fashioned skirts loudly to express her extreme disapproval. It took more and more provocation to achieve that these days.

Isangell poured herself a second cup, relishing the fact

that she had perhaps twenty whole minutes before her maids returned to dress her formally for the day.

'As for you,' she said aloud after a long blissful moment, 'have I ever told you how much I dislike being eavesdropped on?'

The curtains at the back of her sitting room moved slowly aside, revealing an abashed Ashiol. He looked like hells. His arms were scratched and torn, and he was clad in the half-shredded remains of a black shirt and leather breeches. His feet were bare, so scratched and swollen that it made Isangell wince to look at them.

'How did you know I was here?' he asked.

'My curtains have been known to smell of orange blossom and freshly laundered linen, but rarely of sweat and leather. Luckily my mother has almost no sense of smell.' Isangell poured cream into her second cup of tea and held it out to him. 'Here, you need this more than I do.'

'Thanks.' He moved towards her, limping a little, and sat beside her.

'Do I even want to know?' she asked.

'Doubt it.'

She looked at him for a long while, taking in everything while he drank the tea in two or three gulps. Wordlessly, she pushed the remains of the toast and fruit towards him, and he attacked it with military precision.

'I could ring for more breakfast, if you like,' she said.

'I don't want anyone to know I'm back.'

'Ashiol, you live here. This is your home.'

'No. It really isn't.' He lay back against the settee, resting his shoulders on the soft cushions. 'I'm sorry, gosling. This isn't how I wanted this to turn out for either of us.'

She moved to the chair so he could stretch his legs out. 'I thought you were going to be my knight in shining armour,' she said. 'You were supposed to stand at my side and glare at

my mother and give me the strength to make the hard decisions. That was the plan, wasn't it?'

'That was the plan,' he agreed, closing his eyes.

'I shouldn't have asked you to come back to Aufleur. It's
happening all over again, isn't it? The gangs —'

'They're not gangs,' he snapped, then reconsidered. 'Oh,
hells, maybe they are. I thought I could come and be the
Ducomte without all that street mess, gosling. I really
thought I could do it, or I wouldn't have inflicted myself on
you. But things changed.'

'At the Floralia parade.'

'Yes.' He gazed at her for a moment with his very dark
eyes. 'I'm sorry about your dress.'

'It would have wilted anyway.'

'Then I'm sorry about the public humiliation.'

'Apology accepted.'

He looked so exhausted lying there on her floral cushions.
There was something else, as well. 'You're glowing,' Isangell
said, tilting her head at him.

'Sorry about that.'

'No — there's something about you. A strength you didn't
have when you turned up on the Palazzo threshold a few
days ago.'

'Yes.' There was something almost childish about the
expression on his face, a mixture of guilt and enthusiasm. 'I
lost part of myself before I left Aufleur the last time.'

'And now it's back?'

'Back with a vengeance. But it comes with responsibilities...'

Isangell slid forward, from the chair to the carpet,
pushing her hand into his. 'You're not going to be here,' she
said. 'When I need someone to rant at about my mother, or
to help me decide which treaty to sign, or to pick which

TANSY RAYNER ROBERTS

useless noble I should marry and bear children to, you're not going to be here for me.'

'Nope,' he said, tracing the back of her hand with his finger. 'Whenever you really need me, I'll be somewhere else.'

'But you'll turn up like a bad smell whenever it's least convenient, when I'm truly busy, or when I just don't want a big brother cousin beating down my door and making his opinion heard.'

'It's the least I can do.'

'If you can keep yourself alive, I'll take what I can get.' She squeezed his hand, then let go. 'I don't think I ever will understand why you need to be with them rather than us.'

'I'm a better person there than I am here,' he said, watching her through half-lidded eyes. 'I can do more for this city you love so much. And... they need me. You don't, Isangell, you really don't. You're strong without me.'

'Am I now?'

'You were taught by the best. Just try and stay alive for another decade or two, will you? I would make a very bad Duc.'

'Well, we all know that.' Isangell watched him relax into the cushions, a rare sight. 'Ashiol?'

'Mmm?'

'Did you like my Floralia dress?'

'Very pretty,' he mumbled.

'I was thinking of getting that dressmaker to make me something spectacular for the summer solstice — she's very good.'

'She'd like you. You'd like her too, I think.'

Isangell was losing track. 'Who would I like, Ashiol?'

He opened his dark eyes for one more brief moment before closing them with an air of deep finality. 'My King.'

It made no sense, but she was used to nonsense from her cousin.

When his breathing slowed into deep sleep, Isangell got to her feet and rang for her maids. They were quiet, blank-faced demoiselles, hand-picked by her mother. Isangell had tried learning their names, but they stared at her when she made an effort at conversation. Today, she didn't bother. 'There's a lunch with the Edoran ambassador, but I'll dress for that later,' she said to the expressionless mass in morning dresses. 'Just a day frock for now, and send for my steward and his scribe to attend me in the library. I have some proclamations to send to the Heads of the Great Families.'

'Yes, high and brightness.' The maids moved around her in their coordinated routine. One bent over the tea table to clear the tray, and covered her reaction to the snoring nobleman in torn black leather sprawled on the Duchessa's pretty floral settee.

'The Ducomte will need a change of clothes and some more breakfast when he wakes up,' Isangell tossed over her shoulder as she headed for her dressing room. 'If someone could be here to remind him where his own rooms are, that would be wonderful.'

Her thoughts were already turning towards the politics and civil manoeuvring that the day would bring. There was no time to roll the mystery of Ashiol Xandelian around in her mind, as she had been doing since she was old enough to recognise that he was not like ordinary people. That other Ashiol, the nox version of her cousin, was an intriguing individual. The Duchessa d'Aufleur shouldn't be tempted to get to know him, but Isangell couldn't help wondering if that dark world of his was more interesting than the one she inhabited.

She only hoped he didn't get himself killed before she had the chance to meet that other Ashiol.

~

IT WAS a little after dawn when Velody returned home.

She stopped by the public baths first, with a handful of centi she had borrowed from Crane. Her dress was practically glued to her, there was blood and gunk in her hair, and by the time she came out of the water she was trembling as if she hadn't slept in a week. She washed the dress too, rather than let the sky filth touch her skin again, and wore it home wet.

Now Velody stood in the doorway of the kitchen, hoping her friends wouldn't hate her.

Delphine and Rhian were at the table with a pot of mint tisane, as if they had been sitting there for a long time. When they saw her, they both reacted hard.

'What the buggering hells!' said Delphine. 'What happened to you?'

Rhian was at Velody's side instantly. 'Are you hurt?' she said, then looked more closely at the state Velody was in. 'Out of those clothes,' she said firmly. 'What were you thinking? Something dry, and then bed.'

It was so close to having the old Rhian back that Velody wanted to cry. 'I'm supposed to be looking after you,' she said weakly.

'Doing seven hells of a job of it,' snapped Delphine. 'You heard the demme. Move it.'

In Velody's bedchamber, she stood passively as Rhian stripped the wet dress from her and found her a thick, old-fashioned noxgown. Delphine brought linens to dry Velody's hair, and then the three of them climbed together into Velody's nest of quilts and blankets.

'So,' said Rhian, her head on Velody's shoulder. 'Got anything to tell us?'

Velody laughed, and it came out as a sob, but she managed to rein it in before completely falling apart. 'A lot has changed this Floralia.'

'No shit,' said Delphine. 'Come on, darling. Don't we tell you all our secrets?'

Velody leaned back against the headboard, very aware that there were mice watching them from every corner and cranny of the room. 'Not sure where to start, except... well, I found out why we can't remember where we came from, before we started our apprenticeships. I can remember now. I remember everything. Your parents, Delphine, your aunt.' She squeezed Rhian's arm a little. 'Your brother. My family. I don't know if you're going to believe me, but I want to tell you about Tierce...'

Delphine and Rhian listened as Velody poured out everything — the oaths and the dreams, the little brown mice, and the Creature Court. Of the sandstone walls of Tierce, of Cyniver and Delphine's aunt. She was half-convinced that they thought she was crazy, or they would be angry about what she had done.

They didn't say much of anything. They listened. And finally, when her words ran together and her eyelids fluttered, they left her alone to sleep. Velody heard them murmuring together as they closed the door behind them.

She dreamed of Garnet.

TWO DAYS AFTER THE
NONES OF LUCINA

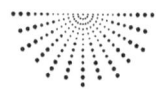

NOX

*M*acready had missed the beginning of summer this year. He blinked twice and suddenly the sunlight was stretching later into the evenings, and nox no longer had that sharp chill to it. Considering how many noxes he saw from beginning to end, clambering on the rooftops with Velody or Ashiol or the both of them, you'd think he would have picked up on it earlier.

Everything was about Velody. There was nothing but Velody for the whole of Floralis and a market-nine of Lucina. The sentinels and Ashiol were on constant alert for one or more of the Lords and Court to challenge Velody's authority, either in the open or on the quiet, but no hint of an attack had come as yet.

Macready had been thinking about the Silver Captain lately. The Court was so different when he was alive. There were three healthy young Kings, one of them Power and Majesty, the other two supporting him. There were five

Lords then as now, and more sentinels than the Lords and Kings put together.

We were a team then, so we were. The sentinels meant something other than damage control and clean-up crew.

The Captain was a right bastard, true enough. He rode his sentinels harder than some Lords rode their courtesi, but there was a method behind it. The Captain hated the Creature Court, the whole lot of them, Kings included. Genuinely hated them. He watched them like dangerous children, noting their every move and counter move. He would not only have dug out what Poet and Priest were up to by now (not to mention Livilla, Dhynar, and Warlord) but he would have turned his attention to Ashiol and his motives, then to Velody herself.

'We're loyal to them,' he would grunt at least once a day. 'Don't mean they're loyal to us. Remember that, men.'

The sentinels were all men to the Captain, especially the women. The fact that nearly half his fighting force was female had been a source of deep pain to the old coot, and he grimly ignored it whenever possible.

Say what you like about the Silver Captain, you rarely lost anyone on his watch. After he was gone — and that was the one thing Macready could never forgive Garnet for, if he lived a century or more — the rest of them fell so fast it was frightening. It was luck that had left Macready, Kelpie and Crane standing. Macready had no illusion it was because they were the best that the sentinels had to offer. His mammy always said her boy had a mean streak of luck in him. He preferred to think it was that keeping him alive rather than any particular talent. Talent was a fickle mistress, but you could count on luck for longer.

Macready offered the captaincy to Kelpie once it was only the three of them, and she'd thrown it straight back to him. In the end, they agreed that neither would hold it. 'We'll wait until Crane's of age,' Kelpie grinned.

Mac and Kelpie had never liked each other much until they were the only ones left. Now, they had been hanging on to each other for so long that it was impossible to bring like or dislike into it. She was his, like those four gabbling sisters back home were his.

Crane was playing on the rooftops with the Kings this nox, and Kelpie crashed out in her nest after two solid days without sleep. Neither of them had remembered what day it was. Why should they? It was stupid and maudlin to keep commemorating it year after year, but what else was there to do?

Macready lifted his mug solemnly, toasting the wiry, angry Silver Captain and the end of life as he knew it. Three years ago this nox. 'Happy Vestalia, you old bastard,' he said, and drank deep. The festival of virgins and peasants was tomorrow, which made it more appropriate to break a barley roll in honour of the Captain's anniversary than to raise a mug, but what the hells. He felt like drinking. He could break a bread roll for breakfast.

Everything was changing in Aufleur. The daylight Duc's death last year pushed the changes along at a dizzying rate. Nothing like the death of an elderly monarch to make a society self-conscious about being modern, clever, fast.

Take this bar — the Pretty Princel on the riverside of the Lucian district. In the old days it was the sort of place where the dregs of society went to drink alone, keeping a knife handy at all times. The sentinels made a habit of gathering here after a hard nox because the Princel served drinks until sunrise, and because it was too grotty a hole for any of the Creature Court to wander into by accident. They liked their glamour spots, did the Lords and Court.

Look at it now! The walls were painted purple and rouge,

adorned with amusing frescoes and hangings. There was a piano in the corner, and bright young things filled the place with laughter, dancing, new fashions. They ate oysters with triangles of bread and butter as if the recipe had only just been invented.

There was a gang of them in here now, four hours before dawn — coves in bright striped suits and demmes in beaded dresses, drinking flame-and-gin and taking turns to tinkle the piano now the hired player had gone home for the nox. Macready felt old just looking at them. He should have picked somewhere else for his drink, somewhere that had the feel of the old place even if it wasn't exactly here. Too late now. He took another swig.

Hard to tell if they were a literary set, theatricals, or just good old social parasites. Everyone acted like toffs these days. One of the coves sat at the piano, playing it with both hands as a cigarette twitched between his lips. The others exploded into gales of giggles, as if someone had said something frightfully funny. The melody was one of those uneven jazz things that were so popular nowadays.

Macready finished his drink and decided not to order another. If they started singing, he'd have to go and punch one of them, and he wanted to avoid that. The Captain would have done it by now, which was the best possible reason to hold back.

One of the demmes raised her voice in song, matching the snappy beat of the piano music with sharp, cynical lyrics.

Macready was still.

Who was she? The corner was badly lit. All he could see was a slender lass with streaky make-up, an expensive dress and bobbed blonde hair. Nothing special about any of that. She was one of a thousand trashy flappers in this city. Her voice caught him though — full-bodied and beautiful with a sharp line of desperation running through it. *That lass needs rescuing*, he thought, and almost laughed at himself. Like he needed another person to save.

He tossed a shillein on the counter for another drink. No particular reason.

The lass slumped away from the piano as if the song had drained all the energy from her. The others laughed and dragged her back. The striped suit at the piano began a duet and the lass shrugged, playing along. It was a funny flirt of a tune and didn't suit her at all. She sulked through the second half, and only recovered when another of the coves bought her a gin cocktail.

At the end of the song, as she tossed her bobbed hair back to slug down the drink, Macready finally saw her face properly. It was Delphine.

He hadn't seen anything of Velody's two demmes since she claimed her place as Power and Majesty. Velody made every Lord and their courtesi swear on their own blood, and hers, that Delphine and Rhian were off limits. Dazed with power and the aftermath of battle, each had sworn docilely. Macready barely gave much of a thought to Velody's demmes after that — the Court were untrustworthy, but none of them would be stupid enough to break a blood oath. Velody's friends were safe, so why think of them at all?

Delphine was thinner and harder than he remembered. Had she changed so much in the last month, or was she just a mean drunk? Hard to tell.

'Beautiful, darlings, but does it mean anything?' asked one of the striped suits in a lazy drawl.

Delphine lit a cigarette and gave him a dirty look. 'If you start talking about Society again, Villey, I'm going home.'

'Sorry for boring!' he chuckled, and the others laughed along.

The cherry-pink striped suit at the piano grabbed

Delphine and hauled her into his lap. She slumped against him, unresisting. Saints, how drunk was she?

'The ladies don't like to hear about your philosophies, Villiers,' said the suit. 'Their brains are too small.'

'Beast!' said another demme, a redhead with a long cigarette-holder and a fringed dress so short she was barely fit to be seen in public. 'He only has one philosophy and we've heard it so many times we can all recite it in unison.'

'Nothing means anything!' Delphine slurred. 'We celebrate the great emptiness because we've nothing truly important to care about. Life is too easy, milk and honey and lovely, lovely strawberries.' She made kissy noises.

'Festivals and ribbons,' said the redhead. 'We need something important to bring our lives into sharp focus.'

'We need a war!' Delphine screamed, and the redhead shouted it with her. They both collapsed into hysterical giggles.

Macready raised his mug slowly to his lips. Villiers was looking annoyed at the teasing. Was Delphine making trouble for herself? Macready reminded himself that all this was none of his business, but that kind of thinking had never worked for him. He'd have to stick around now, to make sure she got home safely. This lot weren't to be trusted.

Hard to see how his calm, sensible Power and Majesty had paired up with a mess of a lass like this one.

'I don't make fun of your singing,' said Villiers.

'Don't be sour,' said Delphine. 'If you repeat yourself so often, how can we help but tease?'

'I don't know about the rest of you,' said Cherry-Pink Stripes, 'but I don't want a war! I wouldn't know what to do with one. I'm quite happy with a meaningless life, thanks very much.'

'And that's why no decent poetry has been written in a

hundred years,' sighed Villiers. 'Men like you, Teddy, with nothing to write about.'

'But there is a war,' said Delphine in a clear voice. 'Didn't you know?'

Macready almost choked on his drink as the lass turned her head and stared straight at him.

'How many gins have you had, little one?' said Villiers, not taking her seriously.

Delphine lifted herself from Teddy's arms and rose unsteadily to her feet. 'I'm telling the truth. The skywar has been back for years, raining death on the streets of Aufleur.' She swung around on her high heels, advancing on Macready. 'We could be under attack right now, and we wouldn't know a thing about it unless we suddenly dropped dead of the Silent Sleep. Isn't that true, seigneur?'

There was a chill in her voice that stung Macready. He drank from his mug, trying not to show how bothered he was by those sharp, hurting blue eyes. 'Whatever you say, lass.'

She faltered, and her voice rose an octave higher. 'Would you deny it to my face? Are you a liar as well as a thief?'

One of the striped suits — not Teddy or Villiers, one with peppermint stripes on his breeches — skipped forward to grab her around the waist. 'Don't frighten the customers, Dee-dee. Come away and dance with me, you know you want to.'

She cradled her head against his chest as he guided her away from Macready, back to the others. Macready heard Peppermint Stripes hiss to the redhead, 'What pills did you give her?'

The redhead laughed at him. 'Nothing she hasn't had before, sweetling.'

Macready finished his drink and set it down purposefully, then circled the bar. Easy enough to find a dark corner where he could wait them out without being seen. It wouldn't be long, by the look of it. Delphine's outburst had shaken her crowd a little.

'Kiss and make up, little one,' said Villiers, taking her arm in a proprietary fashion. 'I'll see you home.'

'I'll do it,' said Teddy. He collected his hat and a feminine wrap from the stand at the door. 'It's on my way,' he added, draping the filmy cloth around Delphine's shoulders.

'As you like,' said Villiers, releasing her. An unfriendly look passed between the two coves before they broke apart.

'Lisette's tomorrow?' called the redhead as she pranced up the front steps, tucked between Villiers and Peppermint Stripes.

'See you there,' agreed Teddy in a cheerful voice, steering Delphine out the back way.

Macready waited a few moments and then followed Cherry-Pink Teddy, just to be sure.

There was a narrow lane running along behind the Pretty Princel. Delphine had trouble negotiating it, even with Teddy's arm around her waist.

'Come home with me, darling,' Macready heard Teddy say. 'I'll look after you.'

'No!' Delphine said, pushing him away. 'You'd only want to fumble, and I'm not up for it right now.'

'Never stopped you before.'

'Charming, aren't you.' Her words all ran together in one long drawl. 'That's exactly the right way to talk a demoiselle into bed.'

Macready couldn't move from the doorway without making his presence obvious. Their every step took them further away from him.

'Bit late to pretend you're not a tart,' said Teddy. It was hard to tell if he meant to insult her, or if it was the sort of thing this crowd said to each other.

Delphine didn't take offence. 'Don't feel like being one now, that's all.'

'Not with me, you mean.' He sounded disgusted. She shrugged a shoulder. 'Bored already?'

'You said it, not me.'

Macready rolled his eyes. This lass didn't need rescuing. Spanking, maybe.

Teddy moved fast, pinning Delphine hard against the alley wall with his body. Macready was about to leap to the rescue when he realised that the bint was laughing.

'What do you think you're doing, you beast?' she shrieked, not taking her attacker at all seriously.

'Isn't this the way you like it?' Teddy grunted. 'Fontaine told me about the first time he had you, Dee-dee. He showed everyone the scratch marks.'

Delphine wasn't laughing any more. 'You're too light-weight to play rough,' she said in a voice worthy of a Duchessa. 'Let me go. I feel sick.'

He let go, and she slid towards the ground. Chivalry was obviously ingrained deeply in Teddy for all his attempts to come off as a hard man. He leaped forward to catch her, just as she threw up violently. He was in exactly the right position to receive the full force of her vomit, down his pink-striped suit and soft silk shirt.

'Bitch!' he screamed, and backhanded her. Delphine rocked back against the wall and fell in a crumpled heap.

Right, well, that was enough of that.

'Get yer filthy hands off her!' Macready yelled, striding towards them. He was too short to be intimidating, but the accent usually did the trick for him. Everyone in Aufleur knew that Islandsers were crazy.

'Who the hells are you?' asked Teddy.

The fop hadn't even glanced at the moaning figure of

Delphine on the ground. He was far more concerned with shaking vomit from his pretty clothes.

'I'm the feller who's telling you to leave the lass alone,' Macready said with just a touch of menace.

Teddy looked uncertain. 'I said I'd see her home.'

'Fine job you're doing of it too,' Macready laughed. 'Get out of here, friend. That shirt of yours will need to soak.'

Teddy glanced down at the horror show that remained of his very expensive suit. 'Real silk,' he muttered. 'Fine, you're welcome to her.' He walked away, putting his hands in his pockets.

Macready muttered a word that would have made his mammy bat him around the head with a ladle. He stared down at the crumpled heap that was Delphine. 'And luckily,' he said with heavy irony, 'I know where you live.' He knelt, brushing back her short blonde hair. 'Come on, lass. Let's have those lids open.'

She moaned as she recognised him. 'What are you doing here?'

'I'm a free service they offer with every twelve tots of gin. Can you get yourself to your feet?'

'Noooo.'

Macready pulled out a handkerchief and rubbed vomit from her lips. She had managed to keep her dress completely clear of it — obviously the lass had hidden talents. 'Be glad your stomach's empty. If you wish to be carried, it'll be over my shoulder.'

'Go away,' she sighed, closing her eyes again. 'Leave me here to die.'

Macready looked up and down the little alley. No one in sight, and they were a long way from the safety of her front door. 'Sadly, my lovely, that's not an option.'

TWO DAYS AFTER THE
NONES OF LUCINA

NOX

*A*shiol fell out of the sky and crashed hard on grass and stone. This was someone's elegant courtyard garden, set into the steepest side of the Avleurine hill. He spat blood, and gasped for air. When he recovered enough strength to move his body, he rolled on his back and stared up.

Velody was still fighting the terrors above. She soared across the blistering sky, her talons outstretched. It was beautiful to watch her. She danced back and forth as lightly as that needle of hers when she was hemming cloth. Ashiol breathed in and out for a few moments, noting a new rasp on one of his lungs, and watched Velody save the city.

'Quite a sight,' said a light voice above him as Poet melted out of the shadows.

Ashiol chose not to sit up. He was comfortable where he was. 'She doesn't do too badly.'

'Indeed,' said Poet, his eyes following their Power and

Majesty as she wrestled with the spreading sky pattern they had always called the burnplague. Motes of light spat from Velody's fingers, quenching the dangerous mass blister by blister. She was careful, as ever, not to let any of the acid touch her. 'Why, she scarcely needs the Lords and Court to support her at all. Which would be why we have remained uninvited to join you in the sky for nearly four market-nines.'

'She has to learn everything the sky has to throw at her,' said Ashiol, trying not to sound defensive. 'It's more of a challenge if she handles it alone.'

'You fight at her side,' said Poet.

Ashiol swallowed an angry retort. 'She is still in training.'

'Of course. You wouldn't want her to have to handle such business *all* alone.' Poet's narrow eyes blazed down at Ashiol. 'She should be accompanied by a warrior she can trust at her back. And that would not describe any Lord of our Court, naturally.'

Now Ashiol sat up, if only to place his back to Poet. 'When Velody is more comfortable with the Court, she will make greater use of your talents.'

'How is she to become more comfortable with us, my King, if she avoids us?'

Ashiol had known this was coming. 'She must build up her strength and skills before she is ready to deal with the Court.'

'The Court who swore allegiance to her as Power and Majesty?' said Poet. 'Yes, I can see why you might wish to shield her from us.'

'Lords and Court have forsworn themselves before,' Ashiol growled. 'She's not like us, Poet. She doesn't know the intricacies of the Creature Court, the challenges and pissing contests, the language of body and blood —'

'And how, my King, shall she ever learn our dance if she is

not allowed to take that first step?' Poet was so close behind Ashiol that his breath tickled his ear. 'I want this demme to rule us, truly rule us as our Power and Majesty should. Do you want the same?'

Fury rose up in Ashiol's chest. He restrained himself from swinging around and punching Poet through the face. 'Do you presume to know better than me?'

There was no response. When Ashiol did look behind him, Poet was gone. 'Damned rat moves faster than I do,' he muttered.

Velody swooped overhead, catching Ashiol's eye as she blasted the last of the burnplague blisters back where they came from. For a moment, his blood sang with pride. *Why in hellfire shouldn't I try and keep her away from the monsters for as long as possible?*

Poet's taunting voice still gnawed at him, somewhere low in his spine. *So what's going to happen, little King, when she finally has to dance with the monsters? You'll have a fight on your hands to stop them eating her alive. The moment your back's turned, who'll keep her safe and whole and sane?*

He had to put that out of his mind now, he had to. When things got rough, Velody would be strong enough to handle it. She'd have to be.

FINALLY, the sky was clean and clear. Velody withdrew from chimaera shape and glided down through the nox air to where she had left Crane and, more importantly, her clothes. She was glowing with triumph. She hadn't panicked when Ashiol was hurled out of the sky, and she definitely outclassed him in this particular battle.

'Did you see?' she called out eagerly to Crane as her feet touched down on the soft lawn of the highest slope of the

Alexandrine, in the grounds surrounding the Church of the Faceless Child.

The sentinel brought her silk coat to her and stood behind her to wrap it around her bare shoulders, helping her shrug into the sleeves. 'Very nice.'

'Is that the best you can do?' she asked indignantly, turning so fast that she didn't give him time to lower his arms. She stood for a moment in his loose embrace, breathing hard. His eyes held her, and she backed away a step or two. *Careful, Velody. You're power-drunk after battle. Keep the flirting to a minimum.*

She was beginning to understand why half the Court had fallen into bed with each other. It was heady and rich, this afterglow of battle. Nox after nox, Velody fought her instincts to throw herself into Ashiol's arms and find out if their bodies would choreograph as well together in private as they did in the sky. A sense of self-preservation kept her from making that particular move. Ashiol was a predator through and through; she was vulnerable enough without making it a hundred times worse.

Crane was another matter. Oh, so pretty, and she didn't miss the look of admiration that filled his eyes when he was near her. Every pore in her body told her he was safe, that he would never hurt her.

Still, she had promised herself to resist this new sensuality as much as possible. The last thing she needed was complications, and sleeping with one of her sentinels would create more complications than even she could imagine.

A teasing look came over Crane's face. 'What do you want me to say, Majesty?'

Velody belted her coat firmly. 'Perhaps a more effusive compliment than "very nice"?'

Crane hesitated.

'What's wrong?'

'Nothing. You don't need me to tell you how good you are in the sky.'

'I suppose not.' She frowned. 'So what aren't you saying?'

'Majesty?' he replied innocently.

'Don't "Majesty" me. You've got doubts. Tell me what they are.'

'It's just... you haven't been down below yet, have you?'

Velody's lips thinned a little. It was a sore subject. Ashiol had described the underground city of the Arches so well that she thought she could find her way through the Shambles to the Haymarket without a map to guide her, and yet there was always an excuse to prevent her from setting foot in the place.

'He doesn't think I'm ready yet to deal with the Court in their territory,' she said.

Too much time spent with the sentinels lately. When any of them said 'he', they meant Ashiol. She would not be surprised to learn that an unqualified 'she' meant Velody every time. Strange, to be the centre of somebody's world after barely a month of acquaintance. Stranger, perhaps, that Ashiol and the sentinels had so quickly become the centre of hers.

Crane's head snapped up. 'Not their territory, Velody. *Yours*. I don't think you should be waiting for Ashiol to tell you when you're ready to deal with the Court, above or below. You're the Power and Majesty. Aren't you?'

She sucked in a breath. That *Aren't you?* was verging on rebellion. How long had Crane felt like this? Would Macready and Kelpie back him up if they were here? 'The Court haven't touched me yet. None of them have challenged my authority. I've barely seen any of them since that nox in the Gardens.'

'They're frightened of Ashiol,' said Crane. 'He keeps them at bay. Half of the Creature Court think he's still out for revenge for what happened to him last time he was among us, and the other half... they're biding their time. As soon as they think you're worth ripping apart, they will. The minute Ashiol's back is turned.'

'You have a great deal of faith in my abilities,' Velody said sharply.

Crane clenched his fists. The look he shot her was so blazing that she was surprised it didn't burn her skin. 'This isn't a game, Velody.'

'I never thought it was.' She used what she had come to think of as her 'political' voice, the calm and measured speech of a King to her subjects. So far she had only been able to try it out on the sentinels — it had little effect on Ashiol. 'Your concerns are genuine, Crane, but your anger... I don't understand where your anger is coming from.'

The voice did its trick. Crane breathed in deeply, his fists uncurling. Finally he sighed and dropped to his knees. 'Forgive me, Majesty. I forgot myself.'

Velody bit off an entreaty to drop the formality. If he felt the need for it, who was she to deny him? She moved towards him and laid her hands on his fair hair. They touched each other so easily, Ashiol and the sentinels, and she had no doubt that it reflected the way the whole Creature Court were with each other. There was an entire language to touching that she was slow to learn. Living with Rhian had schooled her to avoid even the most casual of touches for the longest time.

His sigh told her that the touch was appropriate. The tension was already leaving his body. She stroked his hair gently. 'What's wrong, Crane?'

'I'm on edge.'

'Really?' she said in mock surprise. Crane laughed at that, which she saw as a positive sign. She knelt beside him, taking his hands in hers. More touching, carefully calculated. 'You don't have to tell me if you don't want to.'

'This is how you should win over the Court,' he said, half-serious. 'They've been bullied and ruled and kinged over for so long. I don't think anyone ever thought of mothering them to death.'

'Tell me what's wrong, or I'll send you to bed without supper.' That joke didn't go down nearly as well.

Crane's face was still. 'Our Captain died three years ago this nox. The eve of Vestalia is a hard anniversary. That's all.'

Velody squeezed his hands between hers. 'Is that why Macready was like a bear with a sore head all day?'

'And why Kelpie worked herself to exhaustion over the last market-nine, so she wouldn't even be awake for it. Yes.'

'I'm sorry. I've never lost anyone close. You've all lost so much.'

It wasn't entirely true. She was still troubled by the dreams, the overlapping memories of the family who had loved her. Several times she caught herself about to relate an anecdote about one of her brothers, and then she would press her lips together and walk away. It was an old hurt even if the memories were fresh.

Crane's hands were hot under hers. At least, she thought they were. It was hard to draw the line between her ordinary Velody senses and the otherworldly senses that belonged to the Creature King and the Power and Majesty. Heat poured off the young sentinel in waves.

'There are compensations,' he said, and there was a tremor in his voice. Slowly, he lifted her right hand and kissed it across the knuckle.

It occurred to Velody that the heat might not be coming from Crane after all. It was her. She was overwhelmed by the scent of him, sandalwood and wool and skin. *I promised myself I wouldn't do this,* she thought desperately, but the thought wasn't enough to stop her kissing him back as his mouth tipped up to hers and his hands slipped around her.

Too much touching, far too much touching! Her flesh came alive with the thought of how easy it would be for him to unknot the belt of her silken coat and have her naked in his lap...

Ashiol's nearby presence was like a bucket of cold water. Velody drew back in a hurry, brushing her coat as if to erase Crane's fingerprints from the fabric.

'You did well,' said Ashiol as he came out of the darkness, unclothed and glowing like a Lord. The burns from the skyblisters still marked his torso, but he was oddly calm. Last time he was thrown from the sky in mid-battle, the anger had rolled off him for hours afterwards.

Crane hesitated for a fraction of a moment before he grabbed Ashiol's long black coat and handed it to him.

Velody took advantage of the moment to look for the rest of her clothes. She found them neatly piled in the shelter of the church's portico. The combination of skirt and wraparound blouse was the best arrangement for these noxtime romps — she was able to slide on the wool skirt without disrupting her long coat. Normally she could cope with being naked around Ashiol, but it seemed inappropriate right now. The mere thought of nudity was enough to make her blush hotly.

If she had sensed Ashiol approaching, what had he sensed? Did he know what had been going on with Velody and Crane? Saints, did he know what she was thinking? That would be so much worse.

Ashiol was also fully clothed when she returned to the two men. 'I liked the way you did those rapid transformations,' he said. 'You're more relaxed in the sky these days.'

'Yes,' she said.

Crane didn't seem bothered by their near miss. Was it

usual for sentinels and Kings to be physically close in all senses of the word? Velody knew there had been something between Ash and Kelpie.

'When was your birthday?' Ash asked suddenly.

Velody blinked before realising that it wasn't her he was talking to.

'Lupercal,' said Crane, a little defensively.

'You're overdue for your swords. Shall we see the Smith tomorrow? If the Power and Majesty approves.'

Velody nodded. Ashiol had a tendency to let her know of her duties in this roundabout manner. He really was the Power and Majesty in all but name. She didn't have the knowledge or confidence — let alone the desire — to do it alone yet.

I have to face the Court sooner or later.

Perhaps if they continued in this fashion for long enough, Ashiol would realise that he could do a perfectly good job himself as Power and Majesty. Velody could go back to her life as if all this had been a strange, dreamlike holiday. It was difficult to imagine this otherworldly rooftop existence as being anything but temporary. Apart from anything else, the life expectancy wasn't all that promising. Except for Priest, every member of the Court was under forty years old.

At Ashiol's mention of swords, Crane's lovely face lit up with joy. He was glowing. It had never occurred to Velody that it wasn't his personal choice to wear only daggers while Macready and Kelpie had swords.

'Get some rest then,' Ashiol was telling Crane. 'We'll have to be there at noon. I'll see Velody home.'

Crane bowed his farewell to Velody in a suitably formal manner, but she could tell he was no longer thinking of her. Did kisses mean so little in this world, and swords so much? She cautioned herself for being even slightly offended. What did she expect — a duel over the honour to walk her home?

All this animor was going to her head. She was turning into one of those melodramatic heroines from the newspaper serials.

'Why hasn't he had swords before?' she asked Ashiol on their walk back to Via Silviana.

'Sentinels are usually too young for long blades when they join our world — no point giving a thirteen year old a sword he'll outgrow in six months. Crane should have got his on his last birthday, but Garnet had already forbidden blades to the sentinels.'

'Which birthday?' she asked before she could stop herself.

Ashiol shot her an amused look that left her in no doubt that he had some idea of what had been happening between Velody and the sentinel in the church grounds. 'We figure their bones have lengthened enough by seventeen years.'

Velody almost stopped breathing. She had been groping a child. 'How can he only be seventeen? How long has he been a sentinel?'

'Let's see. He arrived in the same year Garnet became Power and Majesty — that would be seven years ago. I'm pretty sure he was about ten. Young for a sentinel, but not exceptionally so. Kelpie was about twelve, I think, when she joined us.'

'You like them young, don't you?' said Velody shortly.

Ashiol shot her a biting grin that made her regret the entire conversation. 'Funny, I was going to say the same to you.'

Velody clamped her lips together. She had avoided suitors in recent years, telling herself it was for Rhian's sake. Why should things be any different now just because she spent most of each nox naked in the moonlight? *It's all the touching*, she decided. *I have to cut down on the touching.*

'Where do we find the swordsmith?' she asked, to change the subject.

'Down below,' said Ashiol.

Velody looked at him in surprise. 'The Arches? You're letting me —' Too late, she bit back the words.

Ashiol winced. 'I'm not *letting* you do anything,' he grunted. 'You're the Power and Majesty, it's up to you to do the letting.'

'You said I wasn't ready.'

'You're not. That much I'm sure of. But you won't get ready without being in the middle of it all, dancing the dance of the Court.'

Velody shivered. For a moment, she wanted to beg him to catch her if she fell, but she thought better of it. *Don't fall*, she told herself fiercely. *You can manage that much, surely.* 'What changed your mind?'

Ashiol's mouth twisted. 'Wisdom from an unexpected quarter,' he admitted. 'Either that, or I was persuaded into letting you walk into a trap. One of the two.'

'Well, as long as that's clear.'

'Just... remember that the Arches, the Shambles, all of it is yours. You are the Power and Majesty, and they live there at your sufferance. If you're not sure how to react to something, try being arrogant, or violent.'

Time to walk into the tiger's mouth, little mouse.

'What should I wear?' Velody asked.

TWO DAYS AFTER THE NONES OF LUCINA

NOX

*I*t was a miserable hour for Macready. Delphine could walk with a little help, but she resented every step and made sure that he suffered along with her.

Finally they turned into the alley that ran behind Via Silviana. Macready let go of Delphine for a moment to turn his attention to the kitchen door, putting his set of latch hooks and picks to good use. They didn't work. He stared at the door in amazement, and tried again. None of his usual tricks made a dent in the damn thing.

'New locks?' he asked Delphine.

She was curled up on the cold path, half-asleep, but she managed to raise a giggle.

Macready rolled his eyes. 'And that would be my fault for breaking in a while back, am I right?'

Hadn't Velody told the lasses that they were safe from the Creature Court now? He didn't know how much she had told them about her new life.

He knocked loudly on the door. 'Velody?'

Too much to hope she was at home. It was still hours before dawn. That left Rhian inside — scared and overprotected Rhian, who jumped at the sound of a male voice.

'Get up here,' he snapped at Delphine. 'Call your friend to the door.'

Delphine made a soft noise, but didn't stir. She was either slipping in and out of consciousness, or faking it really well. Macready rolled her on her side in case she was sick again, then went back to the door. 'Rhian?' he called, trying to make his voice unthreatening. 'Rhian, sweetness, it's Macready. I've got your lass Delphine here.'

He looked at the upstairs windows, but didn't know which room he should be aiming for. Surely the timid lass would have a bedroom overlooking the quiet alley rather than the main street? 'Rhian?' he called again, louder this time. 'I won't come in. I know you won't have men in the house. I respect that, honest to the saints. But it's not the warmest time of nox and she's sick. If you don't let me in, I don't know what the devils to do with her.'

His nearest nest was another long walk from where they were — and it could take twice the time with Delphine stumbling along beside him, if she was even up to walking any further this nox. He couldn't just leave the lass here even if she was the stupidest female he had ever met in his life. Velody would skin him if she found out.

'Rhian, if you'll come to the door, I'll go and leave you alone!' he promised.

There were footsteps in the kitchen, and Macready almost collapsed with relief. 'She's here,' he said through the door. 'I'll back away while you fetch her. I won't come near you.'

There was a series of soft clicks as the locks and latches were undone. The door opened. Macready looked up into

Rhian's face, her eyes troubled beneath her close-cropped red hair. She was a big lass, wide-shouldered and taller than him, though she stood as if trying to make herself smaller. *A few weeks of sword training and you'd stand up straighter, my sweet*, he found himself thinking.

'Macready,' she said.

Remembering, he backed away from the door. 'I'll keep my distance, lass. I know the rules.'

She took in the sprawled figure of Delphine, and sighed. 'You'll have to help me inside with her,' she said.

Macready had been thinking much the same, but he was startled at her matter-of-factness. 'Are you sure?'

Rhian gave him a look he couldn't quite define. 'Velody said I can trust you.'

Macready couldn't think of what to say, but he managed something of a smile. Rhian came out in her noxgown and a shawl; Macready took hold of Delphine's arm, but he needed Rhian to steady her other side.

'Shall we wake her?' he asked.

Rhian gave Delphine a shake. 'She's out like a blown lantern. I could drag her inside by her feet and she wouldn't wake up.'

'Now there's a thought,' muttered Macready.

Rhian almost laughed, but caught herself. 'You take her shoulders and I'll take her feet. I know the house better, and I think I can manage to walk backwards.'

'Sounds like a plan.'

Macready was starting to like this lass now she was coming out of that frightened shell of hers. It was enough of a mystery to him that Velody and Delphine were friends, but here was another anomaly. What did Rhian and Delphine have in common, apart from both being somewhat broken?

Rhian seemed less nervous if he said nothing, so he did his best to keep his mouth shut as they manoeuvred

Delphine into the house. They stopped in the kitchen for Rhian to relatch the door, then headed for the stairs.

It wasn't in Macready to keep quiet for long. 'I was wondering, so I was,' he said, halfway up the stairs. Delphine's head was lolling around, but he couldn't think of a way to protect it except by holding up his knee, which wasn't practical. 'Did Velody say you could trust all the sentinels, or just me?'

'You,' Rhian said, and again there was that brief waver of a smile. 'The others as well, but particularly you.'

'Here was I thinking it was Crane she had the soft spot for,' Macready said, a little smug.

'She does,' said Rhian. 'But she thinks he's reckless. He doesn't always think things through. She said you're always thinking, especially about other people. That's why you're the one she'd trust most with our lives, as well as her own.'

Hard not to be flattered by that. Macready found himself grinning as they swung Delphine's limp body into her room and laid her on a bright blue and green bedspread. The room was messy, full of dresses and shoes scattered any old how, and a dressing table so heaped with cosmetick products he might sneeze once and find himself fully made up in powder and colours.

'So,' he said as he pulled Delphine's shoes off, tossing them among the mess. 'She talks about us, does she? I wasn't sure if she would.'

'She tried,' said Rhian, sinking down on the bed beside Delphine. 'We couldn't understand most of it, and we reacted badly. I... closed off. The thought of Tierce, of everything we've lost, was too much. Delphine refused to acknowledge it at all. She finds it hard, I think, to believe there's another world around us that we can't see or hear. She has enough trouble dealing with this one. Now Velody doesn't say anything, and we can't even imagine what she's doing out there, what dangers she faces.'

What could Macready say to that? Should he apologise for taking Rhian's friend away and throwing her into danger and strangeness? It would sound as stupid out loud as it did in his head. Besides, it wasn't him that Velody owed her new life to. That was Ashiol all the way — and Poet, as well, had stuck his hand into the mix. Macready was still trying to figure that one out.

Rhian raised her troubled eyes to his. 'I'd like you to leave now.'

'Of course, lass.' He backed towards the door, but couldn't resist one more attempt to put her mind at rest. 'Whatever dangers Velody faces, she can handle them, so she can. She's stronger than she used to be. She has all of us looking out for her. What I mean to say is — I'd worry more about Delphine if I were you.'

'I do,' Rhian said softly. 'But I know Dee, inside and out. I know what she does to herself and I know why she does it. I don't know Velody at all any more.'

'I'm sorry,' he said, and he was right, it did sound stupid.

'I know,' said Rhian. 'I'd still like you to leave.'

38

TWO DAYS AFTER THE NONES OF LUCINA

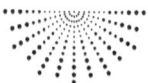

NOX

*V*elody let herself in the back door and made straight for the workroom. She couldn't believe she had left it so late. The couriers would be coming to pick up Vestalia gowns for Madame Miesje, Lady Anya Paucini and Lady Camellie in the morning, and she had hours of work ahead of her to finish the commissions on time.

Velody glared at the shadowed gowns on their mannikins as she lit the lamps. The Paucini demme's milkmaid outfit was complete, and the hems of the gowns for the older ladies were basted, but there was still finishing work to be done. It didn't help that the refined women of the court liked their festival peasant garb to be made from slippery, expensive fabrics.

She pulled Lady Camellie's gown from the mannikin and settled at the iron sewing machine to edge the hems with lengths of lace she had already cut and basted into place. If she worked fast, she might just be done in time to catch an hour or two of sleep before she had to prepare herself for her first visit down below. It was considered ill-luck to use machines after noxfall, but she would have to risk it.

Macready's scent alerted her to his presence as he came down the stairs. Her foot slipped from the treadle. He stood in the doorway to the workroom and coughed, a dry little sound, as if he didn't know she had sensed him coming.

Velody forced herself to keep working, eyes on the fine lace trim, foot moving steadily back and forth 'I know you have a good reason for being here,' she said in a measured voice. 'You wouldn't disobey my orders for anything other than a very good reason.'

'Rhian let me in,' he said.

Velody's fingers were cramping, still twitchy from her outdoor antics. She let go of the lace to stretch them a little. 'Why would she do that?'

'Brought your lass Delphine home.'

'Oh.' Velody concentrated on sewing a straight line, though her foot kept urging the machine to work too fast. 'She usually brings herself home.'

'Couldn't see how she was going to be managing it this time.' He glanced at the armchair opposite Velody's.

They never asked, these sentinels. She wasn't sure if it was an exaggerated courtesy or a leftover wariness from the days of Garnet. If they wanted any kind of favour or indulgence, they merely hinted at it and waited to see if an offer would be forthcoming.

Velody nodded impatiently at the chair. 'If you want to talk, then stay, but I have to keep working.'

'I wouldn't want to disturb,' he said, but sat.

The machine made a comfortable, noisy hum as Velody worked, while Macready watched her.

'If it's the lecture about how I shouldn't let Ashiol dictate my level of involvement with the Court,' she said when the silence got too much for her, 'I've already had that from Crane.'

'Have you now?' replied Macready.

'I don't know what you people want from me,' she said in frustration. 'How can I possibly be a good Power and Majesty if I don't have the faintest idea where to start? Of course I have to take my cues from Ashiol.'

'Stands to reason,' said Macready.

She glared at him. 'What did you want to talk about?'

'This and that.'

'I'm going down below tomorrow, as it happens,' she said. 'Well, later today.'

Macready leaned back a little in the chair, settling himself. 'When?'

Velody finished one hem and started measuring out the lace for the other. 'We're visiting the... Smith? For Crane's swords. Ashiol said noon was the time to go.'

'Indeed. About time,' said Macready.

She glanced up and saw that he was grinning broadly. 'You approve?'

'Swords are a fine thing for a grown lad.'

She congratulated herself on not blushing at the use of the word 'lad'. Seventeen. Oh, my. *Delphine will laugh herself sick about this one.* 'I suppose it's safer during the day,' she said. 'The Court will all be asleep.' It was a bitter thought, that the indulgence Ashiol had finally granted her was tempered by a safety net.

'As long as they don't wake up,' said Macready. 'The timing of it wasn't chosen to coddle you. The Smith's only available for one hour of each day, so he is.'

'Oh.'

Velody worked in silence for a little while longer. The satin of the gown was striped, cut in a bawdy fashion that no noble lady would dream of wearing on any day other than the Vestalia. When the festival was over, it would probably be tossed to a lady-in-waiting who would cut it up for cushions, or pass it on to a poor relation.

'When does all this have to be finished?' Macready asked, breaking the silence.

'The couriers are due an hour before noon,' Velody said around a mouthful of pins.

'Will you be done in time?'

'If I don't fall asleep and accidentally stitch the gowns together, yes, I expect so.'

'It must be difficult, so,' he ventured, 'working so many hours on these gowns of yours when your nox is taken up with other responsibilities.'

She gritted her teeth. 'Are you saying a Power and Majesty shouldn't be distracted by daylight concerns?'

'Of course not!' He sounded quite outraged. 'You have to earn a living, Majesty. Saving the city is a grand pursuit, but it puts no food on the table.'

'How do you manage?' she asked. How had she never thought of this before? 'There are only the three sentinels now, and you work day as often as nox when you're needed. How do you put food on the table?'

Macready didn't answer at first. 'There's an allowance paid,' he admitted finally. 'Enough to get by. In the old days, when there were a dozen of us, some had other jobs and lives as well.'

'The Creature Court pays you an allowance?' Velody asked, confused. At the pained expression on Macready's face, her mind cleared. 'Ashiol.'

'Garnet before him.'

'The Kings support the sentinels. Of course they do.' She turned back to her pinning, furious. 'No one told me!'

'Why should they, Majesty? You've enough to do supporting yourself. Ashiol has gold to spare.'

'That's not the point. Someone should have told me.'

Once again, Ashiol was usurping her responsibilities, wrapping her in cotton blankets to protect her from the reality of her position. *If he wants to be Power and Majesty, why didn't he damn well take it when he had the chance?*

Macready sighed. 'I didn't mean to get into all this.'

'What did you mean to do?'

'I'm worried about you, Majesty. And I'm not talking about Court politics. I mean you.' He took a long, slow breath. 'We broke something when we brought you into this new life, did we not? Yourself and your lasses. You had something important there, a fine balance, and we've shaken it all to pieces.'

Velody concentrated on her work. The machine made rapid, small stitches, more evenly than she ever could by hand. He wasn't talking about her dressmaking commissions, or her erratic income. He was talking about Velody, Delphine and Rhian.

'It was already in pieces,' she said. 'But you're right — the pieces were in balance. The daylight isn't just festivals and honey cakes, you know. There are darknesses in this world too, crime and violence. Men who think they're entitled to take anything they want from a woman, no matter her wishes.'

'You're talking about Rhian. I'd guessed as much, love.'

Velody laughed hollowly. 'Your guess is as good as ours,' she said, fighting to keep her voice steady. She kept her head turned away from him. 'She's never told us what happened, not really. From some of the things she has said while waking from bad dreams, we know there were men, more than one. We know they held her down. The rest was left to our imaginations. All we see is what was left behind.' She swallowed hard, but focused on the hemline and kept sewing. 'We all deal with horrible things differently, don't we? Rhian withdrew, more and more each day, until she had imprisoned herself in this house, hiding behind padlocks and bolts. The midwife thinks we should encourage her to do more for herself, to challenge her boundaries. We didn't mean to make it so easy for her to bury herself.'

'She's not the only one who buried herself,' noted Macready with a pointed look.

Velody slid another pin out and dropped it into the small padded box that she kept them in. 'True enough. I closed myself off to everything but my home and my work. Crane kissed me this nox, and I let him. It's the first time I've let a man do that to me for more than a year.'

'Gods, lass. What a waste.'

Velody couldn't help grinning at that. 'Kissing Crane, or not kissing anyone?'

'Both,' he said firmly.

Velody ducked her head away, glad that the lantern light was too dim for him to detect extra colour in her cheeks. 'Delphine dealt with it rather differently.'

'Aye, I've seen how she handles her pain.'

'Glad you brought her home. That set of hers can't always be trusted to do as much.'

'I saw that too.'

Velody sighed. 'You're right that becoming Power and Majesty has broken something, Mac, but I'm not sure it's such a bad thing that it's broken. We've been walled up in this house for too long. I know I should turn my back on the Creature Court, go back to looking after Rhian and Delphine like always, but I need this. I've tasted the sky now, and I want more of it. I want to be something bigger and better for once in my life.'

'Being the most sought after dressmaker in the city wouldn't do it for you?'

Velody slid her foot from the treadle, finally looking at

him. 'I always thought so. But when all those letters of commission started flooding in, the grand career I've always wanted, something inside me just sighed and said, "More work". Fighting the sky makes me feel alive. I want to be the Power and Majesty. I *need* it.'

Something powerful lit up Macready's eyes. 'Then *be* it,' he said, tripping over his tongue in his haste to get the words out. 'Be the Power, Majesty. You're not there yet, and you know it. Ashiol is cushioning your feet as you walk. Be who you need to be, throw yourself as far into the sky as you want. The sentinels will be there to catch you if you fall.'

It was a beautiful idea, and something inside Velody woke up and thrilled at the thought of it. *Stretch your hands as high as you like, sentinels. I won't fall.* 'What about Delphine and Rhian?'

'Ah,' said Macready. 'As to that, I have something of a plan.'

39

VESTALIA

THREE DAYS AFTER THE NONES OF LUCINA

DAYLIGHT

'*I* won't do it,' said Delphine, pouting like a six year old. 'You can't make me.'

It was an hour before noon and Velody still hadn't slept.

After Macready left she was swamped by a wave of tiredness that slowed her nimble fingers. The dresses were completed on time for the couriers, but there was little margin for rest.

Neither Delphine nor Rhian had work today, as there were no garland traditions for the Vestalia. Their next important festival was the Matralia in two days time, when mothers and maternal relatives everywhere would be crowned with silverbreath and ivy.

'Please, Dee,' said Velody, trying to smooth all irritation out of her voice. Without meaning to, she slipped into her Power and Majesty cadence. 'I need you with me today.'

'I don't see why,' said Delphine. 'You've got all your new friends to watch out for you.'

Velody glanced at Rhian, who was staring at the kitchen table as if it were fascinating. 'If we're going to keep living together, you have to understand what's changed in me,' she said. 'I need you to see it for yourself. I can't take Rhian, but you're not afraid of anything, Dee. Please come with me today.'

Delphine's head snapped around. 'If we're going to keep living together? You would *leave*?' she said incredulously.

'I can't stay if you hate me all the time,' Velody replied.

'I think you should go,' Rhian said unexpectedly.

'You're not serious?' said Delphine.

'Perfectly. I want to understand what's happening to Velody. I can't... I can't go, but you can.'

If there was one thing Delphine hated more than being told what to do, it was being told what to do by two people. 'You go if you're so keen to find out,' she shot at Rhian.

Rhian replied with surprising warmth. 'Velody's been looking after us for years, Delphine. Both of us. If it's our time to look after her, we need to know how. And why.'

Delphine glared at them both. 'Will *he* be there?' she asked after a moment, pronouncing the 'he' quite savagely.

Velody was amused at the venom. 'Macready? Yes, I think so.'

'I don't like him. He's smug.'

'What exactly did he save you from last nox?' Velody asked.

Delphine obviously didn't want to answer that one. 'What should I wear?' she asked with a sigh.

'What you're wearing is fine.'

Velody had gone for a plain green festival dress with a looping overskirt that implied an apron even though it wasn't strictly designed for the Vestalia. *They'll have to get used to me being me, not some strange, primped-up stage act.*

'Are you joking?' cried Delphine, jumping to her feet.

'These people eat and drink glamour. We can't wear *any* old thing!'

～

ASHIOL ARRIVED at the alley behind Velody's home to find the sentinels waiting for him. Kelpie looked the better for some sleep, wearing a crisp uniform and all four of her blades beneath her leather coat. Crane was bright-eyed and tense, only his strict sentinel training preventing him from fidgeting. Macready was Macready. Obviously the bastard wasn't human.

Ashiol already wished he hadn't let Poet's sly words push him into this.

Velody opened her gate and came out to greet him. She wore her hair up in businesslike fashion. No grandeur. Then her blonde bint of a housemate joined them, bright in a pale blue festival gown that barely covered her knees.

Ashiol turned on Macready, his eyes flashing dangerously. 'What is she doing here?' he hissed.

'Nature of an experiment, my King,' said Macready, not even flinching.

'You thought it appropriate *today*?'

'Our job isn't just to look out for the Power and Majesty,' replied the sentinel in an undertone. 'We also tend to the welfare of Velody.'

'Well?' began Velody, standing at the gate and pretending not to know about the tussle going on between the two men. 'Which way is it?'

'I thought we could walk across the city and go down below in the Lucian district,' said Ashiol. To his annoyance, Velody's gaze flicked to the sentinels as she considered her response.

'Why do Macready and Crane think that's a bad idea?' she asked.

Ashiol swung around to glare at Macready, who shrugged innocently.

Crane answered the question, little traitor that he was. 'It means you enter the old city almost immediately above the Killing Ground, which is where we find the Smith. You can probably get through today's ritual and be above ground again before any of the Creature Court even sense you're down there.'

'I see,' said Velody. Her eyes rested on Ashiol again. What was it about those grey eyes of hers? They were impossible to argue with. 'That would be appropriate, Ashiol, if I were a cat-burglar creeping into someone else's home. Somewhat less appropriate for a Power and Majesty visiting her own territory for the first time.'

The blonde was smirking. Had she forgotten her ordeal in Poet's dressing room so quickly? Daylight folk found it so easy to ignore what they did not understand. That was why they were bait and meat. Not warriors.

'What would you suggest, Macready?' Velody asked. Ashiol resisted the urge to bite her face off.

'The main entry isn't far from here, Majesty. You can walk up through the main tunnels and cross old Aufleur from one end to the other. Show them all you aren't afraid of making a bit of an entrance, so it will. You'll have to decide quickly, though, if we're to make it to the Smith during the hour after noon.'

Velody smiled that sweet smile that Ashiol was starting to hate. 'We'll follow you, Macready. Show us the way.'

Ashiol choked down the chimaera beast that rose inside him. *Let her be the Power and Majesty then, if she's a mind to it,* said a jealous voice inside him that could not belong to him.

Possibly it spoke in Garnet's accent. *See how far she gets before she needs to scream for help.*

This was what he had wanted. He had to remember that.

IT WAS A DARK PLACE, and dripping. They all stepped carefully along the dim tunnel, keeping their feet out of the water. Each of the sentinels carried a lantern on a pole, which sent shimmering patterns of light over the walls, ceiling and water.

Velody wanted this. Every little brown mouse within her tight human skin was squeaking with excitement. Her fingertips tingled. The old sensible part of her was a little concerned at how easily she had adapted to this life, but only a little.

She liked this new Velody.

'Is this where you've been spending your time?' Delphine asked as they made their way up the long, broad tunnel into old Aufleur, down below.

'This is my first visit,' said Velody.

Crane, walking ahead of them beside Ashiol, turned his head to grin at Velody. She smiled uncomfortably back.

Delphine had not missed either look, Velody knew, but mercifully she didn't comment. Velody was all too aware of the watchful Kelpie and Macready bringing up their rear. Seventeen. *Oh, saints.* Nearly ten years younger than herself.

There was more than Crane's puppy lust to think about today. Velody knew that in the days of the old skywar, Aufleur had been an underground city, housing a huge population. She also knew now that the remains of this once great engineering masterpiece served the Creature Court as a home. Still, it came as something of a shock when the tunnel opened out into a magnificent gallery, with an ornamental bridge cresting the sluice river. There was the cathedral. Velody hadn't expected a cathedral. It was as grand and imposing as anything she had seen in Aufleur above, for all that the points of its highest spires disappeared into a ceiling of dirt and cracked marble.

As she gazed up at the majesty of the architecture, a flock of pigeons burst out from an upper eyrie of the cathedral, descending to the bridge in a fall of graceful plumage. Ashiol and the sentinels all tensed at this first sign that they were not alone down here. Delphine giggled and pointed. Velody stared, only remembering a moment too late that the Creature Court included a Pigeon Lord.

Priest emerged from the flutter of pigeons in glowing Lord form. He swept a tapestry cloak from the floor of the bridge and wrapped it around his nakedness.

For my benefit? Velody wondered, not sure whether to be amused or wary.

Delphine's giggles had turned into a choking sound. Velody reached out absently and took her hand, squeezing it a little. 'Greetings, Lord of Pigeons,' she said aloud.

'Greetings of the day to you, Power and Majesty,' replied Priest in a deep, sombre voice. 'And what a fine day it is for a visit to your territories.'

Velody was not imagining that emphasis on 'day', she was certain. Neither had she missed the unspoken, 'And about time too', that he would never, of course, be impolite enough to speak aloud.

This one would disembowel me as soon as look at me, Velody decided. But he would display impeccable manners while doing it.

'We have brought our sentinel for a long-awaited appointment with the Smith,' she said aloud, trying not to sound as if she was explaining herself, or, worse, asking permission.

Priest's face did not falter. 'Indeed,' he said. 'We are not to be graced with a Court then, Majesty?'

'I would not be so discourteous as to call a Court during your time of rest, my Lord,' Velody answered diplomatically.

'We are at your call day or nox, Majesty,' he replied, bowing low. 'May I ask when we are to be thus honoured?'

Velody paused for only a moment. She could blaze with anger at the Pigeon Lord's effrontery, thus avoiding answering his difficult question. That was what Ashiol would want her to do. That's how he would handle it. *What would I do?*

She smiled sweetly and answered the impertinent question. 'This nox, my Lord. If it is not too short notice?'

She had the pleasure of seeing Ashiol's shoulder-blades stiffen.

Priest's whole demeanour changed. 'No, indeed, Majesty. We shall be prepared for your grace and presence.'

Velody inclined her head, feeling like a pantomime dame.

Ashiol turned around and looked at her, his face calm but his eyes burning. Velody nodded to him. 'We must not keep the Smith waiting,' she reminded him.

'Indeed not, Majesty,' Ashiol grated, and set off at a blistering pace, Crane hurrying to keep stride with him.

As Velody dragged Delphine after them, Macready and Kelpie close at their heels, she heard the cries of a flock of pigeons. It sounded remarkably like human laughter.

'It's some kind of cult, isn't it?' Delphine said breathlessly.

Velody rolled her eyes. 'In a manner of speaking.' She heard Macready's snort of laughter behind her. 'You needn't contribute.'

'A thousand pardons, Majesty,' he chuckled.

Ashiol led the way through a cluster of many small

cottage terrace buildings jammed up against each other and separated by narrow, oddly proportioned streets lined with round cobbles.

'Is this the Shambles?' Velody asked.

'We haven't time for a guided tour,' growled Ashiol. Obviously he wasn't going to berate her while there was a chance any of the Court might overhear.

They moved in silence now, into an awkward-shaped square in the middle of the Shambles, then through more tangled streets. When they emerged, it was into a strange, earthy place. It smelled of rot. Pinpricks of daylight shone through glass tiles in the ceiling.

'Where is this?' Velody asked, looking around in awe.

Macready sidled up beside her, swinging his lantern forward. The remains of dirt banks and landscaping were visible now — even the twisted remains of once-living trees. There were stones everywhere, each carefully placed. 'The Angel Gardens, so,' he said quietly. 'A grand place once. Food was grown here, and children played.' For a moment it seemed as if he was going to say more, but changed his mind.

'Why didn't anyone keep it going?' Velody asked, recognising that the place had once been beautiful.

'Eh, none of the Court are well-known for their green fingers,' Macready said. 'That's more of a daylight skill, would you not think?'

'It's getting warm,' said Delphine. 'I'm not shivering any more.'

'We're close then,' said Macready. 'Step lively, lass. Don't want to keep the man waiting.' He eyed Velody for a moment. 'I wouldn't practise your Power and Majesty airs on the Smith, lass. He's not where you might expect him to be in the pecking order. He's more alongside.'

'Doesn't react well to intimidation?' Velody replied, widening her eyes innocently.

Macready laughed in a sharp, surprised bark. 'Gods, lass. If our Crane didn't need his swords so much, I'd be tempted to see you try. What a show that would be!'

As they crossed the Angel Gardens, the sounds of a forge filled the air: metal striking metal with hollow, hot echoes. A gust of warm air breathed over them from ahead. Velody could smell coals and steel.

Ashiol halted in mid-stride, swinging around to face Velody. The glare still had not eased from his face. 'You lead us,' he said sharply.

Her confidence drained into somewhere near her feet. 'I don't know the way.'

Ashiol stared at her, implacable.

It was Crane who broke the silence, holding his hand out to Velody. 'I know the way, Majesty. We've been here before. You have to present me though. It's... the way it is.'

There was a note in his voice she had not heard before. Something very like fear. This was important to him, but it wasn't until now that she realised just how important. Slowly, Velody let Delphine's hand drop and reached out to Crane. Together, hand in hand, they walked into the dark.

The smell of the place was all heat and danger. Hair prickled all along Velody's skin. Her mouse-selves did not like this at all, though her inner chimaera uncurled at the scent of hot metal and the biting sounds.

She squeezed Crane's hand, and he led her towards a glow at the far side of the darkness.

A huge figure loomed up in the orange and grey shadows, large muscular arms pumping as he slammed hammer to anvil, turning a glowing blade as he worked. He did not look up as Velody and Crane approached.

Velody's mind had gone blank. Had Ashiol even told her what to say? Crane gave her a warning nudge in the side and the words came back to her in a merciful rush. 'Master

Smith, I bring you this loyal servant to be armed as is fit for a sentinel of the Creature Court of Aufleur.'

The ringing beat of hammer to anvil did not even slow. The Smith did not look up. 'A new Power and Majesty,' he grunted. 'Go through them like water, you do. Wasteful.' He glanced up in a moment between hammer strikes, and his cutting blue eyes swept over Velody to fasten on Crane. 'You're late,' he said.

'I was delayed,' said Crane.

'Don't mince words with me, boy. I know all about Garnet's game. No blades for the sentinels!' He turned back to his work, shaking his massive head. 'As if the Power and Majesty has a right to change such ancient traditions.'

'You don't seem surprised,' Ashiol's voice came clearly through the darkness, only a little way behind Velody and Crane, 'that our new Power and Majesty is a woman.'

The Smith plunged the blade he was working on into a water butt, and for a moment there was nothing but the hiss of steam in the air. 'Creature Kings,' he muttered. 'Forgotten more about your own selves than you ever knew. She's not the first.'

'Not —' Ashiol struggled to recover himself. 'Not the first?'

'How long have you been the Smith of Aufleur?' Velody asked.

The Smith turned to her, his blue eyes gleaming in his shaven head like the coals in his brazier. 'Since the first Creature King set foot on this piece of land, missy. When the city above was nothing but a wagon full of bricks and a plan scrawled on parchment. Before the skywars, before the old city below, before the world changed for the better and the worse, I was here.' He laid his cooled blade aside on a workbench. 'She was a lady, so she was,' he added, to no one in particular.

'The first female Creature King?' asked Velody. She wasn't sure whether to be shocked or pleased that she wasn't unique.

'Aye. Nice dame. Didn't last long.' The Smith shrugged a shoulder in Ashiol's direction. 'Don't trust their stories of the past, missy. They've never been good at holding on to their own history, the Creature Kings. Comes from feeding the Court with children. No perspective.' He stepped out from behind his anvil and looked Crane up and down. 'Blue-hilted daggers, wasn't it?'

Crane drew them from his belt and displayed both blades.

'I remember,' said the Smith. 'I've a nice spike of fresh skysilver that might suit you. Let's get you measured up, lad.'

Velody stepped out of the way as the Smith went through the solemn business of measuring Crane, testing his muscles to see what weight of metal would best suit him. The other sentinels and Ashiol came closer, watching the process with ceremonial gravity. Even Delphine seemed fascinated when the Smith brought forth the lengths of glimmering skysilver for Crane to choose from. The stuff made Velody's skin crawl.

She moved into the darkness away from the braziers, trying to find a space where she could sit quietly out of the way. When she found the outline of a heavy door, she only hesitated for a moment before pushing it open to escape the close heat of the forge.

Outside, she breathed shakily for a moment or two, her eyes closed against the glare of the sunlight as she took a moment to appreciate fresh air.

Sunshine and fresh air? She opened her eyes hurriedly. They were still underground, weren't they? But there was no denying the blue sky and the bright noon sunshine that blazed, a little pale for summer, overhead.

She stood in an empty arena, the ground scattered with a

367

light layer of sand over firm stone. Tiers of raised stone benches lined the arena, with a line of tall pine trees as their backdrop. When Velody turned back to the forge she saw nothing but a blank grey wall.

This was ridiculous. If she was above ground again, where was the city? They hadn't walked far enough for Aufleur to be completely out of sight. From what Ashiol had told her, they should be directly under the Lucian district, still within the curve of the river. There was nothing on the horizon but scrubby plains and distant mountains that were not at all familiar. Where was this place?

'The Killing Ground,' said a light voice. When Velody looked up at the stone benches again, she saw the spindly figure of Poet lounging on the topmost tier. 'It's not exactly part of the real world, if you're wondering. And yes, we are still underground.'

The pale sunshine was warm on Velody's face. 'Just when I think I'm getting used to all this...'

Poet laughed and rose to his feet, stepping down the banks of benches. 'I'm not supposed to be here, by the way. The Killing Ground is sacred to the Kings and sentinels. No lesser ranks allowed without express permission.'

She moved to the lowest tier of seats and sat down, stretching out her legs along the cold stone of the bench. 'If you hadn't told me, I wouldn't have known. Are you so keen to be punished?'

'A good subject should be truthful as well as loyal, don't you think?'

She was not being as careful as she should be, but it was hard to see Poet as a threat. She stifled a yawn. 'I'll get back to you on that one.'

He sat near her, crossing his legs under him like a child. The pale sunlight reflected off his spectacles. 'I hear you're honouring us with your presence this nox.'

Velody smiled. News certainly travelled fast in this place. 'Have you come to ask me for fashion advice?'

'I never take advice,' said Poet breezily. 'I only give it.'

'How would you advise me?'

'Wear something pretty.'

This time she laughed, and caught a strange look in his eyes as she recovered herself. *He's looking at me like I'm something good to eat. Oh, help.* She cleared her throat. 'I haven't had a chance to talk to you lately...'

'Whose fault is that? You've been hiding from us all, my Lady Power.'

'I've been wondering about the nox they made me Power and Majesty.'

Wondering was something of an understatement. Her memory of Poet hanging limply in the air, his body twisted around Ashiol's harsh chimaera claw, kept invading Velody's dreams.

'I remember the nox in question,' said Poet, not quite mocking her.

She was no good at dancing around subjects, and he had no respect for her attempts. Blunt was best, perhaps. Start as you mean to go on, she urged herself.

'I can't help thinking that someone wanted things to turn out the way they did that nox,' she said. 'That I was being manipulated into place. How much of it did you orchestrate?'

'Did I have ulterior motives for taking a claw to the gut?' Poet laughed softly. 'What a nasty mind you have, my Lady Power. I think you're going to fit in just fine around here.'

She wasn't put off, not now that she finally had a chance to resolve it in her own mind. 'At first I thought Ashiol had planned it that way, playing the monster to convince me I could do better. But he seems to be regretting the decision made that nox. I don't think he was in control at all.' She looked straight at Poet. 'Why on earth do you want me to be the Power and Majesty? Is it because you think I'm weak, or because you think I'm strong?'

His smile lit up his face, engulfing his entire body in a halo of charm. 'I haven't the faintest idea.'

She shook her head, more annoyed at herself than at him. What had she expected? Some grand revelation?

'Of all the Lords,' Poet said after a moment, in a voice accustomed to storytelling, 'Priest has the edge over the rest of us. Want to know why?'

'I'll take any information I can get.'

'Good choice. It's because he arrived in Aufleur as an adult, as a Lord in all his power. The rest of us are a family of squabbling brats who watched each other grow up and stumble over our first attempts at wielding power. Each of us, even the mighty Ashiol, has served as courteso or courtesa to at least one Lord, and had our share of public humiliations along the way. But there's still a touch of mystery about old Priest.'

'And that's what I am,' Velody said. 'A King that no one knows.'

'A Power and Majesty no one knows,' Poet corrected. 'We never saw you on your knees in service to a Lord or King — or in any more inventive positions, come to that. None of us knows your strengths and weaknesses and history. And, my Lady Power, you don't know ours.'

'You just like chaos,' she accused.

'I do have a taste for the unpredictable,' Poet admitted. 'Also the absurd, the decadent and the extreme. I'm a man of many tastes.' He reached out and touched her face. 'I like to throw the wildest dice I have, and stand well back to watch the results.'

This was ridiculous. At his touch, an inner heat filled her body, making her crave far more than the touch of his hand to her face. What was wrong with her? Bad enough that she had been running around the rooftops allowing herself to seduce a teenager, but she was damned if she was going to be attracted to this strange and dangerous specimen.

'You go too far, Lord of Rats,' she said haughtily, borrowing the voice pattern of an elderly Baronille who had once examined every inch of Velody's studio for dust before condescending to have a dress pattern commissioned.

Poet withdrew his hand and slid back on the bench, increasing the distance between them. 'Indeed I do, Majesty,' he said, bowing his head in the perfect semblance of humility. 'Your forgiveness?'

She pressed her lips together, trying not to laugh. 'I'm not entirely sure that you deserve it.'

He tilted a wicked grin up at her. 'Quite right, my Lady Power. I wouldn't trust an inch of me, if I were you.'

'Velody!' called a familiar voice. Delphine stood at the doorway to the forge, which had opened out of the blank grey wall.

'Calling for your blood,' said Poet. 'You'd better not keep them waiting.'

Velody pushed away from the stone bench and walked towards Delphine. When she looked back, there was no sign of him.

'You were talking to him,' Delphine said in an outraged hiss, 'like he's normal!'

Of course. Delphine had met Poet before. The explosion of white rats in the Orphan Princel's dressing room seemed years ago. 'Nothing about any of this is normal,' Velody said, too tired to explain further.

BLOOD, as it turned out, was exactly what they wanted from Velody. The Smith took it for granted that she knew she must donate her own essence to the quenching barrel that would cool Crane's swords at the end of the crafting.

'How much blood?' she asked, trying not to let her revulsion show.

'As much as is needed,' said Ashiol in a hard voice.

She rolled her eyes at him. 'I don't have to fill the whole barrel, do I?'

4 0

VESTALIA

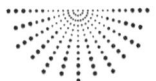

THREE DAYS AFTER THE NONES OF LUCINA

DAYLIGHT

*M*acready trailed behind Velody and Delphine as they walked home, arm in arm like any two young lasses out for an afternoon stroll. After Velody and Crane donated blood to the quenching barrel, the Smith made it quite clear that he did not require an audience for the entire swordmaking process. They were sent away before the hour ended.

To her credit, Delphine did not scream or faint when Crane opened Velody's vein with the skysilver blade, then his own with the steel, so that they could bleed simultaneously into the murky black waters of the quenching barrel. That lass had more backbone than Macready had ever hoped for. The plan might not be a total waste of everyone's time.

When they reached the kitchen door, Macready was prepared to melt off into the shadows and leave them all be, but Rhian opened the door before he had a chance.

'You'll join us for tea,' she said in a steady voice, meeting his eyes with her own.

How was a man to turn down such an offer? Ignoring startled looks from both Delphine and Velody, he sat at the kitchen table.

'It wasn't as bad as I expected,' said Delphine, as Rhian poured hot mint and lemon for them all. 'They're all quite nice.'

Macready blew a little on his own tea to disguise his grin. 'Not exactly the worst of them that you saw today, lass. Those were Velody's friends and allies, not the ones you have to worry about.'

'That Orphan Princel is pretty bad,' sniffed Delphine. 'Even he seemed almost civilised today.'

Macready gave Velody a hard look. 'When exactly did you see Poet, my Lady Power?'

Velody put her cup down. 'The Killing Ground, I think it's called. Behind the forge.'

Macready was outraged. For Rhian's sake he tried to keep his voice steady, but it still came out as something of a yelp. 'Poet invaded the Ground?'

'I don't know about invading it. He told me he wasn't allowed there.'

'Courteous of him, to be sure.' Macready was shaking. 'The Killing Ground is sacred to the *sentinels*, Majesty, not the Creature Kings. It's your duty to enforce the law that no member of the Lord and Court besides Kings may set foot in that place.'

'I'm sorry,' Velody said, eyes wide. 'I didn't know it was important.'

'There are few enough places where we're safe,' he muttered. 'Don't let Poet sweet-talk you, my Lady. He was born vicious, that one.'

Rhian's hands were trembling around her cup, so

Macready fell silent. How the angels was a fellow supposed to impress the danger of the situation on two women while reassuring a third that all was well?

Delphine broke the uncomfortable silence. 'What are you going to wear this evening, Velody?'

Velody took up the distraction. 'I think I have to go for something awe-inspiring. The Court are impressed by appearances, and they've never exactly seen me at my best.' She paused, thinking. 'Something loose and comfortable, in case I have to take it off in a hurry.'

Both Rhian and Delphine coughed on their tea.

Macready grinned, and refilled his cup from the pot. 'Avoid black and silver,' he advised. 'They're Livilla's colours. There's no competing with her on them.'

'Saints preserve that I compete with Livilla,' Velody said dryly.

'We should go up and look through the wardrobes now,' said Delphine. 'It will take ages to pick exactly the right thing, and we don't want to clash.'

Velody looked at her, startled. 'What do you mean, clash?'

'I'm coming along, aren't I?'

Now it was Macready's turn to splutter his tea.

'No,' said Velody. 'You're really not.'

'I came today,' Delphine argued. 'You can't just show me some of this Creature Court you're running around with and leave out the rest.'

Velody looked to Macready with a pleading expression on her face. 'Can you explain it?'

'You're the Power and Majesty, lass.'

'Now I know how Ashiol feels,' she muttered. 'Dee, you can't come. It's dangerous.'

'I don't see why,' said Delphine. 'We've been with those people half the day and not one of them tried to kill us.'

'The scary ones were all asleep!'

Delphine crossed her arms, defiant. 'If it's so dangerous, Velody, why are you going?'

Oh, yes, thought Macready in admiration. This lass was smarter than she looked.

'Because,' said Velody, 'I need to prove to Ashiol that I'm not afraid of any of them.'

'You're throwing yourself into the lion's mouth to impress a boy?' crowed Delphine. 'That's almost worthy of *me*!'

∾

HELIORA KNEW ASHIOL'S ANGER; it was as familiar to her as the rest of him. He vibrated with it, furious at her.

'If you're not going to do your duty as a seer, I don't know why you invited me here,' he said.

Heliora glared back at him. 'The seer is never obliged to put herself in danger at a King's request, particularly when the King in question is being as stupid as a bucket of bricks. You want me to check the futures to make sure your precious new Power and Majesty isn't going to die this nox? Do you have any idea how ridiculous that sounds?'

'I have a bad feeling.' Ashiol's eyes were rimmed with shadow and his whole body was tense.

Hel buried her hands in her gauze skirts to prevent herself from reaching out to rub his shoulders. 'You made her Power and Majesty, Ash. She has at least as much animor as you.'

'None of the experience though.'

'How is she going to get experience unless you throw her to the wolves from time to time?'

He gave her an exasperated look.

Heliora shook her head. 'She's not going to turn into Garnet the minute you stop trying to control her, you know.'

'So how do I stop *me* turning into Garnet?'

She busied herself with the teapot and cups. 'Idiot. Not being Power and Majesty is a good start. Not trying to manipulate everyone into doing things your way might also help. And then there's not being dead.'

His laugh was reluctant but genuine. 'You're good for me, brat.'

'Someone has to hold you back from the brink of total self-indulgence.' She watched him carefully as he swallowed his first mouthful of tea. 'When did you last eat?'

'I was going to stop by the Palazzo kitchens before I go back to Velody's.' He grinned at her, already looking more relaxed. 'My party clothes are still in my rooms there.' He stared at his cup. 'Hel, this is real tea. Where did you get hold of it? Can you let Isangell's steward in on the secret? The poor dope's going mad trying to secure a new supply line with the shortages this season. A fine thing when a fortune-teller's larder is better stocked than the Duchessa's.'

'It was a gift from a friend.'

'A well-connected friend,' Ashiol said with a yawn.

Heliora reached out to touch his hair. 'You've got hours and hours before noxfall. Why don't you rest here?'

'Might just do that.' His arms were crossed over the table top and his head drifted down to rest on them. 'For a little while. You'll wake me a couple of hours before sunset, won't you?'

'You've always been able to trust me,' she said in a voice so quiet that even she could barely hear it. *Oh, Ash. I'm so sorry.*

He began to snore. She sat on the floor beside him for several minutes, until the tent flap was pulled aside to reveal Poet. She glared at him, hating him only slightly more than herself. 'I can't believe you talked me into this, rat boy.'

Poet checked Ashiol's eyelids in a businesslike manner, then caressed his hair, unknowingly copying Hel's earlier gesture. 'You agreed we had to prise his hands off Velody's reins, even if only for one nox,' he said.

She gazed at him with bleak eyes. 'And where are your hands, Poet?'

Poet reached down and drew her to her feet like a true gentleman. Gravely, he kissed her on both cheeks. 'You know we have to do this.'

'If you use this opportunity to kill him,' Heliora said fiercely, 'I will hurt you in ways you cannot imagine. I will search the futures for the worst death anyone will ever experience and visit it upon you tenfold.'

He dabbed her on the nose with his thumb. 'You're very cute. Has anyone ever told you that?'

She looked past him to his courtesi, the bulky Halberk and the boy, Zero. Between them, they carried a hessian package. As they lowered it to the floor, Heliora caught a glimpse of the shiny silver contents and her blood went quite cold within her veins. 'Poet, no!' She lunged past him, but he held her wrists so hard that his fingers bruised her bones.

'Has to be done, little one.'

'Not the net,' she pleaded, struggling in his grip. 'Poet, please. It was the worst of all the things Garnet did to him! I promised you I would dose him for the whole nox!'

'So you did,' said Poet pleasantly. 'But you can see why I don't trust you. Your loyalty is to Ashiol first and the Creature Court second. You only agreed to help me so as to give your precious Ash the escape route he desires, to ensure that Velody truly succeeds Garnet as the Power and Majesty. You already regret what you have done — how am I to be sure you didn't give him half a dose, so that he had time to wake up and save the day?'

'You can't do this!' she screamed, still wriggling to get free. Poet was using his whole body to keep her still now and, for all his lack of bulk, he was remarkably strong.

'Hel, you know that you will die between now and Saturnalia,' he hissed in her ear. 'It doesn't have to be this nox.'

'Swear you won't kill him while he's helpless,' she sobbed. 'Swear by your blood!'

Poet pushed both her hands behind her back and held them fast with one of his own. With the other hand, he used a long fingernail to nick a cut in the soft flesh of his lower lip, allowing blood to well up there. He leaned in and kissed Heliora, not a polite kiss this time, but a hard melting of lips and tongue. His blood tasted of power, and his skin smelled of cinnamon. 'I swear on my blood that I will not kill him while he is helpless, and my prisoner,' he murmured into her mouth. 'Where would be the fun in that?'

Hel wrenched herself away from him and watched, helpless, as the two courtesi handled the shimmering net of skysilver, spilling it all around Ashiol's body and binding it fast with ropes and hessian. They were careful not to touch it themselves, their hands protected by thick gloves.

Ashiol twitched and shuddered as the net engulfed his skin, but the potion Hel had put in his tea was heavy enough that he did not regain consciousness. He would dream of burning pain, she had no doubt of that. He would wake screaming.

'I hate you for this,' she said to Poet.

'Not as much as our Ashiol is going to hate you when he wakes up,' Poet replied cheerfully.

VESTALIA

THREE DAYS AFTER THE NONES OF LUCINA

DAYLIGHT

*M*acready knew which way the wind was blowing — fringed shawls and beaded head-dresses — and he was quite happy to leave Crane to watch the lasses while they played dress-ups, thank you very much. Also he could do with a change of clothes himself, which meant a return visit to his nearest nest.

Two blocks from Via Silviana, Macready smelled ferax and slowed his trot. It was late afternoon and there were too many people around for him to comfortably draw his blades in preparation for an attack.

He might be safer if he kept to the populated streets, but if he dived into the nearest side alley now, he could have the comfort of Tarea and Jeunille to counter whatever Lord Dhynar was planning to throw at him.

It was too long since his lasses saw action. Macready headed for the alley, sliding his hands under his thick brown cloak to find the green hilts of his skysilver blades.

Five ferax bodies fell from the rooftops above to land at the far end of the alley, shaping themselves into the gleaming Lord form of Dhynar Lord Ferax. 'Macready,' he said with one of his more annoying grins.

The long blade of Tarea snicked out from under Macready's cloak. He held her steadily, aimed straight at Dhynar's bare chest. 'Something to say to me, my Lord?'

A soft padding sound alerted Macready to the presence of Dhynar's courtesi. He knew without looking that there were nine creatures filling the alley mouth behind him: two brighthounds, two darkhounds, two stripecats and three slashcats. He wasn't outnumbered. In their animal form, courtesi were particularly susceptible to the bite of a skysilver blade — even attacking him all at once, they would be cautious enough that he would have the advantage.

'I don't bandy words with servants,' said Dhynar lightly. 'I want something that belongs to you.'

'It's considered polite to ask before borrowing a man's possessions,' growled Macready, swinging his sword in a slight arc.

Dhynar stepped back in a graceful motion, as if he had all the time in the world. 'You're right, sentinel. I'm mortified by my own lack of manners. Throw down those shiny trinkets of yours and I might let you live.' He grinned a little harder. 'Please.'

Macready braced himself. His first move would have to be to throw his back against one of the side walls of the alley, to give himself the best chance against attack from both directions. 'You know you're going to have to make me.'

'So I am,' said Dhynar, and he took another leisurely step backwards.

'I have to say, your battle tactics are none too intimidating at the moment,' said Macready. 'A true challenge means stepping forward, don't you know?'

'Giving my friends some space,' said Dhynar. 'It's their party.'

Shapes twisted around the ferax's ankles and crept forward into the alley. A group of slender greymoon cats and brocks gathered at Dhynar's feet. Warlord's courtesi. Nasty. No one had seen that particular alliance coming.

Macready breathed out, tensing himself for a more challenging fight than he had expected.

The shadows moved again, and two large young-eyed wolves joined the cats and racoons. Livilla's boy.

Macready swallowed. Movement above caught his eye. The sky was full. Livilla's ravens and Warlord's bats lined the guttering on the buildings, rubbing wings with a mixed flock of gulls, plovers and sparrows. Priest was in on this too. Either that, or Dhynar had the power to control nearly all the courtesi of the Creature Court. Macready wasn't sure which was the more unpleasant thought.

'As I said,' Dhynar said cheerfully, 'I want your blades. They're necessary for this evening's entertainment.'

'You know you'll have to take them from me,' Macready repeated. His voice was only slightly hoarser than before; he was rather proud of that.

Dhynar shrugged and stepped even further back into the shadows. 'As you wish.'

The hounds leaped first, a beat ahead of the others. Macready swung his back to the wall and brought his sword around to slash at the creatures. The wolves pounced from his right side, even as the lower creatures swarmed at his feet and the vicious stripe- and slashcats screamed into view.

With rapid, stabbing sword and knifework, Macready managed somehow to hold his own, until the flying creatures descended and he went down beneath a harsh cloud of beaks and feathers. Teeth sank into his legs and, torso, and as he bent his head down to protect his eyes from the screeching hordes, long claws raked agonisingly into his back.

Somewhere beyond the mêlée, Dhynar Lord Ferax was laughing.

PREPARING Velody for the Court was, at least, a project all three women could share. When Rhian and Delphine had finished with her, Velody was sheathed in a sapphire flapper frock, an inch or two shorter than she was comfortable with, edged with fine silk fringe. Delphine begged it from Velody for her last birthday, even paying for the expensive fabric herself. She never wore it because the loathed Maud, one of her dance-club cronies, acquired a similar dress and wore it first in public. That, and as Delphine discovered upon first trying on the dress, the sophisticated dark jewel colours had the unfortunate tendency to make her look washed out.

With Velody's dark hair and grey eyes, the sapphire dress was inspired. Despite the various glittering and impractical shoes Delphine offered her, she chose calf-high boots with a sensible heel, keeping in mind the long walk underground to reach the centre of the old city.

Velody hadn't specified where the Court was to take place, and was uncertain where would be most appropriate. She would have to ask Ashiol when he arrived.

She wore shining paste earrings that were quite convincing as sapphires, and a long necklace of dark mock-pearls that could, she supposed, be used in a pinch as a weapon.

'I wish you'd let me cut those locks off,' Delphine sighed, but Velody was still unwilling to go that far in the name of fashion. She dressed her hair in the silvery net of a snood to keep it out of the way. The darkness of her hair was set off by a garland of summer violets. Rhian had sent one of her street runners to the docks to purchase the flowers especially.

It was dusk by the time Velody descended the stairs, and found Crane waiting for them at the foot. He had slicked up for the occasion, dressed all in black, his knives prominently displayed and with no sign of the usual ratty brown cloak. His stained-glass saint of a face took her breath away as he gazed up at her, but she kept a firm hold on herself. *No more flirting with teenagers. You've got enough problems.*

'No swords?' she asked as she reached him.

'Good smithery takes longer than a day,' said Crane with obvious regret. 'I wish you'd told Priest next week for this Court. I'll be properly armed by then.'

'Can't be helped. Where's Ash? I need to talk to him before we go below.'

'Kelpie's looking for him. He gave her the slip after we came up from the Arches, but she reckons she'll catch up with him when he swings by the Palazzo for a change of clothes. He hasn't got any stashed anywhere else.'

There was something troubling about Crane's face, or perhaps the set of his shoulders. 'There's nothing wrong, is there?' Velody asked.

'I don't think so. But they should be here by now.'

Delphine barrelled down the stairs wearing a shameless faux-silk wrap that covered almost everything, but looked as if it might not at any moment. 'You look pretty,' she said, eyeing up Crane. 'Where's the short one?'

'Macready? He takes a little longer to get pretty,' said Crane with a straight face.

'Doesn't surprise me in the least.' Delphine scrabbled around for the nearest pair of street shoes and pulled them onto her feet.

'You're not going out like that,' Velody protested.

'Just down to Maia's. I need to see if she has my white

frock.' The laundress whose home and business occupied the premises only two doors down was a useful friend of Delphine's.

'What's the rush?' said Velody. 'You're not going out this nox?'

'Why shouldn't I?' Delphine shot over her shoulder. 'If I can't come to your party, I'll find one of my own. Back in a minute!' She scrambled towards the back door.

Velody sighed. 'It's not a party!' she yelled for the dozenth time that afternoon. 'Oh, what's the use?'

She could see a filtered pattern of sunset-coloured light through the workroom windows. It was getting late. 'When was Ashiol going to meet us here?'

'Long before now,' said Crane. 'Something must have happened.'

'I don't like the sound of that.' She knew she was starting to sound panicky, but couldn't bring herself to try and preserve false majesty in front of Crane. 'I can't hold Court without him. I don't even know where to go. Where is it usually held?'

Crane stared at her. 'What do you mean, usually?' Now he was sounding panicky.

'I don't know,' she said. 'I mean, I assume down below, but that place is a labyrinth...'

Crane was horribly pale. 'You didn't specify a place when you called the Court? How did none of us notice that?'

'If you mean when I told Priest we could have a Court, you were all too stunned to notice much of anything.'

'A time,' he went on urgently. 'Did you specify a time?' Velody had never seen him look so fierce.

'Of course I did,' she said crossly. 'This nox.'

'Velody, that means you've given them free rein to obey your call to Court at any time this nox — and anywhere. I can't believe we let you do this,' he added.

'Not here,' she whispered. Her insides felt cold. 'Crane, they wouldn't come here. They couldn't. Each of them swore a blood oath to keep their distance —'

'The call to Court overrides all oaths,' he said grimly. 'Even those made in blood. It's their sacred duty to attend you — and without limits placed upon them, they can interpret that duty any way they like.'

Delphine's name caught in Velody's throat and stayed there. 'Stay with Rhian,' she flung over her shoulder as she headed for the kitchen.

'I shouldn't leave you!' he protested.

'I'll only be a minute!' She tore out the back door and through the yard, out into the lane. 'Dee!' she shrieked. 'Delphine!'

Halfway down the lane between Maia's laundry and their own gate, a crumpled faux-silk robe lay in the dirt. There was no sign of its owner. Velody swung back through her gate, and almost smacked into the chest of Dhynar Lord Ferax.

He wore red leathers, his gingery hair slicked back in something like a formal style. His eyes gleamed dangerously at her. Even as Velody took in the shock of him being here, here, he fell to his knees and bowed his head to her. 'Majesty. I see I am the first to obey your summons.' He flashed a toothy smile up at her. 'I wasn't always known for my extreme piety. You must bring out the best in me.'

His ferax scent was all around her, and there was nothing of a fight in it. She glared down at his innocent face. 'Where is Delphine?'

Dhynar's smile creased into a puzzled frown only momentarily before bouncing back into a wider grin than ever. 'I don't think I know a Delphine.'

She smiled back, grimly. 'I think you misunderstand me.' Her right hand shaped itself into a chimaera claw, blazing with power. She reached down and pressed the claw into his face. 'Where is my friend?'

'Oh,' he said, as if the thought had only just occurred to him, 'you mean the little blonde. She tried to stop me getting through the gate. You really should have warned her about that. Trying to stop a loyal member of the Creature Court fulfilling his sacred duty — well, that's just about the worst crime there is. She had to be punished.'

Velody let out a wild scream that was more bird than mouse — a primal sound of pain. She slashed Dhynar hard across the face and threw herself on him.

'Velody, not like that!' yelled someone — Crane — from a long way away.

She was beyond thinking. Her chimaera hand carved chunks out of the Ferax Lord, but the rest of her was human and scrabbling with pure rage.

He punched her in the stomach, and everything fell away from her. He had won the fight — she could tell that by his triumphant scent if nothing else. How was that even possible? A single punch. But he was still punching her, wasn't he? The pain was tight and hot and continuous in her stomach. As she rolled free of Dhynar, her body sagging on the hard paving stones, she saw the green leather-wrapped hilt of a knife sticking out of her flesh.

She knew this knife. Her name was Jeunille. It couldn't be her steel twin, as Velody was all but immune to the touch of ordinary metal now. Skysilver though — oh, yes, it was burning like skysilver.

'Macready,' she said in a gasp that barely managed to emerge from her dry throat.

'Oh, yes,' smirked Dhynar. 'The lovely Delphine isn't the only one of your friends I've seen this nox.'

Velody wasn't alone with the Ferax Lord. There were others around them, leaning in to see her pitiful state for themselves. Mars the Warlord's dark features, the painted face of Livilla, the curious smile of Priest, and finally Poet, who blew her a kiss.

'Don't be sad, Lady Power,' he said brightly. 'We're not planning on losing you. This is just another lesson in the life of the Creature Court. I'm afraid Ashiol has neglected your education.'

Velody coughed, and tasted blood on her lips. She was cold all over. *Do they really think a belly wound won't kill me? It feels pretty bloody mortal. Ash is going to be furious when he finds out...*

'I suppose we must let him through,' drawled Livilla.

'It would rather spoil the joke if we didn't,' said Priest. There was the sound of a scuffle, and then Crane was with Velody, kneeling over her, his own knife drawn. It was the steel knife. She didn't know if he had a stupid pet name for it, as Macready did. Saints. Was Macready dead? She couldn't imagine him giving his lasses up so easily.

'Won't do much damage with that,' she managed painfully.

'It's not for them,' said Crane. He held the steel blade to the side of his throat, pressing it hard until blood welled along the edge. 'Do you trust me, Velody?'

She stared at the bright red tear in his skin. *What is this — a suicide pact?* 'I...' was all she managed to say. Pain twisted in her belly.

He lowered his throat over her. Even with a knife in her gut, the close proximity of his body was disturbing. His blood smelled fresh and exciting. 'Drink,' he urged her.

She stared at him in horror. The vision of Poet's limp body in Ashiol's arms, feeding from him like a greedy spider, flashed into her mind and would not leave. It was one thing to offer her blood to others, but to drink it herself? What the seven hells had Ashiol turned her into?

'Velody, please. With mortal blood the skysilver can't hurt you. The wound will heal. It's the only way.'

The blood was dripping from the cut in his throat down onto her collarbone, onto the beautiful dress. The thought of tasting it revolted her. But she was so cold, and the blood was so warm... *I didn't think I'd like raw steak*, she reminded herself, and it almost made her laugh. Almost.

'Velody, now!' Crane demanded, in a rage worthy of Ashiol. 'Feed!'

She raised a numb hand to the side of his head and guided his wound to her mouth, closing her eyes as she did so. The blood tasted of life, and of warmth that went beyond sunshine.

To think she had spent so much time worrying about a stolen kiss on the rooftops! This was far more intimate. She suckled on the cut in Crane's throat, swallowing him by the mouthful. He was the freshest of fresh meat, the richest wine, the thickest and sweetest blood. Her body responded to him with a shudder and she pulled him closer.

The fact she was lying on her back in the yard, surrounded by people she barely knew, was there in her mind, but it was difficult to see it as being at all relevant.

Crane's body covered hers, his muscles pressing into her soft curves, and there was one muscle in particular that she could feel, hard and urgent against her. *Definitely going too far*, she thought, even as she raised her chimaera claw to slice his clothes from his body.

It wasn't there. She could not remember consciously changing and yet the claw had withdrawn back into her own narrow, stub-nailed fingers. She stared at them for a moment, and withdrew her bloody mouth from Crane's throat.

He kissed her mouth in what could only be a ceremonial fashion, tasting himself on her lips.

She reached for her familiar shape of little brown mice and could not find them. In a panic, she tried to shape herself into Lord form, then chimaera, and remained nothing but Velody. 'What have you done to me?'

Crane opened his mouth to speak, but she shoved him away and sat up, her mind racing. She was in a yard filled with the most powerful members of the Creature Court — with all of them, in fact. The courtesi lined the shabby fence, naked or dressed in elaborate finery, and all five Lords were in attendance. Everyone but Ashiol. *They're all here and I'm powerless.*

Priest was the first to speak — or laugh, rather. 'Darling demoiselle, did no one ever tell you what sentinels are for? You can't have honestly thought they were there as your bodyguards.'

'They're food,' broke in Livilla in her usual sneering drawl. 'A particularly convenient food, reserved for those of the highest rank. Their blood can save you from most of the deaths of our kind, even the skysilver wounds that can heal no other way.'

'Didn't do Garnet much good,' said Velody.

'He found the one death we couldn't save him from,' said Crane in a small voice.

She looked down at herself. Macready's green-hilted knife still rested in her stomach, pinning the dark sapphire dress into her flesh. It didn't hurt. She didn't even feel short of breath. 'How?'

'Skysilver wounds those of the Creature Court,' said Crane. He took hold of the hilt, pulling out the blade. It emerged smoothly from Velody and her dress, leaving a hole in the fabric. 'Drinking me made you mortal.'

She swallowed. Was it as easy as that? 'I'm not your Power and Majesty any more then. You can all leave. Make sure you close the gate on your way out.'

Now it was Poet's turn to laugh. 'Oh, you're still queen of the castle, precious one. Your animor will assert itself over the mortal blood within a day or so.'

'I'm supposed to believe that you won't kill me in the meantime?'

'Why should we?' asked Warlord. He had a rich voice heavy with a Zafiran accent. 'We cannot quench a mortal. Your death would serve no purpose but to make the Court weaker.'

Velody squeezed her eyes shut for a moment, then opened them again. 'Fine. If I'm still your Power and Majesty, you can start by telling me where Delphine is.'

'Her,' said Livilla with disgust. 'You can have her back. She's been nothing but trouble.'

She moved aside, and the taller and darker of her two courtesi dragged a struggling Delphine out from a corner of the yard, pushing her roughly to the ground. Delphine wore only a faded camisole slip, so thin as to be indecent, and the clumpy street shoes she had pulled on to make her dash to the laundress's. Her hands were tied in front of her and a rough gag had been shoved into her mouth. She looked more angry than scared.

Crane passed his steel knife to Velody, who slit the cords that bound Delphine's wrists. Delphine pulled the gag from her mouth herself. 'What the hells —' she started to say.

'Go inside,' said Velody. No time now to collapse in relief that her friend was not dead. There were other friends at risk this nox.

'If you think I'm leaving you alone with these maniacs —'

'Please, Delphine. Now.'

Reluctantly, the blonde pushed herself to her feet, glared around the yard at the intruders, and headed for the kitchen door.

'And now,' said Velody in a voice so calm that it frightened her, 'perhaps one of you can tell me if Macready is alive.'

Delphine turned at that, and sat suddenly on the steps, eyes wide.

Velody looked straight at Poet, eyes locking hard with his. 'Well?'

'No point in asking me, little miss,' he said insolently. 'I wasn't there.'

Her eyes passed over each face of the Creature Court until she reached Dhynar. 'Well?' she said again.

The Ferax Lord shrugged and grinned. 'He was breathing when we left him, Lady Power.'

'There's dried blood on the hilt of his dagger,' she said.

Dhynar's grin widened, and he opened his long red leather coat to reveal a second skysilver blade — Macready's sword. 'Even more blood on this one, Lady Majesty.'

'He was bleeding, all right,' said one of Dhynar's courtesi, a young man with white hair and strange, pale eyes. 'Bleeding from every bit of him.'

'Breathing may be a luxury he has since learned to do without,' Dhynar admitted without shame.

Velody rose to her feet, fury crackling under her skin. 'One of you will fetch him to me,' she ordered in a strong voice. 'Now.'

There was a long pause. 'I think you have failed to understand us,' said the rich Zafiran accent of Warlord. 'You are still our Power and Majesty, Lady, but if you want us to obey your commands, you must make us do so.'

'You have to bully us into it,' said Priest, sounding amused. 'Scare us enough to force us to do your will, or convince us by any other means you have at your disposal. Since you are currently powerless, we're all rather interested to see how you manage it.'

Solemnly, he raised his eyes to the sky. They were all looking upwards, even Crane. Velody was the last to realise.

Even as the last light of evening faded into darkness, thin veins of light crackled along the clouds. How had she missed it? Ashiol had trained her so well that she should have tasted the coming of a silverstorm long before the attack began.

But she had no animor to hear the sky's warnings. This nox, she was mortal.

42

VESTALIA

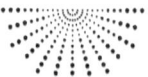

THREE DAYS AFTER THE NONES OF LUCINA

NOX

*T*he air was cold for a summer evening. Shapes moved across the dark sky; stabbing shapes like spikes of ice. Ashiol was nowhere in sight, and Velody didn't have enough animor in her to produce a single little brown mouse.

'Ouch,' said Poet with some satisfaction. 'This is going to hurt.'

Velody sighed. 'I suppose there's little chance of convincing you all that you should leap into the sky and defend the city simply because it is your sacred duty?'

'I like her,' said Priest. 'She's funny.'

Velody stared helplessly at their hostile faces. 'What do you want from me?' she asked finally. 'What will it take to get you in that sky?'

The clouds were screaming now, and there was a nasty orange glow to the south, which meant that fireworms were a definite possibility.

'More than you have, pretty lady,' said Warlord.

Very deliberately, Livilla spat on the ground. Priest took two steps away from her, but said nothing. Dhynar grinned so hard that it was surprising his face didn't fall off. The courtesi were blank-faced, waiting for their Lords to make the decisions.

Poet sank to his knees before Velody. Behind him, both the giant Halberk and skinny boy Zero followed suit. 'Lady,' said Poet. 'My courtesi and I are at your command.'

Velody blinked. 'What?'

'Only say the word, Power and Majesty, and we three will hurl ourselves into battle against the sky, or obey any other command you choose to make of us.'

'Poet, this is not what we agreed,' Livilla said sharply.

'Speak for yourself, sweetie-pie,' he tossed over his shoulder. 'I just got a reputation as her Ladyship's most loyal follower.' He smirked at Velody. 'I told you that you could count on me when things got difficult.'

'So you did. I might be flattered if I didn't think you arranged these fun and games just to produce this particular result.'

'You wound me,' he said happily. 'Are we taking to the sky?'

A sizzling bolt cracked over their heads, slicing down into the nearby neighbourhood. There was an explosion, and skysilver shards burst into the air. 'Go!' Velody ordered.

'You heard the lady,' Poet told his courtesi. He fell apart into a horde of white rats that soared up into the empty air as if they weighed nothing. Halberk became a bear and leaped after his master, while Zero shaped himself into a gang of weasels and followed suit.

For a moment, Velody could hear nothing in the yard but Delphine's shaky breathing. She was quite shaky herself.

'His effort was wasted,' sneered Livilla. 'One Lord cannot

hold the sky alone. Without the rest of us, the fool will die up there and the city shall fall.'

'Well, then,' said Velody, 'Poet must have a great deal of faith that I can convince the rest of you to join him. Shall we open the negotiations?'

The four remaining Lords stared at her.

'Well?' she continued defensively. 'Obviously I can't threaten you into this. I'll have to bribe you. What do you want from me?'

Warlord unfolded his body from the nearest fence, a superior look upon his face. 'Blood,' he said.

Velody still held Crane's steel knife. She tilted it obediently towards her wrist. 'How much?'

Warlord spluttered with something like laughter. 'Mortal blood is of little use to me, Lady Power. When you are Creature King again, your blood will be worth something.'

She gazed steadily at him, pleased with her ability to do so. 'I can't spare all of it.'

'A goblet will be sufficient.'

Velody couldn't help the look of distaste that crossed her face. 'Fine, just don't tell me what you plan to do with it. I may throw up.' Until now, she had managed to ignore the fact that her own face was encrusted with dried blood from Crane.

Warlord was still staring at her. 'What?' Velody said impatiently.

'You agree to my request?'

'I just said so, didn't I?'

'You will truly give me a goblet of your blood — of Creature King's blood?'

'I expect you to work for it. But yes, if you fight the skybattle this nox, to the best of your ability, I will reward you as you ask.' At his disbelieving expression, she jabbed the tip of Crane's steel dagger into her thumb, drawing a dot of blood. 'Blood oath, if you like. It seems appropriate.'

After another startled pause, Warlord bowed low. 'Majesty,' he said. He nodded to his courtesi, and they all took to the sky in a tight military formation: a hardened gang of brocks, greymoons and bats led by one powerful black panther.

Velody looked around the remaining Lords. 'Has no one thought of giving you presents before?'

'The courtesi give offerings to the Lords, and the Lords give offerings to the Kings,' said Crane, sounding amused. 'It never happens the other way around.' The ugly wound in his throat no longer bled.

'Well,' said Velody, 'the idea was for me to be a different Power and Majesty, wasn't it? This sounds like a start.'

'I have a request,' said Livilla suddenly.

'Ask away,' said Velody.

The female Lord swayed forward on unwieldy heels. She wore a revealing black flapper dress — the flapper fashion as interpreted by high-class brothels. The dress was made of a satin so fine that every contour and detail of her rail- thin body was visible.

If I ever retire as Power and Majesty, Velody thought giddily, *I could have great fun designing wardrobes for these people.*

'I want a promise,' said Livilla. She eyed the red dab on Velody's thumb. 'A blood oath, of course.'

'Of course,' said Velody as if she did this every day.

Livilla raised a pencilled eyebrow and pursed her wine-red mouth. 'When Ashiol Xandelian fucks you for the first time, I want to be there.'

For a moment, Velody thought she had had a stroke. There was a strange buzzing in the back of her head. '*Excuse* me?'

'You heard,' said Livilla. 'Everyone knows it's going to

happen sooner or later. I want a front-row bench to the action.'

'Everyone knows...' Velody repeated. She stared wildly around the yard. 'Does everyone really think I'm going to end up in Ashiol's bed?'

Delphine's hand shot up. The Lords and Court looked amused, all of them.

'Wonderful,' Velody muttered. The very thought of it made her skin crawl. Ashiol Xandelian. It would be like embracing a rabid lion in a snake pit — insanely dangerous.

She turned her glare back to Livilla. 'It's never going to happen.'

'So you say.'

'I mean it!'

'Well, then. The vow earns you my obedience on this one nox and costs you nothing.' The wine-coloured mouth curved into an unpleasant smile. 'It seems to me you have the best of the bargain.'

Grumbling, Velody jabbed her thumb with the dagger again.

'Velody,' Crane said in a low warning. 'Ash won't like this.'

She shot him a scornful look, and displayed her bloody thumb to Livilla. 'I swear that in the very unlikely event that Ashiol and I have sex, you can witness it.' Ha, that would be a nice little insurance policy, at least.

'Thank you,' Livilla said sweetly. She returned to her two courtesi. With solemn precision, the three of them stripped their clothes from their bodies, making sure everyone had a good view of the show, and then shaped themselves into animal form. Several wolves leaped into the sky, surrounded by a flock of ravens.

Velody looked at Priest and smiled her best smile.

He shook his head. 'No point in that, little miss. I cannot

be bought off by trinkets like the young ones. You have nothing that I want.'

Velody looked up. The sky was ablaze with light and colour. She might not be a Creature King right now, but Crane's blood had left her with the basic senses of a sentinel — the awareness of skybattles, for a start. You couldn't see much from down here, but an occasional familiar shape would dart across the clouds straight above them, battling a power tendril or chasing a skybolt. Poet, Warlord, Livilla and their courtesi had their work cut out for them.

'The fact that your friends need help means nothing to you?' she asked.

'They're not my friends,' said Priest.

'The city may well be destroyed.'

'It's not my city.'

That was true enough. Ashiol had told her that, of all of them, Priest had the least allegiance to Aufleur as he had arrived only a little over a decade ago, a fully developed Lord.

Velody nodded. She moved towards Priest, looking him up and down. Hard to tell if he was playing a game like Poet, or if he truly meant what he said. Perhaps meaning what he said was the game. 'Nice waistcoat,' she commented.

Priest eyed her suspiciously. 'You've been doing so well with honesty this nox, Lady Power. A shame to act the coy demoiselle now.'

'No, really. I like it.' She reached out and tugged a little at the green velvet that enveloped his paunch. 'Good fabric. Shame about the cut.'

Priest shifted in annoyance. 'This was made by the finest tailor in Aufleur.'

'Oh, Donagan,' she agreed. 'His work stands out. I recognised it instantly. A master craftsman, I agree. His designs have stood the test of time.'

'If you're suggesting my tailor is old-fashioned,' he growled, 'I prefer last century's styles.'

'Of course.' Velody nodded. 'They suit you. But as I was taught as an apprentice, the older styles can be made so much more comfortable and flattering by applying a little modern technique. Poor old Donagan still uses all the stitches that his grandfather taught him. Classic, of course, but hardly cutting edge.' She smiled at her own pun.

Priest tipped his head back, looking her over. 'What exactly are you offering, little miss?'

'A waistcoat, of course. I have a peacock design that would suit you so beautifully, and I think you'll have trouble going back to Donagan after you feel the results of my tailoring.'

'You'd make it for me with your own two hands?' he demanded roughly.

She wiggled her fingers at him. 'The only hands I've got.'

'You strike a hard bargain, Lady Power.'

'Power and Majesty,' she corrected in a firm voice.

Priest shook his head and smiled. 'Power and Majesty,' he agreed. 'I look forward to collecting my waistcoat.'

'My best work,' she promised him.

'Come, ladies,' he called to his courtesi. 'We've got a sky to fight.'

As Priest and his women scattered upwards in a cloud of feathers, Velody turned her attention to Dhynar. Crane came to her side, his skysilver blade held loosely in his right hand.

Dhynar smirked, his four courtesi flanking him. 'And what are you going to offer me, *little miss*? I've got a few ideas on how you can please me enough to send me into battle.' He jerked a head in Delphine's direction. 'You can have her giftwrapped, for a start.'

'Oh, you misunderstand,' Velody said sweetly. 'You're not fighting the sky, Dhynar. I have another use for you. You're going to show me exactly where you left Macready. If he's still alive, you can survive the nox.'

Dhynar laughed openly. 'And what exactly are you threatening me with, princessa? Your boy's stabbing knife? I could break his neck before he got anywhere near me.'

'True enough,' said Velody. It was amazing, really, the senses at a sentinel's disposal. She had never wondered about the extent of their powers, but now she was wholly reliant on them. She could feel Crane's entire presence, his every reaction, without even looking at him. She knew exactly where he was and what he was ready for. She was aware of another presence, beyond the wooden fence, and was just as aware that Dhynar remained oblivious to that presence. Interesting, the limitations of a Creature Lord. She had thought them able to sniff out any danger.

Perhaps the pervading scent of blood and skybattle in the air had clouded his senses.

'Crane is not the only blade at my disposal,' she said quietly.

'Oh, please,' Dhynar laughed. 'Let the little blonde come at me with a kitchen knife. I'll enjoy that.'

A long blade blossomed in his chest, sliding through the leather as if through butter. He staggered, unable to fall. The sword pinned him through two palings of the firm wooden fence, from the other side.

'You forgot to count, Ferax,' snarled Kelpie as she strolled through the open gate a moment later. 'You only disarmed one sentinel.'

'Been out there a while, have you?' Velody couldn't help asking.

Kelpie turned unfriendly eyes on her. 'I like to know what's going on.'

Blood dribbled out of Dhynar's mouth. Velody stared at

him. It was hard to find sympathy for his belly wound. 'He has Macready's sword,' she said.

Kelpie patted her victim down dispassionately and removed the sword from under his coat. 'Now he's got mine instead,' she said. 'Fair trade.'

Dhynar's four courtesi hung back, unsure what move to make.

'Now,' said Velody, staring at Dhynar. If she could get through this without her legs collapsing from under her, she would be happy. 'I want to know where Macready is.'

'Ashiol too,' broke in Kelpie. 'They've done something to keep him out of the way.'

Dhynar smiled fiercely. 'Don't know anything,' he coughed, and there was more blood in his mouth now.

'Let him die,' said Kelpie. 'We've got five skysilver blades between us. We can cut the truth out of his courtesi.'

'The Creature Lords serve me,' Velody said between gritted teeth. 'He will answer my question.'

Dhynar's eyes flashed defiantly. He pushed his hands back against the palings of the fence and took one staggering step forward, then another, dragging his body painfully along the long blade of the sword.

'Oh, no!' Kelpie shoved her hands against his shoulders, pushing him hard against the fence again. 'No quick death for you. Answer the Majesty's question.'

Dhynar was too far gone to talk. His whole body convulsed. His courtesi crept near him, huddling at his feet, each of them trying to touch him.

'Can they help him?' Velody asked in an undertone.

'They can help themselves,' Kelpie spat. 'Parasites. There's nothing they can do to heal him from a skysilver wound — they're staying close so they can quench him when he dies.'

Velody made her mind up quickly. 'Crane, remove the sword. Kelpie, open a vein.'

Crane hurried through the gate. Kelpie whirled around, fury on her face. 'What?'

'I need him alive. If there's one thing I've learned this nox, it's that sentinel blood can heal skysilver wounds.'

'We don't give our blood to scum like him!' Kelpie was horrified. 'It's a sacred gift, only meant for the Creature Kings.'

'I'm a Creature King and I want your blood,' Velody demanded. 'In him. Now!'

'I won't do it!' Kelpie screamed.

The sword blade slithered back through the palings as Crane drew it out from the other side of the fence. Dhynar fell forward onto the ground, blood gushing from the wound in his stomach.

'Am I your Power and Majesty or not?' Velody thundered. The Creature Lords were not the only ones who had to learn to obey her.

Kelpie shook with rage, but she took her steel knife and sliced into her own wrist. She went down on her knees and thrust her bleeding wrist against Dhynar's face.

He gasped like a starving man and his mouth locked over her. Kelpie gritted her teeth as he suckled from her wrist.

Crane returned with Kelpie's bloody sword, heading directly to the kitchen steps. 'Do you have any rags?' he asked Delphine.

Silently, Delphine went inside and returned with a handful of torn cloth. Crane began to clean the sword.

After a few minutes, Kelpie shoved her other hand in Dhynar's face and broke his grasp on her. He rolled over obediently, and she clutched her wrist to her body. 'That's it,' she snapped. 'I'm not giving him any more.'

'Will he live?' Velody asked.

'If I don't get tempted to stick another blade in him.'

'Good.' Velody eyed Dhynar's four courtesi. 'What do you have to say for yourselves?'

'Our Lord is beaten,' said the white-haired courteso. 'We submit to the service of the Power and Majesty.'

The other three nodded in hasty agreement.

'I see,' said Velody. 'Good choice,' she added. 'Two of you can help your Lord to his feet, and the other two can lead the way. We want our fallen sentinel, and we want him now.'

THEIR NAMES WERE SHADE, Lennoc, Grago and Farrier. Without their Lord to lead them, they were utterly submissive. Velody didn't trust them an inch.

Kelpie was clearly angry. Her whole body language screamed fury. She hated that Crane had been left behind to protect Delphine and Rhian, she hated that all four of the courtesi had been brought on this march to the spot where Macready had been left in a pool of his own blood, she hated that they were being slowed down by the stumbling, powerless figure of Dhynar Lord Ferax, and she hated that Dhynar had not been allowed to die. Most of all, it seemed to Velody, Kelpie hated taking orders from anyone who was not Ashiol.

Overhead, the sky was bleak and angry. The quick movements of the swooping figures battling the storm spoke of urgency and desperation. Velody tried not to look up. She didn't want to think about how differently the battle might be going if she and Ashiol were up there in chimaera form, putting her training to good use.

Where was Ashiol? What had they done to him to keep him away from her while all this was going on? She dismissed the fleeting idea that he might have been in on this plan to force her independence. The flames of the seven hells would freeze solid before Ashiol Xandelian voluntarily relinquished control over anything.

Was he dead? Was Macready?

Kelpie sucked in a breath as they turned into a narrow alley off Via Leondrine. Velody, still unused to the duller senses of the sentinels, took longer to smell the blood. It didn't take sentinel senses to see the ugly dark smear on the uneven cobbles though, or the marks that showed where a badly beaten body had forcibly dragged himself along the ground.

Macready lay just beyond the first curve of the alley, his body crumpled where he had run out of strength. His clothes were in tatters, clawed and scratched from his body in thin strips. Every inch of his visible skin was bleeding, with hundreds of tiny wounds and several larger, angrier gouges. Kelpie was the first to reach him, tears streaming down her face as she turned him over. His face was unrecognisable beneath the swelling, the blood and the claw marks. His eyes were closed.

'He's still warm,' she said. 'Velody, there's no pulse.'

'There is a pulse,' corrected Lennoc, the white-haired courteso with calm eyes. He tilted his head a little as Velody swung around to stare at him. 'He lives,' he said.

'He's not breathing!' Kelpie said in a ragged voice.

Velody's eyes fixed on the strange, pinkish irises of Lennoc. 'Feed him,' she said in a low voice.

'No!' snarled Dhynar. The two smaller of his courtesi held him against a wall for support. He was recovering more slowly from his skysilver wound than Velody had, perhaps because Kelpie had stopped the blood infusion so soon. Crane, Velody remembered, had encouraged her to be greedy. He would have let her drink him dry if she had wanted it.

'Did you say something, Ferax?' Velody asked coldly.

'You do not order my courtesi to do your bidding, Lady Power,' he growled. 'That is not your place.'

Velody made eye contact with the two young men who supported their Lord and master. 'Let go of him,' she rapped out.

They obeyed without question, opening their hands and stepping aside from Dhynar. He half-slid down the wall and steadied himself with his own hands. 'You can't do this!' he all but wailed.

Velody turned back to Lennoc. The albino had a strange face, delicate but unpretty. 'Please feed him,' she said again. 'Just a taste of your blood.'

Intelligence gleamed in Lennoc's eyes. 'As you wish, Power and Majesty.'

The courteso went to Macready, kneeling beside Kelpie. He sank teeth into his own lower lip, then leaned down to press his mouth to Macready's. When he drew back, he gathered more welling blood on his finger and pushed it gently inside Macready's mouth, touching his tongue.

Kelpie turned her head away as if she could not bear to look.

Shade, Lennoc's dark-eyed partner, moved next. He copied Lennoc's gestures entirely, biting blood from his own mouth, bestowing a bloody kiss on Macready's unconscious lips, and pressing a blood-stained finger inside the sentinel's mouth.

'Why are you doing this?' Kelpie asked resentfully.

'Lord Dhynar took us in when Lord Lief was killed,' said Lennoc calmly. 'Our loyalty is to him, who saved our lives. He is our Lord, for as long as he breathes. But she is our Lady. She is the Power and Majesty, and our Lord gave oath to her, as did we all.'

Shade nodded in agreement.

Velody only had to glance at the two younger courtesi,

Grago and Farrier, and they left the side of their Lord and master. Both bit into their own wrists with surprisingly sharp teeth, and took turns to hold them over Macready's mouth.

Macready twitched once and his mouth opened a little further.

'She doesn't even have any power,' Kelpie said in frustration. 'You're all obeying her like she's done something special.'

Whose side are you on, sentinel? Velody thought angrily, but she didn't need an answer to that. She had always known it. Kelpie resented the idea of serving a woman.

'Farrier and I have never known a Lord but our Lord Dhynar,' said young Grago, who must have been all of eighteen. Fifteen, Velody revised, remembering her earlier guesses about Crane. 'But she is our Lady. Our Power and Majesty.'

'She saved his life when you would have taken it,' added Farrier.

Kelpie had nothing to say to that.

Macready's body shone with fierce energy as the combined blood of four courtesi did its work on him. He panted as if he had been running hard.

'Do you really think you can rule us with bribes and kisses?' Dhynar sneered, more in control of his body now. 'Do you think tender mercy will give you an edge over Garnet's strength and cruelty?'

'My flesh is unmarked,' Velody said. 'Your courtesi obey my commands, and your life was mine to spare this nox. Are you so sure that my heart is tender, my Lord Ferax?'

～

CURLED up in Velody's favourite chair by the fire, Delphine did her very best not to chew off her manicured nails. She splayed her fingers on her lap, silently reminding herself how much the shaping and polishing had cost her. A ridiculous extravagance for someone who made her living stitching ribbons and winding garlands, but she had spent half a week's income on it, and it was hers to protect.

Velody's protectors were falling like rose petals. The Ducomte Ashiol was missing, Macready was probably dead... Delphine had seen the face of Velody's new world this nox and it was horrifying.

They toy with each other like cats and mice, and sometimes they die.

Crane, hovering in the doorway of the workroom, looked as nervous as Delphine felt. He had checked the perimeter of the house several times, and would not admit to being shaky from his earlier blood loss. Delphine should tell him to sit down, but she didn't want to dent the boy's ego. Right now, he was the only thing standing between herself, Rhian and whatever new dangers the Creature Court had to offer.

At least they left me something pretty to look at, she thought, and stifled a crazy giggle.

Rhian was coping. She had remained inside while all the drama was going on and Delphine could not be sure how much she had heard or seen, despite the fact that Rhian's bedroom window overlooked the backyard. Delphine could only hope that Rhian had not witnessed the one scene she herself was desperately trying to forget — that of Velody writhing beneath Crane, her mouth locked over the wound in his throat and desperately suckling.

Rhian allowed Crane's presence in the house, but would not make eye contact with him, or acknowledge his existence. She sat with her feet tucked up under her on an old pattern-strewn couch at the far end of the workroom.

The kitchen door crashed open. Delphine yelped even as Crane whirled around with both blades drawn.

An albino man — one of the Ferax's courtesi — carried the limp figure of Macready in his arms. Crane fell back, allowing the man to bring Macready into the workroom.

It was on the tip of Delphine's tongue to order them out, to keep this new stranger away from Rhian and let them dump the corpse in someone else's house, but Rhian was already moving. She swept the patterns from the couch on which she had been sitting and motioned for the albino to bring Macready to her.

A nursemaid was required then, rather than a hasty funeral. Delphine watched helplessly as the albino laid Macready's body gently on the couch.

'He will heal with sleep,' he said.

'What else can be done for him?' asked Rhian, in a cool and practical voice she had not used in years.

'Nothing but that, demoiselle. He may have a little fever — cool it if you can, though it may not make a difference. He will live.'

Rhian turned her attention to the patient. Macready was bruised and bloodied in so many places that Delphine could not stand to look at him. Rhian had little trouble with it.

'We'll need clean cloth and hot water to tend these wounds,' she said. After a moment's pause, she looked up and met Delphine's eyes. 'That means you.'

'Oh, right.'

This strange new Rhian would take some getting used to. Delphine turned to the kitchen, allowing a small ember of hope to burn within her for the first time in as long as she could remember. It wasn't a strange new Rhian at all. This was the Rhian who had been banished by more than a year of panic attacks and fear. Still, Delphine made sure to herd both

Crane and the albino into the kitchen ahead of her. No need to press Rhian too hard.

Velody was waiting in the kitchen. 'Thank you, Lennoc,' she said tiredly. 'You and Dhynar's other courtesi should take your Lord back to home territory now.'

The albino was surprised. 'You do not wish us to take to the sky, Majesty?'

Velody blinked. 'Without your Lord?'

'We serve the Creature Court and the city of Aufleur, Lady, as well as our Lord.'

She nodded. 'You and Shade take to the sky. The other two can help your Lord down to the Arches and keep him there. I don't want him prowling the streets this nox.'

Lennoc nodded solemnly. 'We shall ensure he rests, Lady.' It might have been irony.

'You do that,' said Velody. She might have been amused.

The albino courteso bowed his head, and left just as that cranky female sentinel stormed into the kitchen. 'What about Ashiol?' she demanded, her tone of entitlement making Delphine bristle.

Velody sounded close to breaking point. 'I don't have the faintest idea where he is, Kelpie. Do you?'

'If you'd let me use my knives on Dhynar and his scum we might know!'

'I'd like to manage without torturing people if at all possible.'

'Even if it means Ashiol's death?'

'Seven hells, Kelpie, he should be able to take care of himself!'

'It would be easier for you with him gone,' Kelpie accused.

Velody didn't even bother to retaliate. She pulled out a chair from the kitchen table and sank down on it. 'I'm not an idiot. I've seen the state of the sky. We have four Creature

Lords and more than a dozen courtesi in the air, and even I can see that they're losing the battle.'

Kelpie's lips were thin and pale. 'Last time I saw the sky this bad, it lasted until dawn,' she admitted quietly. 'At the end of it, Garnet died. He was the best we had, and the sky took him. The Lords can't hold the sky alone this nox.'

Velody buried her face in folded arms. 'I'm powerless for now, so we need Ashiol. That's hardly groundbreaking news, Kelpie. How about you stop bitching for half a minute and think about where we need to start looking?'

Good. If Velody was willing to tell Kelpie she was a bitch, Delphine wouldn't have to. Delphine lit the stove, and filled the kettle from the pump. She felt less stupid and useless when she was doing something.

'There is one thing,' Kelpie said.

Velody lifted her head a little. 'Yes?'

'Ash deliberately gave me the slip after we left the Arches. He was going somewhere he didn't want me to know about.'

Velody tilted her head a little. 'The sentinels, or you in particular?'

Crane coughed discreetly. 'Got to admit, Kelpie, there are certain occasions when he doesn't like you to know where he's going.'

Kelpie's eyes blazed. 'I know where to look,' she said, and swung towards the door.

Crane took a step after her, but Velody stood in his way. 'I'll go with her. You need to stay here to guard the others.'

'Again?' he protested.

Kelpie was already gone, the kitchen door and back gate swinging behind her. Velody followed, dragging the door closed behind her.

Crane stared sullenly at Delphine. Oh, he was even pretty when he pouted like a baby.

She gave him her best smile. 'You can help me make bandages for Rhian.'

43

VESTALIA

THREE DAYS AFTER THE NONES OF LUCINA

NOX

*V*elody matched Kelpie's pace as they moved past the Piazza Nautilia and on through the residential streets that curved around the side of the Lucretine hill. Though they weren't following the more straightforward route, it was evident that they were heading for the Forum. It was strangely pleasing that, although Velody sorely missed her powers as a Creature King, she still had the strength and stamina to keep up with Kelpie.

'He doesn't always like having sentinels tagging along,' Kelpie said, not even out of breath as the Gardens of Trajus Alysaundre came into sight. 'Lots of reasons — playing the Ducomte with his real family, or just wanting to be alone. But usually he tells us to get lost. If he wanted to get rid of me without saying why, that means he was going to see one of his women.'

Velody couldn't help smiling at the note of disgust in Kelpie's voice. 'Are there so very many?'

'There used to be. I haven't exactly been keeping track lately, but there's one in particular who's stood the test of time.' Kelpie sounded grim.

This could be the appropriate time to ask a question Velody had been wondering about for quite a while. 'Are you and he...?'

Kelpie let out a sharp laugh. 'Not since his exile from Aufleur. I plan to keep it that way too.' She tilted her head in Velody's direction. 'He's never let you near the seer, has he?'

'No,' said Velody. Ashiol had only mentioned the Court's seer once or twice, and never suggested she and Velody meet face to face.

'Thought not,' said Kelpie with some satisfaction.

They moved briskly through the ornate gates of the gardens and made their way down the grassy slopes. The Lake of Follies shone out below them, lit up with green paper lanterns for the Vestalia.

'Typical Ash,' muttered Kelpie. 'Likes to keep the women in his life separate.'

Velody thought carefully about how to phrase what she was going to say next. 'You know I'm not one of his women, don't you?'

Kelpie shot her a wicked grin. 'Not after that little promise you made to Livilla anyway. Hope I get to see his face when he finds out about that one!'

'There's never been anything like that between Ashiol and me,' said Velody.

'So you say. But somehow he always ends up with a gaggle of women who care what happens to him, whether or not they share his bed. Or will in the future.' Velody opened her mouth to protest this, but Kelpie cut her off. 'I'm only teasing, Lady Power. I know Crane's the one whose virtue is in danger from you.'

Velody found herself blushing. 'I didn't know he was seventeen.'

'You do now, and you still think he's cute.'

The sky was dark and glowering. Velody had never seen it like that before. Shapes rumbled across it, without the usual flashes of light and threadbolts of a skybattle. This was altogether more ominous.

A swooping figure she recognised as Poet passed in front of a swirl of purplish clouds, and disappeared within them. A few moments later, a swarm of white rats exploded out of the cloud, which dissipated.

'Staring up there all nox won't do anyone any good,' said Kelpie impatiently, seeing that Velody had stopped. 'We have to find our man.'

'I'm coming,' said Velody, pulling her eyes back to ground level. She flexed her mind within her body, searching for some sign that animor was thrilling in her blood again. But no. She was stuck with being mortal for now.

At the foot of the gardens, they walked around the lake to reach the Forum. The domed Basilica loomed over them, and Kelpie led them in that direction.

'If the women in Ash's life aren't all his lovers, why is he so desperate to keep them separate?' Velody asked. She wanted to get as much information as possible before Kelpie remembered that they really weren't friends.

'He hates the thought of us talking about him behind his back. As if we don't have better things to talk about!'

'You haven't talked about anything else since we set out.'

Kelpie gave her a vicious grin. 'I know. Doesn't it make you sick?'

～

HELIORA DIDN'T NEED to stand outside the canvas roof of her tent and the domed stone roof of the Basilica to know that the sky was falling. The futures were hard work, but her visions of the present came easily these days. Too easily, to tell the truth — every time she closed her eyes, she saw Poet and the other Lords fighting the sky, struggling to stay alive and defend Aufleur from the fate that had befallen Tierce.

It had gone on too long. She had to do something. She rose to her feet, only now realising how dark it was, and headed for the entrance flap of her pavilion just as it was ripped aside. Heliora was momentarily blinded by the light of a torch, and it took her a few moments to recognise the face that was leering at her. 'Kelpie.' She was relieved not to have to try to free Ashiol on her own.

A hand lashed out, cracking her across the face. 'Bitch. What have you done to him?'

As Hel fell back to the floor, a vision assaulted her mind, almost as painful as the blow itself. She could see Ashiol's body tormented by the burning strands of the net, twisting into pieces even as his mind still struggled against unconsciousness. 'Poet,' she whispered.

'What's that?' It was another voice, less harsh and certainly less familiar than Kelpie's.

A second torch-lit face loomed near, and only when Heliora could focus did she recognise the woman. It was Ashiol's demme, the Power and Majesty. Her skin was paler and her hair darker than Heliora remembered from the futures, but it was certainly her. Velody.

'Poet,' sneered Kelpie, her foot pressing firmly against Heliora's abdomen. 'Is he the one who came up with this charming scheme?'

'He wanted to give Ash a chance to be free,' Heliora spat, trying to sit up. Kelpie's foot was making it too difficult.

'Wanted to give himself a chance to play at being leader of

the pack,' said Kelpie, rolling her eyes. 'Do you really think Poet did all this to help Ash?'

So little made sense these days. Why was it so hard to believe that Poet had good intentions?

'They promised they wouldn't hurt him,' Hel said.

'And did they keep that promise?' Velody asked.

Heliora squeezed her eyes tight. 'They used the net.' Kelpie swore. She pulled away from Heliora and stomped around the tent. 'Skysilver net,' she said finally, in explanation to Velody.

Now it was Velody's eyes that blazed with anger as she looked down at the crumpled, flattened figure of Heliora. 'Where did they take him?'

'He must be imprisoned,' said Kelpie. 'No guards spare, not with Poet and his boys both fighting the sky.'

'I know where,' said Heliora, hardly able to get the words out through her scraped-dry throat.

Even without the visions of Ashiol's pain and the image of his prison clear in her mind, she would have guessed where Poet had taken him. Why else keep a cage wrapped in skysilver wire in his attic?

'Tell us,' said Kelpie.

'Show us,' corrected Velody, pulling Heliora to her feet.

WITH THE CREATURE Court up above, struggling in skybattle to defend the city, the Arches were empty and silent. Strangely, it felt less safe down below than when Heliora knew there were half a dozen courtesi waiting to pounce on her at any moment.

She led the way to the Shambles and to the abandoned grocer's shop that Poet had set up as his own personal palace. Finding lanterns by the door, they lit these and abandoned their torch. The stove was quiet, but the upper rooms were still warm with the heat from it. Heliora nodded miserably at the ladder that led up to the attic.

Kelpie went first, climbing easily. After a moment, she started swearing.

Heliora was the second up the ladder, followed by Velody. Lantern light swung in patterns against the attic walls.

Ashiol, still slumped within the tangles of the net, was locked within Poet's cage. The bars were wrapped with skysilver wire, but beneath those silvery curls was cold iron.

'The key must be here somewhere,' Kelpie said, already beginning to search the chests.

'Why must it?' asked Velody. 'For our convenience? Poet's not that stupid. He'll have it on him.'

Heliora placed her palm to the wire-wrapped bars, staring at the fallen figure of Ashiol. 'They could have taken the net off him once he was inside,' she said. The skysilver had burnt lines into his skin.

Kelpie upturned a trunk of women's clothing in disgust. 'So what do we do? If we peeled off the skysilver wire he could walk through the bars — but only if he could stand and free himself from the net.'

Heliora had not thought that the cage would be locked. Such a mundane problem. 'If we peel off the wire, Velody can walk through and free him,' she suggested.

'Not for another day I can't,' Velody said, frustrated. 'I drank sentinel's blood.'

Heliora sank to the floor, her fingers still wrapped up in the bars of the cage. 'Well, then. We must wait for him to wake up.'

'No,' said Velody fiercely. 'You two stay here. I'm going to get the key.'

She intended to head back to the upper city through the tunnels again, but Priest's cathedral called to her. She ran up elaborate staircases and along musty corridors until, finally, near the very top, she found a ladder leading into the cathedral ceiling.

There was a hole in the roof, covered only by a curtain light enough to be nudged open by a flock of birds. Velody climbed out into an ordinary warehouse stacked with crates. The doors were locked, and she didn't believe in her ability to do anything clever about that. The windows had no glass in them, but they were too high.

The sky outside was dark and threatening. Ominous shapes boiled back and forth out of the clouds. There was no sight of any Lords or Court up there, and she had a horrible feeling that they were losing the battle.

'Poet!' she screamed at the top of her voice. 'POET!' After a long silence, she tried again, waiting impatiently. A shape fell through the stone ceiling, long and black and dripping with a substance like tar. It crashed to the floor of the warehouse, and sneezed.

'Poet?' Velody said in disbelief.

'My Lady calls?' The effect of his gallant comment was spoiled as he coughed several times and tried to stand up. He was a mess. The black substance that clung to his naked body made a nasty fizzing sound when it hit the cement floor. He staggered, but stayed on his feet.

'It's bad up there, isn't it?' she said.

Poet laughed, and almost choked on the merry sound. 'You called me away to ask me that?'

Her hackles rose at his tone. 'I'm not the one who chose to remove my powers this nox.'

'Do you think I don't know that?' he retorted. 'Saints and devils, woman, we're dying up there!' He gave her a sketch of a courtier's bow. 'I humbly crave my mistress's pardon for my foolish, rebellious tactics, and beg her in all her gracious mercy to let me go back to the battle before our frigging city gets eaten alive.'

'Where's the key, Poet?' she asked.

'What key would that be, Lady Power?'

She glared at him. 'Don't tell me that you don't need Ashiol up there. We know about the cage and the net, but we need the key.'

The mocking look eased from his face. 'I didn't know it would be this bad,' he said. 'It's usually months between the real massacres, and it's less than two since we lost Garnet. It's getting worse, faster.'

'Where's the key?' Velody repeated.

A wave of dark matter, similar to the substance already caking Poet's body, dripped through the ceiling, dissolving holes in Priest's boxes. Poet pulled Velody out of the downpour, his hands leaving dark sticky stains on the front of her dress.

'It's in the tea chest,' he said breathlessly.

She stared at him. 'What?'

He leaned in and kissed her on the mouth, smearing the black substance over her face and tongue in the process. It tasted of salt and danger. He pulled away, grinning boyishly at her. 'The tea chest. Near the stove. You can't miss it.' With that, he flung himself upwards, pulling his body up into the ceiling as if he were climbing a rope. There was a loud sucking sound and he disappeared from view.

'The tea chest,' Velody muttered to herself. 'Marvellous.'

BY THE TIME Velody returned to Poet's attic, Kelpie was half-hysterical. She was using her skysilver knife to pry the wire from the bars of the cage, having hacked at the lock so often that her abandoned steel knife was looking worse for wear.

Heliora gave up even the pretence of being useful. She sat on the floor in the midst of a heap of theatrical dresses, utterly miserable.

'Well?' Kelpie demanded as Velody's head emerged through the trapdoor.

Silently, Velody held up the key.

Kelpie snatched it and put it in the lock with a hand that trembled only slightly. She had done such damage to the lock that opening it was hard work.

Finally, the door swung open. Kelpie hurled herself at Ashiol, sliding her fingers into the webbing of the skysilver net. 'I'm going to need help with this.'

Velody stepped inside the cage as well, and together they lifted and unpeeled the net from Ash's burnt and tortured skin as gently as if they were undressing a baby. The net hissed and bubbled against Velody's fingers but did not burn her. She still counted as a sentinel, it seemed. When Ashiol was finally free, Kelpie gathered up the net and hurled it hard out of the cage door.

'Now what?' Velody asked.

'Same as before,' said Kelpie. 'We wait for him to wake up. Without the net, his body can work on throwing off the damn potion that the seer poisoned him with.' She shot Heliora a dirty look. 'At least he won't be in any more pain.'

Velody gazed at the harsh ridges on Ash's face, neck and arms. 'That pain is mild compared to what I have to do to him when he wakes up.'

44
VESTALIA

THREE DAYS AFTER THE NONES OF LUCINA

NOX

 he pain tore in burning rivulets across the surface
of Ashiol's skin so that he could not move even a
fraction without starting a chain reaction of white-hot
agony. He knew this pain. Not quite an old friend, but a
comrade of long standing. He could endure it. He had
endured it before.

His eyelids screamed as he forced them open. He was in a
cage in Poet's loft — he remembered the cage, but it had been
a feature of the Haymarket when he saw it last. One of
Garnet's toys. Velody sat cross-legged in the mouth of the
open cage door. Her elegant evening gown was stained with
blood. Crane's blood, and her own. Kelpie crouched near
Velody, unusually close. Heliora sat further back from the
others, watching the room with wary eyes. Had he been
unconscious long enough for these three to become allies?

'I'm in the seventh hell,' he muttered. 'The one with all the
demoiselles.'

'Can you stand?' asked Velody.

He could not taste her. For a moment, he was paralysed by the fear that he had lost it again, that his animor had been ripped from his veins by another cruel master. But no, he could still feel his own power pulsing beneath his skin. It was Velody who was empty.

'So,' he managed through cracked and blistered lips, 'that's why Kelpie hasn't been allowed to give me her blood and spare me the pain. Good decision.'

'I knew you'd like it,' said Velody, her voice shaking only a little. 'Ash, the sky's falling.'

His voice was a rasp in his throat, but he mouthed the words, 'How bad?'

'Worse than when Garnet was taken,' said Kelpie.

'We have four of the Lords and their courtesi in the sky already,' said Velody, sounding strangely in charge. *Idiot. Of course she's in charge. Who else could be at a time like this?* 'When I last saw Poet, he was barely holding on.'

She rubbed at a small black smear on the side of her face. Ashiol recognised it as the glutinous substance they called star tar. That hideous muck only oozed through the cracks in the sky during the worst of battles. She was right. It was bad.

The pain made every thought a little slower than usual. 'You've lost your powers,' he said.

'Yes,' said Velody impatiently.

'So how did you put four Lords in the sky?'

Velody's smile broke open and her eyes danced. Had he ever seen her look so totally alive before? 'I asked nicely.'

Ashiol laughed, and that was the worst pain yet. He kept laughing until the shock waves in his body forced him to stop. 'I can stand,' he said, hoping it wasn't just bravado.

He could, though it took all three women crowding into the cage to help him to his feet. He couldn't help noticing that, even as she assisted, Heliora's face was constantly turned away as if she expected him to hit her.

On his feet, there were new waves of pain and it was a few moments before he recovered enough to speak. 'Which Lord is not in the sky?'

'Dhynar,' said Velody.

He looked closely at her. Through the shimmery gown he could see a shadow of the skysilver blade that had punched a hole through her stomach. He reached out, his fingers finding the rent in the fabric. 'He's dead then.'

Velody tilted her head up to his, her steady hands still supporting him from the front even as Kelpie and Hel held him up from behind. 'Kelpie gave him a taste of skysilver blade, but I made her give him blood to keep him alive. Like me, he's powerless for a day or so.'

'I would have killed him,' Ashiol said. It came out as a rebuke, which wasn't quite what he intended. It was hard to think past the pain and the rage. He had been stupid enough to leave Velody vulnerable to the Court.

Her chin went up defensively. 'I think we've established that I'm not you, Ashiol. Wasn't that the whole point of making me Power and Majesty?'

There wasn't a breath of animor about her and yet she was more Power and Majesty than he had ever imagined. *I got it wrong*, he thought numbly. *I got it wrong, and almost got her killed.*

He managed a step or two, and waved the women off him so he could do it on his own. He made it out of the cage, careful not to touch the bars that still had skysilver wire wrapped around them. He staggered after another few steps, but stayed on his feet.

'This is ridiculous,' said Kelpie behind him. 'Velody, he's not up to it. You can't expect him to fight the sky in this condition, Creature King or not.'

'We haven't a choice,' Velody snapped back. 'The only way to cure his pain is to make him not a Creature King right now, and I need him in the sky.'

'Let those bastard Lords suffer up there without his help,' said Kelpie.

'And let the city fall?' Velody responded angrily.

'Shut up, both of you,' Ashiol commanded. It was taking all his energy to control the pain. The last thing he needed was this bickering. His head felt fuzzy and strange, but for the first time since waking in the cage, he remembered drinking tea with Heliora. He swung around fast, his eyes blazing into hers. She looked utterly miserable. 'You betrayed me,' he said.

For a moment, anger crossed Hel's face. Then she retreated into a different expression, the insolent brat with nothing to hide. 'Yes, I did.'

'We'll talk about that later.'

She shrugged, pretending not to care. 'If you like.'

Ashiol flexed the animor within him, and that flare of power made the burn lines on his skin scream harder. Skysilver loved to torture animor. The more powerful you were, the harder it hurt.

'You will be careful,' said Velody. 'You won't take any unnecessary risks up there?'

Ashiol gave her a dirty look. 'You know better than to ask something like that.'

'You can try not to get killed at the very least.'

'I'll see what I can manage, Majesty,' he said, not quite mockingly.

Velody obviously knew he was making fun of her and opened her mouth to retaliate. Ashiol changed quickly, shaping his body into his horde of cats and streaming in a long caravan of fur towards the trapdoor. Saints and angels, it hurt. Power blazed like scalding syrup across his

skin as he burst out of the attic, leaving the three demmes
behind.

Talking about him, no doubt.

45

VESTALIA

THREE DAYS AFTER THE NONES OF LUCINA

NOX

*P*ain thudded through Macready as he awoke.

Beyond that, the first thing he was aware of was the heady combination of Rhian's rose-scented skin and Delphine's extravagant perfume.

'Well, now,' he said. 'What's a man done to warrant this kind of close attention from a pair of demmes?'

Delphine's bright blue gaze shone at him, so bright it hurt his eyes. 'We thought you were dead,' she said.

'Eh, well, it wouldn't be the first time.' He switched his attention to Rhian, but she avoided his gaze.

'I'll bring you some heal-leaf tisane,' she muttered, drawing herself away and moving to the kitchen.

'She bandaged you up and made poultices,' said Delphine. 'I watched. I never knew she was so good in an emergency.' She hesitated. 'Well, she used to be. I'd forgotten.'

'So you've just been sitting there, pining for me to awake?' Macready teased her.

Delphine made a face. 'This happens to be the warmest room in the house.'

Macready stirred a little, testing his arms and legs. An image of the courtesi creatures descending on his helpless body with their claws and fangs and beaks shuddered through his mind for a moment, but he shook it away. He couldn't move his limbs. Someone had tied him down. 'What's this?'

Delphine rested her chin on her hands, looking rather pleased with herself. 'Kelpie warned us that our only chance of making you rest until you were fully healed was to tie you to the bed.'

'Indeed?' It wasn't even a bed, but a hard couch in Velody's workroom. He struggled against the bonds, but they were secured tight. *Garland-makers*, he remembered. Of course they would be good with knots. 'You'd better tell me what's been going on, had you not?'

Rhian returned with a steaming cup of something herbal that didn't smell entirely nice. 'Your blades are with Velody,' she said, more confident than on the previous occasions he had met her. Having a grown man tied to a couch was doing wonders for her self-esteem. 'She thought that was particularly important for you to know.'

'All right, then,' said Macready, doing his best to sound non-threatening. 'Now you've unmanned me twice over, is there anything else you want to tell me? Like what in the seven hells has been going on since I was taken out?'

'You want to know everything?' asked Delphine.

'If you wouldn't mind, lass.'

She took a deep breath. 'Well, for a start, Velody almost got killed with that skysilver dagger of yours...'

WHEN HE WOKE for the second time, Macready felt stronger and less groggy. There was a different scent in the room, overriding the lingering traces of Delphine and Rhian. He shifted, and gasped a little as his battered flesh came into contact with the ropes. 'Would it be too much trouble to untangle this poor prisoner, Majesty?'

Velody was barely visible in the darkness. 'I suppose I can trust you to stay still now?'

'No one to chase now you're well and safe,' he replied, keeping his voice low so they didn't wake Crane, who was cocooned nearby in a makeshift bed of two armchairs and several blankets.

Velody untied the knots. 'How do you feel?'

'Like a man mauled by wild animals and put back together with a very blunt needle. Yours, I expect.'

She touched his face in that casual way she had developed, brushing his curls back out of his eyes. He was glad of that, as a stray lock had been itching his nose for some time.

'Delphine and Rhian looked after you?' she said.

'I wasn't much of an entertaining invalid, now you come to mention it. Both of them went to bed hours ago, so they did.'

She drew his two daggers from a makeshift belt she wore over her bloodstained dress. 'You'd better have these back.'

'Much obliged, Majesty. My other lasses?'

He was amused to see that she wore both his swords in harness. Luckily she wasn't much taller than Macready, or she might have done herself a mischief.

Velody unbuckled the harness now, with a sigh of relief as she laid the two swords on the floor beside him. 'I'm not sorry to see the back of these lasses of yours.'

'Eh, they can be kind mistresses if you treat them right.' At her serious look, Macready ventured a question. 'All well in the sky?'

'Ashiol's still battling — it's bad, from what I can see. Kelpie's up on the roof now, watching. I think I'd rather not know if the worst is coming.'

'We're to be swallowed in our beds before dawn then?' He tried to speak lightly, but it was evident from her haunted eyes that it was a possibility.

'I don't know.' Velody sighed, and the last pulse of energy seemed to sag out of her. She leaned forward, folding her face against Macready's chest. 'I wish I could do something.'

He stroked the back of her head, holding her close for comfort. Strange to feel her so near and not taste the crackle of animor that usually lit her skin from within. 'Now you know how we sentinels feel, watching the Great and Mighty fight our battles for us nox after nox.'

She tilted her head back, her eyes finding his in the near-darkness. 'Now I know how the Creature Court felt all these market-nines while Ashiol and I kept them out of it. No wonder they were all so angry at me.'

'You won't be letting that happen again,' he assured her. 'You know better than to let our Ashiol make your decisions for you again, do you not?'

It was an important question, and he waited anxiously for her answer. *Keep Ash's hands off the reins, lass. You're doing fine.*

'Oh, yes,' she said fiercely. 'I've had a taste of what it really is to be a Power and Majesty, Mac. I won't let that go again, not in a hurry.' She grinned suddenly, making an absurd face. 'Look at me, all puffed up with my own importance and I haven't even tortured anyone yet.'

'There's still time,' he told her. He pulled his hand back from her hair. His joints were stiffening up again and his muscles ached as if he had been running all day and nox. 'If you don't mind, Majesty, I could do with a wink or two more o' sleep now. If the city falls before daylight, I'd rather not know of it.'

'Of course.' She drew away from him, pulling up the blankets that Rhian and Delphine had left for his comfort. 'If we're still here in the morning, I'll make you breakfast.'

He smiled, his head already descending muzzily into sleep. 'Ah, love, I'll hold you to that promise.'

The city would not fall. Not this nox. Macready just plain hurt too much to expect the luxury of oblivion. He'd settle for an hour or two of troubled and broken sleep.

46

VESTALIA

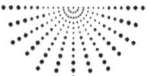

THREE DAYS AFTER THE NONES OF LUCINA

NOX

*A*fter Velody and Kelpie left, Heliora stayed in Poet's attic for a long time. Where else did she have to go? The seer was no use during full skybattle.

What use had she been in recent times? Garnet was swallowed by the sky and she didn't see it coming. Now she had betrayed Ashiol.

If she returned to her pavilion in the Basilica, Ashiol would come to her when the battle was won, assuming it could be won. She would have to explain how she was convinced so readily that he and Velody should be separated, so that she could come into her own as the Power and Majesty. So that Ashiol could be free. Somehow, she didn't think he would be all that understanding.

Heliora paced the attic frenetically. Her impending death had affected her more deeply than she had guessed. Every choice she made took on an air of urgency, even desperation.

I wish I could get it over with.

A true and loyal seer would appreciate this chance to train a successor, to prepare the Court for the time when she was gone. But Heliora had long since lost any sense of loyalty to the Creature Court; any sense that she was of value to them.

She would die, and few would note her passing.

She climbed down from the attic, glad to leave the looming shape of the creature cage behind, but her feet froze on her when she tried to leave the grocer's shop. The streets of the Arches were dark and the sky was falling. She climbed back the stairs to Poet's cosy living space, and curled up in one of his sumptuous chairs. She should not be here, but where else did she have to go? Would Poet be furious that she had helped Ashiol escape? Would he take his anger out on her? *Is that how I die?*

Velody was a revelation. Heliora had viewed her as an abstract concept, the first female Power and Majesty that anyone had ever heard of. She had seen a thousand different Velodys in the future, killing and dying and turning inside out with power. Some were benevolent ruling ladies, others were vicious monsters. This Velody was just a woman. How could she be the brightly burning figure of Heliora's visions? *It doesn't matter, I suppose. I won't be here to see it happen.*

It was all too much to bear. Too much to think about. Heliora was crushed and wrung out, beyond the point of endurance. There was only half a year until Saturnalia, and she could be taken any time between now and then.

Of all the deaths she had seen for herself, all the moments that occurred before darkness and oblivion fell, one possibility stood out more bright and fierce than the others, blazing with light. *Let the futures take me. Die as I have lived. Leave the Court and the promises and the obligations. Never have to look Ashiol in the eyes and admit to my moment of weakness.*

Heliora pushed her mind open to the sky, and fell forward into the futures.

Colours blazed before her eyes. She saw Dhynar killing a blonde flapper and laughing about it to his men. Warlord and Livilla, hands around each other's throat, daring each other to make the deadly squeeze. Priest ruling them all, in a sea of blood. Poet weeping and biting and giggling and singing. Ashiol sane, Ashiol insane, Ashiol ruling, Ashiol dying, *Ashiol Ashiol Ashiol.*

Heliora felt her body convulse even as her mind sped faster and harder into the no-longer-infinite possibilities of tomorrow and tomorrow and tomorrow...

Pain brought her out of it, a sharp crack across her face that sent her spinning back to the present version of herself, the body on the couch. For a moment she grasped a handful of reality, but then the futures had her again, swirling crazily into festival after festival and several darker, stranger futures in which there were no festivals at all and a cold light held sway over Aufleur.

Smack! and Hel's mind was dimly aware again that something was happening to her body. A third blow hurt her arm, and a fourth her stomach. She blinked back into the present long enough to register that she was on the floor and Poet's familiar silhouette was bending over her.

'Do you want to die?' he grated. 'Just let me know and I'll leave you to it.'

Helplessly, still half-ensnared by the tangle of future possibilities, she tilted her head up to him, waiting for the bruising kiss, the suddenness of his body pressed against hers, pulling her back from the edge.

How long have I wanted that from Poet? she thought in shock.

Visions of Ashiol's death, of Velody's destruction, of the blackness that came just before Heliora's own obliteration, all blotted her vision. She felt Poet's hands on her body, but could not see him any more. It was all the more shocking when he did not pull at her clothes, paw at her breasts, bite at her throat. Instead she felt him lift her, as gently as if she were a child, and then let go with a savage thrust that thudded her back to the floor. Her visions snapped away as her spine jarred and her head cracked against the carpeted floorboards. She stared up at him, so stunned that she barely noticed that the futures had ceased to torment her.

'I'm not Ashiol,' Poet said with a sneer. 'I'm not going to ravish you back into sensibility, whether you want me to or not. Do I need to hit you again?'

Her mouth was muzzy, and her head was worse, but she was grounded for now. Slowly, she shook her head.

'Good.'

He leaned down to briskly assist her to her feet. Heliora's whole body ached as he drew her upwards, then shoved her at the couch. She crumpled into it. Poet sat beside her. He wore battle dress — silks and leathers, all scuffed and filthy. He took some time over removing his boots, ignoring Heliora's presence.

'What happened?' she asked finally. The skybattle was won. She knew that much now. There was nothing but quiet vibrations coming to her from the world above. 'You seem more psychotic than usual.'

'I lost a courteso,' he said shortly. 'Halberk. My bear. A lash tendril got him in the heart.'

'I'm sorry,' she said after a moment.

Poet gave her a grim smile. 'Why? You don't care. I don't care much. It's just the way it is. What are you still doing here?'

She blinked at the question. 'I didn't have anywhere else to go.'

'Wonderful. Were you actually trying to kill yourself, here

on my good carpet? Or were you hoping your dark Ducomte would swoop in to save you at the last minute?'

Another difficult question. 'I don't know.'

Behind the glaze of his wire-rimmed spectacles, Poet's eyes were hard and chilly. 'I don't console lonely women, Hel. It's not my style.'

She had never seen him so bitter before. He was usually laughing at the world, and himself most of all. Heliora's masochistic streak still tempted her to flirt with him.

'So you're not into rough sex, or consolation. What is it that you do like, Poet?'

He stared at her, and she was mesmerised by him. Slowly, he drew her mouth towards his and gave her the kiss of a tender lover. She tasted his tongue and teeth and the intense burn of his animor. One hand caressed her knee and moved around to the small of her back, pulling her closer into him. She responded with passion, her whole body awake to him.

An instant later, Poet had snapped away, pushing a distance between them again. His head tilted mockingly at her, even as the warmth drained from his eyes. 'I like to torture people. Out you go, Heliora. Try not to throw yourself off a bridge on your way home.'

47

FOUR DAYS AFTER THE NONES OF LUCINA

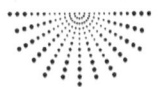

DAWN

*V*elody planned to sleep away the last few hours of the nox in her own bed, but made the mistake of sitting at the kitchen table to drink a cup of milk. As the first light of dawn crept into the room, she woke to find her head resting on her arms on the table.

'It's over then,' she said, knowing Ashiol was there.

He stood exhausted in the kitchen doorway, lit up like the southern stars. A fierce energy surrounded him like a halo. *No wonder the sentinels follow us*, she couldn't help thinking. *If this is the usual effect Creature Kings have on others, I'm surprised they don't worship us as devils and angels.*

Perhaps they did. There was something either devilish or angelic about Ashiol right now, as he strode to the kitchen table and sprawled in a chair. His face was fierce, exuding a ripe power.

'Cup of tea?' Velody suggested.

Ashiol gave her a look that made her shiver. 'It's over,' he said. 'Full retreat. The sky's so calm you wouldn't know it had even rained.'

'How many did we lose?' Her voice was surprisingly steady on that question.

'Halberk, Poet's bear. Quenched, not swallowed. One of Priest's courtesi is in a bad way, she might not make it. All Lords accounted for. So it's not all good news.' Ashiol's grin might have been harsh if she couldn't see how drained he was, right down to the bone.

Velody was tired too. She could think tomorrow about the courtesi that she had sent to their deaths. Right now, she needed to get to bed before she fell apart, a heap of flesh and bone.

'Do you want to stay the nox?' she asked. 'The morning, I suppose I mean. There's at least one armchair that Crane's not sleeping in.'

Ashiol's eyes were glowing coals, bright and haunted. 'I need to say something to you.'

'It can't wait? Ash, you're shaking. You need to rest.'

He shrugged her suggestion off, though he couldn't stop his hands trembling. 'You did well this nox. Better than well.'

'I wasn't fighting the battle.'

He met her gaze with that intent look of his, the one that was so hard to look away from. 'I got the story from them, Velody. You put them in the sky, played the real Power and Majesty without so much as a teaspoon of animor to your name. You're the real thing.'

It should have meant more, hearing that from him. Instead, it came with a wave of disappointment. 'You didn't think I had it in me,' she said quietly. 'Why put me in this position if you didn't believe I could be the Power?'

'I didn't think you couldn't,' he said. 'I just... I didn't know.

438

I didn't even think about it. I was so desperate for it not to be me.'

Oh, that. Did he really think it was a surprising admission?

Velody sighed. 'That's why the seer sided with them, you know. She thought she could save you from yourself. Everyone else expected you to come blazing forth and be the real Power and Majesty, leaving me in a crumpled mess at your feet.' She shook her head. 'Everyone except Poet, which is so bizarre I can't begin to figure it out.'

Ashiol looked alarmed. 'Don't trust him, no matter how much he seems to be on your side.'

Velody was sick of being underestimated. 'Do you think I don't know that? I am the Power and Majesty. I proved that, if it needed proving. Once my animor is back I will prove it again and again if I have to. This is who I am now, and I am not giving it up to anyone, least of all you.'

Ashiol nodded, but said nothing.

Velody had given up on all diplomacy. 'Is that it, my Lord Ducomte? You wanted to pat me on the head, tell me how well I did? Because if there's no other old news you'd care to share, I need to sleep.'

His eyes flared up at the formality, as if she had insulted him. Perhaps she had. 'Has anyone told you about Tasha?' he asked abruptly.

'You,' Velody sighed. 'You told me.'

'Not this story.'

She rested her arms back on the table and stared at him. Her skin ached. *Sleep.* Why wouldn't he leave? How did she know this story wouldn't leave her in a happy bedtime mood?

'Tasha turned viciousness into an art form,' Ashiol said. 'I hate to think what she could have achieved if she knew it was possible for females to be Kings. Livilla's a pale shadow of what our mistress was like.'

'You and Livilla were courtesi together?'

That was the hardest part of coming to this game so late. Velody had no idea of the history of these people, their past alliances and enmities. She knew that members of the Court might serve as courtesi to two or three Lords before coming into their own Lordship — and, of course, they would have close relationships with those courtesi who shared the same Lords. She was going to have to write a list somewhere to keep track of the histories as she learned them.

'Livilla was Tasha's,' Ashiol confirmed. 'As well as me, Garnet, Lysandor who left us... and Poet.'

Velody lifted her eyebrows. 'All at the same time?' Five courtesi. These days, Dhynar having four was apparently a big deal.

'We were her cubs,' said Ashiol with a bitter smile. 'That's what she called us. She drew her power from us. Tasha knew — thought — she could never be a King, let alone Power and Majesty, but she found her power in other ways. She was charm and poison and sex and claws. She had all kinds of dirty tricks that no one else ever figured out. She didn't have more animor than the other Lords, but the way she used it... ingenious and nasty. No one dared cross her, not even the Power himself.'

Velody rose and found the bottle of brandy that Rhian had been hiding from Delphine. She poured a measure for each of them in square green glasses, and passed Ashiol his across the table. 'Why are you telling me this? What does it matter now?'

Ashiol tasted the brandy, blinking as if surprised at the quality. *We might not all live in a Palazzo, seigneur Ducomte, but that doesn't mean we don't have a taste for the finer things. This* bottle was a gift from a satisfied customer. Velody sipped her own drink. Alcohol didn't hit her as fast these days.

Finally, Ashiol spoke, his voice low and uneven. 'A boy came to us once. He was about eight or nine years old — Garnet found him somewhere. We knew by looking at him that he was one of us — or, at least, that he would be. In a few years, he would awaken the animor within. But that was too long for Tasha to wait. She wanted him to be hers.'

Velody frowned, but said nothing. The less she interrupted, the more likely he was to get this over with before it really was the new day.

'She did something to him,' said Ashiol, his voice stumbling a little over the words. 'I still don't know what — we'd never seen anything like it before. She dragged the animor out of his skin. Made him a courteso, years before his time. I've always wondered... what if she'd let him be, sent him away until he was ready. Would he be more or less powerful? For all we know, he could have been a sleeper; never awoken at all.' He drummed his fingers against the glass. 'I think he would have ended up less twisted. No one should have to deal with the Court at nine years of age.'

'I don't know that twelve or thirteen is so much better,' Velody said sharply. It still appalled her that they were introduced to this world as children. She was barely able to deal with it as an adult. 'So Tasha had six courtesi?'

'No,' said Ashiol.

She stared at him. Far, far too tired for this. 'Poet,' she said finally. 'Saints, that was Poet?' Nine years old. It made her shudder to think of it.

'You were a sleeper,' he said. 'You...' He swallowed, and stared at the glass before draining it. 'I need to know if I did this to you. Whether I awoke you. I know it was hardly before your time, but... I wanted another King so badly.'

Velody started to laugh. Maybe it was the brandy, but

she'd barely tasted it. She looked up at him and cackled harder. 'Ash,' she said when she could breathe again. 'Saints and angels. I don't think I've ever met anyone more self-absorbed than you.' He looked offended, and that only made her laugh harder. 'Of course it wasn't you, you colossal thimblehead. It was Garnet.'

Ashiol stilled. It felt for a moment as if all the heat had left the room, had been sucked directly into his skin. 'Garnet?'

Velody wasn't laughing any more. 'Of course Garnet. Isn't everything about him? He... I... I've only been remembering since the Floralia, when I got my animor back. It comes in bits and pieces. But I've been dreaming of the skies of Aufleur most of my life. I think I woke up the first nox I came to this city. Came into my powers. I saw the box sky explode into colours. I saw a naked boy fall from the sky.' Her eyes met his. So very dark and unrelenting. 'I saw his friend transform into a cloud of cats. It's so strange... it feels like a story someone told me once. But I do remember it now. Garnet caught me out on the balcony and he...' She hadn't thought it through, hadn't put the fragments of dreams and memories together, and now the answer was so very simple she almost choked with it. 'He took what was mine.'

Ashiol's gaze only became more intense. 'He took — he couldn't, not without your consent, not unless...' His face blazed with anger. 'What did he do to you?'

Velody was taken aback. 'Nothing. He kissed me, and he took — he asked first. I had no idea what he was asking, or taking. He was half-insane, or seemed that way. I think he was high,' she added, with rather more knowledge of such things now, thanks to Delphine's habits. 'He asked me to give it willingly, and I did. He was right, Ash. Your world, the Creature Court — I was so young. I would have been chewed up and spat out.'

'You think you won't now?'

She rolled her eyes. 'Oh, hush.'

Ashiol stood, anger pouring off him. 'He took your animor? No wonder — we were equals and then we weren't. He outstripped me. He became Lord first, and King. I couldn't keep up, couldn't fucking compete. Now I know why.' He turned on her, his animor lighting his skin up from the inside. 'You gave him that.'

'I didn't know,' she protested. 'In any case, he's dead. Don't you think maybe he's not winning any more?'

Ashiol moved fast, too fast for her to react, grabbing both of her arms and pulling her to her feet. 'You have no bloody idea.'

'I know he hurt you,' she flung at him. 'I'm not defending him, Ashiol. But it's over. He's gone. Can't you let him be gone?'

His hands trailed heat up her arms. 'How can he be gone? Your animor still stinks of him. So does mine.' But something else crossed his face, a pain Velody couldn't begin to understand. 'Don't want him to be gone,' he muttered.

'Forgive him,' she whispered. 'You have to forgive him for everything. Including leaving you in this mess. Or you'll never be free of this... thing that weighs you down.'

Ashiol gave her a frantic look, and he still wasn't letting go of her. Why wasn't he letting go? Then he moved, his mouth forcing heat against the pulse point on her throat, and oh. *This.* Velody could feel the deep power of his animor through his lips and tongue as he sucked lightly on the sensitive skin there, making her gasp.

She leaned back against the kitchen table. His body was hard against hers, his fingers still pressing into her arms, but she worked one wrist free to hook it around his neck, pulling him closer. Ashiol let out a noise, somewhere between a moan and a snarl, and lifted her onto the table, his hands tangling in the soft fabric of her dress as his mouth moved, kissing along her collarbone, then further down...

Velody almost cried out as his lips traced the swell of her breast, right at her neckline, as his fingers pushed her dress up, bunching it around her hips. Thoughts such as not being alone in the house were... not relevant, somehow. Velody could hear every heartbeat, knew where every creature slept, and none of them were here. Here was about Ashiol, his fierce kisses against her cool skin, his fingers working their way up her thighs. With a small sound of frustration, she slid further back on the table, dragging him with her. His body covered hers, and the room spun around her with the dizzy heat of wanting him. She could feel the hard outline of his cock digging into her thigh, and she guided his hands to the fastenings of her dress. One hook, then another, and she was spilling out of it.

Velody closed her eyes as his fingers and mouth worked over her breasts, and a vision swept through her mind. A different mouth, different pair of hands... She gasped as Ashiol's tongue flicked against the edge of her breastband, then ran over the fabric.

Red hair, black hair, skin hot against skin, limbs tangled...

Ashiol was actually sucking on her breast now, his mouth hard on her nipple, wetting through the breastband to the sensitive skin below... and his fingers were lower, sliding between her thighs.

Velody opened her eyes, a deeper vision spearing through. Every suck of his mouth, every caress of his fingers, brought Garnet into her head. Not the Garnet she had met, a bright-eyed boy taunting her on a balcony. An older, sharper, more fierce warrior.

Red hair and black, one body covering another, hands on skin, heat...

Pain.

Velody gasped aloud, and not because Ashiol's fingers were pressing inside her, not because his mouth was tugging fiercely on her breast. She shoved him hard, and if she had even a breath of animor at her disposal, she would have used that too. Ashiol tumbled onto the floor, staring angrily up at her. 'What the frig —'

'You,' she said, shaking, pulling her dress back to cover her breasts and legs, fastening hooks back where they belonged. 'You and Garnet were *lovers*.'

He touched the back of his hand to his mouth, eyes darkening at her. 'Yes,' he said sullenly.

'I saw —' She clenched her hands into fists, to regain some kind of control. 'He did something to you. When you put your mouth on me, I saw it! He took —'

'He took my animor.' Ashiol stood, his body bristling. 'Is that what you want to hear? *You knew that.*'

'How did he take it?' she snapped out, angry because she saw the truth finally. If he didn't admit it to her now, she was going to hate him forever.

'Kings,' he said, and then stopped. 'Kings shouldn't fuck each other,' he said finally. 'Leaves them vulnerable to attack. In the moment... one can steal animor from the other. Rip it right out of them. That's what he did to me. What I thought he'd done to you.'

Velody glared at him. 'So if we finished what we started on this kitchen table... if you made me come, you could take my animor?'

'You drank sentinel's blood, you're not —'

'Don't give me that,' she said, breathing hard, still feeling the imprint of his mouth and fingers on her skin. 'You should have told me. You know you should have told me what I was risking.'

'Believe me,' he growled, 'it won't be an issue in future.'

Velody crossed her arms over her body, afraid at how

close they had got. 'It had better not,' she said. Especially considering — hells, Livilla's blood oath. 'I think you should go, Ashiol.'

He nodded, formality restored between them. 'My Power. My Majesty.'

She couldn't breathe properly until he was long gone.

FOUR DAYS AFTER THE
NONES OF LUCINA

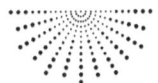

DAYLIGHT

*D*elphine awoke to the sound of someone shuffling about in her wardrobe. As she peered sleepily across the room, several garments flew out, adding to piles already heaped on the floor and across her bed. 'Velody, it's too early for a fashion crisis,' she groaned.

'It's past noon, so it is!' The voice that emerged from the wardrobe was definitely not female. 'Have you nothing at all practical to wear? Honestly, lass, there's nothing in this cave of yours that isn't tangled in beads and ribbons, or made of fabric so fine one good sneeze could tear it to shreds.'

Delphine pulled the covers defensively over her breasts. 'Macready?'

The Islandser's tousled head emerged from the wardrobe. 'You had no brothers, I take it? Why Velody couldn't have had a tomboy or two as friends, I don't know. Trews, lass, trews.'

Delphine summoned as much poise as she could manage

with a sleep-encrusted mouth, unbrushed hair and no cosmetick. 'What the seven hells do you think you're doing?'

Macready backed out of the wardrobe dusting off his hands. His face was unaccountably serious. 'You were a liability last nox.'

'What?'

'Dhynar took you down as easily as breathing. Used you as bait to trap our Majesty into worrying more about you than herself.' Macready rolled his eyes. 'You haven't the sense you were born with. Rhian's no use in a brawl either, but at least she doesn't step out from these walls. I may not be able to do much with her right now, but, by the saints and angels, I can do something with you.'

Delphine sat up, letting the covers slide down to her lap. Whatever he was up to, he wasn't in this room to get an eyeful of her in her noxgown. 'What exactly do you have in mind to "do" with me?'

Macready grinned suddenly, the expression lighting up his hazel eyes. 'I'm teaching you to defend yourself.'

There was a flashing movement as he tossed a silvery knife at her. Delphine squeaked and threw the covers up. The knife hit the bedclothes with a soft thump. 'Very funny.'

Macready moved towards her, reclaimed his knife and sat on the bed. 'Not being able to stand up to Dhynar — well, that's not entirely humiliating. The man's an animal, no joke intended. But you couldn't even hold your own against a drunken fop who wanted to fumble you up against a fence.'

Heat rushed to her face as she remembered that nox. 'I know how to kick a man if he gets too close.'

'Do you now? Didn't see much kicking at the time, lass. Seemed to me the only defence you had was to retch all over him, and that made him more of a mind to hurt you.'

She opened her mouth to protest, but he tapped her lower lip with his finger. 'When I'm finished, coves like your Teddy

448

boy won't be able to lay a hand on you unless you want them to. And as for the Lords and Court...' Macready's smile was a slightly evil one. 'Let's just say you'll be able to hold your own. What do you say, lass?'

'Why are you doing this?' she accused. 'Why do you care what happens to me?'

The smile drained from his face. 'As long as Velody is fretting about you and your lass Rhian, she cannot truly be our Power and Majesty, and she cannot keep herself alive as best she can. We're down to three sentinels, and if we have to keep diverting one or two to watch out for daylight folk, we're not protecting our Kings.'

'So it's for Velody,' Delphine said sharply. Well, what had she expected?

'For you all,' and it was annoying how damned sincere he sounded. 'You're part of this world now, like it or not. Unless you want to cut Velody out of your lives altogether, you have to be prepared for danger.' Macready shrugged. 'What I'd really like is to get my hands on that Rhian of yours. She's got a nice core of anger under all that shying and shuddering. Imagine what she'd be like with a knife in her hands and some idea of how to use it.'

Delphine felt almost dizzy at the thought of the difference it would make to their lives if Rhian felt confident enough to defend herself against attackers, confident enough to step out into the streets and take her life back into her own hands. 'You think if she sees you teaching me, she might agree to learn herself?'

'Worth a try, is it not? If she cannot bring herself to learn from me, maybe you could teach her in time.'

Delphine made up her mind. 'Fine. If you're so set on the idea, I'll do it.'

And there was that smile again, so friendly and warm it was hard to believe it hadn't been there a moment ago. 'Good for you. So what can we find you to wear that won't rattle out a tune when I wrestle you to the ground?'

~

WHEN VELODY AWOKE in her bed, it was well and truly daylight. Afternoon sun streamed in through her window. It was with some effort that she peeled back the many layers she had burrowed under hours earlier.

She went to sleep leaving the house full of men. How was Rhian dealing with all this?

A clash of blades alarmed her. She rushed to the window, dreading what kind of confrontation she might see as she looked down at their small yard.

Delphine and Macready were fighting with knives.

Velody blinked, not sure if she was quite awake. The vision failed to fade. Delphine wore one of last season's dryad tunics with a pair of leggings Velody had only ever seen her wear around the house and never in front of male visitors. Macready spoke in a steady, low voice even as he jabbed a knife repeatedly in Delphine's direction. She was actually rather good at deflecting it, although her expression suggested she couldn't quite believe what she was doing.

The world was full of wonders. Velody pulled on her favourite faded blue workdress and headed downstairs. Her animor was still dormant, though she could feel something tingling in her bones that reassured her that it wasn't too far away. In the meantime, she had at least one new commission she had to get started on — the waistcoat for Priest. If one of his courtesi had been wounded in battle, it was all the more important that she begin work on the gift she had promised him.

In the kitchen, she found Rhian standing where she could watch the antics in the backyard through the window as she kneaded bread dough. She looked surprisingly relaxed, especially since the back door was wide open and Kelpie and Crane sat on the steps, cradling mugs of hot ginger and calling out helpful remarks (Crane) and sarcastic comments (Kelpie) to the two duellists.

Velody opened her mouth to ask what was happening, then shook her head. 'Forget it. I just don't want to know.'

Rhian tossed a rare smile at her. 'Macready said we should be able to defend ourselves. I'm not quite sure how he got Dee to agree.'

'Dared her into it,' Kelpie suggested from the steps.

'He promised her she'd have a chance to carve a chunk out of him if she got good enough,' said Crane, turning around to give Velody a melting smile. 'How did you sleep?'

'Eventually,' she said, joining them at the doorway. She preferred not to go into the details of what had kept her awake.

Macready and Delphine stopped their formal fight and just yelled at each other, waving the knives for emphasis.

'Uh-oh,' said Crane. 'Here they go again.'

Even with the limited senses of a sentinel, Velody felt Ashiol enter the kitchen behind her a moment before he spoke.

'Post's in.'

She turned to see him holding out a sealed letter. He had a strange look on his face. The seal was gold-white wax, with the ducal rings clearly marked on it.

Velody took it from him, cracking the seal open. 'Did you arrange this?'

'The Duchessa rarely consults me on her dress choices,' he said with a touch of humour.

'I'm not surprised, considering what you did to the last festival dress I made for her.' Quickly, Velody read the letter of commission. 'She wants me to make her a gown for the

Sacred Games of Felicitas,' she said finally. 'Something extraordinary, she says, but a touch more robust than the roses of Floralis.' She bit her lip.

'That was a joke,' said Ashiol.

Velody eyed him. 'You think?'

'It's *wonderful*,' said Rhian.

Velody read the letter through again. 'She wants to meet tomorrow to discuss the commission. I've got to get some samples together!'

She started towards the workroom, but Ashiol caught her by the arm. 'This really matters to you?'

Velody barely saw him. Already she had a dozen fabrics and designs floating before her eyes. 'Of course it matters,' she said impatiently, and shook him off, eager to get started.

As she left the kitchen, Velody heard Ashiol say, 'We've never had a Power and Majesty who cared about anything other than himself and the Court and the sky.'

'Maybe that's where you've been going wrong all these years,' said Rhian.

DELPHINE WAS DOING BETTER than Macready had ever expected. Her reflexes were sharp and she was remarkably fit — probably from all that dancing she did, though he was surprised her taste for cocktails and party drugs hadn't slowed her body down more. What might she achieve if she gave up those indulgences?

She was tiring now after several hours of training, but he didn't want to stop. This was too important... like he was on the edge of discovering something magnificent. A thought, half-crazy, intruded on his mind and would not let him go. Delphine was too good to be wasted.

'Macready, I'm tired,' she complained.

'Take a rest for a minute then.'

'Can't we stop for the day? You can't expect me to learn everything by noxfall.'

He ignored the whining tone in her voice. She was better than that. She just had to figure it out for herself. 'Kelpie, lend me your steel Sister,' he said.

Delphine wiped a sweaty tendril of hair back out of her face and gaped at him. 'Her sword?'

'Why?' demanded Kelpie.

'I want to test a theory.'

Delphine stepped back. Gripping the hilt of Macready's steel dagger Phoebe at a mostly professional angle, she looked for a moment as if she wanted to use it on him for real. 'Why do I need to learn to use a sword? It's not like I'll be wearing one on my hip when I go out at nox.'

'You never know,' Macready said lightly.

'No!' Kelpie had never been slow. She stood up with her back straight against Velody's kitchen door, her eyes burning at him. 'You can't be serious.'

'Why not?'

'She's a vapid, useless, drugged-up flapper with no more sense than what she was born with!'

A thwacking sound made them all jump. Macready stared for a moment at the knife that now quivered in the door only inches from Kelpie's face. He turned around and glanced at Delphine, who stared back in shock that she had thrown the thing.

'She has terrible aim,' continued Kelpie, as if this proved her point.

'She wasn't aiming for your face,' said Macready. 'Were you, my lovely?'

'Not exactly,' said Delphine, her voice shaking. 'But I wouldn't have been heartbroken if she moved her head at the last moment.'

'There you are,' said Macready with a broad grin. 'Sentinel material if ever I heard it.'

Delphine paled. 'What?'

'It's a stupid idea,' Kelpie said flatly. 'The stupidest.'

'We need new blood,' said Macready. 'You know it. We've had none in five years now, and three sentinels was barely enough to keep up with one King, let alone two.'

'She's too old to start now.'

'Do you not think it's time we stopped sacrificing children to the nox?'

'She's not up to it.'

'I think she is.'

'Will you both just shut up!' It was Delphine, blistering with fury. She stormed up to Macready, ignoring Kelpie altogether. 'What makes you think you can go around deciding things for people? I don't want to be part of your crazy nox life with the blood and the death and the danger! You've already got Velody tangled up in your web — what's next? Will you be slitting Rhian's throat at the next full moon?'

'You've got it in you to do this,' Macready said urgently.

'No, I don't,' Delphine snapped. 'I'm a demme who's good at making festival garlands and likes to have a good time when I'm not working. That's all I am.'

'But you're not content. You're not happy with yourself. What's the harm in trying something else — something extraordinary?'

'Because I'm not extraordinary.' Her mouth had twisted into something ugly — quite an achievement with a face like hers. 'I'm not special. I'm not *Velody*. I don't want to save the world. Half the time I don't even want to live in it.'

'So you won't try,' Macready said softly.

Delphine's blue eyes blazed at him. 'You can keep your knives and swords and self-defence, and the ghosts of your dead friends who used to be sentinels. I have better things to waste my time on.' She stormed towards the house.

'Like what?' he called after her.

'There's a new club opening this nox!' she yelled without even turning around. 'I intend to wear something fabulous and get thoroughly smashed. If anyone wants what's left of my body afterwards, they're damned well welcome to it. Except you.'

'Oh, nice,' said Kelpie sarcastically. 'Any more booze-addled tarts you want to add to our number, Macready?'

'I believe in you, Delphine!' he shouted as she reached the kitchen door.

That made the lass pause, at least. She whirled around, her body trembling with rage and disbelief. 'How could you *possibly*?'

49

FOUR DAYS AFTER THE NONES OF LUCINA

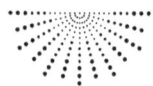

NOX

*V*elody dragged her sketchbooks and favourite fabric swatches up into her room to work in the quiet, gathering ideas for the Duchessa's gown. Only when it was so dim she had to light a lantern did she realise that evening was upon her.

That, and the tingle in her veins. She tried to ignore it at first, continuing to sketch out the bell shape of a skirt, but her hand trembled so greatly that she had to drop the charcoal. Animor. How had she survived without it for so long? Her skin glowed as the power lit up her blood from within. The sky was open to her and the world was her own. She was herself again, burning brightly.

Velody gazed upon her sketchbook with flinty eyes. Scribbles. What did they matter? Only the sky mattered; the sky and the city and the Creature Court.

Ashiol was nearby, and getting closer. She could sense his presence like an intense beacon, far more compelling than when she was limited to the half-senses of the sentinels. She slipped from the bed and went to the window.

Crane entered the yard, two blue-wrapped sword hilts on his back. He glanced up at her, grinning like the boy he was, delighted with his new toys. Her eyes flicked past him. He wasn't important.

Ashiol was behind him, and his eyes promised something marvellous. He looked briefly up at the sky. Velody followed his gaze. The sky was quiet. If ever she had wanted a catastrophe to fall from above, it was this nox. The power hummed in her ears, so sweet and silken that she longed to put it to good use.

'Are they ever going to leave us alone?' Delphine complained at the doorway. 'The house is full of them. I can't believe you had to hide up here to work. They're not living with us now, are they?'

Velody turned. For a moment, she saw everything through animor, which made Delphine a bright silver stain in the doorway. Velody concentrated until she could see her friend's silhouette, her facial features, the detail of her clothing. 'Are you going out?'

'I won't be trapped in here like a rat in a cage,' Delphine said petulantly. 'So the streets aren't safe — big surprise. I've got somewhere to be.'

She was wearing silver, a shimmering dress of glass beads on white fringe layers, and a skullcap of fine metallic lace. Her dancing heels were lethally steep. Her cosmetick was aggressively perfect, her face so primped and refined with heavy lines of kohl in the Zafiran fashion that she hardly looked like Delphine at all.

'Some of them might hunt you down, hurt you in order to hurt me,' said Velody. It was a struggle to form the words, let alone phrase them in her own voice. The animor was screaming in her head and heart and flesh, desperate to be spilled out into the sky.

'Then you'll be hurt,' said Delphine.

Velody blinked, and suppressed the staggering power a little. 'Are you angry at me?'

'I'm angry at the world. Don't mind too much. A cocktail or three will make me loveable again.'

Velody tried to think of the right thing to say, but it was so hard to focus on the daylight world when the nox was calling to her. 'Be careful,' she tried, and knew that she sounded distant and insincere.

'Why bother?' replied Delphine, and flounced out.

Velody breathed out with a rush of relief as she was left alone. The air was a multitude of colours, bouncing before her eyes. She peeled off her dress and boots and under-clothes, and stood naked before the window.

Ashiol was below, staring at her with darkened eyes. Velody barely even noticed Crane, his mortal form dimming his image so that he was a blur before her eyes. Ashiol was sharp and defined, his every breath and heartbeat visible to her. The faded lines from the skysilver net were faintly evident on his face and skin beneath his clothes.

Velody opened the window and threw herself into the sky, shaping herself into her glowing Lord form as she flew upwards. She did not care whether or not Ashiol followed her. The sky was hers.

THE BEST CLUBS weren't in the usual places, the trendy hot spots of Aufleur. The new fashion was to be unfashionable, to make a happening happen where everyone might least expect it. Bars and house parties were out. The best music and dancing and drink and powders could be found in unheralded nooks of ageing industrial areas, in streets no one knew the name of, in places where the best sets would not normally be seen dead.

This nox, the club had taken over a cramped cellar belonging to a musty old bookshop. Coloured glass lanterns flickered in the darkness, sending strange gold and scarlet shapes to dance along the bare walls. The air smelled of gin and aniseed and sweat.

Delphine was dancing and, for once, she was not enjoying herself. Her arms ached from her afternoon of knife and hand-to-hand exercises. All the time she was training with Macready, deflecting his blows and learning how to twist and kick out of his firm grip, part of her had been thinking about this nox. She looked forward to it as her only chance to get rid of the twist of anxiety in her stomach.

Maud was here, in a new emerald fringe dress. Villiers was here too, and Peggy, and the adorable Lars whom Delphine had been trying to get to notice her for months. The cellar was full of the bright young things that she loved to play with, some she had long considered to be her friends, but it wasn't the same any more. All she could think about was being grabbed by that grinning ferax man who treated her like so much rubbish.

As the musicians raised their beat and she danced faster, Delphine remembered the way her blood chilled when she thought Macready was dead.

Bloody Macready. He was the reason she hadn't picked up a drink this nox. Wasn't he? Delphine preferred to think that her new sobriety was a reaction to finding out about the terrors that lurked in the streets and in the sky above, but that was hardly realistic. Drowning in spirits and dancing with strangers was her favourite way of dealing with danger and fear back in the long and horrible months after the attack on Rhian. Why would she break the pattern now?

Had Macready made the difference? Delphine hated it if it was true. She hated him — his smug little Islandser accent, and the glint in his eye that said... She had no idea what it said. It wasn't a look she was used to seeing in the eyes of men. Nothing to do with desire or greed.

I believe in you, Delphine.

How could you possibly?

No one noticed she wasn't drinking. She acted the way she always did, dancing as if she had already lost all hold over herself. She was a fake, showing them the wild and abandoned Delphine they expected so she could hide her own whirling thoughts from them.

How long had she been faking this other Delphine?

That thought startled her. The walls pressed in tightly and she was overwhelmed by the urge to escape. She let an expression like nausea cross her face, and used it to twist away from Villiers without explanation.

When she found the stairs up to the bookshop, Delphine kept going higher and higher, into storerooms and up until she found herself pushing open a door and stumbling out into a forgotten flat space that might once have been a roof garden. All that was left were a few half-dead vines and a rickety railing, but it was open to the sky and she could breathe again. Delphine stood at the roof's edge and kicked off her beaded high heels, watching them clatter into the street below. No one yelled.

A ventilation shaft led to the cellar. She could hear the laughter and piano music vented out into the nox almost as loudly as when she was among the pressing bodies. It was better here. Delphine gulped in the cool air, both hands gripping the railing as she gazed into the sky. She stood for what felt like hours, until she could assemble a rational thought or two.

It was frustrating to know that there might be a whole

new world of madness up there between the drifting moonlit clouds, but she would never see it. She squinted into the sky. Was Velody up there, struggling to keep the city in one piece?

'It's a quiet nox, my lovely. In case you were wondering.'

Delphine deliberately didn't turn around, even when Macready tossed her recovered shoes at her feet.

'Lost something?'

'Me,' she said wretchedly.

'Ah, now I can't have that.' Macready joined her at the railing, his face sombre. 'You look the same as you ever have.' He eyed her up and down, sniffing the air pointedly. 'A little less gin-soaked than I'm accustomed to, so it seems.'

'Lost the taste for it.'

He looked faintly startled, and a little smug. 'But that's grand.'

'No, it isn't!' She turned on him angrily. 'I'm loose and out of control. It's what I *do*. I don't have anything else except my work, and what the seven hells is that? Stitching ribbon after ribbon for empty festivals.'

Macready gave her an odd look. 'You're bright and you're beautiful, lass. You can be anything you want.'

'I just wanted to dance,' she said, sounding pathetic. The piano music filling the nox air was a particular torture, one of her favourite songs.

'Well, then,' said Macready, 'that's easily fixed. Dance with me.'

'You can dance?'

'I'm an Islandser,' he laughed. 'Dancing is in our blood.'

She nodded her head to the ventilation shaft and the cheerful jazz music. 'Even to this?'

He winced, but rallied. 'Even to this newfangled noise, my sweet, I can make the effort.'

Strangely, she was cheering up. 'You're too young to be such an old grouch.'

461

'You're too young to be such a cynical hag, so you are,' he countered. 'Will you dance with me, lass, or break my heart?'

'I can do both.'

'Works for me.'

He held out his hand and she took it. The world shifted a little.

50
FOUR DAYS AFTER THE
NONES OF LUCINA

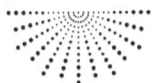

NOX

*V*elody danced the quiet sky and Ashiol watched her. There was no doubt now. She was Creature Court. Her sheer exultation at the return of her animor put him to shame. She embraced the whole thing as he hadn't since he was a teenager. *Since Garnet and Lysandor ran at my side, brothers at arms...*

Ashiol still hadn't mourned for Garnet, for the man and King who had been his in all senses of the word. *Broke me, twisted me into something harsh and scarred.*

Now Garnet was in his head all the time. He could think of nothing else. Garnet was dead. Swallowed by the sky. Ashiol could still smell him on his skin, if he let the memories last too long.

Velody had no frigging idea what she had done to him. There she was, swooping and spinning indulgently through the sky, shaping herself from chimaera to Lord form to her hordes of little brown mice, then back again. Part of him hungered to join her, to be part of her play. But he held back, watching his Power and Majesty glorying in her own power.

'Ever seen anything so beautiful?' someone asked behind him.

Ashiol barely resisted a growl. 'Poet.'

'Not forgiven me yet, kitten? Ah, that's a shame.' The Rat Lord emerged over the crest of the roof, clad in one of the whispering white silk burnoose garments that were fashionable in the city at the moment with the new Eastern craze. 'We need to talk, you and I. Can't do that while you're hissing and spitting. Would you feel better if I let you bite me a few times, for the sake of equality?'

'Drugging you, wrapping you in a net that burns your pretty skin to shreds, and sticking you in a cage of skysilver might redress the balance,' suggested Ashiol.

'Perhaps it would,' agreed Poet. 'But that would make you a monster, and isn't that the very reason you chose not to be Power and Majesty?'

Right now, with Garnet in Ashiol's head and the shade of Tasha not far away, it was hard to look at Poet without hearing the boy's screams when his animor was released before its time.

'You don't mind being a monster.'

Poet lifted his eyebrows. 'Old news, kitten. I'm on the side of the angels now. Try to keep up.'

Ashiol said nothing.

Poet took this as encouragement to come over the roof and sit beside him, dangling his bare feet in the gutter. 'Heliora's hurting,' he said after a silence that was either seething or companionable, depending on your point of view.

Ashiol grinned bitterly. 'If you look closely enough, you

can still see the map of scars on my skin from that fucking net. I don't need to look. They still burn.'

'Not that kind of hurt,' Poet said, rolling his eyes. 'Everyone knows about your pain threshold, kitten. We're not impressed. Our seer is in agonies of the heart, and all over you.'

Ashiol said nothing. Sooner or later, Poet would reveal whatever he had come here to tell him, and he wanted it sooner.

'She tried to kill herself this morning,' said Poet in a voice so light that he might have been remarking on the weather.

That got to Ashiol, but he was damned if he would let Poet see it. By 'tried' he assumed an unspoken 'and failed', which was something at least. 'Hel's doomed anyway,' he said. 'Dead by Saturnalia, she saw it herself.'

'Ouch!' Poet exclaimed. 'Now I know what all the demoiselles see in you, you charming devil.'

Ashiol clenched and unclenched his fists.

Poet clicked his tongue. 'Go to her, you fiend. Forgive her before you lose her altogether.'

'What exactly are you getting out of this friendly advice?' demanded Ashiol. 'Since when have you cared about Heliora?'

'All of the Court are obliged to see to the needs of the seer,' said Poet primly. 'In a technical sense, of course. To be honest, I'm hoping that if she's back in your good books, she might stop trying to seduce me. The woman's a menace.' He nodded up at the whooping, tumbling figure of Velody. 'I can keep an eye on our Majesty this nox if you really think she needs it.'

'And I should trust you why?'

Poet leaned back on his elbows. 'I have everything I want. Enjoy the sight, kitten. I'm content.'

Every instinct told him that Poet was manipulating him into something, but Ashiol's obligations to Heliora went far beyond those of a Creature King to the seer. She was his oldest friend who had stayed.

Poet's eyes followed Velody as if she were the most magnificent thing he had ever seen. 'Heliora regretted it the moment she betrayed you,' he said. 'If you can even call that a betrayal. Your beloved brat only wanted to release you from all this.'

If there was anything Ashiol hated more than Poet, it was Poet being right. 'I'll be back,' he muttered, levering himself up off the roof.

'As you like,' said Poet. 'I'm sure our Power and myself can manage without you for an hour or two. She can take care of herself, animor or no animor. Surely she's proved that by now.'

Ashiol shot him a look of pure loathing, and went to find the seer.

HOW HAD Macready ended up with this lass in his arms? Dancing to jazz music on a rooftop with Delphine pressed hard against his body was the last thing he expected to be doing this nox.

The slow song was a relief, as he couldn't keep up with the rapid steps she came up with for the faster, crazier numbers. As she tried and failed to teach him, though, he had discovered how much he liked the sound of her laugh. Now the music was slow and measured, and he had her in his arms as they moved back and forth on the rooftop.

He inhaled and caught a faint smell of roses — but no, that was Rhian's scent still mingled with Delphine's own. A borrowed scarf, perhaps? Delphine's scent was richer, a purchased glaze of unguents and potions he wouldn't dare guess at. The perfume was worth every centi she had spent on it — the smell of her lifted his blood and sped up his pulse.

'You're not so bad at this type of dancing,' she said lightly.

Macready turned his face towards her, wanting to say something, but the breeze brought another scent to him that made his body react with wary tension. 'Ferax,' he said beneath his breath.

Delphine was startled. 'Here?'

'Come on,' he said, scooping up her fallen shoes before he grabbed her hand and pulled her back down into the bookshop.

'We could stay,' she protested as they reached the front door. 'He won't come through a whole club of people to get to us, will he?'

It was a good thought, but... 'After last nox, he'll be monster enough to do anything, even slaughter a roomful of drunk jazz junkies.'

Macready gritted his teeth. He was stupid to linger with Delphine, enjoying her company instead of taking her home straightaway. He had known Dhynar would be out for retaliation this nox and that Velody's pretty blonde friend was the most obvious target. Not to mention that Macready himself was on the Ferax Lord's list of unfinished business.

'A whole room of people?' Delphine repeated, not believing it.

'He's done it before,' said Macready, and pulled her out into the empty street.

They ran for several blocks. Well, Macready ran as best he could, hustling a limping and complaining Delphine along beside him. It started to rain, a cool early summer rain that dampened the cobbles and slicked back Delphine's hair beneath her silver-lace headdress.

The scent of ferax was all around, like the young Lord had rubbed himself over every wall and fence to show them they were trapped. Where was the cur? Macready could feel their pursuer everywhere, but could not hear or see him.

Macready's nearest nest was close, but this too was a danger. He was heading this way last time, when Dhynar and the courtesi set upon him. They knew where he was going then and they would know it now. Especially if Macready and Delphine were being lured in a particular direction.

Still, the temptation of his nest, knowing they would be safe once they were inside, was foremost in Macready's mind.

Even as late as this, there were shopfronts open along Via Leondrine. The wide thoroughfare was bright with lampboys and passing trade. If they stayed on this main street until the very last moment, there was a chance Dhynar would not pounce until the.

'Where are we going?' snapped Delphine, shaking her arm from his. After hurrying several blocks away from her friends without any sign of their pursuers, she had lost the initial burst of fear.

'Be honoured,' he said shortly. 'You're going to learn one of the secrets of the sentinels.'

Past the candlemaker's and the hot-wine bar, Macready's eye fastened on the narrow opening between shopfronts. It didn't look wide enough to be an alley or a side street, and most people walked right past without even seeing it.

The smell of ferax was ever more powerful. All ferax, which made little sense. Where were the brighthounds and darkhounds, the stripecats and cats? Surely Dhynar wasn't tracking Macready and Delphine on his own, without the help of his courtesi?

'Now,' Macready hissed suddenly. Even as Delphine opened her mouth to protest, he whisked her through the narrow opening in the street and pulled her along the back lane.

The back of his neck prickled as he remembered the mass of courtesi descending on him last time, snapping and scratching and swallowing bites of his flesh...

They were five steps from safety. Three. One. At a battered and dented stone wall, Macready plunged a hand out, palm up. 'Get in,' he urged Delphine.

'There's nothing there!'

He rolled his eyes. 'Will you not trust me for once?' He gave her a sharp shove in the small of her back, pushing her face-first into the wall. Delphine threw up her arms to protect herself, fell forward and vanished.

Macready followed her, sliding through the stones to the quiet place of safety on the other side. There was no scent of ferax here, and he sucked in the clean air gratefully. Had he really thought Dhynar might have breached this most ancient form of sanctuary?

Delphine was looking around at the small space. There was a stuffed mattress on the floor, a chair, a cupboard, a few storage trunks. The space was shabby and spare, with little in the way of home comforts. 'Where have you brought me, Macready?'

'Somewhere safe,' he said, trying to sound reassuring. 'This is my nest.'

Safe, indeed. No one could find this place unless the sentinel who made it led them through the wall. Even if they watched him enter, they could never find the entrance on their own. Nests were designed to be inviolate, not for the sake of the vulnerably mortal sentinels, but so they could more effectively protect their Kings in times of danger.

But while the enemy could never find the entrance, they could certainly lie in wait outside the approximate area, ready to pounce as soon as the sentinel and his charges emerged. Macready had no doubt that this was what Dhynar had in mind.

'Make yourself comfortable, love,' he advised Delphine. 'We'll be here until morning.'

For some reason this brought a light to her eyes.

51

FOUR DAYS AFTER THE
NONES OF LUCINA

NOX

*V*elody watched Ashiol leave, so that only Poet remained on the rooftop watching her. She felt unbelievably light. A week ago, Ashiol would not have willingly left her alone in the sky at nox, let alone within the reach of one of the Creature Lords. He finally had some trust in her power and abilities.

That reminded Velody that she had promises to keep. She must start on Priest's waistcoat, to show her goodwill. The Warlord would be coming to her some time this nox for his goblet of blood.

At least Poet had extracted no promises from her. His support was unconditional. Yes, that did make her suspicious. How could it not?

As if he sensed her watching him, Poet stood up on the roof, his silken white garment flapping around him in the cool breeze of the evening. He stepped into the sky, soaring up towards her like a saintly cloud. 'It's many years since I was last without animor, cut off from the blood of the Court,' he said as he floated close to her. 'Must taste like the food of angels to have it back.'

'Food of devils and angels and saints all rolled in together,' Velody admitted.

She felt a new sympathy for Poet, knowing he had been part of this crazy, twisted world since such early childhood. What had it done to him, that exposure to power and danger and perversion at nine years of age?

It began to rain, slowly at first. A true and natural rain, nothing of the skybattles about it. Small droplets hung on Poet's long eyelashes and left translucent spots on his silken white burnoose.

For the first time since she had escaped through her window, hours ago, Velody was very much aware that she was naked.

'Come,' said Poet, for once without a teasing note in his voice. 'I want to show you something.'

The sky was quiet, and yet... Poet had somehow found the one tiny patch that was still very much alive. It was a small hollow of darkness. Now they were close, Velody could hear a subtle fizzing sound from it, a hissing and bubbling.

'See?' said Poet. 'It's never truly over. Even now they're wriggling and scheming to find a way in.'

'Do you really think there's a mind behind it all?' Velody asked in surprise. 'Ashiol talks in terms of war and battles, but he never refers to the enemy as if we were fighting real people.'

'Ashiol doesn't know everything,' said Poet. 'Do you really imagine that this falling, fighting sky of ours is some kind of natural event, like a bushfire or an earthquake?'

Velody had thought about it, but come to no conclusions. 'There's no strategy behind it. No plan. Everything just gets thrown at us in random patterns. If we beat it back long enough, it goes dormant. It doesn't feel organised.'

'Maybe that's the strategy,' said Poet. 'It wants us to think that there's nothing there, that we're fighting air and light. Then, when we least expect it... the invaders will march in to conquer us.'

Velody looked sidelong at him. 'How much sleep have you had lately?'

He gave her a sudden grin. 'Sorry, was I rambling?'

'A little.'

'It's the unseen battles that bother me,' he added.

'They're harder to catch, harder to fight.'

'Unseen battles?'

'Didn't Ash tell you? The seen battles are the lights in the sky and the tendrils and the falling fire — those bright and burning dangers that make our noxes so very interesting. But every now and then something subtle sneaks past and we miss it. It can take days or weeks or months, but something insidious is down there among us, and we have to find it before we can even think about destroying it.' He shuddered a little. 'I prefer the bangs and flashes, thanks very much.'

'How often do they happen, these unseen battles?' Velody was angry. Yet another thing that Ashiol hadn't prepared her for. She resented that she had to look ignorant in front of Poet.

'From time to time, when we least expect them,' Poet said airily. He gestured at the sizzling, seething dark patch in the sky. 'That, for example, is a trap.'

'How do you know?'

'Because it's been singing to me for the past three hours. It called me here.' Poet gave Velody a smile that was not entirely his own. 'It's powerful, this sky of ours. Never forget how powerful. It lured me here, and made me bring you. Could an earthquake do something like that?'

473

Alarmed now, Velody swung back in the air, keeping the white-robed figure of Poet between herself and the black patch. 'We have to get out of here!'

'Too late,' said Poet sadly, just as the sizzling sound reached a high-pitched intensity and the patch burst open in a spray of blood.

~

MACREADY WAS uneasy as he saw that light in Delphine's eyes.

'You know,' she said, taking a step or two towards him, 'I half-believed you were making all that up about us being chased by the Ferax Lord.'

'Why would I do a thing like that?' Macready replied incredulously.

She tilted her head, making her silver headdress sparkle. 'It got me here, didn't it? Alone with you, in your nest? Cosy.'

'You're not my type,' Macready assured her. 'Fancy something to eat? I've got some apples around here somewhere...'

Delphine gave him a knowing look. 'So what is your type?'

'Unavailable.'

'Oh, you like the prim and buttoned-up variety. Or do they have to have husbands at home?'

Damn it all, she was still flirting with him. This was not the plan. 'Both, ideally.'

'So someone like me wouldn't be of any interest at all?' Somehow, without moving a muscle, she slid her dress a little way off her shoulder, and bit her lower lip so that it was swollen and inviting...

Macready reached out a firm hand (look, Ma, no tremors) and pulled her frock back into place. 'If you valued it more, it would be a tempting offer, lass.'

Delphine's warm blue eyes turned instantly cold. 'Fine,'

she said angrily. 'You won't mind if I go home.' She stepped around him, towards the door.

'I'm not trying to trap you, lovely. There are real dangers out there.'

'I don't believe you,' she flung at him, scrabbling at the wall for the way out.

Macready grabbed for her arm. 'Stop that. Don't be a little idiot.'

'Don't touch me.'

'You were keen enough to be touched a minute ago!' Oh, and wasn't that exactly the wrong thing to say?

'Let me out of here right now,' she threatened, 'or I'll scream so loud that the whole city will know you're keeping me here against my will.'

'Dhynar's out there,' Macready said desperately. 'I can't let you out while he's prowling. He'll hurt you to get at her.'

Delphine stared at him. 'Back to Velody, are we? It's always about your precious Power and Majesty. Is she unavailable enough for you, Macready?'

'It's not like that.'

'I'm not part of these stupid Court games you play, I'm not part of that world. I'm going back to the club where my real friends are!'

Delphine lunged for the wall again, and Macready was alarmed to see that she was close to the catch that would open the nest up to the alley outside. He grabbed for her, trying to hold both arms back, but she twisted and wriggled. Her elbow met his jaw in a move he had only taught her that morning, and he skidded back, falling.

He was still gripping her wrists, and pulled her with him as he fell. It was his skull that cracked painfully on the wooden boards, and he rolled fast to pin her to the floor beneath him. They were both breathing hard. Macready tried desperately to think of the right thing to say to convince her to listen to him, to make her believe that he was trying to protect her. Instead, he gazed at her angry eyes and cosmetick-flecked eyelashes. *Saints and devils*, he thought as his mouth closed over hers and Delphine responded passionately with teeth and tongue. *Do I never learn?*

He could feel the contours of her body under his, her beaded party dress like rough, flimsy cobwebs under his hands, the heat of her as she writhed under him.

The heat was coming from Macready too. He was hot and hard, and already possessed her with his hands and mouth. It would be so easy. A few lacings here and there, her dress pushed up another inch or two on her thighs, and she would be his.

An image of that drunken idiot in the alley flashed into his mind, followed by a chilly thought. *I'm supposed to be rescuing this lass.*

That was enough to bring him to his senses. Even as Delphine's hands wormed inside his shirt to touch his skin, he pushed himself away from her.

She looked stricken for a moment, then flushed and angry. 'What's your problem, Macready?'

'Not a good idea, love.'

'That isn't the impression you gave me a few seconds ago.' She sat up like a pouting child whose favourite doll had been snatched from her. 'Are you afraid your precious Power and Majesty would think less of you if she knew you were frigging me, or would you just think less of yourself?'

Oh, this one would be a peach to wake up to in the morning. 'Neither,' he said, trying to salvage the situation. 'But you'd think less of yourself, sweetheart, and I'm not sure that's what you need right now.'

Delphine's blue eyes flashed angrily. 'Who the saints are you to tell me what I need?'

She propelled herself up off the floor. Macready prepared

himself to fend off an attack, but Delphine took off running for the way out — and damn it all if she didn't find the catch in her scrabblings this time. She fell through the wall and was gone.

Macready ran back to where he had placed his sword harness and daggers, grabbing the two skysilver weapons. If Dhynar was still lurking out there, he would need to be armed.

The delay cost him. When he burst out of his nest into the alley, there was no sign of Delphine. He couldn't even smell her perfume. The scent of ferax hung in the air though. This time it was mingled with the scent of hounds and cats. Dhynar was nearby, and so were his four courtesi.

'Feck!' Macready swore.

52
FOUR DAYS AFTER THE
NONES OF LUCINA

The sky burst open in a sharp explosion of blood
that engulfed Poet, wrapping itself stickily around
his skin. Velody, protected mostly from the blast by his body,
received only a spattering over her hair and arms. She
grabbed Poet by his flimsy burnoose and threw him through
the air behind her, then reached out to the gaping source of
the explosion.

It crackled and spat at her, and the flecks of red liquid on
her skin began to frizzle and burn. Behind her, she heard
Poet cry out in agony. She tapped into the glowing animor
within her, pouring a steady stream of it into the open hole
in the sky. The hole swallowed the animor easily, and only a
few ragged fronds of sky around the edge began to heal
despite the heavy onslaught of her power. The gaping wound
bulged and bubbled, as if it were about to explode again.

Velody went chimaera. Tapping into her animor after a
single day of mortality had been heavenly, but this was
beyond the seven heavens, beyond anything saints or angels
had to offer her. Her body exulted as her wings beat the air,
her scales slithered out to protect her spiky skin, and her

talons extended into the dark mass of the skywound itself, scorching it with the highest power of all. The power that was hers to wield.

Bone-thin bolts of blue light flew from her claws and spikes and skin, slamming into the skywound again and again. It screamed as if it were a living thing — or something screamed, deep within that seething space — and slowly the sky began to heal over it, like fresh skin after a burn. The bubbling, bloody hole shrank into itself until it was only the size of Velody's head, then her heart, then her hand. Finally it was only a fingernail-sized speck of redness.

She threw another burst of animor into it, relentlessly holding the pressure of her burning light against the blood-stain until the hole dwindled to a spot, and finally vanished. Even then, Velody held her burning animor over the place where it had been, sealing the sky over tenfold, reluctant to stop until she was certain it was gone.

Only then, in the blissful silence, did she realise that the skywound had been singing to her as well as Poet. Its persis-tent hum had hung in her ears throughout the entire battle, tempting her to come closer, to surrender peacefully to its bloody siren call and allow herself to be swallowed. She had been fighting that too, without even realising it.

She relinquished her chimaera shape in a rush, reshaping herself as Velody in Lord form, glowing brightly in the dark-ness. She looked around for Poet.

He had not fallen, which was a mercy at least. Still covered in the sticky blood from the skywound, he hung in the air as a huddled mass, cringing and moaning to himself. His skin, where it was visible beneath the coating of blood, was bone white.

'What can I do?' Velody demanded. She snapped her fingers in front of his face, trying to get his attention. 'Poet, tell me how I can help you!'

As she watched, the dark skyblood moved as if it were alive, forming a pattern like a spider web, fringed and ominous. Poet's eyes fluttered but he did not register her presence. She reached out to touch him and he jerked backwards, away from her, whimpering.

'Touching him would be a mistake,' said a rich, accented voice. A masculine figure dressed in bright Zafiran silks rose up from beneath them, his sandalled feet expertly treading the sky. Warlord smiled at Velody, an entirely unfriendly smile. 'I came for the drink I was promised. But I see you are busy with blood of a different kind.'

'I suppose it's not in your interests to help Poet survive this,' Velody said sarcastically.

Warlord ran his dark eyes thoughtfully over the bloodied, moaning figure. 'This alone would not kill him, only weaken him,' he said. 'It is true that it makes him more vulnerable, which is not displeasing to me. I could kill him now, I imagine, without him lifting a paw to stop me.' He turned his dark eyes on Velody and she forced herself not to shiver under his gaze. 'You, however, would protect him from me, would you not?'

He was handsome, this Warlord, but there was a hardness that made him less than attractive to Velody. As with the others, she could not help but think, what kind of person was he before the Court poisoned his soul? What kind of man would he have been if he had not been taken by the monsters?

'It does not suit me for him to die this nox,' she said.

Warlord looked intrigued. 'You seem ruthless enough, Lady Power. I wonder if you are?'

Velody wrapped the lingering presence of the chimaera around her naked body. 'Last nox I promised you a price of blood, which I will pay. This nox I offer no bribes, no gifts. I am your Power and Majesty, and you will show me how to save Poet from this blight.'

'Such knowledge is valuable,' the Warlord said.

She glared at him, allowing her animor to glow from her eyes. 'So is my friendship.'

He acceded with a bow, after a very long moment of consideration. 'As my Lady demands.'

Between them, Velody and Warlord carried Poet to ground level without laying hands on him. They dragged him down out of the sky by wrapping tendrils of animor around his wrists and ankles.

They came to earth near the Lake of Follies. It was late enough that the last of the revellers had abandoned the lakeside, with only a few stray garland and ribbon fronds clinging to the empty pavilions.

Poet still twitched and moaned within the blood that stuck to him. He did not react when they lowered his curled body over the water.

'Are you saying we can wash it off?' Velody asked.

'Not entirely,' said Warlord. 'But it's a good place to start.'

With a snap, he withdrew the animor he had been using to hold Poet's top half in midair. Poet's head and shoulder-blades smacked back against the water and went under.

'Won't it pollute the lake?' Velody still held Poet's feet with her own animor.

Warlord grimaced. 'You mean, more than the toffee apples, ribbons and other festival paraphernalia dumped in here nearly every nox? Watch and learn.'

Velody peered into the water. Beneath the surface, Poet clawed free of the skyblood that matted his hair and clung to his skin. It fell away from him like old paint peeling under turpentine, rising to the surface of the lake in strips and flakes. His skin glowed with a black cobweb pattern, mimicking the lines the blood had marked upon him, and then that was gone too. His skin was pinker than usual, as if he had been scrubbed fiercely.

'Does water always have that effect on the... sky substances?' Velody asked.

'It's no ordinary lake,' said Warlord. 'The Lake of Follies isn't the frivolous ornament that everyone thought it was when Trajus Alysaundre poured half the city's grain budget into building it.'

Velody wanted to ask more, but Poet started struggling against her bonds and she dropped his feet. He bobbed up, sputtering water into the air. 'Yagh, that piss burns like acid.'

'You were lucky,' Warlord said seriously.

'Don't do me any favours,' Poet shot back, still scraping the blood from his limbs and clothes. He managed a watery smile at Velody. 'Give me a hand out of this birdbath, pretty lady?'

'Not until I'm certain that you're clean, inside and out,' she said firmly.

'You'll be waiting a long time,' Warlord muttered.

'This isn't exactly what I had in mind,' said Warlord, looking around Velody's stark backyard.

She sat on the back steps, refusing to compromise. 'As soon as this is done, I'm going straight to bed. I'm not going to walk all the way to the undercity just so you can sit on your favourite cushions and use your favourite crockery while you drink my blood.' She held out a small pewter cup that Delphine had won in a darts match between the Guild of Ribboners and the Guild of Spinners an age ago. 'I think this qualifies as a goblet, no?'

'I accept the conditions,' said Warlord, sounding suspicious.

'He still doesn't think you'll do it,' said Poet, an exhausted and damp figure leaning against the back fence. 'He's waiting for you to break your word.'

'Doesn't know her very well then,' grunted Crane, who stood in the kitchen doorway.

Velody took Crane's skysilver dagger and sliced down into her left wrist. The blade burned against her veins, and she felt a hollow numbness swim in her head.

'Steady,' said Crane. He sat behind her on the steps, cradling her as the blood ran into the goblet.

Warlord and Poet both stared at the trickle of blood, unable to take their eyes off it.

'A goblet,' said Crane, leaning his chin forward to rest it on Velody's shoulder. 'Why the saints did you have to volunteer a goblet? He'd have accepted a spoonful.'

'Now you tell me,' she said, and laughed.

After a moment, Crane laughed with her, a soft and happy sound that sustained her while the goblet filled.

Once it was brimming, Velody held the vessel out to Warlord, who brought it to his mouth, gulping greedily. Somehow, the sight of him drinking made her sick to the stomach where the loss of the blood itself had not. She swayed, and Crane held her tightly, closing his fingers around the still-bleeding cut.

'Get out of my way,' said Rhian, standing over them both with the kitchen lantern light behind her. Armed with bandages and a dish of hot water, she set to cleaning and wrapping Velody's arm.

Warlord drained the last drop from the goblet and threw it aside. His dark skin glowed as if sunlight was shining on it. 'Seven hells,' he gasped. 'That's a draught for the angels.'

'Devils, surely,' said Poet.

Rhian finished bandaging Velody's arm, and briefly laid her cheek against her friend's shoulder. Velody inhaled the scent of roses and herbs that was so familiar to her.

'You need hot, sweet mint, and something to eat,' Rhian said finally. She cast her eye around the yard — to the bedraggled Poet, the protective Crane, and Warlord who had splashes of Velody's blood clinging to his upper lip. 'You are all invited to join us,' she said quickly.

Warlord and Poet exchanged a look, obviously puzzled. 'You're joking,' said Crane doubtfully. 'Aren't you?' Rhian turned without speaking further and went into the kitchen.

53

FOUR DAYS AFTER THE NONES OF LUCINA

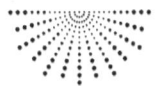

NOX

*T*he scent of ferax overwhelmed Macready. He took a deep breath, forcing himself not to panic or to call out Delphine's name. With his two skysilver lasses bared and ready, he moved further into the narrow alley.

A bright ginger ferax trotted out to greet him, and it was a moment before Macready realised it wasn't Dhynar but an actual ferax. Just as cats clustered madly around Ashiol when his animor was in full bloom, and mice hovered whenever Velody was near, so the ratbag urban ferax liked to be near the Lord who bore their shape.

'Go on then, my fine furry friend,' Macready said lightly. 'Take me to your man.'

The ferax gave him one of those chilly 'you are not important' looks that animals were so good at, then turned and padded back the way it had come.

Macready followed, expecting an ambush. He wasn't disappointed.

The first thing he saw as he rounded the curve of the alley was Delphine, limp like a broken doll on the ground. *Dead*, he thought, and his mind went numb at the realisation. *Oh, my poor sweet lass.*

'Haven't you had enough of me, Macready?' teased the voice of Dhynar.

'Aye,' breathed Macready, his hands loosening and tightening on the hilts of Tarea and Jeunille. 'So I have, my Lord. Time to put an end to it.'

Brighthounds and darkhounds emerged from the shadows, staring at him. Golden stripecats and silver slashcats peered at him from various windowsills.

'Sure about that?' asked Dhynar. He came forward, stepping with distaste over Delphine's crumpled body. He was clad in red leather, immaculate in his battledress.

The cats and hounds shaped themselves into their Court form — dark-eyed Shade and albino Lennoc, seasoned veterans of the Creature Court, with the young and hungry Grago and Farrier only just behind.

'Only your own courtesi this nox?' asked Macready. 'Hardly seems worth the trouble.'

Dhynar smiled. 'She didn't scream, you know. Barely a whimper. They don't build demoiselles like they used to.'

I'm going to skin you alive and feed you to Priest's bird women, Macready thought in a haze of anger. He forced himself to be calm. 'Still the bully-boy tactics, my Lord? This is no playground. You think killing the Power and Majesty's friend will win you points? She won't be merciful when she sees the mess you made of that lass of hers.'

Dhynar laughed. 'You think I care about that bitch's regard of me? She makes a mockery of the Creature Court.'

'She humiliated you and you can't take it,' Macready said in disgust. 'You made a blood oath that Delphine and Rhian would not meet harm at your hands. So easily forsworn, boy?'

'An oath to a demme means nothing,' said Dhynar. 'She is not my Power and Majesty.'

'You broke a blood oath,' Macready repeated. 'No angels and devils for you, my son. No sweet saints to sing you into the afterlife. The city owns your soul now. Velody owns your soul. If you think she'll be kind with it, you're more of a fool than everyone says.'

For a moment, something like doubt crossed Dhynar's face. Then he laughed. 'I don't believe in fairytales. But my blood oath's only half-broken, you know. I believe in doing things completely. There's still a trembling florister with my name on her.'

Blood buzzed in Macready's ears. 'Stay away from Rhian, you ginger bastard.'

'Oh, she'll open up for me like a rose, petal by petal. If she doesn't... I'll tear her up by her roots.' Dhynar sniggered.

The younger courtesi shared the joke, but neither Shade nor Lennoc reacted to it. Good men, both of them. Macready hoped he wouldn't have to kill either of them to get to Dhynar. Not that he wouldn't.

'You won't touch a hair on that lass's head,' he said slowly. 'You won't be touching any more women, Dhynar Lord Ferax, this or any nox.'

'Such fine words for a shortarse,' Dhynar mocked. 'What are you going to do on your own, little man?'

'He's not on his own.' Kelpie rounded the corner of the alley, the hilts of her Sisters plain on her shoulderblades and the Nieces on her hips. 'I've been looking all over this saints-forsaken city for you,' she muttered as she came to a halt alongside Macready. 'Tell me you weren't on a date with the chickadee.'

'Don't joke about Delphine,' Macready growled, voice cracking a little. 'The bastard killed her.'

Kelpie turned her mouth to his ear, speaking so quietly that even he could barely hear her. 'You always were blind when it came to women, Mac. The demme's not dead.'

Dhynar and his boys moved in that instant, so Macready didn't have a chance of finding out if it was true, but his mind cleared for the first time since he saw Delphine's crumpled body in the alley. It was time — long overdue, in fact — to let his lasses do the talking for him.

It felt good to be fighting back to back with Kelpie, skysilver blades whirling as they fended off Dhynar's snarling, swiping courtesi. The fight was a blur of adrenalin and blood.

Macready miscalculated against Lennoc and lost Jeunille when the albino kicked the dagger out of his hand and it went skittering across the cobbles. Macready used his bare hand to punch the courteso in the throat and then the face. Lennoc went down and was still.

Shade pounced, shaping himself into two darkhounds as he attacked, but Macready brought Tarea up and slashed both bellies. The hounds fell back, whimpering, and crouched over the unconscious Lennoc. Macready spun around to help Kelpie, but she was finishing off Grago in a haze of elbows and blades. Farrier already lay on the ground, dead or knocked out.

'What were you saying, my Lord Ferax?' Macready breathed.

'So pleased with yourself, mortal,' said Dhynar in a deadly voice. 'I am a Creature Lord and you cannot touch me.'

'Tarea begs to differ,' said Macready.

'You broke a blood oath to a Creature King — to your own Power and Majesty,' Kelpie said scornfully. 'That makes you a dead man walking. No one's ever survived it for more than a day.' She quirked an eyebrow. 'You might want to think about asking the saints of Aufleur for forgiveness — you know what happens to the Blood Forsworn if they die without repentance.'

Macready extended his sword tip, close enough to Dhynar that the skysilver buzzed at the proximity. 'I'd take a hint from the sentinel, so I would. Make your amends to the sky and the city, or so help me, I'll make you share Tasha's fate.'

Dhynar moved back in a sweep of red leather, grasping Delphine by the shoulders and hauling her upright in front of him. She gasped and her eyes opened wide, though they were still dazed. Her face was bruised, and blood matted her hair on one side of her skull.

'Ah, me,' said Dhynar, 'it seems I forgot to kill this lass of yours. This, my friends, is what we call leverage.'

Thank you, saints and angels. I'll show you proper gratitude once I've a minute spare. 'You're still forsworn,' Macready said steadily. 'The oath was not to hurt either of Velody's lasses, or allow them to be hurt at your will.'

'You think I care about being forsworn?' Dhynar demanded. 'Once your precious Velody finds this one gutted on her doorstep, and what's left of the shrinking violet when I'm finished with her, she'll throw herself at my feet. Can you imagine how good the animor of a Power and Majesty will taste when I'm the one who ripped her heart out?'

Kelpie and Macready shared a look. 'She'll eat you alive,' said Kelpie. 'She'll slice you into pieces and sew you back up as a *coat.*'

Dhynar stared back, bemused. 'A demoiselle,' he said. 'How strong can she be?'

'Oh, lad,' Macready said under his breath.

'Where's Ashiol in this grand plan of yours?' Kelpie asked.

'Where's Poet, come to that? Not to mention, where's your frigging brain?'

Dhynar smiled cheerfully. 'Better be nice to me, sentinel. I'm going to own this city by the time the nox is through. You'll be in service to me.'

Kelpie blinked. 'I honestly don't know what to say to that.'

'I have a fair idea,' said Macready, grinning hard. 'How about this? I can run you and Delphine through with this skysilver sword of mine and only one of you will bleed. I wonder which one?'

Delphine's dazed expression sharpened at that and she glared at him.

'I can tear her throat out before you get near me,' Dhynar said pleasantly. 'So what's our next move, sentinel?'

Delphine threw up. Vomit flew down the front of her dress and drenched both of Dhynar's arms.

'Bitch,' he gasped, but didn't let go of her. 'You'll bleed for that.'

She threw her head back, butting him in the face, then pirouetted and stabbed him in the throat.

Only then did Macready realise why he hadn't seen his dagger Jeunille after Lennoc kicked it out of his hand. The lass he thought was a corpse had grabbed it for herself.

Dhynar opened his mouth, as if he still had something to say. He staggered to his knees.

'Repent,' Kelpie said urgently. 'Voice or no voice, the saints will forgive you if you want it hard enough. Don't die forsworn, boy.'

In all this, Macready had forgotten quite how young Dhynar was. No matter. He would get no older.

The light went out of the eyes of Dhynar Lord Ferax and he fell back against the cobblestones of the alley. The body twitched and glowed for a moment. Macready knew what it meant. The animor was detaching, to scream itself through the city and be quenched by the Creature Court.

He had other things to think about. The sight of Delphine, alive and homicidal and stinking with her own vomit, was by far the most important thing in the alley right now. He went to her and caught her up in a bear hug. 'Who the devils taught you moves like that, my lovely?'

'Don't take too much credit,' Delphine shot back, but smiled shakily at him. Proud of herself, he hoped.

'You're fecking miraculous,' he told her, and couldn't think of anywhere to look but right there, into her bright eyes.

'Hate to interrupt this moment of yours,' said Kelpie acidly. 'You do realise that when the Court finds out that some little garland-maker from the daylight killed a Creature Lord, she'll be fair game.' She gestured to the empty corner of the alley where the wounded Shade had been guarding the unconscious Lennoc. Somehow, they had both crept away while the attention of the sentinels was elsewhere. 'It won't have gone unnoticed. The blood oath not to hurt her is void now she's taken one of them — they'll rip her apart to make an example of her.'

'She's not a daylighter,' said Macready, grinning fit to burst. 'She's a sentinel. Killing Creature Lords who betray their Kings is our solemn duty.'

He winked at Delphine, and she gave a startled little laugh, then threw up again. He was learning to recognise the signs and managed to skip out of the way.

54

FOUR DAYS AFTER THE
NONES OF LUCINA

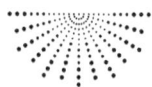

NOX

*E*very step towards Heliora told Ashiol that there was somewhere else he needed to be. Aufleur was calling him, trying to warn him of something important. For once, he ignored it. He had a responsibility to fulfil, and he was sick of dancing to the fucking city's tune. If there was a real problem, Velody could handle it. It was her job, not his.

In these early hours before dawn, the Basilica market was quiet, though there were still some lanterns and chatter near the worst of the grease-trap food stalls and the pay-by-the-hour tents.

Ashiol stopped outside Madama Fortuna's Pavilion of Mystery. If he concentrated hard enough, he could sense Heliora breathing through the thick fabric of the tent walls. Kicking himself for not remembering that the seer was the least nocturnal of any of the Creature Court, he didn't recognise the significance of the perfumed smoke approaching him until Livilla was close enough to touch.

'Hello, darling.'

He turned slowly, steeling himself not to make any sudden moves. No reason for her to know that he hadn't smelled her coming a mile away. 'Livilla. No boytoys with you this nox?'

She extended her black leather boot in front of her and wiggled her foot. 'All better. I can look after myself now.'

'Yes, because women walking alone in Aufleur dressed like that have such an easy time of it,' said Ashiol sarcastically.

Livilla glanced down at her sparkling black dress. 'What? It's fashionable. It even covers my knees; it's almost conservative.'

'It shows everything else. That bloody jewellery of yours — how many daylighters have tried to jump you since you came above?'

'Ten or twelve. I mostly let them live. You can't be worried about my wellbeing...'

'Old habit. Surprised your boys agreed to let you out though. That raven of yours is trying so hard to be an alpha male.'

Livilla smiled that sweet, bright smile that had somehow survived her years as Garnet's moll. 'They tried to stop me. Anyone would think they had forgotten who the Lord is. Men tend to do that, I've noticed, when a woman is in charge.'

'You beat up your own courtesi?'

'Of course not. I drugged their syrup and left them snoozing in a puddle together. Buy me a drink, Ashiol?'

This was getting far too comfortable. 'I'm busy,' he said shortly.

'So predictable, my cat. If you must wake the seer, don't you think you could wait an hour or two? She's not going to kill herself in her sleep.' Livilla indicated a nearby gin stall with a swish of her shiny black bobbed hair. 'I'm thirsty.'

Ashiol gave up. 'Do you know everything, Liv?'

'I'm the only female Lord in a sea of men, darling. I hear all the gossip.'

They went to the gin stall together. He bought her a deep cup of something expensive that smelled of booze and pears and burnt sugar, and a single shot for himself. Livilla sprawled on the bench provided for patrons and Ashiol sat beside her without thinking about it. She put her feet in his lap and he didn't push her away.

'So what pretty piece of poison did you come here to spout in my ear?' he asked her.

She pressed her heavily painted lips together. 'Oh, that's right. I wanted to tell you that your sweet little Velody is frigging Mars and I'm not happy about it.'

Ashiol closed his eyes. 'You've based this on the evidence of what? No, don't tell me. He's an hour late for an assignation with you.'

'Two,' she pouted. 'I know he's with her. He went to get his precious cup of blood.'

'Not that fidelity has ever been an issue for either of you, but Velody isn't likely to —' Her words caught up with him. 'His cup of what?'

'Didn't you know?' She smiled wolfishly, and drank from her cup. 'She promised him a goblet of her blood, as a bribe to take to the sky. Back when you were playing bondage games with Poet in that cage of his.'

Ashiol swore. 'What is she thinking? Doesn't she have any idea of what that blood of hers is worth?'

'Obviously not.' Livilla yawned and leaned back on her arms. 'Anyway, you know how horny Mars gets around blood. If he didn't tear the sky apart in his speed to get back to me, that means he's between her thighs right now, showing her why Zafiran men are so very popular with the ladies.'

'You're enjoying this way too much,' Ashiol accused. 'You don't care who Mars is screwing — you know he always comes back to you. You just want to see if I give a frig.'

'You're no fun,' she sighed, and nudged his groin with the heel of her boot.

Ashiol leaped to his feet and handed his cup back to the gin man. 'Game over, Liv.'

'Don't you want to know what gift Velody gave me?' Livilla whined.

'Hells, no.' He thought about it. 'Tell me. I'd better know the worst.'

Livilla stood, making the entire process a slinky, sensuous moment. She leaned into him, nuzzling her face into his neck. 'You're never going to have her, Ash.'

'What?'

'The wide-eyed little dressmaker. You're not going to get to be the one who wakes her up to what the Court is really all about. One of us is going to slide her out of her daylight knickerbockers and unpeel those innocent layers until she cries for more, more, more! But it won't be you. Maybe Mars. Maybe that adorable little boy sentinel. My money's on Poet. There's a glint in his eye I haven't seen in a very long time.'

'That's the venom I've missed,' said Ashiol with a grin, moving away from her. 'Not everyone's a succubus like you, love.'

'Are you telling me you haven't wanted her in your bed since the moment you first saw her?' demanded Livilla. 'Or maybe up against a wall — that's more your style.'

'I'm not having this conversation with you.'

'Poor Ashiol. She doesn't want you. Not even a little bit. If she did, she would never have made me that promise.'

'What promise?' He grabbed her wrists, and was annoyed to see that the violent gesture made her eyes shine and her breath come a little faster. She might be a vicious harpy now, but Ashiol remembered when Livilla had been sweeter than Velody and Rhian put together...

Livilla laughed delightedly. 'When you frig her for the first time, I get to be there as witness. She swore a blood oath, Ash. You know what that means.'

A female scream cut through the Basilica. 'Hel,' Ashiol breathed, and started running.

RHIAN'S bizarre little tisane party remained civilised for about ten minutes before Warlord cracked and tried to put Poet's face through a window. It took all of the animor that Velody could summon (short of changing to Lord form right there in the kitchen) to drag the two men apart, all the time wondering exactly what it was Poet had said to set Warlord off. It was remarkably easy to tune out Poet's snark, and she hadn't been listening to a word he said.

Warlord was literally glowing with rage. Velody shaped her power into a tight, cold burst and thumped him hard in the forehead with it. He sat down in a hurry on the kitchen floor. 'Devils, woman. I would have killed Garnet for trying something like that on me.'

'No, you wouldn't have,' she said firmly. 'And you're not going to raise a hand against me, my Lord. Get back to the table and finish your biscuit, or walk out that door right now.'

Warlord shot her a scorching look, but returned to his chair. 'Good biscuits, demoiselle Rhian,' he said politely.

Rhian gave him a strained smile. 'I'll give you the recipe.'

'You,' Velody said, pointing a figure at Poet. 'Haven't you

ever heard that if you can't say anything nice, you shouldn't say anything at all?'

Poet looked faintly puzzled. 'What's the punchline?'

There was a knock on the kitchen door and it swung open. Priest stood there, resplendent in a bright scarlet waistcoat with gold cranes embroidered on it. 'Ah,' he said happily. 'So this is where the best people are. I thought as much.'

Velody stared at the waistcoat for a moment. She had seen a few swatches of Isharo fabric in the markets, enough to recognise the style of the design, but it had never been fashionable in Aufleur. *Until now*, she thought, with a sudden blinding inspiration for the gown she had to make for the Duchessa to wear at the Sacred Games of Felicitas. Her fingers twitched, and she resisted the urge to throw everyone out of the house so she could get to work.

Too long a moment had passed. There was no getting rid of Priest now. 'What are you doing here?' she asked belatedly.

The large man smiled at her. 'There's something in the air, my dear. Can't you feel it? The sky is shivering. It's all very ominous, and I felt the need for protection from my Power and Majesty. Ah, biscuits. Splendid.'

Rhian stood with great poise and fetched Priest a cup. 'Mint or ginger?' she asked politely.

Velody stared at her friend, not sure whether she was really getting better, or had cracked under the pressure. Rhian was wary around these men and never allowed any kind of casual contact, even the brush of a sleeve against a hand, yet she seemed calmer than she had in months. *Perhaps we've frightened her so much, she's come out the other side*, she thought, passing her own cup to Rhian for a refill.

Priest smiled around the table. 'Isn't this cosy?'

Something was wrong. Velody swayed, and flung an arm

out to steady herself. An unfamiliar taste burned hard in her throat for a moment.

'Are you all right?' Crane asked with concern.

'I don't... know,' she gasped. 'What is that?' The others knew. She could see it on their faces. 'Tell me!'

'If you'll excuse me, demoiselles,' said Priest, moving towards the door, peeling off his clothes as he went.

Warlord said nothing, but shoved his way past Priest on the way out.

Poet gave Velody a courtly bow, face only slightly strained. 'You'll be wanting to join us, my lovely. One of us is dead and it's time to lick the corpse.'

'Stay with Rhian,' Velody told Crane, then followed the Creature Lords out into her backyard.

Priest took to the sky, shaping himself into the flock of pigeons as he went.

Warlord folded down into the body of a sleek black panther and loped away through the gate.

Poet simply stood there, his arms stretched up to the sky. 'I didn't know he had that much in him,' he said in surprise, and then tipped his head back as if expecting to be kissed. 'Delicious.'

'Who's dead?' Velody asked, the words choking in her throat. *Ashiol*, she thought for one awful moment. *Saints, what have you done to yourself now?* As soon as she asked the question though, she knew. 'Dhynar.' She could taste the absence of him in the air.

There was something else too — a tension that hummed and crackled under her skin. With a shiver, she remembered standing in the Forum, waiting for the Duchessa's pavilion to pass by. She had felt something similar then, though she had not had any reason to know what it was. She knew now. Dhynar was coming to be quenched. His animor had been released into the air, in bursts and splashes like mud under the wheels of a cart. For a moment, it blanketed the entire city with a very thin film of his essence and power.

Velody found a thread of it and tugged it towards her. It came willingly.

They were all doing it, she realised. Even as she captured some of Dhynar's released animor, she could feel the Lords and Court in their various positions above and beneath the city, gulping and chewing at strands of what was left of their fallen comrade. Only Livilla and Ashiol were absent from the feast.

For a moment, Velody fought revulsion at how easily the Creature Court cannibalised the dead. *Thimblehead*, she chided herself. *You let a man drink a goblet of your blood this evening. This is hardly the time to be prissy.*

She remembered Ashiol talking about Garnet, and what a waste it was that his animor had been swallowed by the sky. The Court needed this — needed Dhynar's strength to be shared among them instead of being lost to the enemy.

Velody pulled the thread of animor hard inside herself and reeled with the strength of it. Saints and angels! It felt like sex and death all at once. Light burned inside her body as she swallowed Dhynar down. For a moment, she was overwhelmed by the scent of ferax, but she pressed her sense of self into the foreign animor and made it hers.

She wanted to break apart in an army of little brown mice.

She wanted to go chimaera and tear the sky into fragments.

She wanted to throw the nearest man to the ground and ride him into insensibility...

The fact that the nearest man was Poet brought her back into some semblance of control. Even as she did, he turned to her with fierce eyes and kissed her hard, pulling her body into his.

Velody sent him flying with a hard push of her animor. 'Keep your tongue to yourself, Lord of Rats.'

Poet laughed at her. 'Worth a try, my Power.'

She shuddered, still warm inside from the animor she had quenched from Dhynar. 'Have I been doing that my whole life without knowing?'

'You're very good at repressing things,' Poet suggested.

He wasn't wrong there. 'Has anyone been... promoted?' she asked, with visions of a dozen brand-new Lords all powered up and ready to attack her.

'You tell me,' shrugged Poet. 'Proximity matters. If any of his courtesi were close to the action, they might have been boosted up to Lord. We'll have to wait and see.'

'You could find out for me,' Velody said, making her voice firm.

Poet gave her a look of disbelief. 'Are you giving me a direct order?'

'Yes, I think I am.'

'Right, then.' He grasped his ear in a mock salute. 'Off I go then, my Power and Majesty. Your loyal servant.'

'Why does that make me suspicious?' she called after him, and heard his lilting laughter all the way down the lane.

55
FOUR DAYS AFTER THE
NONES OF LUCINA

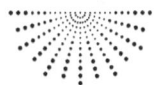

NOX

*H*eliora was screaming, and she couldn't stop. The terrors that broke into her dreams still had hold of her. For a few moments, she could see everything, and it hurt her so much that if she'd had an axe handy, she would have broken open her own skull just to make the pain stop.

'Hel, sweetling. I'm here.'

She fought her way out of the strangling blankets to stare at Ashiol. For a moment, she was confused, thinking that he should still be outside the city and safe, as he had been for the last five years. Even as she remembered what he was doing here, all the other events of the last few days crashed in on her. She groaned. 'Go away, Ash.'

'There's gratitude for you,' said a sharp female voice.

Heliora peeked through her fingers, wary of Kelpie or Velody, but it was much worse than that. 'Hello, Livilla.'

'Everyone's always so pleased to see me,' said Livilla Lord Wolf, lighting a cigarette.

'What did you dream about?' Ashiol asked Heliora, ignoring Livilla despite his hatred for those cigarettes of hers.

Heliora scratched at her stubbled scalp, feeling awkward. 'Aren't we fighting?'

'I'm over it. You did something stupid, but you meant well. Tell me about the dream.'

'I don't remember it.' Strangely, that was the truth. Heliora hadn't forgotten a dream since she was a teenager. 'It was about blood, I think.' She searched back through the vague images she could still hold on to. 'Dhynar broke a blood oath. Oh, saints and devils. This is happening right now, Ash.'

'The little fucker,' Livilla said loudly. 'I knew we should have squashed him like an ant when he took that fourth courteso. Who the seven hells does he think he is?'

'Where is he?' Ashiol asked Heliora urgently. 'If I can get him to repent in the name of the city, it could make all the difference.'

The futures folded in on Heliora. 'Too late,' she told him. 'The Ferax Lord is dead.'

Livilla howled. Her skin burst into a blinding glow of light and she spun towards the opening of the tent.

'No!' Ashiol leaped after her, shaping himself into Lord form and grabbing her by the shoulders. 'You can't quench him, Liv. You can't afford to take in any more animor.'

She snarled at him, her usual glamour discarded for a wolfish, furious face. 'Haven't you heard the news, my cat? Women can be Kings now.'

'They can also destroy themselves by taking too much power,' Ashiol yelled at her. 'Velody doesn't cancel out what happened to Samara.'

'I don't give a damn about Samara!' Livilla screamed. 'I want to be Velody. You are not stopping me.'

She tore out of the tent, shaping into two silvery wolves as she did so. Ashiol shaped himself into a mob of black cats that swarmed after the wolves, catching them up and bringing them down with vicious, easy power. The wolves and cats snapped at each other, rolling and fighting with wild violence.

Heliora wrapped herself in a large shawl and stood at the opening of her tent, watching Ashiol and Livilla tear each other to pieces. She found a stray shoe and used it to put out Livilla's fallen cigarette.

Dhynar's animor floated overhead, veiling the city. Neither Ashiol nor Livilla was aware enough to latch onto it, too busy biting and snapping at each other.

As Heliora watched, the veil of animor broke up into pieces and was divided and quenched between those members of the Creature Court who weren't currently trying to kill each other. It took only a few minutes and the last breath of Dhynar was gone.

Heliora wondered where Poet was, whether he was feasting on his share of Dhynar's power. She had been thinking about Poet a lot lately. That wasn't a good sign.

Something bad was coming, and Heliora didn't have to look into the futures to see that. Blood oaths were not made to be broken, and last time it had happened, Aufleur had come the closest it ever had to total destruction.

She closed her tent flap, not really wanting to see what happened when Ashiol and Livilla regained their human forms, naked and in each other's arms. Then she slid out of her shawl and went back to bed.

∾

RHIAN AND CRANE looked up as Velody returned to the kitchen. 'Dhynar Lord Ferax is dead,' she told them.

Rhian's gaze was steely. 'Should I sacrifice a honey cake?'

'Four Lords instead of five,' said Velody. 'That should be easier to juggle, right?'

'Depends,' said Crane. 'They'll each be more powerful. Dhynar might have been the wild card, but that doesn't make the others less dangerous. And... assuming they didn't die with him, there are four courtesi out there without a Lord.'

'What does that mean?' Velody asked. 'Will they make trouble?'

'Not them, but the other Lords will all be angling to take them in. You'll be lucky if you don't get a turf war out of this.'

Velody sighed. 'It never stops, does it?'

'There's a reason our Power and Majesties mostly go mad,' Crane said, then looked horrified at having said that out loud.

Velody reached out and patted his hand. 'I'm not Garnet.'

'No,' he said. 'You're not.'

They looked at each other for a moment, and Velody realised with a sinking feeling that she was very lucky he hadn't been the nearest man to her when she quenched Dhynar.

'Who killed him?' Rhian asked suddenly. 'If Dhynar died, who killed him? And... I know this might be a stupid question, but why?'

Velody hadn't even thought to wonder about those things. She closed her eyes, trying to open her mind to the city again, but she could no longer feel the presence of each of the Lords and Court.

'I'm not good enough at this yet,' she said in frustration. 'I'm a baby when it comes to understanding Aufleur and the animor. Some Power and Majesty.'

'Be patient,' said Crane. 'It will come.'

'How many more will die before I figure it all out?'

There was a quiet knock at the kitchen door. Velody noticed that Rhian didn't even flinch as she went to let Ashiol in. He looked exhausted, his clothes torn and dishevelled.

'We have a problem,' he said, as he collapsed into one of the kitchen chairs.

'Start at the beginning,' said Velody. 'Simple vocabulary. I'm feeling dumb and uneducated.'

He lifted his eyes to her. 'I hear you've been making blood oaths. Want to tell me about them?'

'You know about them,' she said uncomfortably. 'We made the Lords and Court swear with their blood that they would not hurt Delphine and Rhian.'

'Those were blood oaths made to you,' he growled. 'What have you been promising to other people?'

'Oh.' Velody could feel her face flaming. 'I had to convince the Lords to fight the sky when you were in that cage. Livilla and Warlord wouldn't settle for less than blood oaths. I honoured his this nox.'

'Well, I hope the promise you made Livilla isn't too onerous,' he told her. 'You can't break it, ever.'

'I know,' she said uncomfortably. 'I mean, I assumed —'

'An oath is never taken lightly, Velody. A blood oath least of all. It ties your soul to that of the city. If a blood oath is broken, Aufleur demands a life in return. I've never known anyone to survive breaking a blood oath for more than twelve hours or so.'

'I see.' *A good thing I plan on never sleeping with you then.* They'd been so close to it the other nox, and she hadn't thought twice about breaking her word to Livilla. Holy hells. 'Perhaps you should have explained that earlier.'

'Perhaps so.' Ashiol's face was guarded. Did he know the terms of her oath to Livilla?

'Does that mean I didn't need to promise them anything? They would have obeyed me eventually, or been forsworn?'

'Maybe. Allegiance isn't a cut-and-dried concept, and you may have noticed that the oath to serve you as Power and Majesty was not made with blood. They can bend that particular oath pretty far without it breaking, especially when it comes to self-preservation. Arguably, it's their duty to stay alive. Likewise, they won't lie to you, but they'll conceal the truth and they're damn good at blurring those lines. But, for the most part, they will obey direct orders, especially if reinforced by a push of power.'

'I didn't have any power at the time!'

'I know,' he sighed. 'There's more, Velody. Being forsworn from an ordinary oath can be uncomfortable for one of the Court, but betraying a blood oath — if the person forsworn doesn't fully repent their action before death catches up with them, it's not only their life that's forfeit but their soul. There aren't any saints or angels for them, and what happens next makes the seven hells look like a holiday camp.'

'That's superstition, surely?' Rhian asked. 'I mean, how can you know for certain what happens to them after they die?'

'It happened to my first Creature Lord,' said Ashiol. 'Tasha. She broke a blood oath and she died. It didn't stop there. The broken oath kept her shade from moving on — she haunted the city for weeks afterwards. We heard her every scream, her every agony. There was a plague that month — do you remember the Weeping Fate? I don't think it was a coincidence. Death followed Tasha's empty footsteps wherever she wandered. Whole streets were wiped out.'

Velody shuddered. 'I get the message. Never make a blood oath you can't keep.'

'We never knew whether it was the sky or Aufleur itself that was doing it,' Ashiol went on. 'But it took everything we had to exorcise her from the streets. Those of us who remember that would never break an oath.'

'You can stop lecturing me,' Velody snapped. 'I understand.'

'I'm not lecturing, Velody, I'm trying to explain. Dhynar joined us *after* Tasha. He may have heard the stories, but he wasn't here. He didn't see it. He can't have taken it seriously enough, or he would never...'

'Would never what?' Velody asked. She felt cold. 'What has he done, Ashiol?'

'He died this nox — after breaking a blood oath. The seer told me — he brought his death upon himself.'

'What oath did he break?' Rhian asked suddenly. 'Has he made any blood oaths other than the one not to hurt Velody's friends? Where's Delphine, Ashiol?'

'It's going to happen all over again,' muttered Crane. 'Dhynar's shade will bring death to the city.'

'I don't care if Dhynar's shade is on fire!' Rhian yelled. 'Where is Delphine?'

'Macready was trailing her this nox,' Crane assured them. 'He'll see she comes to no harm.'

Rhian was furious, something Velody had not seen in a very long time. 'Last time Macready went up against Dhynar, he was brought back in *pieces*!'

Velody heard a faint noise outside in the alley. *Saints, but my hearing's getting good.* She glanced at Ashiol to confirm that he had heard it, and he nodded a little.

'It's all right, Rhian,' Velody said. 'They're home.' She opened the kitchen door just as the back gate swung open. Delphine, fragile and battered, was only on her feet because both Macready and Kelpie supported her arms. The three of them looked like they had been through all seven hells.

Rhian ran past Velody to Delphine, unwound her from

the two sentinels and led her inside. Delphine sank into a kitchen chair and Rhian fussed over her.

'We have to talk, so we do,' said Macready, unsmiling as he and Kelpie reached the kitchen door.

'No,' Velody said, remarkably calm considering the circumstances. 'No, we don't. I want you out.'

'Majesty,' he said, startled.

'No. Not Power, not Majesty. Not any more.' She turned to Crane. 'And you. Out.'

Crane, just as surprised as Macready, got to his feet. 'Stay where you are,' Ashiol growled.

Crane hesitated.

Velody rounded on Ashiol. 'Don't think I've forgotten about you. Ever since that first time you broke into my house, you've put me and my friends in danger. It's all about you, Ash. Your power games. If the blood oath can't protect Rhian and Delphine, they will *never be safe*. That is not acceptable.'

'No one could have predicted what Dhynar would do,' Ashiol protested.

'I should have predicted it! But no, I was too busy trying to learn the rules for this twisted world of yours. It's over.'

Ashiol remained sitting. 'You don't mean that.'

Velody glared at him, then looked at each of the three sentinels. 'Kelpie. Crane. Macready. This is my last order to you all. Escort the Ducomte Ashiol Xandelian out of this house.'

There was a discernible pause. Kelpie moved first, stepping into the kitchen and laying her hand upon Ashiol's shoulder. 'Time to go.'

'You're taking her side?' Ashiol asked in disbelief.

'You're King, but she's the Majesty,' said Macready, who still stood in the doorway.

Ashiol shrugged off Kelpie's hand, his eyes burning into

Velody. 'You'll never be safe. We've tried this before. Whether we're around or not, whether you accept it or not. If the Court don't force you into action, the sky will. You can't escape it.'

'You did,' she said calmly. 'You escaped it for five years. You left the city. So that's what we're going to do.'

Ashiol's face froze. 'You can't.'

'We'll leave Aufleur, and we won't return.'

'You're sure about this, lass?' Macready asked.

'I don't have a choice, Mac,' she said helplessly. 'I have to get out from under this before it eats us alive. I can live without being the Duchessa's dressmaker, and I can certainly live without being the demi-monarch of a crazy bunch of reprobates. I can't live with risking the lives of Delphine and Rhian.'

'The city will fall without you,' Ashiol said flatly. 'One morning, you'll wake up and no one around you will ever have heard the name of Aufleur. The animor in you will keep the memory of all these dead souls in your mind, but you'll be the only one who knows this city ever existed. Can you survive that?'

'If I have to,' said Velody, trying not to let her face crumple.

'This is what you both want?' Macready asked softly, his eyes going from Delphine to Rhian and back again. 'You'll give up everything to follow Velody away from the city?'

'I have nothing in Aufleur to give up,' said Rhian, still holding Delphine protectively. 'I have Velody and Delphine. That's everything.'

'Me too,' said Delphine between bruised lips. 'We're family.' It evidently hurt her just to talk.

Velody reached out and held her friend's hand. 'You'll leave now. All of you.'

She glanced at Crane and then wished she hadn't. His face

509

looked like someone had killed orphans in front of him. She raised the animor within her to force them out if she had to.

'No need for that, my lass,' said Macready lightly. 'We'll be going now.' He stepped forward and stood beside Ashiol. 'My King?'

Ashiol stood up and pushed back his chair. 'I'm coming.' He kept his eyes on Velody all the way to the door.

Crane reached out as he followed the others, and Velody squeezed his hand quickly. 'Goodbye.'

'Did you mean that?' Delphine asked after Ashiol and the sentinels were gone and Velody had latched the door behind them.

'I don't see any other way,' Velody said helplessly.

'It's a good idea,' said Rhian. 'Why don't you get some sleep? I'll make soup for Delphine. After we're all rested, we can make our plans.'

Velody smiled. 'That sounds wonderful.'

56

FOUR DAYS AFTER THE
NONES OF LUCINA

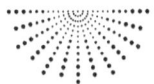

The house was quiet as Velody went up to her room. She hadn't felt so peaceful in the longest time. She looked longingly at her bed and the messy tangle of quilts and blankets. But she couldn't lie down quite yet. There were little brown mice along her shelves, floor and window ledge. She had finally trained them to keep off her bed, but that was little comfort now.

Velody went to the window and pulled it up sharply. 'All of you, out. This is no longer the rodent hotel. Sorry and all that. But it's over.'

She reinforced her words with a little push of animor, and watched with some satisfaction as two lines of small brown mice scampered up her wall and out her window.

As the last one crept away, Velody was startled by a meow. She spun around and saw a ginger tom glaring at her from the top of her wardrobe. 'Are you still here?' she said in amazement. She hadn't seen hide nor hair of Old Tom since Ashiol gave him to her, though Rhian had reported stolen bacon, milk and biscuits from the pantry on a regular basis over the last month. 'The eviction goes for you too, puss-

puss. The last thing I need is one of Ashiol's spies watching over us as we make our getaway.'

Scornfully, Old Tom leaped down from the wardrobe and loped towards the window.

Velody turned around and saw nine black cats settling themselves on her bed, even as Old Tom climbed out of the open window. 'Oh, no, Ash,' she wailed. 'This isn't fair. Dramatic exits are non-refundable.'

The cat shapes blurred together, shifting into a single, male human figure. 'We still have things to talk about, Velody.'

She glared at him. 'If we're going to have this conversation, I want you to put some clothes on.'

He shrugged, utterly comfortable in his skin. 'I forgot to bring them with me.'

'I'm tired, Ashiol. And I'm done. This is it for me. Why is it so hard for you to accept that?'

He didn't smile. 'Maybe because you leaving is pretty much the end of the world? I can't have that.'

Every inch of her was aware of the violent potential of his body. He was a lethal creature, and had one distinct military advantage over her: he was more prepared to hurt and maim and kill. 'Are you going to try and force me into changing my mind?'

'No.' He moved from the bed with animal grace to stand near the window. 'I'm going to beg you.'

This was unexpected. 'You? Beg?'

'Us. Beg. Look outside.'

Suspicious, she moved to the window and looked down to the courtyard below. It was full of people. The Creature Court — or, at least, Warlord, Livilla and Priest, surrounded by their respective courtesi. They all knelt on the cobbles, heads bowed.

'This is not what we agreed,' Velody said angrily.

'We agreed nothing. Look at them. Really look at them. They're on their knees to you.'

'Oh, they make a fine show of penitence,' she raged. 'When you all want something from me.'

'We want everything from you,' he said quietly. 'I don't deny that. We need you. Even now, Dhynar's shade is latching itself to the streets and walls of this city. The days after Tasha died forsworn were the worst that any of us has ever seen. They were worse than anything Garnet did to me at his craziest. Anything the sky ever threw at us. We need a Power and Majesty to save us, to protect us, Velody.'

'You expect me to believe all this?' she asked. 'That somehow, as soon as I make up my mind to leave you, there's a great threat that only I can be equal to?'

'There will always be a great threat that only you can be equal to. That's what Power and Majesty means.'

Velody shook her head. 'No, Ash. Let's not play this game any more. We've been going through the motions, pretending that I could play the lead, but it's not true. It's time for you to take your rightful place.'

'I'm not strong enough. I'm not good enough. If I were, I would never have let Garnet drive me into the ground and chase me out of the city five years ago. I gave up. You're better than that.'

It began to rain. The back gate opened and Poet stepped into the yard, his boy courteso only a step or two behind him. He looked up at the bedroom window and smiled. It wasn't a particularly nice smile, but he joined the others on their knees, and his boy mimicked him.

'Over-beading the hem, aren't you?' Velody muttered.

'Are you going to turn your back on us?'

She glared at him. 'Macready wants Delphine to be a sentinel! Saints only know what he has in mind for Rhian. If I don't get them out from this web now, we'll never escape.'

'I understand that Delphine and Rhian are family to you,' said Ashiol. 'Family is important. But they aren't the only ones due your loyalty and protection. They aren't your only family. Not any more.'

Velody closed her eyes. She couldn't take much more of this.

'Be our Power,' said Ashiol. 'Be our Majesty.'

'They don't want me,' Velody said, and she hated that she could hear her voice wavering.

'Their knees say otherwise. Would you rather they opened a vein?'

Velody shuddered. 'We've had enough of that sort of thing for the time being.'

Rain splashed against the window and down to the yard below. The air smelled salty and stale. Velody held a hand out, and looked at the rain as it pelted against her skin. It was dark red, and definitely not water. 'The sky's bleeding.'

Worse than that. She could hear the blood calling her, whispering to her in a familiar voice.

'Not so smug now, are you?' Ash started to say something, but Velody held up her hand. 'Not talking to you.'

She clambered up to the window ledge and stood with the cold blood blowing around her for a moment in droplets and spirals. She could hear Dhynar's voice, crying out to her. *I'm sorry, I'm sorry, I'm sorry...*

'Too late,' she said sadly. 'I can't save you. I don't know how.'

A slight sound made Velody turn, and she saw a long line of little brown mice crouching along the thin ledge that ran across the buildings. Some of them nibbled on fragments of food. Others just stared at her, unblinking. 'Oh.'

'Velody,' Ashiol started.

'Shh. I'm thinking.'

A few times before, she had tapped into the mind of the

city, if only for a moment. She could feel it now, the beat of Aufleur. If she opened her mind and her animor to it, she could feel the pulsing streets, like veins, and the sparks of life that denoted daylight people going about their business. Most of them were sleeping now, and that gave a warm hum to the city.

The Lords and Court below her burned like fierce candlelight, all heat and nervous tension. She ignored them, trying to see beyond into the dark and breathing city. She found Dhynar's body easily enough, a withered husk of dry skin and splintered bones, barely even recognisable as human once the animor had abandoned him. *So that's how we all end up — those who aren't swallowed whole by the sky.*

Dhynar's shade was nowhere near his body. Velody breathed with the city, searching for the wrongness that was causing blood to fall from the sky like rain. She found it in a narrow street near the Forum, moving at a disturbing pace. It was not just wrong, but devastating. There was something corrupt and rotten about it, a soul-stench that trailed along the cobbles with easy, careless pollution.

Velody removed her dress and let it float on the blood-soaked breeze down to the yard full of Creature Court below. 'Come, if you like,' she said. 'I doubt you'll be able to keep up.'

Then she was swarming, tumbling, a raging race of tiny paws and quick-beating hearts, a cloud of streaking brown fur and paws that danced so much faster than your average mouse. She was as fast as a breath, as quick as a thought. Her paws did not touch the ground as she tore across the city as a blur of little brown mice.

The Thing that remained of Dhynar had covered three more streets in that time. The cloying pollution of him clung to the stones and bricks and Velody pursued him. She burst into an open piazza, not yet populated by the early-morning crowd. She shaped herself into Lord form and called his name, though she was well aware that it wasn't his name any more. 'Dhynar! Dhynar Lord Ferax!'

The Thing turned and regarded her. It was as thin as a whisper, translucent enough that Velody could see the cobbles through what served it as skin. 'I am not that Creature,' it said in a rasp.

'You still wear his shape,' said Velody, though the shape in question was a bastardisation of the real man, more ferax than man, with long orange fur and a ragged half-face. The real urban feraxes that had so loyally dogged Dhynar in life now hung back at the darkest edges of the piazza, whining. Some were dead already, and others oozed with sickness.

'Not for long,' gasped the Thing, and a foul breath billowed out from it with those words. 'I will feed soon, and then there will be countless shapes to choose from.'

Velody shuddered. 'I can't let you do that.'

It took a step towards her, and pestilence boiled out of the print left behind on the cobbles. 'It hurts.' That sounded more like Dhynar himself. There was still some of him there within the wrongness.

'I know,' she said, compassion flooding into her voice. 'I know, sweetling. I'm here to make it better.'

'Bring me back to life,' he moaned.

'I can't do that. It isn't possible.'

Thing again, its eyes glowed with a blinding whiteness.

'Then I will eat this city whole. I will be flesh, or I will have flesh. You decide.'

Velody's mind was open to the Thing as well as the city. She could see how to end it, as easily as breathing.

'I can make the pain stop, Dhynar. I can make everything stop. Oblivion is the best I can offer you. Will you take it?'

'No!' he howled.

She ate him anyway.

It was a fierce meal. Velody was not quite little brown mice, or Lord, or chimaera, but some strange combination of the three. She tore at the foul Thing that had once been Dhynar Lord Ferax, and with each bite and gulp she consigned him to oblivion. 'Nothing, be nothing, be gone,' was her mantra as she consumed his soul.

Velody was not human any more. That much was obvious, for she could sense every pulse of her body just as she could sense every pulse of the city, and she could feel her animor working on the fragments of soul and shade as she ate them, changing the pestilence into something else.

She wasn't sure exactly what that something else was, but it tasted like power. Power and honey.

When it was over, she collapsed into a scattered pile of little brown mice with full bellies and splitting headaches. She moaned and wriggled in that mass of tiny bodies, allowing herself to rest for a few precious moments before she scanned the city for traces of Dhynar.

He was gone. Completely gone. Not a breath of him remained in Aufleur. The pestilence that still daubed the streets he had polluted was already beginning to lose its potency.

With a word and a thought, Velody killed every one of the feraxes. Better safe than sorry.

That last burst of animor was too much for her. The horde of little brown mice collapsed back into a single, clumsy human female body. The cobbles were cold against her breasts and stomach and legs. She was willing to sleep right there.

Cool hands found her and drew her to her feet. The scent of roses and foreign tinctures enveloped her as Rhian wrapped a shawl around her waist, and Delphine pulled a soft shirt over her head.

That made no sense at all. How could they have found her

here? Velody leaned against them, not asking questions. The nox was beginning to fade and there would be daylight people filling this piazza soon. She still wasn't enough herself to recognise which piazza it was, though she knew them all so well.

'What day is it?' she asked, and laughed at herself. A fine thing for a woman of their house to have forgotten her place on the calendar. 'Was there work today? Garlands?'

'Shh,' said Delphine, and held her closer.

They were all there. Not just Rhian and Delphine. The Creature Court clustered around them, keeping only a slight distance. The Lords came forward hesitantly. Livilla brushed her dark mouth to Velody's cheek and then retreated hastily. Warlord brought a heavy man's coat, and Velody allowed him to slip her arms into it.

Ashiol was there, further back from the others, flanked by the sentinels. Velody had no idea what he was thinking — even if he was pleased or angry — and found that she didn't overly care.

'You, my dear,' said Priest, Lord of Pigeons. 'You are more than we deserve.'

'I'd agree with that,' said Poet. 'But what in seven hells has she done to deserve us?'

Velody had no answer for that. Exhausted, she reached her arms out to Delphine and Rhian again and allowed them to lead her home.

The Creature Court followed. But there was time enough to worry about that later.

VELODY'S BATTLE CONTINUES IN
THE CREATURE COURT BOOK TWO
The Shattered City

CALENDAR NOTES

The Ammorian calendar, or Fasti, has three named days — the Kalends (first day of the month), the Nones (nine days before the Ides) and the Ides (full moon — which falls more or less in the middle of the month). Generally people refer to days in relation to these, e.g. "four days after the Ides," or "two days before the Kalends."

The day after each Kalends, Nones and Ides is considered nefas/unlucky.

Market-nines or nundinae are the closest thing they have to the idea of weeks — these refer to the markets held in the city every 9 days regardless of other festivals.

MONTHS OF THE YEAR:

Venturis (winter)
    Lupercal (winter)
    Martial (spring)
    Aphrodal (spring)
    Floralis (spring)
    Lucina (summer)

Felicitas (summer)
Cerialis (summer)
Ludi (autumn)
Bestialis (autumn)
Fortuna (autumn)
Saturnalis (winter)

GLOSSARY

- **Alexandrine Basilica** — once the largest church in the known world, constructed by the fourth Duc d'Aufleur, mad old Ilexandros. His successor, Duc Giulio Gauget, declared the Basilica to be an unholy abomination and stripped its rich furnishings to ornament his own Palazzo. The hollowed-out and falling-down Basilica is now used as a marketplace, and a merchant's lot here is worth a small fortune.
- **Ammoria** — a principality once consisting of three duchies: Silano (capital city: Bazeppe), Lattorio (capital city: Aufleur) and Reyenna (capital city: Tierce). When the city of Tierce vanished, Reyenna became one of the baronies of Lattorio.
- **Animor** — the energy/power contained within the bodies of all full members of the Creature Court. Seers and sentinels do not hold animor, though they are touched/contaminated by it, which gives them a status between the nox and daylight worlds.

- **Ansouisette** — a fashionable cocktail of aniseed and lemon liqueur.
- **Arches, the** — ruined city that exists below Aufleur, where the city's inhabitants once lived after being forced underground during the old skywar. Now inhabited by the Creature Court. Also known as 'the undercity'.
- **Artorio Xandelian** — former Ducomte d'Aufleur, son of Duc Ynescho Xandelian and Duchessa Givette Camellie. Artorio refused to marry in his youth, but at age thirty-three was prevailed upon by his father to marry nineteen-year-old Eglantine in order to produce an heir. A year later Isangell was born. Artorio died of the Silent Sleep when his daughter was thirteen.
- **Ashiol Xandelian** — Ducomte d'Aufleur, son of Augusta and Bruges, stepson of Diamagne. Cousin to Isangell, Duchessa d'Aufleur. Member of the Creature Court; rank: King; creature: black cat.
- **Atulia** — region to the north of Ammoria.
- **Aufrey** — one of the twelve Great Families of Aufleur.
- **Aufleur** — capital city of the duchy of Lattorio in the principality of Ammoria. Ruled by Isangell, the daylight Duchessa.
- **Augusta Xandelian** — second child of Duc Ynescho Xandelian and Duchessa Givette Camellie. Married Bruges Lanouvre and had one son, Ashiol. A year after Bruges's death, Augusta married the Baronne di Diamagne and retired to his estate. She and Diamagne had four sons: Bryn, Keil, Jemmen and Zade, and a daughter, Phage (Pip). Now widowed again, her official title is the

Dowager Baronnille though she is technically entitled to use the title Ducomtessa.

- **Avleurine** — one of the hill districts of Aufleur; location of the Temple of the Market Saints.
- **Bridescake** — ornate wedding cake traditionally covered in spring flowers.
- **Bruges Lanouvre** — late husband of Augusta Xandelian; father of Ashiol (died when Ashiol was seven years old).
- **Burnplague** — a spreading sky pattern of blisters that spit motes of light and acid.
- **Camellie** — one of the twelve Great Families of Aufleur.
- **Camoise** — country to the far east of Ammoria. One of many cultures that trades extensively with Aufleur. Providers of the exotic and expensive 'real tea', the best of which is Camoiserian leaf.
- **Carmentines** — bright scarlet flowers with long stems.
- **Cathedral of Ires** — place of worship dedicated to the Crone Ires, who is venerated by the Irean Priestesses. Place where wills are lodged for safekeeping.
- **Celeste** — former Lord of the Creature Court who left with Lysandor during the tyrannical reign of Garnet as Power and Majesty.
- **Centi opera** — portable stalls featuring puppet shows. Sometimes a young female performer, an ingénue, performs among the puppets.
- **Centrini** — affluent mercantile district in the centre of Aufleur.
- **Cheapside** — part of the market district of Tierce, where Velody's family own a bakery.

- **Chimaera** — a monstrous dark shadowy shape with claws, teeth and scales; an amalgam of every devil and forbidden creature imaginable. Only Creature Kings are able to take chimaera form; used in battle.
- **Church Bridge** — traditional starting point for festival parades; finishing point is the Forum. One of two city bridges across the River Verticordia, the other being the Marius Bridge.
- **Ciocolate** — a very expensive delicacy brought over from Nova Stella. Served as a fondant or as a hot, spicy drink called ciocolata.
- **City Fathers** — the members of the City Council, who meet in the Curia: this group is made up of the Duc's Ministers, a Proctor for each of the city districts, and the three senior priests who between them form the ruling body of the city, under the hand of the Duc or Duchessa. The three senior priests are the Matrona Irea of the Irean Priestesses (the only woman allowed to be a city father), Brother Typhisus of the Silver Brethren, and the Master of Saints.
- **Clara** — member of the Creature Court; rank: courtesa to Warlord; creature: greymoon cat.
- **Coinage** — the coins of Aufleur are divided into gold ducs, silver ducs, copper shilleins and copper centi.
- **Columbine** — a female dancer who performs in musette and theatre revues.
- **Coronets** — delicious lemon-glazed breakfast pastries, shaped like crowns and unique to Aufleur.
- **Courtesi (courteso: male; courtesa: female)** — the lowest rank of the Creature Court; must ally

themselves with a particular Lord for protection. Too vulnerable to exist alone.

- **Crane** — youngest of the surviving sentinels. Weapons: blue-hilted daggers and swords.
- **Creature Court** — the courtesi, Lords and Kings who hold animor within their bodies, belong to the nox and have the ability to fight the sky. Ruled by the Power and Majesty, the highest ranked of their Kings. Peripheral members of the Court include the sentinels and the seer, but they often consider themselves separate from the Court.
- **Crossroads** — any part of the city where two streets meet is considered sacred to the protective spirits or household gods of Aufleur. Casual sacrifices (for example chickens or honey cakes) are often made here for greater effect.
- **Curia** — slope-roofed building in the Forum that houses meetings of the City Council.
- **Cyniver** — brother of Rhian and lover of Velody; lost when Tierce was swallowed by the sky.
- **Damascine Virgins** — an order of priestesses in service to Damascus the war-angel. They sacrifice to him on the eleventh day of Martial.
- **Dame** — appropriate form of address for a respectable matron, diminutive of 'madame'.
- **Damson** — member of the Creature Court; rank: courtesa to Priest; creature: gull.
- **Delphine** — friend to Velody and Rhian; ribboner and garland-maker.
- **Demoiselle** — unmarried (young) woman; 'demme' for short.
- **Duc/Duchessa d'Aufleur** — ruler of the city of Aufleur.

- **Dhynar — member of the Creature Court**; rank: Lord; creature: ferax.
- **Diamagne —** farming and wine region south of Aufleur; part of Lattorio. Also the name of the Baronne di Diamagne (now deceased), who married Augusta Xandelian (Ashiol's mother) as her second husband.
- **Donagan —** reputed to be the finest tailor in Aufleur, a master craftsman.
- **Dottores —** medical practitioners, mostly male. The only women allowed to practise in Aufleur as dottores are those registered as midwives, although many of them dispense other forms of medical advice on the side.
- **Edore —** region to the north of Ammoria and Atulia.
- **Evander X —** a popular writer of newspaper adventure serials, pen-name for Evanderline Inglirra.
- **Farrier —** member of the Creature Court; rank: courteso to Dhynar; creature: slashcat.
- **Floralia —** six-day festival commemorating the glory of spring and the fertility of the coming summer. It begins in the month of Aphrodal and ends in the month of Floralis. Honours maidens, sweethearts, brides, household gods, passion and abundance, each on a different day. The first day (maidens) is celebrated with a public parade by the Spring Queen (the highest-ranking female in the city) and her Spring Consort, both dressed in pink and white.
- **Flame-and-gin —** common bar drink.
- **Florister —** artisan who works with plants and flowers; often works in conjunction with a

ribboner or garland-maker to produce festival garlands.

- **Fornacalia** — festival from the sixth to the seventeenth of Lupercal in honour of the harvest saints, and the baking of the corn. Citizens wear ceremonial baking aprons for the rituals. Overlaps with the Parentalia, Quirinalia and Lupercalia.

- **Forum** — the public centre of Aufleur, a large area lined with temples and public buildings such as the Alexandrine Basilica and the Curia. The city market is held here every nine days, events such as the apprentice fairs are held here, and this is the traditional climax of most public parades and pageants. The Duchessa's Avenue connects the Forum to the Lake of Follies. Other cities, such as Tierce, also have a Forum, though the Forum of Aufleur is unusually large.

- **Gardens of Trajus Alysaundre** — gardens covering one side of the Lucretine hill in the centre of Aufleur; built over the top of the decadent public baths established in honour of the third Duc d'Aufleur, Trajus Alysaundre. The gardens face on to the Lake of Follies and the Forum.

- **Garnet** — member of the Creature Court; rank: Power and Majesty; creature: gattopardo (mountain cat). He is the son of the cook and the groundskeeper on the Diamagne estate, and was Ashiol's boyhood friend.

- **Giacosa** — bustling merchant district at the southern end of Aufleur.

- **Giulio Gauget** — fifth Duc d'Aufleur. Known for excessive modesty and piety in contrast to his predecessor, Ilexandros Alysaundre.

- **Givette Camellie** — the Old Duchessa, wife of Duc Ynescho, mother of Artorio and Augusta, grandmother of Isangell, Ashiol, Bryn, Keil, Jemmen, Zade and Phage. Became Regenta when her late husband was mentally incapacitated; pre-deceased him after a long illness.
- **Gleamspray** — a rare and lethal element of the skybattles which is known for killing daylight folk; victims appear to succumb to the 'Silent Sleep'.
- **Grago** — member of the Creature Court; rank: courteso to Dhynar; creature: stripecat.
- **Great Families** — the twelve Great Families of Aufleur: Xandelian (ducal), Leorgette, Lanouvre, Gauget, Paucini, Aufrey, Alysaundre, Vittorio, Giuliano, Camellie, Delgardie, Octaviano.
- **Halberk** — member of the Creature Court; courteso to Poet; creature: bear.
- **Harlequinus** — a sad dancing clown, main male role in the harlequinade, a regular feature of musette revues.
- **Haymarket** — located in the Arches. Formerly a packing and storage facility; now a large space where the Power and Majesty resides. A canal runs water from the River Verticordia right through the Haymarket and down through the Arches, emerging at the Lock in the side of the Lucretine hill, which is the main entrance to the Arches.
- **Heliora** — member of the Creature Court; rank: Seer. Joined Court as a sentinel; became Seer during Ortheus's reign as Power and Majesty.
- **Ilexandros Alysaundre** — fourth Duc d'Aufleur; also known as 'mad old Ilexandros'. Built the Alexandrine Basilica, largest church in the known world, in the Forum of Aufleur.

- **Imperium** — a distilled alcoholic beverage made from fermented grain mash.
- **Inglirrus** — a small country across the strait from Orcadia.
- **Irean Priestesses** — powerful priestesses who venerate Ires the Crone, otherwise known as Saint Grandmere. The priestesses wear white and are said to have communion with the dead. Wills are lodged with them for safekeeping, and the priestesses are responsible for public readings of said wills. Their chief priestess is the Matrona Irea, one of the three priests included in the City Fathers.
- **Ires** — the Crone, or Saint Grandmere, worshipped in the Cathedral of Ires and venerated by the Irean Priestesses.
- **Isangell** — Duchessa d'Aufleur (full name/title: Duchessa Isangell Xandelian d'Aufleur, First Lady of the Silver Seal); daughter of Artorio Xandelian and Eglantine; granddaughter of previous Duc d'Aufleur, Ynescho Xandelian, and his Regenta, the Duchessa Givette.
- **Isharo** — an island country to the Far East, a trading partner with Aufleur, particularly for flowers and fabrics.
- **Islandser** — a person from the Green Islands, to the west of Inglirrus, with a distinctive accent.
- **Janvier** — member of the Creature Court; courteso to Livilla; creature: raven.
- **Jardin Falcone** — editor of the Aufleur Gazette, a popular city newspaper.
- **Kelpie** — sentinel. Refers to her swords as her 'Sisters' and her daggers as her 'Nieces': hilts are wrapped in dark leather.

- **Lanouvre** — one of the twelve Great Families of Aufleur.
- **Laudinon** — the capital city of Inglirrus
- **Lemuria** — festival during Floralis to placate the shades of dead ancestors and lost loves.
- **Lennoc** — member of the Creature Court; courteso to Dhynar (formerly courteso to Lief); creature: brighthound.
- **Leorgette** — one of the twelve Great Families of Aufleur.
- **Librarion** — Aufleur's city library.
- **Lictors** — honour guard that protects ranks of Duc, Duchessa, Ducomte or Ducomtessa, as well as select City Fathers, priests of high status and the Chief Minister. Lictors travel in multiples of three, carry ceremonial rods of state, are armed with axes and wear black and scarlet.
- **Lief** — deceased member of the Creature Court; rank: Lord; creature: greathound.
- **Livilla** — member of the Creature Court; rank: Lord; creature: wolf.
- **Lucian** — one of the districts of Aufleur, known as the theatre district.
- **Ludi** — as well as being the name of the first autumn month, this word means 'games'.
- **Ludi Aufleuris** — fifteen-day series of games held during the first month of autumn, Ludi. Women traditionally wear scarlet shawls when attending these games and wave the corners of the shawls to favoured gladiators and performers.
- **Ludi Megalensia** — Games of the Great Mother, held in the month of Aphrodal. Unlike other Ludi, there are no fights, animals or mock battles; instead, the games feature theatrical performances.

- **Ludi Sacris** — Sacred Games, held in the month of Felicitas. On the chief day of sacrifice (day four), everyone in the city makes a sacrifice to their chosen saints or gods.
- **Ludi Victoriae** — Victory Games, held in the month of Cerialis, in which favourite historical battles are re-enacted in the Circus Verdigris by gladiators and actors.
- **Lupercalia** — one-day festival in Lupercal during which men carouse in the streets wearing goatskins, goat masks and fake phalluses. Not unheard of for their real phalluses to hang out, for extra authenticity.
- **Lysandor** — member of the Creature Court; rank: King. Fled with Celeste during Garnet's tyrannical reign as Power and Majesty.
- **Macready** — sentinel. Weapons: Alicity (steel sword), Tarea (skysilver sword), Phoebe (steel dagger), Jeunille (skysilver dagger); hilts wrapped in green leather.
- **Margarethe** — one of the lower districts of Aufleur, run- down and poor.
- **Market-nines** — every ninth day (nundinae) is a public market day, regardless of other festival constraints. The phrase 'market-nine' refers to these nine-day groupings. Market-nines fall on different days each year.
- **Mars/Warlord** — member of the Creature Court; rank: Lord; creature: panther (Khatri zaba in Zafiran). Born Maziz dal Sara, he was the son of the Zafiran ambassador.
- **Mask** — an actor who performs with their face covered in musette and theatre revues.

- **Matralia** — festival during month of Lucina, when mothers and maternal relatives everywhere are crowned with silverbreath and ivy.
- **Mercatus** — grand city-wide market festivals held in Cerialis and Ludi, the two months with the most sacred games.
- **Musette** — a theatrical establishment or performance, usually in the style of a music hall, variety show or pantomime.
- **Nefas** — means 'unlucky', particularly in relation to a day; for example the day immediately after the Kalends, Nones or Ides of each month is nefas, and business transactions are rarely performed on these days.
- **Neptunalia** — a winter festival held on the Kalends of Saturnalis, celebrating the ancient Seafather with sweetmeats, sacrifice and rituals involving paper boats.
- **Nova Stella** — a land far to the West of Ammoria, discovered and colonised two hundred years previously by explorers from Stelleza. Source for ciocolate and tobacco.
- **Nox** — the opposite of day.
- **Orcadia** — north-western region, known for its gentle climate and bubbled wine.
- **Orcadian Strait** — a body of water between Orcadia and Inglirrus.
- **Orphan Princel** — Poet's theatrical alter ego, stellar and stagemaster of the Mermaid Revue.
- **Ortheus** — former member of the Creature Court; rank: King; Power and Majesty (before Garnet). Creature: serpent.
- **Palazzo** — home of the ruling ducal family, located on the Balisquine hill and surrounded by other

opulent residences. A former palazzo, now abandoned, is located on the Avleurine Hill.

- **Parentalia** — nine-day festival from the thirteenth to the twenty-first of Lupercal, during which all citizens of Aufleur travel to place flowers and sweetmeats on their family tombs and grave markers. White silk garlands are traditionally worn.
- **Paucini** — one of the twelve Great Families of Aufleur.
- **Piazza Nautilia** — public square at the conjunction of three major streets in Aufleur: Via Delgardie, Via Leondrine and Via Camellie; location of Triton's Church and the best public baths in Aufleur.
- **Poet** — member of the Creature Court; rank: Lord; creature: white rats. Moonlights as the Orphan Princel, a famous musette performer.
- **Power and Majesty** — leader of the Creature Court; must hold the rank of King.
- **Priest** — member of the Creature Court; rank: Lord; creature: pigeon.
- **Proctors** — public officials elected each year; one for each district in Aufleur. Included among the City Fathers.
- **Quirinalia** — One-day festival on the seventeenth of Lupercal, overlapping with the Fornacalia and Parentalia. Bunches of myrtle are exchanged and worn at the belt to ward off ill-luck for soldiers. Vigiles and lictors are allowed this day off public duties for religious observance.
- **Reyenna** — formerly one of the three duchies of Ammoria. After the disappearance of its capital

city, Tierce, Reyenna became known as one of the baronies of Lattorio.

- **Rhian** — friend to Velody and Delphine; florister.
- **Sage** — Velody's brother, who was lost along with the rest of her family when Tierce was swallowed by the sky. Originally a dock worker, he was injured in an accident and ended up taking recreational potions for many years before cleaning up his act and getting factory work.
- **Saints** — worshipped by the daylight folk through rituals and festivals. 'Saints and angels' and 'saints and devils' are two common swearing phrases heard throughout the city.
- **Samara** — legendary former member of the Creature Court; female Lord who took in too much animor and blew apart. Cited as evidence that women cannot be Kings.
- **Saturnalia** — an eight-day festival, held from the seventeenth to the twenty-fourth of Saturnalis, in which masters and servants traditionally swap roles, men and women wear each other's clothing, etc. Also sometimes known as the Feast of Fools, it celebrates all things topsy-turvy. Traditional refreshments include hot cider, bean syrup and roasted chestnuts. An important theatre season.
- **Scratchlight** — weapon used by the sky in battle; kills one in fifty mortals it hits — not as effective as the rarer shadowstreak or gleamspray.
- **Seer** — member of the Creature Court, outside the usual hierarchy. The seer has the ability to look into the future and pull out visions of what is to come.
- **Seigneur** — a polite term of address for men,

which gets politer the higher in rank they actually are.

- **Sentinels** — the loyal armed servants of the Kings of the Creature Court. Each bears blades of steel and skysilver to represent the thin line they tread between the nox and the daylight. They are ready to give up their blood to their masters at a moment's notice.
- **Seonard** — member of the Creature Court; rank: courteso to Livilla; creature: wolf.
- **Serenai** — patron saint of gamblers and good fortune. Friendly bets often include promises for the loser to sacrifice to Serenai or other saints and angels on the winner's behalf.
- **Shade** — member of the Creature Court; rank: courteso to Dhynar (formerly courteso to Lief); creature: darkhound.
- **Silent Sleep** — a fatal illness that tends to affect the very young and the elderly. A side-effect of skybattle, but to daylight folk a mystery illness that attacks without warning and leaves no contamination trail.
- **Silver Brethren** — a chaste order of male priests, who wear silver chains and shave their heads. They never speak once they have taken orders, only sing and chant during their street processions.
- **Silver Captain** — Nathanial, former leader of the sentinels. Died on the eve of Vestalia, three years before the return of Ashiol.
- **Silverstorm** — shards of skysilver generated by the sky during battle.
- **Skybattle** — when the sky opens and attacks the city, using all manner of deadly phenomena. Only happens at nox, and only the Creature Court and

their allies, such as the seer and sentinels, are aware of this. The Creature Court exists to battle the sky and protect the city. Any damage to buildings or other parts of the city is repaired at dawn, and any daylight folk affected by the sky's weapons recover and return to normal. Occasionally there are fatalities if a person has suffered a direct hit, particularly if they are very young or elderly. Such fatalities are referred to by the daylight folk as the Silent Sleep.

- **Skyburn** — the effect of some sky weapons on the sentinels. In its lightest form it is similar to sunburn; more serious symptoms include deeply reddened or bruised skin, fever and weakness.

- **Skyfall** — to be swallowed by the sky. Death by skyfall means a Court member's animor goes with them into the sky and is lost forever, instead of being shared among the survivors of the Creature Court. 'The sky is falling' is an expression often used to indicate that a skybattle is beginning.

- **Skyseed** — a red cloud that is the seed of a deathstorm. Deathstorms bring flaming hail, 'devils' (violent animated dust clouds) and 'angels' (poisonous bursts of steam)'. A skyseed can be destroyed by lancing — similar to lancing a boil, only a million times more disgusting.

- **Skysilver** — a metallic substance that falls from the sky. The Creature Court believes it comes from the stars. All skysilver is the property of Kings and given to the Smith, who forges it into weapons for the sentinels.

- **Slow rain** — a force of destruction from the sky, liquid that can burn a hole right through a member of the Court and give a sentinel skyburn. Usually occurs a couple of times a month, often heralding worse to come.

- **Smith, the** — a figure who is both part of and apart from the Creature Court, only accessible for an hour at noon each day. The Smith crafts the skysilver into weapons for the sentinels, and has been around since before Aufleur was built.
- **Songbird** — a singer who performs in musette and theatre revues.
- **Star tar** — hideous black muck that oozes through the cracks in the sky during the worst skybattles.
- **Stellar** — the most prominent and popular performer in a musette or theatre revue.
- **Stelleza** — an affluent country to the west of Ammoria, known for its adventurers and explorers. Strong trading partner with Aufleur.
- **Surrender** — a party potion that makes the user high and giddy.
- **Sweetheart Saints** — patron saints of romance and sweethearts.
- **Tasha** — former member of the Creature Court; rank: Lord; creature: lion. Recruited Ashiol, Garnet, Lysandor, Poet and Livilla as her courtesi. Died forsworn, and returned as a shade who dragged corruption and disease through the city before she was stopped.
- **Temple of the Market Saints** — located on the Avleurine hill. The Market Saints are the patron saints of all traders and merchants.
- **Tierce** — capital city of Reyenna, and where Velody, Delphine and Rhian come from. When Tierce disappeared, Reyenna became a barony of the duchy of Lattorio.

- **Trajus Alysaundre** — third Duc d'Aufleur; see also 'Gardens of Trajus Alysaundre'.
- **Velody** — friend to Rhian and Delphine; dressmaker. Member of the Creature Court; rank: King; Power and Majesty; creature: little brown mouse.
- **Vestalia** — a rural festival on the ninth day of Lucina in which people dress up in milkmaid costumes, aprons and other 'peasant' attire. Other features are green paper lanterns and sacrifices of honey, cake, bread and salt. The day is sacred to bakers and millers.
- **Via Ciceline** — a vibrant shopping strip in the heart of the wealthy Centrini district.
- **Via Silviana** — a narrow street crammed between the affluent Vittorine hill and the shabby, bustling Giacosa commercial district. The shop belonging to Velody, Rhian and Delphine stands at the halfway point between Vittorine and Giacosa, under the Sign of the Rose and Needle.
- **Vittorine** — one of the hill districts of Aufleur; also extends below the foot of the hill into an upmarket shopping district that meets the thriving merchant district of Giacosa.
- **Vittorina Royale** — a theatre in the Vittorine district, currently managed by the Orphan Princel, and hosting the Mermaid Revue. Current and former performers at this theatre include Christophe, Sunshine, Ruby-red, Zephyr, Topaz, Bart, Adriane and Madalena.
- **Warlord** — member of the Creature Court; see 'Mars'.
- **Xandelian** — one of the districts of Aufleur. Also the name of the current ruling ducal family, whose

members include Ynescho, Augusta, Artorio, Isangell and Ashiol. One of the twelve Great Families of Aufleur.

- **Ynescho Xandelian** — the Old Duc, grandfather to Isangell, Ashiol, Bryn, Keil, Jemmen, Zade and Phage, father of Artorio and Augusta. Ruled with an iron fist until his wits gave way; his wife, Duchessa Givette, took over as his Regenta.
- **Yvette LeBeau** — former mistress of the Old Duc and former columbine; in her retirement she owns a house on the corner of the Marius Bridge over the River Verticordia and entertains theatricals.
- **Zafir** — an eastern country rich with culture, source of the popular 'princessa and djinn' plays that are a regularly revived trend in the Aufleur theatres and musettes.
- **Zero** — member of the Creature Court; rank: courteso to Poet; creature: weasel.

THE CREATURE
COURT CONTINUES

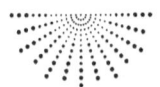

BOOK 2: THE SHATTERED CITY

Daylight and nox collide as Ashiol and Velody's uneasy alliance fractures. The Creature Court try to fight the war with theatre instead of bloodshed... but they still have to deliver a sacrifice.

Will Delphine and Rhian escape the dangers of Velody's new world, or be consumed by them?

Get your copy of *The Shattered City* today. You can pick up a signed copy at the Teacup Magic Emporium.[*]

---

[*] tansyrr.com/collections/dark-divine

BOOK 3: REIGN OF BEASTS

With three kings at war over the title of Power and Majesty, someone's going to bleed. A final battle is coming, and the Creature Court must learn from their past to save their future, before they lose everyone.

Saturnalia will change the Creature Court and the city of Aufleur forever.

Get your copy of *Reign of Beasts* today. You can pick up a signed copy at the Teacup Magic Emporium.*

---

* tansyrr.com/collections/dark-divine

CABARET OF MONSTERS

A PREQUEL NOVELLA TO THE
CREATURE COURT TRILOGY

Saturnalia in Aufleur is a time of topsy-turvy revels, of the world turned upside down and transformed before your eyes. The city's theatres produce an annual display of reversals, surprises and transformations. In Aufleur, flappers can transform into wolves. Even the rats are not what they seem.

Evie Inglirra is on a mission to infiltrate the theatrical world of Aufleur and discover what lies beneath their glamorous cabaret costumes and backstage scandals. What secrets will she uncover?

Get your copy of *Cabaret of Monsters* today. You can pick up a signed copy at the Teacup Magic Emporium.*

---

* tansyrr.com/collections/dark-divine

ABOUT THE AUTHOR

Tansy Rayner Roberts is an award-winning Australian science fiction and fantasy author who does not make her own gowns, or run across rooftops. She lives with her family in Tasmania and has been known to pick up the occasional embroidery hoop.

Listen to Tansy on Sheep Might Fly, a podcast where she reads aloud her stories as audio serials.

What tea is Tansy drinking? Find out at when you subscribe to her excellent newsletter.*

Follow TansyRR at:
tansyrr.com

Visit the Teacup Magic Emporium† to get signed paperbacks, bundles, magical merch and bonus content direct from the author!

---

* tinyurl.com/tansyrr
† tansyrr.com/collections/dark-divine